BY ALEXIS HALL

A Lady for a Duke
Something Fabulous

LONDON CALLING
Boyfriend Material
Husband Material

WINNER BAKES ALL
Rosaline Palmer Takes the Cake
Paris Daillencourt Is About to Crumble

MORTAL
FOLLIES

MORTAL FOLLIES

ALEXIS HALL

NEW YORK

A Del Rey Trade Paperback Original

Copyright © 2023 by Alexis J. Hall

Published in the United States by Del Rey,
an imprint of Random House,
a division of Penguin Random House LLC, New York.

DEL REY and the CIRCLE colophon are registered
trademarks of Penguin Random House LLC.

Library of Congress Cataloging-in-Publication Data
Names: Hall, Alexis J., author.
Title: Mortal follies: a novel / Alexis Hall.
Description: New York: Del Rey, [2023]
Identifiers: LCCN 2023012831 | ISBN 9780593497562 (trade paperback) |
ISBN 9780593497579 (Ebook)
Subjects: LCGFT: Fantasy fiction. | Romance fiction. |
Lesbian fiction. | Novels.
Classification: LCC PR6108.A453 M67 2023 |
DDC 823/.92—dc23/eng/20230327
LC record available at https://lccn.loc.gov/2023012831

Printed in the United States of America on acid-free paper

randomhousebooks.com

9 8 7 6 5 4

Art from wooster, TWINS DESIGN STUDIO, Murhena © Adobe Stock Photos

Book design by Sara Bereta

To my lord Oberon,
in the hopes that this tale will remind him of better times

AUTHOR'S NOTE

Please note, *Mortal Follies* includes a number of themes some readers may prefer not to engage with. These include but are not limited to sexual content, threat of violence and danger (including a wasp attack and near drowning), animal sacrifice, mentions of one of the main character's deceased family and how they died (stabbing, drowning, burned to death), accusations of familicide, transphobia (challenged), social non-acceptance of LGBTQ+ relationships, slavery/transatlantic slave trade (discussed), sexual harassment and threat of sexual assault, murder, severe illness (magical), smoking.

PROLOGUE

I ntroductions, gentle reader, are in order. I am that knavish sprite
that frights the maidens of the villagery. I am Oberon's jester—
was Oberon's jester, that's rather the issue. I am called hobgoblin by
some and, contrary to what certain people might have told you, it
is *not* a name I like and you shall *not* have good luck if you repeat it
in my hearing.

I am also your narrator.

For reasons that are none of your concern and, more impor-
tantly, not at all my fault, I am somewhat on the *outs* with my patron
at present. Where once I sat by his side on the arm of an elfin
throne in the twisted, thorny bowers of his court, I am now living
in a tiny flat in Putney with rising damp and leaky windows and I
am forced, for the first time in the millennia of my existence, to pay
what I understand you mortals call *rent*.

It is vile.

But I am nothing if not resourceful and so I have struck a bargain with some particularly impressionable mortals at one of your "publishing houses" and have agreed to share for their readers some of the many stories of misguided passion, murderous intrigue, and other tomfooleries that I have gathered down the years. Hopefully this will go better than it did the last time—I gave an excellent story to a mortal playmaker around 1600 and the bastard didn't even give me a co-writer credit.

The particular tale I have chosen for you is one that I collected in the year of our lord (or I suppose *your* lord, some of your lord at least—although I've never really understood why your kind is so keen to believe in immaterial deities when there are so many material ones right in front of you) 1814, shortly after the first abdication of Napoleon but a little before his immediate escape from Elba. It is my understanding that there is, in the present market, a particular fondness for tales from this era. Something about the dresses perhaps? Or the balls? Or perhaps you're all just nostalgic for the staggering social inequality. I wouldn't blame you, I found it *hilarious* myself. The Corn Laws, for example, were a masterpiece of comic invention; raising the price of grain so much that the people who grow it can't afford it? Genius! Of course we live in more enlightened times now. And I'm sure you will never again engage in such foolishness.

But I am digressing.

The tale that follows is one of ancient gods, malicious curses, and forbidden romance. I tried to work in a bit with a dog, but there was never a moment where it really came up.

I hope it meets with your approval. Especially because I have just received a letter from a corporation telling me I owe them money for water. Apparently you *pay* for *water* in your world.

The naiads must be running a scam.

I am digressing again.

Enjoy the story. Be assured that it involves unpleasant things happening to other people. I know that there is little you mortals enjoy more. In that regard, at least, you are much more like my own people than either of us might care to admit.

MORTAL FOLLIES

CHAPTER

1

When Miss Mitchelmore arrived at Lady Etheridge's ball, she was resplendent in a gown of silver French gauze over a silken slip, her hair styled à la Grecque and decorated with roses. She caught even my eye, and I sometimes find it a little tricky to tell mortals apart. Which, I'll admit, may have caused the tiniest of problems in the past.

For much of the evening I watched her from across the room while an elderly colonel opined to me at length regarding the French emperor. It was not, as you may imagine, a topic about which I cared in the slightest. See above regarding my difficulty distinguishing mortals from one another, even short Corsicans. Eventually I extricated myself from the conversation by enchanting him with a slight but persistent itching between the shoulder blades.

Thus freed, I found myself following the pretty Miss Mitchelmore. I am, amongst other things, a collector of stories, and my instincts told me that she was either the kind of lady who did interesting things or the kind to whom interesting things happened. Or, at a pinch, the kind to whom they could be made to happen. I am not above interfering in mortal affairs if it seems truly necessary, or if it would be mildly entertaining.

Initially it seemed the evening would be a profound disappointment. Miss Mitchelmore danced with several gentlemen, but never twice with the same one. She conversed with a number of ladies but said nothing that might be scandalous. There *was*, however, something strange about her gown. After her first dance I noticed a tear in the hem. After the second I caught sight of a stray thread trailing from her glove and saw petals falling from her hair. I should at this point make clear to the reader that the lady's dress, while fine, was decidedly *not* of fairy manufacture. The works of my people have a wholly undeserved reputation for coming apart unexpectedly or transforming into leaves and cobwebs at the slightest provocation. In fact, such disasters tend to require *considerable* provocation. The problem is that mortals are exceedingly provoking.

But on this evening, at this ball, Miss Mitchelmore's dress was most certainly dissolving into something. A snag here, a run there—it swiftly added up to a problem that first she, and then the general assembly, could not ignore. The loss of a headdress might be explained away as youthful high spirits, but by the time her gloves had frayed to the elbows it was clear she was in no fit state to be in mixed company. And since in her present circumstances mixed company could scarcely be avoided, she was, to put it bluntly, fucked.

To her credit, but my disappointment, she did not panic. I have, over the centuries, seen a number of mortals deprived unexpectedly of clothing (there are some jokes, after all, which never fall out of fashion) and their responses are almost always hilarious. But once Miss Mitchelmore's skirts had begun to go the way of the rest of her ensemble, she retreated quietly to the garden and took shelter behind an ornamental bush.

I followed her, of course. Slipping my mortal guise, I became first a shadow, then a sparrow, then a raindrop on a chestnut leaf. I have a fondness for scenes of mortal misadventure, especially those that befall preposterously, and I had the sense that this lady's life was soon to become *extremely* preposterous.

Not having had the foresight to bring a needle, thread, and several yards of spare fabric to a society ball, Miss Mitchelmore's efforts to conceal the dishevelment of her garments were growing increasingly futile. The fine cloth of the dress was crumbling beneath her fingers, and it was not long before she stood alone in the dark attired only in her corset, stockings, and chemise. Having been raised never to curse, she heaved a sigh and kicked a pebble.

Some minutes passed, during which she recovered a little of her composure but none of her clothing. Her dilemma was a simple one. She could return to the party in her undergarments and suffer the immediate loss of her status and reputation. Or she could wait in the garden until somebody found her and suffer the mildly delayed loss of her status and reputation.

Poor Miss Mitchelmore. She was, by any measure, having a pisser of an evening.

The door to the terrace opened and a figure emerged. She was, to Miss Mitchelmore's great relief, a woman, meaning immediate scandal had been averted. Or would have been, were it not for the specific woman it turned out to be. To the wags of the ton the lady was known as the Duke of Annadale. She was not, of course. That had been her father. But he had died somewhat improbably of leprosy a few years prior to the events I presently relate, having been predeceased by all three of his sons. The eldest was stabbed in a gaming hell despite never gambling. The next was lost on a vessel crossing the Channel despite the weather being calm and the captain having been diligent in his offerings to Mannanán and Poseidon. The youngest burned to death in the grass fires at Talavera. And thus the title fell into abeyance while the properties and monies fell on a woman who—although scarcely twenty at the time—was at once denounced by polite society as a sorceress. That she continued to be invited to balls despite the broad consensus that she had murdered four men by witchcraft might, perhaps, tell you everything you need to know about the fashionable set.

For a sorceress or a murderess she was a remarkably unremarkable woman—average in most particulars, but for a nose tending towards the aquiline and a hard, cynically set mouth. She wore a gown of dark-green velvet, its demi-train now slightly out of fashion, and a hat adorned with towering white feathers. Leaning back against the trunk of a chestnut tree, she brought a spill to her cigar, lit it, and inhaled. For some moments it seemed that she would not notice Miss Mitchelmore at all or, if she did, that she would ignore her for the sake of propriety. I was just preparing to intervene when the Duke of Annadale looked down.

"If you will pardon the observation, you appear to be in your underthings."

"Yes." In Miss Mitchelmore's defence, I would not have known quite what to say either. Then again, I would have been invisible.

"A bold choice, but perhaps an unwise one?"

Straightening a little, Miss Mitchelmore managed a smile. Her smile was the kind accounted by mortals to be pretty. As, for that matter, was the rest of her. She had delicate features, hair a demure but fashionable light brown, and eyes that, in normal circumstances, sparkled with a kind of innocent joy. "It was not a choice. I—I fear somebody is playing a rather cruel joke upon me."

"Well, if you will buy fairy-woven gowns." I should say that I *intensely dislike* the Duke of Annadale.

"I *have* recently acquired a new modiste, but I am sure she is quite human. Besides, my friend Miss Bickle wears fairy-woven gowns all the time and she has never had this difficulty."

Seeming to tire of the sartorial question, the Duke of Annadale made her way over to the small hedge and, removing the cigar from her lips, proffered it to Miss Mitchelmore. "Smoke?"

"I do not. And, even if I did, I think I would find my other concerns more pressing."

With a shrug, the Duke of Annadale took another lungful of tobacco. "That's one way to look at it. The other is that it can scarcely make matters *worse.*"

Perhaps seeing no point in resisting, Miss Mitchelmore took the cigar, put it to her lips, and sucked awkwardly. I personally found the resulting coughing fit terribly entertaining. "I must say," Miss Mitchelmore sputtered, handing the offending object back to the Duke, "you seem to be taking my present condition remarkably in stride."

"The joy of being a lady is that one may look at other ladies in their underwear and have it accounted no impropriety. The joy of being reviled as a witch is that propriety means little to one anyway."

The mention of witchcraft combined with the slow recognition of a face she would doubtless have seen before, if only from afar, brought Miss Mitchelmore's mind to a belated conclusion. "Then you are—that is—you are the one they call the Duke of Annadale?"

The Duke nodded.

"I'm sorry, I'm sure it is a name you mislike."

If she did, she gave no sign of it. "I mislike the inaccuracy. But *Lady Georgiana* is scarcely better."

"No? I think it rather pretty."

"Really?" The Duke of Annadale seemed to be considering the matter. "And what reason do I have to trust the aesthetic judgement of a woman standing naked in a garden?"

Miss Mitchelmore coloured at that. "I am not naked, I am simply . . . underdressed."

"You are *undressed*, and while it is a style you wear well it is not one that speaks to your good taste more generally."

Running low on patience, or perhaps simply growing weary of the night air, Miss Mitchelmore looked defiantly at the Duke of Annadale. "You are mocking me, and that is unbecoming a woman of your station."

"So was murdering my brothers. Since I am suspected of that already, I fail to see how showing mild discourtesy to a stranger will further sully my reputation."

"Please." It was not a desperate *please* but it was an earnest one. "Lady Georgiana, I am—you must surely realise—in a most compromising position and should any gentleman happen upon me in this state, I would be quite ruined."

"Then you should have had the foresight to be born richer or more male."

Unperturbed, Miss Mitchelmore persisted. "You must have some garment you can lend me?"

"I'm sorry"—for the first time I heard amusement creep into the Duke of Annadale's voice—"are you now attempting to undress *me*?"

"Why would I . . . ? Oh, you are toying with me still." An unfamiliar feeling fluttered in Miss Mitchelmore's heart. You may wonder, reader, how I know such things. Suffice it to say that I am a thing of dreams from a world of passions, and my eyes see much that yours do not. Or perhaps I am simply lying.

"Playing, perhaps. But not toying. I never *toy.*"

Uncertain what to make of that observation, Miss Mitchelmore renewed her pleas for more practical assistance. "Do you not have a cloak or a pelisse or a mantle you could lend me? Something that could afford me at least some modesty while I try to work out how to extract myself from this awful situation?"

There was quiet a moment. "And what would I gain by assisting you?"

"It would be an act of Christian charity."

"Do you really believe I give two figs for Christianity?"

And at last, Miss Mitchelmore was genuinely shocked. "*That* is a wicked thing to say."

"More wicked than *I intend to leave you to freeze to death in your shift and corset?* More wicked than *Hecate of the Crossroads, I shall offer in your name the sacrifice of three pristine oxen if you strike my father down with leprosy?*"

"I believe you would do neither of those things." Miss Mitchelmore was defiant again, standing as tall as she could manage while sheltering out of sight of the house. "But even if you would—yes, I dare say it *is* worse. The old gods may hold sway in this world, and they may have power to harm us while we live, but to reject salvation would be to imperil your very soul."

"And what matters more to you right now, my imperilled soul or your exposed thighs?"

"Happily they have the same remedy." Miss Mitchelmore set her chin in an attitude of ladylike righteousness. "The gospel entreats us to clothe the naked, so by robing my body you will also be uplifting your spirit."

To that the Duke of Annadale gave half a smile, a curt nod, and no other reply before turning and walking back into the house.

Miss Mitchelmore watched her leave with a look of startled betrayal. Then, when she was quite certain that the Duke of Annadale had vanished, she sank down with her back to the hedge and wept. As well she might, because her best hope of rescue had turned out to be a cold and heartless creature. And, worse, one with no appreciation for fairy craftsmanship. I could, of course, have gone to Miss Mitchelmore's aid myself, but I'm here to tell this story, not to participate in it. Besides, you mortals are such helpless things. Once I started assisting you, I'd never be able to stop. And then I'd be stuck making shoes for widowers or spinning straw to gold for ungrateful farmers' daughters. Not that either of these are options for me anymore, which is why I am reduced to, of all things, *professional storytelling*. I assure you I am quite disgusted with myself.

The sound of footsteps on the other side of the hedge made Miss Mitchelmore freeze, uncertain whether it was better to be seen and risk ruin or to remain unseen and live forever in a hedge. Her uncertainty was resolved swiftly, however, when a bundle of cloth fell onto her head.

"My cloak." The voice belonged to the Duke of Annadale.

Trying to stand, turn, and wrap herself in a now quite tangled garment all at once meant that Miss Mitchelmore did not rise with quite the grace or dignity she might have hoped to, but she still managed to demand some kind of answer from her reluctant saviour. "Why did you let me think you had abandoned me?"

"I have a reputation to uphold. And besides"—the Duke of Annadale reached out and wiped a tear from Miss Mitchelmore's cheek—"perhaps I thought you would cry prettily."

Miss Mitchelmore blinked back what remained of her tears. In the Duke of Annadale's defence, she was right—the lady *did* weep most decoratively. Then again, my people have a fondness for tears that may colour my judgement. "That may be the wickedest thing you have said yet. Why would *anybody* wish to see *anybody* cry?"

"For the joy of seeing you impassioned? Or else we met too late and my soul is already tarnished beyond repair. Now, shall we to my carriage?"

Having little choice, Miss Mitchelmore followed the Duke of Annadale through a mercifully discreet side gate and into the street. It was early enough that passersby could not be avoided entirely, but the walk from the garden to the carriage was a short one and a young woman in a cloak drew far less attention than a young woman in essentially nothing. Ordinarily Miss Mitchelmore would not have dreamed of leaving a party with somebody to whom she had not been formally introduced. But forced public nudity, she was learning, suspended many of the rules of etiquette. Besides, the Duke of Annadale was a lady, which meant it was not so much improper as uncommon.

As they climbed into the carriage I followed them, becoming as smoke and commingling myself with the wisps that still rose from the Duke of Annadale's cigar. They settled down opposite one another and the Duke of Annadale permitted Miss Mitchelmore to give the coachman directions to her home.

"Thank you," Miss Mitchelmore said once the carriage had pulled away and Lady Etheridge's townhouse had slipped comfortably into the distance. "I am not certain what I should have done had you not intervened."

The Duke of Annadale shrugged. "You seem resourceful enough. I daresay you would have thought of something."

"Perhaps, but I cannot quite see what. I confess I am perhaps still a little unwise in the ways of the world, but I am sure dresses do not ordinarily dissolve in such a way."

The smoke from the Duke of Annadale's cigar coiled listlessly about the roof of the carriage, and I coiled with it. "Magic," she said. "When in doubt, assume magic."

"But who would stoop to sorcery for something so petty?" asked Miss Mitchelmore in genuine bafflement.

At this the Duke of Annadale laughed, short and sharp. "My dear girl, you really *do* know nothing of the world. Since time immemorial people have used magic for three purposes: personal enrichment, personal vengeance, and sex."

The expression on Miss Mitchelmore's face made all the reply that was necessary.

The expression on the Duke of Annadale's face did likewise, but she replied verbally anyway. "Are you really going to become missish at the mention of sex when my cloak is all that stands between your fair skin and the cold night air?"

"My circumstances are beyond my control. Your speech is within yours."

The Duke of Annadale leaned back. The tips of her feathered headgear passed, for a moment, through my incorporeal form as she moved. "So it is. And I choose to speak plainly. What happened to you this evening was caused by *somebody*, and that somebody wishes either to extort you, to humiliate you, or merely to see you naked." She gave a knowing smile. "The third motivation has at least the virtue of honesty."

"But why me? I am surely not so remarkable as to be worth enchanting."

"Oh, don't be tedious." The Duke of Annadale rolled her eyes.

"I barely pay attention to these things and even *I* have heard of you. Your little clique is quite the talk of the town."

"My clique?"

"Now you are being even more tedious. You are a notable beauty, your friend Miss Bickle is a notable heiress, and your cousin is notably African."

"John is English, Lady Georgiana. He was born in Surrey."

"And his father?"

"Was born in Senegal, but that is surely an old scandal."

The Duke of Annadale drew on her cigar. "Take it from one who knows: old scandals never die, they just acquire embellishments. But either way the point is that you are clearly notable, and somebody has clearly noted you."

Miss Mitchelmore fell silent awhile, not perhaps unexpectedly, given that she had just learned of a hitherto unknown enemy, and her silence persisted until the carriage rounded the circus and turned onto Gay Street. Finally, she asked, "Is that why you have not asked my name?"

"No, that was ordinary incivility."

"Still I feel I should introduce myself."

"You have already introduced yourself. I have seen your knees."

Unable to make any kind of curtsey while sitting and wrapped in a cloak, Miss Mitchelmore extended a hand. "I am Maelys Mitchelmore. It is a pleasure to make your acquaintance."

"I doubt that sincerely." The Duke of Annadale took her hand, raised it to her lips, and kissed it gently. Miss Mitchelmore shuddered in a way that had nothing to do with the cold or the shock.

It was a gesture, Miss Mitchelmore felt sure, that required some form of reply, but before she could work out what it was, the carriage pulled to a stop. The coachman opened the door, and seeing no pressing reason—or at least no proper reason—to dally now she had been delivered safely home, Miss Mitchelmore disembarked, mumbling a repeated thanks.

"Think nothing of it. And I mean that most literally." The Duke of Annadale looked down from the carriage a moment, her eyes moon pale and quite as distant. "You may keep the cloak. I have others."

And then the carriage sped away into the night, as did I.

2

I decided to pay a visit to Miss Mitchelmore the following morning. She was by far the most interesting thing to have happened since I arrived in Bath, and if worst came to worst I would always be able to amuse myself by disarranging her hair or hiding her stockings. Which, yes, may seem petty, but you'd be amazed how boring immortality becomes. Although one does find oneself missing it if it is removed from one.

Entering the house on a beam of sunlight, I became a fly for a while until an overzealous maid attempted to chase me from the room, at which point I briefly became a wasp and stung her. To further discourage her interference I became a mouse, then a rat, then an annoying tune that was stuck in her head. Then, finally remembering that I had intended to observe Miss Mitchelmore, I took a form of mists and shadows, which is close to my natural shape but quite imperceptible to mortal eyes, and slipped into the drawing room.

There I found my target already receiving her cousin Mr. Caesar and her friend Miss Bickle. They made an intriguing trio. Miss Mitchelmore—as the Duke of Annadale seemed acutely aware—was generally accounted a beauty in the slender, symmetrical, but fundamentally biological way that mortals are so fond of. And her friends were likewise decorative, Miss Bickle's undeniable if everyday prettiness half-swallowed by the extravagance of her clothes and Mr. Caesar's patrician elegance accentuated by the tastefulness of his. He was that meticulous sort of man whose breeches were always immaculately fitted, whose boots were always immaculately polished, and whose cravat was always immaculately tied. Or at least it was, but while he stood interrogating his cousin about the events of the previous evening I sidled up to him and began to pull gently on it, introducing a pleasing strain of disorder into his otherwise flawless appearance.

"Why didn't you come to me at once?" he was asking. "You knew something was amiss and you elected to hide in a garden instead of seeking assistance."

Miss Mitchelmore looked exasperated. "And what assistance could you have provided, John? My gown was falling apart under a mystical influence and you are neither a sorcerer nor a seamstress."

"Even so, I should have liked to be informed. One of us could have done something, surely?"

At the pianoforte, Miss Bickle had been playing the same note intermittently for three minutes. "Do you think," she asked nobody in particular, "that the big keys ever get jealous of the little keys? They're higher up and look much cosier. But he's right Mae, we could have helped you."

"I did not want to ruin your evening."

Miss Bickle giggled. "I *was* having a lovely time actually. I danced with a terribly gallant captain just come back from Spain. Which was rather queer because I could have sworn we were at war with France."

"This year, France was in Spain," Mr. Caesar explained.

"Oh I say, how confusing."

At last noticing the alterations I had made to his neckwear, Mr. Caesar made his way grumblingly to a mirror and began to fix his cravat. "Can we, perhaps, return to the question of Mae's vanishing on us yesterday evening?"

"Yes, let's." Miss Bickle played that same note again, for emphasis. "It was fearsomely unfair to Mrs. Wilberforce. A chaperone who loses her charges is ordinarily accounted quite poor at her job."

This occasioned genuine regret in Miss Mitchelmore, who did not enjoy being the cause of misfortune in others (a sensibility that I feel bespeaks a *marked* lack of imagination). "I am sorry, Lizzie, I should not have wished to cause Mrs. Wilberforce difficulty."

Mr. Caesar had finished adjusting his neckwear, and I had yet to find any material with which I might smudge his boots or stain his breeches, so I stood back and let him return to his cousin's side. "You caused us *all* difficulty. I was frantic. I thought you'd been abducted."

"I told him he was being silly," put in Miss Bickle. "I said you'd probably just been taken away by pixies."

"That's still a form of abduction," Miss Mitchelmore pointed out. "And besides I'm not certain that there *are* any pixies in Bath."

Miss Bickle's eyes, already very wide, grew wider. "There are pixies *everywhere*. You just can't see them." To give the lady her due, she was largely right. Although we very seldom steal people.

Sighing, Miss Mitchelmore rose, going first to her cousin and then to her friend. "I am sorry," she said. "I am truly sorry. But I was distressed, and as you might imagine I was not thinking clearly." She sat next to Miss Bickle at the pianoforte and began picking out a tune to which Miss Bickle made occasional and wholly dissonant contributions.

Mr. Caesar lowered himself into the spot on the sofa that his cousin had just vacated. "I understand, cos; I was just concerned. And actually I remain concerned because you still haven't told us how you got home."

"Was it pixies?" asked Miss Bickle. The look on her face said she would be extremely upset were it to transpire that it was *not*, in fact, pixies.

"No, it was not pixies." Miss Mitchelmore took a deep breath. She had already recounted this story to her parents, but since her father was mostly interested in things that could be detonated or electrified and her mother was mostly interested in things that could be dissected, they had taken the news remarkably well. Mr. Caesar, on the other hand, was likely to worry. "It was Lady Georgiana Landrake."

A heavy silence fell over the room. Or as heavy as a silence could be when punctuated by Miss Bickle's irregular plinking.

"The Duke of Annadale?" asked Mr. Caesar, aghast.

"I'm not sure it's right to call her that."

Miss Bickle was already clapping her hands with delight. "That sounds thrilling. Did she put you under a spell? Did she murder you?"

"How could she have murdered me? I'm sitting right here."

"You could be a ghost. The Earl of Innismere attended three society picnics after he died. It was very awkward, especially for his widow." In a spirit of experimentation, Miss Bickle extended a single begloved, bejewelled finger and moved it slowly towards Miss Mitchelmore's face.

"Please don't poke me."

"I have to poke you or else I shan't know you are not a ghost and shall be unable to avenge your murder."

"Lizzie, don't poke me."

She poked her. "Oh Mae, you're alive! I'm so happy."

"That does at least"—Mr. Caesar had shifted to a studied lounge, a posture that said *I care not what you think, but by the way are my calves not excellent*—"spare us the difficulty of avenging your death."

"But don't worry," added Miss Bickle eagerly, "when you *are* murdered, I have simply *hundreds* of plans for vengeance."

"Hundreds?" Miss Mitchelmore was accustomed to her friend's flights of fancy, but some were easier to adjust to than others.

"Oh yes. The first involves scorpions."

Mr. Caesar looked up from the sofa. "And the second?"

"Also scorpions."

Although she could have asked about the third, Miss Mitchelmore chose instead to change the subject, or at least to bring the conversation back to its original course. "In any case, there will be no need. I survived Lady Georgiana's attentions and am quite well."

"I'm not so sure about that." Mr. Caesar was frowning. "What happened to you last night was not natural, and if somebody has used magic against you once I see no reason they would not do it again."

Miss Mitchelmore stiffened at that. It could not have been easy for somebody who had recently survived a magical assault to begin contemplating another so rapidly. "Do you really think I could be in danger?"

"Physically, perhaps not. Socially, certainly." Mr. Caesar's chin came to rest contemplatively and aesthetically on one hand. "Had

you responded less quickly last night you would have been humiliated at best, ruined at worst. Had anybody other than Lady Georgiana found you in the garden, the scandal might have been
irreparable, and even now it may prove costly."

Miss Mitchelmore shivered as though a chill breeze had blown
through the room. I accentuated the effect by adopting the form of
a chill breeze myself and hanging about her for some seconds
before retreating. "We were not seen, I think. And even if we
were . . ."

"I swear, Mae, if you say *we are both ladies,* I shall have Lizzie
poke you again."

Not waiting for the excuse, Miss Bickle poked her friend
anyway.

"But we *are* both la—Lysistrata, please stop it."

Chastened as only the use of her full name by somebody other
than her mother could chasten, Miss Bickle lowered her offending
digit.

"You are both ladies, and Mr. Ellersley and I are both gentlemen. It does not mean that people do not talk. Society may be
blinkered, but it is not wholly blind."

"Surely you *cannot* be suggesting . . ." Miss Mitchelmore's fingertips found their way unthinkingly to the back of her hand where
the Duke of Annadale had kissed it, then to her cheek where she
had wiped away a tear.

Languidly, Mr. Caesar stretched. "I know nothing about Lady
Georgiana. I do not know her habits or her proclivities. And I have
as much cause as any to treat rumours with caution. But were I
struck with a sudden magical curse and then rescued *from* that
curse by somebody who, it is widely speculated, dabbles in sorcery,
I should be at least suspicious."

"She was kind to me. I would not like to think ill of her."

"You are sweet, cousin, but thinking well of bad people never leads to good ends. At any rate, you have been magically attacked. It stands to reason that you need to be magically protected, or else that your attacker needs to be rooted out and made to stop."

"Except"—Miss Mitchelmore remained very tense and rather chill, and I was no longer contributing to that condition—"I haven't the first idea how to do either of those things."

"Pixies?" suggested Miss Bickle. "Or sprites, spriggans, nixies, boggans, naiads, dryads, or kobolds if we could find some caves." She smiled with the contentment available only to fools, babes, and sages. "They made my bracelets." Her bracelets were indeed of fine workmanship, delicate bands of spun gold that wound up both of her forearms and gleamed with jewels in unexpected places.

"Or the old gods, of course," added Mr. Caesar, who had benefited from a classical education. "But for warding off evil I suspect you'd need to speak to Hecate, and that would involve a crossroads, a new moon, and I think at least two dogs. Or you could try Artemis. She has a fondness for virgins, although she might want you to be a touch more athletic."

"I am quite athletic enough, thank you." Miss Mitchelmore bristled, not quite certain if she was being insulted. "I ride well and walk regularly."

"Yes, but how's your archery?"

"Nonexistent."

"There *is* another option." Mr. Caesar sat up, wearing an expression of discomfort that, on this occasion, had nothing to do with my interference. "I am familiar with—that is, I may know how to contact one of the Galli."

"The eunuch-priests?" The tone in Miss Mitchelmore's voice

was not one of shock, precisely, but its pitch rose more sharply than she might have intended. "Are they not . . . that is to say . . . I do not believe they are respectable people. . . ."

Mr. Caesar's eyes narrowed. "Maelys, respectable people, as you are fast learning, do all manner of things that they would never admit to in public. The Cult of Cybele has power, and while they are unlikely to be able to *undo* whatever sorcery has been laid upon you, they may at least be able to offer you guidance." He sat back a moment, then added, "Also they prefer to be called priestesses."

Miss Bickle was looking increasingly put out. "I still say we should visit the fairies. There must be a mound or a hillock somewhere near Bath we could go to, and fairies are *famously* trustworthy." Needless to say I like Miss Bickle very much.

"If you'll pardon my language," replied Mr. Caesar, "they bloody well are not."

"Then *why* do they call them the Good Folk?"

"It's ironic."

"It isn't. Fairies hate iron." This, in point of fact, is a myth, but it is awfully convenient for us to let you go on believing it.

Suddenly restless, Miss Mitchelmore rose and took a turn about the room. "Might we instead think to unmask the culprit? I should sooner not go trafficking with strange cults or gallivanting through fairy rings."

"You should, Mae," said Miss Bickle, "it's *so* jolly."

Mr. Caesar watched his cousin warily. "While I can't quite believe I'm endorsing a plan the first step of which is *go and talk to the pixies,* I do think pursuing *some* kind of supernatural knowledge might be our best strategy. After all, so far we only have one suspect in this matter, and it seems you refuse to suspect her."

"I do not refuse to suspect her." Miss Mitchelmore laid one hand on her breast in a gesture that read half as sincerity, half as an effort to measure the rate of her own heart. "I wish only to keep an open mind. To think charitably of her as I would like others to think charitably of me."

"There is a line between charity and folly, cousin. But perhaps we could compromise. If you will accept that Lady Georgiana is a suspect, I will happily consider any others you can name."

It took Miss Mitchelmore some while to name others, but she eventually managed it. "Mr. Clitherowe? He proposed marriage to me last year, and I refused him."

"*And,*" added Miss Bickle, "he is a clergyman, and clergymen are notoriously weak-willed and subject to temptation. Look at Father Jerome. Or Ambrosio."

Miss Mitchelmore shook her head. "Lizzie, you really need to read more appropriate books."

"You say that, but at least I shall know what to do if a monk with a magical myrtle bough attempts to ravish me."

"The Gothic aside, we shall add Mr. Clitherowe to the list." Mr. Caesar sat up and began to gently massage his temples. "Anybody else?"

"I have recently started attending a new modiste. She might have provided me with a cursed dress for some malicious reason of her own. Or Madame Ebchester may have hexed me in order to throw suspicion on her rival."

Miss Bickle stood rapidly enough to knock over the piano stool. "Ooh, I've just had a thought. What about Miss Worthing? She *hates* you."

"Madeleine Worthing?" Miss Mitchelmore's face fell. "I've always rather liked her."

"I know, but she told me she thought you were a pinch-faced scow who gave no thought to the needs or feelings of other ladies." She smiled again. "So you see, that's good news, isn't it?"

"How, exactly?" asked Mr. Caesar.

"Well, if it's her we can just tell her mama and she'll put a stop to things immediately. Mrs. Worthing is quite fearsome."

For reasons that eluded me but may have been to do with "kindness," Miss Mitchelmore seemed more concerned with Miss Worthing's opinion than with her potential mystical peril. "I still don't understand what I might have done to offend her."

"I think it was something to do with Lady Montgomery's ball last season. The Viscount Fortrose quite ignored poor Madeleine and asked you to dance instead, and you refused him. I think she took that for arrogance."

"She never said anything. Besides, my dance card was already full and it would have been ill-mannered to slight another gentleman for him, even if he *is* a viscount."

"Well, perhaps you should tell her—"

"*To reiterate.*" Mr. Caesar had plainly had enough of the digression. "Our comprehensive list of suspects for the crime of attempting to publicly undress you by magical means are"—he began counting off on his fingers—"a mild-mannered cleric, two dressmakers, a slightly annoyed debutante—"

"She isn't a debutante anymore," corrected Miss Bickle, who could be oddly pedantic about her areas of especial interest.

Unperturbed, Mr. Caesar continued. "Or the mysterious noblewoman who is already suspected—albeit unprovably—of four counts of murder by witchcraft and who was swift to take advantage of your predicament to manoeuvre you into her private carriage, wherein she might have done anything she pleased to you."

"But chose instead"—Miss Mitchelmore was seized by an intense urge to defend her rescuer's honour—"to deliver me safely home at no advantage to herself. You *promised* that you would consider other suspects."

Mr. Caesar was rubbing his temples again "And I am trying, cos, I am truly trying. But on the one hand we have the Duke of Annadale—"

"Please don't call her that, it's cruel."

"Think of it as necessary dramatic emphasis. The point is that on the one hand we have a woman of profoundly dubious character who we already know to be at the heart of one deadly mystery and on the other we have . . . Miss Worthing or a modiste."

"I saw Madeleine Worthing wearing henbane once," said Miss Bickle. "I think she could very well be a witch."

Miss Mitchelmore cocked her head to one side. "Lizzie, why are you so determined for it to be Madeleine?"

"Well . . ." Miss Bickle wriggled a little uncomfortably. "I just think it would be more fun if it were someone from our set. We could have a proper rivalry. We could run out onto the moors and hurl spells at one another."

"What moors?" asked Miss Mitchelmore.

"There are *bound* to be some moors somewhere."

"There's the Cotswolds," suggested Mr. Caesar.

"Don't be silly." Miss Bickle shot him a glance that said *You are very, very foolish indeed.* "You can't have a magical duel on a windswept Cotswold."

Miss Mitchelmore was beginning to get a headache, and not one I had given her. Although I think I would have gone for a toothache in the circumstances. It might have made her speak in an amusing manner. "Since I know nothing of magic and neither, as far as I know, do either of you, perhaps we should avoid plans that involve my having any kind of duel with anybody on any kind of geographical feature."

The level of pout of which Miss Bickle proved herself capable should have been possible only in somebody whose lips had been blessed with a specific pout-enhancing enchantment, but she achieved it quite on her own merits. "Well, then if we are *not* to speak with the pixies and we are *not* to duel anybody anywhere, then it may be best that we do nothing."

"I actually think Lizzie's right on this one," said Mr. Caesar. "Unless whoever it is strikes again—and they very well may not, in which case we have nothing to worry about—we have little to go on. But whatever you do I would make certain to stay away from the Duke of"—he checked himself—"from Lady Georgiana Landrake."

It was, Miss Mitchelmore was eventually forced to concede, the best plan. From my perspective, of course, it was a disaster. There could scarcely be any outcome less conducive to a compelling narrative than the young lady waiting patiently and avoiding confrontation. Still, I resolved to keep an eye on her and her companions in case their lives became diverting again and, to my delight, I found I did not have long to wait.

3

While Miss Mitchelmore remained stubbornly committed to a strategy of keeping her head down until new information emerged, her friends proved less stubborn and therefore more entertaining. Miss Bickle spent the afternoon wandering the woods in a daze trying to talk to tree spirits and jump through rings of toadstools, to limited effect. The tree spirits are real enough, but they are fundamentally *trees* and find conversations with humans even more tiresome than I do.

Following Mr. Caesar proved more fruitful. He spent much of the day in study—knowing that his mother's inheritance could not sustain him all his life and that, should his sisters fail to find appropriate matches, he would one day be responsible for their comfort, he had a notion of taking to the law and, at the time I first encountered him, was working on his application to the Inns of Court.

Come evening, however, he made his way into town and went, somewhat furtively, down a certain street to a certain house, where he knocked, quietly, on a certain door. It was a door on which he had not knocked in some time, and he was not sure how he would be received on his return.

That door opened a crack to reveal a tall man wearing a gown old enough to still have hoop skirts. He eyed his visitor warily for so long that I got bored waiting, transformed myself into a mouse, and skittered past him. "Fuck me, John?"

"Not this evening, Serena." Mr. Caesar gave him half a smile that he hoped signalled both irony and apology. "Now, can I come in or are you going to leave me standing outside attracting attention?"

Serena put out a hand and patted Mr. Caesar on the arm. "Johnny, my boy, everybody knows this is a house full of damnable sodomites. If anything, having you hanging in the window will be good for business. But come in anyway."

Inside, I was soon discovering from my vantage point on the floor, was a coffee house of sorts, full of low tables and soft furnishings upon which lounged gentlemen of varying ages, ethnicities, and degrees of dissipation. It was a liminal space, a twilight world in which men who lived outside the rule of ordinary society could come to re-create a facsimile of that society in their own image. As a dweller in liminal spaces myself, I approved, although I felt the exercise lacked a certain imagination.

"Ladies," Serena announced, clapping his hands loudly enough to command the attention of the whole room, if only for a moment. "Look who's paying us a visit."

The entrance of Mr. Caesar into the parlour attracted somewhat more attention than the return of the host, although the responses he drew were mostly variations on vulgar themes, some of them rather creative, by mortal standards at least.

"I thought we had a deal," said a slender, sharp-eyed gentleman reclining on a chaise longue. He was regarding Mr. Caesar with a heady mix of betrayal and venom. "*You* get the Ganymede Club and Mistress Muff's, I get Serena's and Lord Wittingham's Gentleman's Ball."

This, I would later learn (and would have surmised at the time but I really hadn't been paying very much attention) was Mr. Ellersley, whose relationship with John was still the occasional subject of gossip. The gossip was, I should stress, entirely accurate. They definitely fucked.

Mr. Caesar adopted a tone of strained reassurance touched with what the romantic in me chooses to characterise as wistful melancholy. "I'm not staying, Tom."

"Oh no, *do* stay." This was an older man in a powdered wig that made him look a full two feet taller than he actually was. "No offence, Tom, but he's much more fun than you are."

"Piss off, Lionel," replied Mr. Ellersley, eloquently.

"I assure you I will be happy to leave," Mr. Caesar continued, ignoring the side bickering, "the moment somebody tells me where I can find Tabitha."

A silence fell across the room.

Not one for pleading, Mr. Caesar glared at his erstwhile comrades. "Oh, come on. Somebody must know where she is."

"Tabitha doesn't want anything to do with *us*," Serena explained, rather bitterly, "and we want nothing to do with *her.*"

"But she came here for *years*. And not one of you has so much as written her a letter?" There were layers to Mr. Caesar's indignation that I could have spent happy hours peeling back, had I the inclination. The distaste at being thwarted was part of it, certainly. But so was the knowledge that he had, in many ways, been part of the problem.

Mr. Ellersley arched a thin eyebrow. "Have you?"

"I've been in London."

The man in the wig leaned forwards. "We've *all* been in London, darling. The point is that none of us wanted to see her after she . . . after she went into the service of Cybele." This, I suspected, was euphemistic language. While it was true that to associate oneself with the old gods often meant turning one's back on former acquaintances, joining the Galli often opened a person up to particular scorn. Even—perhaps especially—in a place like Serena's. This was a society that held manhood as paramount and immutable, and resented the reminder that it was neither.

Drawing himself up stiffly, Mr. Caesar looked down at his interlocutor. "I'd have thought, Lionel, that what a lady does with her own life is her own business."

"Oh for fuck's sake, John"—Serena threw herself down in a chair—"she's not a fucking lady, she's a fucking molly. I may wear a dress and call myself Serena but I'm under no delusions that under all of this I'm still a bloody man. But fucking Tabby thought she was too fucking good for us."

A man in military uniform, with insignias that marked him out as holding a captain's rank, downed the last of his coffee. "That's a little unfair, 'Rena. She clearly did what she had to do. Turning to the old gods can't be a step a person takes lightly."

"But there are so *few* of us." Serena's shoulders slumped, and she let her head flop forwards into her hands. "All the old houses are closing down: Mrs. Clap's, Lady Merkin's, the Gadarine Club. Even this place is barely scraping by and we'd have been shut down twice if Lionel hadn't been sucking off the magistrate."

Lionel inclined his head humbly. "I live to serve."

"Which means"—Serena looked up—"that I take it personally when people abandon us."

"Did she abandon us," asked Mr. Caesar, "or did we abandon her?"

"Well, *you* abandoned *all* of us," sniped Mr. Ellersley from his position on the chaise.

Not one to be impugned, Mr. Caesar folded his arms. "Because you *told* me to, Tom. You said, 'I never want to see your smug face again.'"

"Yes, but you shouldn't have *listened* to him," said the captain. "He's a colossal prick."

"Either way, I need to find Tabitha. My cousin is under a curse, and Tabitha is the only person I can think of who might know something about that kind of magic."

Shifting on his seat, Mr. Ellersley sat up. "Which cousin?"

"The one not presently at Eton." For the benefit of the reader, the one who *was* presently at Eton was Miss Mitchelmore's younger brother, who rejoiced in the improbable name of Corantin and whose pertinence to our present narrative is limited.

"Maelys?" Mr. Ellersley looked genuinely saddened, from which I deduced that he had met Miss Mitchelmore, found her personable, and had no desire to see her suffer for his own amusement. This last trait is one I have never quite been able to comprehend, since it is almost wholly absent from my own people.

Mr. Caesar nodded and, being now the only man standing, lowered himself into a free chair, of which there were several— Serena had, it seems, been right about the house's depleting clientele. "It might be nothing," he explained, "but I think she's in danger."

"John, you disgusting creature"—stretching like a cat, Lionel nearly lost his wig—"you're not trying to rescue a damsel in distress are you? We aren't the shining-armour sorts around here."

"Strange as it may seem," said Mr. Ellersley, "I think he might actually be doing something halfway decent."

Mr. Caesar looked at Mr. Ellersley with a scornful weariness. "I've always been decent, Tom. I just didn't have endless time for your nonsense."

"Oh, fuck off," replied Mr. Ellersley, eloquent once again. "But if you really need to speak to Tabitha, last I heard she was living on Westgate Street."

Lionel winced. "My God, who would live *there?*"

"Nothing wrong with Westgate Street," put in the captain. "A lot of my men would *love* to live on Westgate Street. There are far worse places in Bath."

"Not that one talks about in polite society," Lionel observed.

Serena gave a perfunctory laugh. "Darling, as a general rule, polite company doesn't include people whose cocks you've had up your arse."

Sensing that the evening was about to devolve into bickering, and having found the information he had come for, Mr. Caesar rose. "Thank you, Tom. And thank you, Miss Serena, for your hospitality."

Rising also, Serena reached out his arms and pulled Mr. Caesar into an embrace, crumpling his skirts in the process. "Come back to us, John."

And then Mr. Caesar, to my disappointment, left the house of dissolute gentlemen and, like the tiresome mortal that he was, went home. In punishment, I hid one of his shoes.

⸺ ● ⸺

From an abundance of caution, I sought Miss Tabitha's lodgings in advance of Mr. Caesar's and Miss Mitchelmore's arrival. The servants of the old gods sometimes possess capabilities that make my role as an observer, chronicler, and occasional maker of mischief somewhat awkward.

There was a sizeable gap beneath the door of the lodging house, so I was able to inveigle my way inside in mouse form. When dealing with persons who may possess the capacity to penetrate glamours, I prefer small shapes. That way, even an observer who could perceive my true nature would need to peek behind the right chair leg or into the right corner.

I found Miss Tabitha in the house's common room. She— despite Serena's comments, Miss Tabitha most certainly was a lady, in the eyes of the gods at least, and no other eyes truly mattered save her own—was its only inhabitant, perched on a slightly tatty sofa, reading a slightly tatty book next to a window that was saved from tattiness only by that adjective's inapplicability to glass. She wore a yellow dress that managed—within what must have been her limited means—to marry the symbology of her sect with the fashions of the day, and her hair was bound up within a turban, also yellow.

Deciding to chance my luck and test her capabilities, I scampered over to where she was sitting, climbed mousily onto the furniture, and sat by her foot. She glanced down, grimaced in a way that suggested she saw me as a rodent rather than a playful sprite come to torment her with my winsome japes, and nudged me away with her foot.

Comforted that she did not possess the fairy sight, I scampered off, adopted a more normal form of invisibility, and waited for her guests to arrive.

I did not have to wait long. I have always had impeccable dramatic timing.

The knock at the door came as expected and, curious, Miss Tabitha rose from her spot, set her novel aside, and went down to admit Miss Mitchelmore and Mr. Caesar. Assuming the form of a spider, I took up a vantage point in the corner of the room.

"John?" The tone in Miss Tabitha's voice was an admixture of pleasure and anger. "It's been years."

From my hiding place I saw a flash of that feeling you mortals call *guilt* pass across Mr. Caesar's features. "Too many."

"What kept you away?" Despite Mr. Caesar's frankly restrained show of contrition, Miss Tabitha did not seem entirely placated.

"If I admitted it was cowardice, would you be more or less inclined to forgive me?"

"You know, I'm not actually sure." Miss Tabitha gave Mr. Caesar an appraising look, then turned her gaze to Miss Mitchelmore. "And who's this?"

Mr. Caesar straightened his cravat. "Tabitha, may I introduce my cousin Miss Mitchelmore. Maelys, this is Tabitha, an old . . ." He hesitated a moment, caught for words as your kind sometimes are. "An old friend who I have not made time for in far too long, and a cultist of Cybele."

Dropping a flawless curtsey, Miss Mitchelmore smiled. "A pleasure to meet you."

For a moment the three of them hovered in the doorway, and then Tabitha turned and led her guests inside; I scuttled along the ceiling after them. "So," she asked, "what brings you to this part of town?"

"Would you believe me if I said I just wanted to call on you?" asked Mr. Caesar, a note of apology in his voice.

"Not for a second." Tabitha returned to her sofa and sat with her legs outstretched, her skirts draping daintily over the seat. "I'd offer you tea, but I don't have any servants so I'd need to light a fire, boil the kettle, it would all be rather complicated. And my *guess* is that you're here for *her.*" She shot Miss Mitchelmore a warm but cynical glance.

Trembling slightly, Miss Mitchelmore nodded. "Yes. Please don't be angry with him."

"Oh, I'm *very* angry with him." Tabitha laughed and Miss Mitchelmore blanched. "But not on your account. And you don't need to be so frightened."

"I'm not . . . that is"—straightening her back, Miss Mitchelmore made an effort to compose herself—"I've never met a servant of the old gods before."

Tabitha raised a finger. "Not a servant. The old gods aren't like that whiny prick Jesus—"

Miss Mitchelmore gasped.

"I'm joking, dear, just joking. I'm as Christian as you are in a lot of ways. But the old gods aren't like the Creator; they aren't jealous, they don't want our *love.* They're rather like greengrocers: they have something you need, you pay them for it."

If her intent had been to put Miss Mitchelmore at her ease, she had failed rather completely. The lady froze in place. "And what might I have to . . . to pay?"

"Depends on what you want, but in Magna Mater's case it's pretty simple. Want to win a war against Carthage? Build her a temple. Want an empire? Make your emperor's mother her face on Earth. Want answers? Feed the chickens."

Mr. Caesar settled himself uncomfortably on a stool. "Chickens?"

"Sacred chickens. Now, why don't you tell me what's wrong."

So Miss Mitchelmore told her, about the ball and Lady

Georgiana and how they didn't know what to do except to seek help from either the old gods or the fairies and—well, that gets rather personal. Suffice it to say that she went on to say some things about my people for which I shall, from the goodness of my heart, forgive her.

Miss Tabitha listened to the whole story, nodded, and then said, "Well, you *are* in trouble, aren't you?"

"Can you *help* her, Tab?" asked Mr. Caesar, somewhat impatiently.

"Probably not."

Mr. Caesar folded his arms in a way I personally found a little huffy. "Oh, good, I'm so glad I came to visit."

"John," Miss Mitchelmore protested, "we are *guests.*"

"Obviously." Mr. Caesar heaved a beleaguered sigh. "It's also wonderful to see you again, Tabitha, but this is . . . pressing."

"And what," asked Tabitha, folding her hands neatly on her lap, "was pressing you for the last year and a half?"

"I was busy. I was in London, and I hadn't realised how beastly the others had been."

Miss Tabitha looked rueful. "Serena was furious with me."

"Who's Serena?" asked Miss Mitchelmore, who I suspected was feeling a little left out of the conversation. "And for that matter, who are the others?"

"A set of mutual friends," her cousin explained, "and I think they're sorry, or most of them are. They just—didn't know quite how to react."

"They could have reacted by saying *We understand, Tabitha, we support you and won't cut you out of our lives and our homes.*" She sighed. "But you're not here to talk about that, are you? You're here to talk about magic." They were. And I was there to listen to them talking about magic. All of this business with humans discussing their emotions and their personal relationships was inestimably tiresome to me.

Miss Mitchelmore nodded. "Yes. If you—I'm sorry, I don't really understand what's going on."

"Long story," offered Mr. Caesar by way of non-explanation. "And I'm *sorry*," he told Tabitha, "I really am. But—"

"But you need my help. Or the goddess's help, at least?"

"Yes." Mr. Caesar gave a sharp little nod.

Miss Tabitha rose, crossed the room, and then knelt down beside Miss Mitchelmore, peering closely at her. This, I suspected, was mere theatre, since she had demonstrated no extrasensory capabilities when I had tested her, but it made Miss Mitchelmore feel attended to, and that, I understand, is important to mortals. "There are two possibilities," she mused, "although they overlap strongly. It's either ordinary sorcery, or the intervention of some entity."

"Why do they overlap?" asked Miss Mitchelmore, turning her face towards Miss Tabitha's and leaning back slightly for fear of whatever strange powers the priestess might possess.

"Because sorcerers work with entities, and entities instruct sorcerers. If it's ordinary magic, then you want to find a witch, or else go to the crossroads and deal with Hecate directly. If it's some invisible spirit plaguing you"—it was *not* an invisible spirit plaguing her, I am confident that I was the only invisible spirit in Miss Mitchelmore's vicinity for the vast majority of this misadventure—"then find out what it wants or who sent it, and if it's the wrath of a god or goddess then you're probably in real trouble."

"Is that likely?" asked Miss Mitchelmore, displaying, I thought, greater fortitude than many would have in her situation.

"Maybe. Judged any beauty contests lately? Had sex with any attractive animals that turned out to be a disguised deity with a vindictive wife?"

"I most certainly have not and believe it impertinent of you to make the suggestion."

Miss Tabitha smiled. "Just checking."

"So there's nothing you can do?" asked Mr. Caesar.

"Not immediately. I could ask the Great Mother to intervene, but if there *is* another god involved that might start a disagreement and believe me you do *not* want to be in a disagreement amongst divinities. At least, not if you want to keep your topless towers unburned."

"I like my towers as they are, thank you," replied Miss Mitchelmore.

"What I suggest we do," Miss Tabitha went on, "is go outside and consult the chickens. They can't tell you what's happening, but they *can* tell you if what you're going to do next is a good idea or a bad idea."

Mr. Caesar raised an eyebrow. "According to whom?"

"Cybele. But she's normally trustworthy. And you came to me because you wanted to consult the goddess. Let's consult."

The sacred chickens—if sacred they were; chickens look very much like chickens to me—were housed in a small coop in the yard behind the lodging house. Miss Tabitha let her guests out first, then emerged once more with a large tambourine and a paper bag full of pastries.

"Tabby, did you have cakes all this time and not tell us?" complained Mr. Caesar. "You're a terrible hostess."

"I wasn't aware I was *being* a hostess. I thought you came here to consult Mater Magna. Anyway, these are sacred cakes."

Motivated perhaps by curiosity, perhaps by an impish desire with which I strongly identified, Mr. Caesar reached into the bag and drew out a round, golden biscuit. "These are Shrewsbury cakes."

"*Sacred* Shrewsbury cakes."

Mr. Caesar took a nibble. "This has nutmeg in it. I refuse to believe that anything sacred can have nutmeg in it."

"John"—trying to suppress a smirk, Miss Mitchelmore gave her cousin a reproving look—"stop eating the sacred cakes."

"You see, *some* people know how to behave." Miss Tabitha held out the bag. "*You* may have a Shrewsbury cake, Miss Mitchelmore. Since you've been so nice about everything."

Taking a cake, Miss Mitchelmore nodded a polite thank-you. "So, what are we actually going to do?"

"You are going to tell me what you intend to do about your"— she made an encompassing gesture that included Miss Mitchelmore's entire person and, by extension, destiny—"curse situation, and then the goddess will tell us, through the chickens, if she likes it or not."

"This is absurd," said Mr. Caesar, although for all the absurdity of it, he had stopped eating the sacred Shrewsbury cake.

"*This*," Miss Tabitha corrected him, "is the old religion. The temples are smaller now, of course, and I did eat one of the sacred hens last week, but there is power here if you'll stop being such an utter prat about it."

With a level of ceremony that I would have found surprising had I not seen augurs at work before (I have been around rather a long while, did I mention?), Miss Tabitha opened the door to the chicken coop. Then she stepped back, took one of the sacred Shrewsbury cakes in her hands, and crumbled it on the ground before the henhouse. When that was done she stooped, picked up her tambourine, struck it six times, and uttered a wild exhortation to the mother of gods.

Slowly, the chickens emerged.

"Now, Miss Mitchelmore—"

"Oh, please do call me Maelys. It seems wrong to use given names with John and not with me."

"Very well, Maelys, tell me what you intend to do next."

Miss Mitchelmore looked down. The sacred chickens—three brown, three white—were scratching in circles and eyeing the crumbs of Shrewsbury cake uncertainly. "I don't think we'd formulated an exact strategy."

Miss Tabitha looked disappointed. "An exact strategy *would* have been helpful."

"I suppose, perhaps, Lizzie is quite keen to talk to the fairies?"

A chicken gave a disdainful cluck.

"I believe the Great Mother considers that unwise," translated Miss Tabitha.

"Or else, I could simply return to London, hope that the curse is specific to Bath?"

Not even a clucking this time.

"Also does not meet with the approval of the goddess."

Miss Mitchelmore was quiet a moment, thinking. "There is a picnic tomorrow. I had thought I might not go in case something awful happened but—well—can you tell me at least if I will be safe?"

Two of the chickens began pecking at the crumbs. One of them, a white one, picked up a particularly large fragment of cake, then dropped it again and flew back to the coop.

Miss Tabitha made a sound of deep consideration. "Well, that's interesting."

"Don't be dramatic, Tabby," chided Mr. Caesar.

"I'll be dramatic if I want to be. The auspices are complex. You will face danger, but also opportunity."

"Does that mean I should go?" asked Miss Mitchelmore, a note of hope creeping into her voice.

"It means you should consider it. It also means John can finish his cake if he wants."

Mr. Caesar gave Miss Tabitha a grateful bow. "Thank you. Not for"—he waved the Shrewsbury cake—"for helping."

And Miss Tabitha made all of the usual oh-it-was-nothing noises, and the three of them back-and-forthed in that polite way that mortals do (or did, I travelled by underground yesterday and people were *quite rude* to me, but I suppose that's a peril of visibility). When they had finished that particular social dance, Mr. Caesar and Miss Tabitha embraced one another and made promises not to be strangers.

A peculiar promise, for I've always found strangers rather fascinating. They have such a wonderful habit of turning out to be beautiful, unexpected, deadly things.

CHAPTER

4

The next day, the Bickles were giving a picnic by a stretch of the River Avon a mildly inconvenient distance outside of Bath. Several of my mortal aliases were invited but the outdoor setting provided ample opportunities for more entertaining shapes (I have attended picnics before now as an ant, a wasp, an irate bull, and an unseasonable rain, depending on how the mood took me). I began this particular excursion in the form of a robin. Not an inconspicuous bird, of course, but an apposite one.

Affairs thrown by the Bickles were always well attended, primarily because their daughter, Miss Lysistrata Bickle, was their only child and thus heir to a vast if somewhat vulgar fortune founded in tin and, worse, trade. A secondary attraction was the gaggle of artistic notables that, drawn to the Bickles' generous patronage, were more than ready to put up with Mr. Bickle's terrible poetry and Mrs. Bickle's terrible singing. The Mitchelmores, barring the narratively irrelevant Corantin, were of course in attendance, Miss Mitchelmore having been reassured by the highly trustworthy words of an ecstatic cultist and her flock of magic hens that it would profit her to do so. The Caesars had come also, including Mr. Caesar's two sisters, young girls not quite out in society but presentable enough for picnics.

Mr. Bickle had chosen the site of the event for its proximity to what he considered "authentic nature," meaning it was well supplied with water and woodlands and rather poorly supplied with the kind of ground over which one could easily carry multiple large hampers and sufficient dining furniture to lay out a spread for forty people.

"If this clearing"—I heard one of the guests observe as the party stumbled through a seemingly interminable stretch of undergrowth—"is not *exceptionally* picturesque, I shall be asking Bickle to pay for my boots to be cleaned."

The clearing did, as it transpired, prove to be picturesque, although whether it was so pretty as to justify the damage to gentlemen's boots and women's skirts was very much a question of individual conscience. Still, once the tables were set up and the meal laid out and people began to settle down, the walk was soon forgotten by most and forgiven by many.

"You realise," Miss Bickle stage-whispered to Miss Mitchelmore and Mr. Caesar once they had established themselves beneath a tree a little distance from the rest of the party, "that not only are several of our suspects present today but I also saw three fairy rings on the way here."

"None of what you are about to say," warned Mr. Caesar, "will lead us *anywhere* good."

Miss Bickle folded her arms beneath her bosom and pouted. "Well, since *you* went on an adventure yesterday without *me*, I don't see why I shouldn't be able to take Mae to visit the fairies if I want to."

"It was *not* an adventure," Mr. Caesar replied, and not for the first time. "We simply went to visit an old friend and I didn't want to overwhelm her with too many visitors."

"But you got to see *magic*. I didn't get to see magic."

Miss Mitchelmore gave her friend a consoling pat on the shoulder. "It wasn't really magic, Lizzie, more . . . chickens."

"*Magic* chickens."

"And what matters," insisted Mr. Caesar, trying to assert something like control over the situation, "is that the . . . the Goddess Cybele, through the medium of magic chickens, foretold that coming to this picnic would be dangerous to Mae but might also benefit her. So we need to be on the lookout."

At this, Miss Bickle perked up. "Then I propose that we separate and each of us keep a close eye on either Lady Georgiana, Miss Worthing, or Mr. Clitherowe. All three of them are here and that seems a terribly fine coincidence. One of them simply *must* be plotting something."

"Plotting what, though?" asked Miss Mitchelmore. "Poultry aside, I shouldn't recognise sorcery if I fell over it."

"Oh, you know"—Miss Bickle seemed unperturbed—"I'm sure they'll be waving their hands and speaking Latin and things."

"Perhaps it would be safer if we remained together?" suggested Mr. Caesar. "If we split up, then there is one chance in three that Mae winds up following the very one who is trying to harm her."

Miss Bickle looked shocked. "I hadn't thought of that. We should all sit back to back so nobody can sneak up on us."

A tall gentleman with hair shading unfortunately towards ginger wandered over to the trio. "Good afternoon Miss Bickle, Miss Mitchelmore, Mr. Caesar. Fine weather, is it not?" Although he addressed the group his gaze was fixed unwaveringly on Miss Bickle.

"Lovely weather, yes Mr. Fillimore," she replied. Then waited for him to say something else. When he did not, she continued. "And it was equally lovely yesterday, and I hope it shall continue to be lovely tomorrow."

"Yes." The unfortunate Mr. Fillimore stumbled once again before managing to come to something resembling a point. "I believe that your father is soon to begin reciting from the *Lyrical Ballads* if you wished to—that is—I could accompany you to . . ."

"That's sweet of you, but I have heard my father recite Wordsworth many, many times and I am quite comfortable where I am."

After another unpleasant silence, the gentleman left, somewhat abashed.

"Poor fellow," Miss Bickle observed, "terribly gentle but I am sure he's after my fortune."

"Still," offered Miss Mitchelmore, "you should make the most of this afternoon to mingle. You will need to marry eventually, and you can't keep sending eligible young men away."

Miss Bickle screwed up her nose in an exaggerated *thinking* expression. "I believe I can. You see, the thing is I have absolute pots and pots of money."

"It is *vexing* isn't it?" Miss Mitchelmore's tone acquired a musing edge. "If one is poor, one must marry a rich man in order that one might be provided for, and if one is wealthy one must marry a still richer man in order that one not spend the rest of one's days providing for *him*."

"That," Miss Bickle said, "is why I fully intend to run away with the fairies at the first opportunity."

Multiple half-overheard lyric poems, several slices of cold beef, and a helping of blancmange later, Miss Mitchelmore and her companions were beginning to relax into the conclusion that there was not, in fact, going to be a repeat of the disappearing-gown incident. From time to time, Miss Mitchelmore would catch sight of one or other of the "suspects" standing in the shade of a tree or perusing the picnic tables, and would attempt to scrutinise them for any sign of malfeasance but, not being entirely certain what she was looking for, this did not help her. Nor did it help that of all their rogues' gallery, only Lady Georgiana ever seemed to look back. And when she did it was with a coldness in her eyes that Miss Mitchelmore could not help but find disturbing.

As the afternoon wore on, wasps began to gather around the plates and glasses of the increasingly quiescent picnickers. They dragged their sleek, yellow bodies over scraps of pie crust and around the rims of wineglasses, and it was only after a longer time watching than it should perhaps have taken that Miss Mitchelmore realised there were far more wasps gathering about her own particular part of the picnic than were gathered anywhere else.

Cautiously, not wishing to anger the creatures, she rose to her feet. "John," she stage-whispered, "are there—is it my imagination or are we surrounded?"

"Be calm," Mr. Caesar told her with a confidence that I suspect he was not truly feeling. "They're probably much more frightened of you than you are of—"

The wasps did not seem frightened. They rose to follow Miss Mitchelmore, singly at first and then taking off from where they had been crawling in clumps that became clouds that became swarms. They were, unmistakably, coming for her.

"Perhaps"—Mr. Caesar looked up at the wasps with an air of creeping dread—"our remaining together has kept you less safe than we hoped. I suggest you back away slowly and I will try to think of something."

Heeding her cousin's advice, Miss Mitchelmore crept backwards, but the swarm crept after her. Thus far she had at least not been stung, but it was only a matter of time. Looking down, she saw at least three or four wasps crawling across her slipper and felt—or imagined she felt—the prickle of insect legs working their way up her stocking.

The swarm was large enough now, and dense enough, that it was attracting notice, although so far it had attracted no assistance. It had, however, garnered a number of well-intentioned but contradictory shouts of advice, ranging from "play dead" to "scare 'em off." Mr. Bickle's suggestion—which was to remind her that wasps are part of nature's bounty and should be appreciated with as much awe and wonder as the most beautiful flower—seemed wholly unhelpful in the circumstances. While her own father, who had been sat a discreet distance away, keeping an eye on his daughter over the top of a copy of the hundred and third volume of the *Philosophical Transactions of the Royal Society*, contributed the only marginally more useful observation that he had read an article on the subject of *Vespula vulgaris* some months ago but could no longer remember the contents.

Looking from her friends to her family to the fast-growing crowd of observers and the still faster growing swarm of insects, Miss Mitchelmore concluded that there was but one recourse open to her. The River Avon was a few paces away and so, moving as slowly as she dared in order that she might not antagonise any of the hundred thousand venomous insects that had gathered around her, she inched towards it.

Even the slight motions she was making proved, at last, too much for the creatures that had already crawled inside her clothing, and she felt the sharp, hot pain of their stings on her ankles and wrists. Doing her best not to cry out, she made it to within inches of the banks of the Avon and then, taking one last breath, pitched herself headlong into it. Suspecting that this was where the most interesting anecdotes were leading me, I flitted from my bough, took the form of a minnow, and followed her. Or rather I followed her and then took the form of a minnow, since to do otherwise would have meant some undignified flopping around on a riverbank while I searched for a shape that could survive in air.

Although Miss Mitchelmore wore a walking gown rather than an evening gown, her attire was not at all suitable for swimming and, peering up through the surface of the water, she saw that the cloud of insects, far from dispersing as she had hoped, was waiting patiently for her to emerge. Or perhaps not so patiently, for increasing numbers of the furious creatures began to dive-bomb the river in a concerted, if futile, effort to reach and sting her.

And then, of course, there was the current, and the water soaking ever more deeply into her skirt and petticoat. It occurred to me that she would likely drown, which was disappointing because I had come to expect great—or at least intriguing—things from Miss Mitchelmore. Not so disappointing, of course, that I would have bothered to save her. One must take the long view after all, and she would be dead anyway in sixty or seventy years. You mortals are such fragile things, I used to wonder why you bother at all. Still wonder, really, although I now find myself in a similar predicament.

A sudden rip of water pulled her away and I pursued cautiously because this was not a natural current and, while we dwellers in otherworlds tend not to harm one another as a matter of course, accidents can happen and elemental spirits are notoriously careless. Trailing behind her in my fish's shape I watched her struggle for any fragment of control she might have over the direction the river was taking her, and I watched her find none. Not strictly needing to breathe, I did not know for sure how much time she had left but I suspected that it would not be so very long.

It was then that I saw figures moving through the water. Slender, sparkling, and unmistakably feminine figures. I changed my shape to that of a stream of bubbles in order that I might be more inconspicuous. We fair folk are kin to the nymphs, but we are not quite the *same* and they sometimes resent our intrusions into their domains. Godlets, they are, and like most divinities they can be petty unless placated.

From a safer distance, I observed as the naiads gathered around Miss Mitchelmore, and I wondered whether they intended to save her or kill her. In my experience, it is *very* much a fifty-fifty proposition.

I do not know quite how far we had travelled downstream when they finally permitted her to break the surface, but I do know that she was conscious, if barely. When you are in the naiads' clutches you die only if they wish you to, and it seems they did not, in this instance, wish her to. Instead they dumped her onto a muddy bank, where the Duke of Annadale knelt waiting.

"My apologies," she said, uncorking a bottle of Champagne that she had stolen from the picnic. Uncorking, I noticed, in such a way as to be certain that the cork was retained and did not fly into the river. That would have been an insult and, whether she was a witch or not, she clearly knew enough to avoid offending the entities she was attempting to mollify. "It was not this woman's intent to intrude. Another power pursues her and, to my regret, that pursuit has spilled into your river."

The naiads made a high, keening noise. For all their impatience, the apology *was* important. You cannot right a wrong if you do not acknowledge the wrong, and forgiveness comes only if it is explicitly asked for, and with the correct forms. Bringing wine also always helps.

The Duke of Annadale slowly tipped the bottle and let the Bickles' finest Champagne drain into the waters of the Avon. The naiads, now taking the form of fish, now of maidens, and now of a foam on the river, gambolled in it with drunken delight. Not wanting to be perceived as competing for the offering, I hastily exited the water in the shape of a kingfisher.

When she had finished her costly libation—albeit at no strict cost to herself—the Duke of Annadale turned her attention to Miss Mitchelmore, who was slowly stirring at her feet. "I am beginning to think," she said, "that you are just trying to steal all of my cloaks."

Sputtering but still largely alive, Miss Mitchelmore opened her eyes. "So it *was* you."

"What was me?"

"All of *this*." Trying to stand but managing only to kneel, Miss Mitchelmore indicated her general state of dishevelment.

"Now, now, you jumped in the river of your own free will. And it was good thinking, in a way. Apart from the naiads."

Soaked through, missing her bonnet and one of her walking boots, which she felt certain the river spirits had stolen deliberately (she was probably right; they are nasty, acquisitive creatures), Miss Mitchelmore could do little but remain in the mud and look up with as much defiance as she could muster. "For all I know you sent both the nymphs and the wasps against me."

"Ah, yes. Because I am a witch. A witch who has set the full might of her considerable arts against one slightly inconsequential girl."

Miss Mitchelmore made another effort to rise to her feet and, when the Duke of Annadale put out a hand to assist her, started from it as though it were made of hot coals. "I can manage for myself, thank you."

"I am only being courteous."

With much struggle, Miss Mitchelmore eventually brought herself upright, although the mud was surely ruining her exposed stocking. "The last time I gave you my hand, you kissed it."

"Which was also courteous."

"From a gentleman it would be courteous. From a lady it was"—her voice caught in a way I have heard many times before, and which always leads to places worth visiting—"it was peculiar."

"And is a little peculiarity so terrible?"

Having no answer, or perhaps fearing the answer she *did* have, Miss Mitchelmore turned and began to walk away. "I should return to the picnic. I shall be missed."

"The wasps rather did for the picnic. I suspect that they will be sending search parties for you soon enough and then everybody will be returning home."

Miss Mitchelmore winced. "And I shall be the girl who made a scene and ruined the gathering for everybody."

"Don't be so downhearted. For now they think you are the girl who made a scene and drowned in a river. Besides, before your little incident Mr. Bickle was about to recite a composition of his own entitled 'Ode to a Butterfly That Alighted on My Glove One Wednesday Morning.' I think several of the guests will be thankful that you spared them."

The sun had sunk low in the sky and an early evening breeze combined with the river water to send a shudder to Miss Mitchelmore's very bones.

"At *least* let me put my cloak about you. You shall catch a chill."

Hesitant but with enough good sense to set her health above

her uncertainties, Miss Mitchelmore allowed the Duke of Annadale to drape her cloak around her shoulders, and although it
solved the immediate question of the breeze, there were other
problems it decidedly did *not* solve. For the lady was very close now,
and as she fastened the cloak about Miss Mitchelmore's neck, her
fingertips brushed her throat in a way that sparked a certain *awareness* to which Miss Mitchelmore was quite unaccustomed. "Thank
you. I did not mean to be ungrateful."

"You almost died. For your manners to lapse a little is under-
standable. But if you are ready to listen I do sincerely believe I can
help you."

"Because you are a witch?"

"I suppose that depends on what you think a *witch* to be. It
might be better to say that I have needed, over the years, to learn a
number of things about the world that other people seldom need
to learn."

This did not seem to reassure Miss Mitchelmore in the slightest,
but then she *did* have rather a lot to be thinking about at the time.
"What sort of things?"

"When I saw what happened to you at Lady Etheridge's ball, I
formulated a number of theories. I hoped for your sake that you
had simply been the target of some puckish spirit. Such things exist
and will occasionally play tricks on unsuspecting young ladies."
She slanders us a little on that account. Only a little, mind you.

"That seems a strange thing to hope."

"The hobgoblins are malicious," she said. And here I defend
my kind rather more strongly. We are not *malicious,* we simply enjoy
chaos. "But they seldom conceive vendettas unless one of their
kings or queens instructs them to. And I very much doubt that you
have accidentally slighted Oberon or Titania."

In this, the Duke of Annadale vastly underestimates my Lord's capacity for pettiness. As, recently, did I.

"I feel sure," said Miss Mitchelmore, "I should have remembered if I had."

"You might not—fairies are tricky beings—but this does not look like the work of the Other Court. It has a vindictiveness to it that bespeaks a mortal agent."

Recalling a little of her earlier misgivings, Miss Mitchelmore stopped and turned to face the Duke of Annadale. "That much I had worked out for myself. Indeed my friends and I had gone so far as to compile a list of suspects. A list of which you were at the head."

"Really?" The Duke of Annadale gave a knowing smile. "Yes, on balance I suppose that makes sense. But what motive would I have to hurt you?"

"Well . . ." In spite of herself, Miss Mitchelmore looked down, and then up through long eyelashes in a manner that she had been taught to reserve for eligible gentlemen. "We *have* established that you are quite terribly wicked."

"True, but I like to think that there is a difference between wickedness and cruelty."

"And what difference is that?"

"Give me your hand again and I will show you."

Hesitantly Miss Mitchelmore reached out from beneath the cloak and let the Duke of Annadale take her hand. The Duke turned it upwards, as though cradling a baby bird, and then slowly traced her thumb the length of the palm. Through gloves the sensation was muted, but it still made Miss Mitchelmore halt and bite her lip in a—

"*There* you are." Mr. Caesar's voice came first, followed by his person, and followed again by a troupe of other picnickers, including Miss Mitchelmore's own father.

"Maelys," he called in a tone of belated epiphany. "I have remembered what I read, and you should on *no account* attempt to shelter from wasps underwater. They will only wait for you to— I say, is that the Duke of Annadale?"

The two women let go of one another's hands abruptly, although Miss Mitchelmore was still not certain if they were doing anything wrong. "Lady Georgiana rescued me, Papa. It was very kind of her."

"Again, eh?" Mr. Mitchelmore was not given to suspicion. He was the kind of man who prided himself on rationality to the extent of ignoring the obvious. "We shall have to find a way to express our gratitude. Dinner, perhaps? Our normal cook is in London, but the one we found locally is quite adequate."

"Uncle." There was more than a note of warning in Mr. Caesar's voice. "We have every reason to believe that this woman is herself responsible for Maelys's misfortune. I do not think we should be rewarding her."

Although he was, by all available evidence, right, some force moved Miss Mitchelmore to chastise him anyway. "I might have drowned, John. There is a time for accusations, and this is *not* it."

"On the contrary"—the Duke of Annadale gave Mr. Caesar a challenging look—"this is *exactly* the time for accusations. But even so, Mr. Mitchelmore, should you be so good as to extend me a formal invitation to dinner, I would be delighted to accept. Do be aware, though, that much of society feels similarly to your nephew."

Before the situation could deteriorate any further, there was a crashing from the undergrowth followed by cries of "It's all right, I have her," and "Leave go of me, you beastly parvenu" and "Stop that at once, young lady," all in different voices. Then Miss Bickle barrelled into view, holding Miss Madeleine Worthing in a passing approximation of a wrestling lock. The hapless Mrs. Wilberforce followed behind, making sounds of ineffectual disapproval.

Seeing Miss Mitchelmore alive and well, Miss Bickle squealed with delight and dragged her captive forward. "See here, I *demand* you undo whatever spell you have placed upon my friend *at once,* or so help me I shall . . . well, I am not sure what I shall do exactly, but it shall be very unpleasant."

"Mr. Mitchelmore," pleaded Mrs. Wilberforce, "can you perhaps talk some sense into the girl? I tried her father, but he was too busy writing a poem."

By nature, Mr. Mitchelmore was not an imposing man. The angriest his daughter had ever seen him was when a friend of the family had insisted on defending Newton's corpuscular theory of light transmission over Hooke's wave model in spite of the overwhelming evidence supplied by Thomas Young's double-slit experiment. "Now, look here Lysistrata," he tried. "I don't know what you think Miss Worthing has done, but this behaviour is *not* ladylike."

"Well, neither is putting curses on people." Miss Bickle's nigh-preternatural capacity for pouting returned in full force.

"I haven't cursed anybody, you up-jumped collier," protested Miss Worthing, who was still struggling gamely. "I wouldn't know *how* to curse anybody. It isn't a skill we learn in *polite society.*" This was a valid observation. Polite society is woefully deficient in so many ways.

Rubbing her eyes with thumb and forefinger, the Duke of Annadale shook her head. "Just let her go, you neotenous ninny. She plainly lacks the capacity to weave the slightest of enchantments. If you're going to falsely accuse somebody of witchcraft let it be me; I'm used to it."

"We *are* accusing you," Mr. Caesar reminded her.

"And you can't very well accuse us both. If Miss Bickle wishes to wrestle me to the ground as she has Miss Worthing, I would be more than happy for her to make the attempt."

Miss Bickle, it seemed, was not happy to make the attempt. Although whether this was out of an ongoing commitment to manhandling Miss Worthing or the justified belief that the Duke of Annadale would prove more difficult to overpower, I cannot say.

"Then"—the Duke of Annadale nodded curtly—"I shall bid everybody good afternoon and, unless anybody wishes to clap me in irons or burn me at the stake, take my leave of you."

None of the assembly had quite the courage to stop the Duke of Annadale as she swept away, and Miss Mitchelmore took two steps to follow her before realising what she was doing and coming to a stop. "Perhaps," she said to her father, "you might take me home? I am rather damp, and I do not think there is much more we can do here."

"I still have Miss Worthing captive," Miss Bickle offered, wheeling the unfortunate girl into a more visible position, "if we wished to interrogate her."

I would have, in their position. For the fun of it, if nothing else. But Miss Mitchelmore was apparently squeamish. "I don't think there will be much gained by it."

"I am *not* a witch." Miss Worthing was still struggling uselessly.

"That's what you'd say if you *were* a witch," Miss Bickle pointed out.

Mr. Caesar stroked his chin in a studied and, honestly, rather affected manner. "You say that, but the Duke of Annadale might well be a witch and has never denied the possibility once."

With an increasing awareness that he was the closest thing to an authority figure in the party, Mr. Mitchelmore gave Miss Bickle his best stern look. It was not, overall, a very good stern look, but then I have always found sternness an overrated quality. "Lysistrata, I am afraid I have to be firm on this. Please unhand Miss Worthing this instant or I shall—I shall . . ."

"Or you shall what?" asked Miss Bickle with more curiosity than defiance.

"Or I shall think rather ill of you."

"Oh." Miss Bickle released Miss Worthing at once. "Please don't think ill of me; that would be horrible."

Miss Worthing made it very clear that she, at least, thought very ill of Miss Bickle indeed, but Miss Bickle, being a woman of admirable good sense, made it equally clear that she did not care a fig for Miss Worthing's opinion. The rest of the crowd, meanwhile, having been cheated of the opportunity to watch a drowning but being compensated somewhat by the novel and salacious question of a curse, dispersed each to their various homes to better engage in speculation.

And who can blame them? Speculation, after all, often proves so much more interesting than reality.

5

"What exactly is *in* this?" Miss Mitchelmore asked her mother, staring dubiously at the draught she had just been given.

"Ammonium salts, a little saltpetre, syrup of balsam, and almond oil." I hope it goes without saying, readers, but you should not drink this mixture yourselves. If you are going to consume something unusual, wait until a helpful fairy hands you a cup of something strengthening. That *never* goes wrong.

"I'm not sure I even *have* a cold. I think I'm just a little drained."

Lady Jane Mitchelmore pressed the back of her hand to her daughter's forehead. "Well, you don't have a fever, but better safe than sorry, eh?"

Doing her best to look grateful, Miss Mitchelmore downed the concoction her mother had concocted. It tasted less repugnant than it might have, but that wasn't saying a great deal. "Why do we even have saltpetre in the house?"

"Your father is trying to make his own gunpowder."

"Is it going well?"

"Not really. He can mix it readily enough, but kernelling the grains is difficult without specialised equipment."

Miss Mitchelmore had long ago given up trying to follow all of her parents' interests, and besides, she was tired after a long day. "Thank you for the draught, Mama, I feel much better."

Despite her academic proclivities, Lady Jane was not a fool. "You don't, do you?"

"Not really, no. I think perhaps my present predicament is not amenable to conventional medicine."

This was a possibility that Lady Jane could accept in the abstract, but found difficult in the specific. "I'm not sure I hold with curses."

"I'm not sure I hold with them either."

Lady Jane lowered herself into a chair at her daughter's bedside. She had a pained expression on her face that Miss Mitchelmore had seldom seen and knew to be wary of. "I'm afraid I've had a rather dark thought."

"Now would seem a good time for them. I fear dark things are happening."

"You don't . . ." Lady Jane seemed to be having trouble articulating her ideas, which was not an impediment from which she usually suffered. "You don't think it could be Richard?"

"Uncle Richard, you mean?" Technically he was Lord Hale, the rank of Baron being traditionally conveyed by birthright on the eldest sons of the Earls of Elmsley. He is not the most odious mortal you will meet in the course of this narrative, but he is odiouser than many. Worse, he is tedious, but you will be pleased to know he will not appear in these pages for some while yet.

"I know he was . . . chagrined when you married Papa," Miss

Mitchelmore continued, "even more so when Aunt Mary married Mr. Caesar, but surely even he wouldn't stoop to such abominable measures." And it was indeed a vile thing to suspect of one's own family. Still, Miss Mitchelmore could not help but feel a little pleased to have a new suspect who was not the Duke of Annadale.

Lady Jane continued to look sceptical. "I don't like to think it of him. But he has been trying to persuade the earl to disinherit me for years."

"*Sorcery*, though," Miss Mitchelmore replied with an incredulity I found frankly unwarranted for a woman in her position.

"It's improbable," Lady Jane half agreed. "And I would say he lacked the patience for witchcraft, but since I know nothing about it, that would be to hypothesise without data."

Although she herself stored the suggestion away for greater use, Miss Mitchelmore thought it best to reassure her mother on this front at least. Leaning forwards, she patted her on the hand and gave her most convincing smile. "I am certain it is not Uncle Richard. Family may not mean as much to him as it should, but I will not believe it means quite as little as that."

Whether Lady Jane believed her daughter or not, she gave every appearance of putting the thought from her mind. "Miss Bickle is still here," she said, rising. "If you would like to see her."

Having no sisters, and her brother being presently away at Eton, Miss Mitchelmore relied strongly on Miss Bickle for company, and so was pleased to have her sent through at once. Lady Jane kissed her daughter affectionately if absently on the forehead and bustled off to fetch their guest.

Miss Bickle arrived moments later in a flurry of concerned enthusiasm, bouncing through the door like a terrier puppy and then clasping Miss Mitchelmore's hand as though it might fall off.

"Oh *Mae*," she said. "Have no fear, I shall stay by you all night if need be. Indeed, I shall stay right here without moving until you are well."

"Thank you, but I think I am quite well already. I have simply had a nasty shock and got a little wet."

"But you were underwater for a fearsomely long time. Papa was so certain you'd drowned that he began composing an elegy to your death." She looked down a moment. "Actually, I think he was a little disappointed that we found you."

Knowing Mr. Bickle as she did, Miss Mitchelmore couldn't be offended. "But I survived. And I believe we can safely strike Miss Worthing from our list of suspects."

"Can we truly? Perhaps she was playing a very subtle game." And perhaps she was. Certainly I have, in my very long existence, known certain artful witches who feign innocence to mislead others. But they seldom, in my experience, allow themselves to be put in headlocks.

"Madeleine Worthing has the subtlety of a house brick." Miss Mitchelmore shifted uneasily under her covers. "I do not think she would have protested so convincingly had she been guilty. Besides, she is right that the laying of curses is not a skill that she would have had an opportunity to learn, any more than you or I would."

Miss Bickle seemed to consider this deeply. "Yes, I suppose in that regard our education is sadly lacking." I knew she was a lady after my own heart. "Although life would become rather complicated if young ladies were to go around cursing one another all the time."

"Indeed, how would we ever find time to acquire accomplishments?"

"Which . . . well . . . this must mean it *was* Lady Georgiana all along. How disappointing. It seems to me that a mystery should never have an obvious solution. That defeats the whole purpose of *having* a mystery."

Not wishing to inspire her friend to physically attack anybody else, Miss Mitchelmore held off on the subject of Lord Hale, for the moment at least. "Perhaps," she said instead. "But I still feel—that is—it seems so needlessly elaborate. She has no reason to wish me harm, and if she *is* behind all these things that have happened to me, then she has arranged them only so that she can rescue me from them, and that seems . . . I don't know. If she merely wished to ingratiate herself with me, or with my family, there would be simpler ways to do it." Miss Mitchelmore drew her knees up beneath the bedclothes and hugged them thoughtfully. "This may sound strange, but while I can imagine her being cruel, I cannot imagine her being inartful."

"Perhaps she imagines that by rescuing an earl's granddaughter from a wicked sorcerer she might earn her way back to respectability."

"I also don't believe she cares much for respectability."

"Then perhaps she really is looking after you."

"Or perhaps she has placed me under a spell which makes me think well of her when I should not." Such spells do exist. Should you ever need one cast, do not hesitate to ask me.

Miss Bickle's face was even better designed for looking shocked than it was for pouting. Her eyes widened and her lips formed a perfect *o* of surprise. "Gosh. That *would* be a twist. Do you think it likely?"

And that, of course, was the question. One Miss Mitchelmore had been quite steadfastly refusing to ask herself. "I do not know. I—I sometimes sense that she has an influence on me. One I am not sure how to understand."

"Has she transformed you into a stickleback? I hear that sometimes witches transform people into sticklebacks."

"No. No, my back remains largely unstickled. It's more that—it is hard to describe. She kissed my hand once."

"How peculiar."

"Yes." A moment's silence fell between them. "But not unpleasant, I think?"

"Well, I suppose she would have to be very horrible indeed for it to be unpleasant."

The more she thought about the experience, the harder it became for Miss Mitchelmore to put her thoughts into words. "I think it was more than *not unpleasant*. It was almost—a kind of excitement I think?"

"As you might feel with a gentleman?"

Miss Mitchelmore's expression was blank. "In what sense?"

"When a gentleman takes your hand, or asks you to dance, and you feel that"—Miss Bickle put a hand to her bosom—"sort of *skipping* feeling."

And now Miss Mitchelmore's expression had progressed from blank to crestfallen. "I am not sure I have ever felt such a thing."

"Really? I understand it to be quite common."

"When dancing?"

"When dancing. When talking. One afternoon I visited the mines with my father and watched as the workmen heaved great sacks of ore about in their arms and . . . well, I have never envied rocks so much in my life. It gave me peculiar dreams about pickaxes." Reader, it saddened me to hear this and know that it was a dream in which I had missed the opportunity to walk.

To Miss Mitchelmore, however, this was all sounding increasingly foreign. "And you believe most ladies react this way?"

"Most or many. Miss Worthing certainly does. That's why she was so upset when you snubbed the Viscount Fortrose. He's a handsome man as well as a rich and titled one."

"Even if what you say is true, I am not sure this explains the effect Lady Georgiana has on me."

"Might it not be largely the same?" Miss Bickle asked. "But for ladies?"

Miss Mitchelmore's eyes narrowed. "Is that possible?"

"Ah, well." With an enthusiastic spring, Miss Bickle transferred herself onto Miss Mitchelmore's bed. "I've actually been giving this matter rather a lot of thought."

"Have you . . . have I given you cause for suspicion?"

Miss Bickle patted her friend's knee reassuringly. "No, no, no, I mean, it's a simple question of mathematics."

"Mathematics?" It was not a topic that Miss Mitchelmore had ever known her friend to take an interest in.

"Precisely. Suppose we start from the assumption that there is, somewhere in the world, somebody for everybody. A true love, if you like."

This felt like it was going to a place that Miss Mitchelmore either wouldn't agree with or wouldn't understand, but that was fairly common with Miss Bickle's notions. "That seems a large assumption, but let us accept it for now."

"*Well*, I am sure that you know as well as I that one is *never* in a place with exactly equal numbers of gentlemen and ladies. That's why there are always people standing around at dances."

Perhaps it was the day's exertions, but to Miss Mitchelmore's rising concern, her companion was perilously close to making sense. "Go on."

"So it follows that one of two things are true." Miss Bickle held up her forefinger a slightly intrusive distance from Miss Mitchelmore's face. "That either some gentlemen are destined to be with gentlemen and some ladies to be with ladies, or"—she extended a second finger—"the whole notion of love is meaningless and we should all go at once to Beachy Head and leap to our deaths, since life is not worth living."

Miss Mitchelmore tilted her head to one side. "I'm not sure I would present quite so catastrophic a dichotomy."

"All I mean is that it's possible you're . . . one of those ones who are necessary to make up the numbers. There's a perilous shortage of eligible gentlemen this season, and it would be awfully convenient if you were to take up with a lady instead."

Miss Mitchelmore was not convinced. Or perhaps she was uncertain as to whether she wished to *be* convinced. It would make things far simpler in some ways, far more complex in others. I, needless to say, champion the side of complexity. "And you think this . . . mathematical theory of yours is more probable than enchantment?"

The expression on Miss Bickle's face was not reassuring. "*I* think so. But there's a simple test."

"Should I—"

"Just kiss me and see if you feel anything."

This, Miss Mitchelmore was quite certain, was *not* how it worked. "I'm not kissing you, Lizzie."

"Is it my bosom?" Miss Bickle adjusted her gown, then readjusted it. "I sometimes suspect that I have an inadequate bosom."

"No. I think it might be more to do with the fact that I once saw you eat a live slug."

Outrage joined shock and pouting on the list of expressions to which Miss Bickle's face was bizarrely suited. "I was a child. And anyway, it must be quite gone by now. It's been simply years." She opened her mouth wide in order that her friend might inspect it. "Ou ee?"

"You were twelve. Twelve is still old enough to know better."

"But it looked so strange, I felt certain that it would give me magical powers."

"Which is never a good reason to eat anything. But that's the point. I have known you intimately my whole life and I could no more look at you in that way than I could my brother."

Miss Bickle slid up the bed beside Miss Mitchelmore and laid her head on her shoulder. "That makes sense. Although I think Corantin will be a very pretty young man when he is older."

"If you marry my brother, I shall be very cross."

"Really? But it would make us sisters, and that would be wonderful. And *he* didn't see me eat the slug."

A stray thought wandered from the place of dreams where my kind dwells, and into Miss Mitchelmore's mind. "Why *are* you not married yet, Lizzie? For somebody who thinks so much of love you seem to spend little time in pursuit of it."

Miss Bickle sighed. "I know. It's so difficult, isn't it? I do so want to marry for love, but the trouble is that Papa is terribly keen on it as well, and—I mean doesn't that just defeat the entire purpose?"

"In what way?"

"Well, one can hardly elope to Gretna Green if one's father is in the carriage beside one writing poems to read at the wedding. If I went to Papa tomorrow and told him I had fallen for a stablehand, he'd be overjoyed and think it wondrously romantic. Sometimes I think I should set my cap at a sixty-year-old viscount with gout just to surprise him."

"Do you *know* a sixty-year-old viscount with gout?"

"No, but I am sure I could find one."

They passed the remainder of the evening in this manner, lying beside one another and enumerating ever more improbable marriage prospects for one or the other of them, Miss Mitchelmore patiently explaining to Miss Bickle that even if it were possible for her to court a lady, it would be *quite* impossible for her to marry one, even in Scotland. At last, sleep overtook Miss Mitchelmore and Miss Bickle, whose pledge to stay by her friend all night held true only insofar as it seemed truly necessary, retired to the room that had been made up for her.

As for me, I took the opportunity to take a stroll in Miss Mitchelmore's dreams.

And, yes, this is something we do. But before you take offence, remember that when you dream it is *your* spirits that are intruding upon *our* domain.

Dreams are fickle things, and the patterns you give them on waking reflect not one-tenth of the wonders that actually exist in our lands. So it was not the Avon but the Alph by whose banks Miss Mitchelmore walked that night, and the Duke of Annadale was not the Duke of Annadale as she is in life but a figment conjured in part from memories and in part from the dream stuff that is the lifeblood of my kind.

Thus Miss Mitchelmore walked along a river she had never seen, and spoke in a tongue no mortal has ever spoken to the half-conjured shadow of a woman who was coming to occupy all of her thoughts. And when she woke the following morning it was with the fast-fading memory of cold eyes watching her, of fingertips brushing her throat, of lips pressed to the back of her hand.

6

The formal invitation to dinner was offered and accepted shortly after the picnic, and so the Bickles, the Caesars, and the Duke of Annadale descended on the Mitchelmore house. It was an event towards which Miss Mitchelmore looked with mixed feelings. The Duke of Annadale was a confusion at a time in her life when she did not need confusion; society was hard enough when one was not under a curse and had not somehow attracted the attention of a woman who may or may not be a multiple murderess. But she could not deny, at least not to herself, the intense desire to *see* the lady again, if only to ask her what she thought she was doing.

It made for an odd gathering. The Caesars were family and the Bickles as good as, Mr. Bickle and Mr. Mitchelmore having been bosom friends since youth despite their differing temperaments, but nobody in the party was entirely certain how best to behave

around a woman who was at once a duke's daughter and a suspected sorceress. I settled myself within the flames of one of the
candles to better observe proceedings.

"I should begin," Mr. Mitchelmore said, standing, "by offering
my sincerest thanks to Lady Georgiana, without whom it is very
possible my darling Maelys would not have been with us today."

There was a round of general hear-hears, and the Duke of
Annadale gave an arch smile. "Oh, think nothing of it, Mr. Mitchelmore. After all, if I can save just three more innocent lives, society
may consider my scorecard cleared."

Her casual reference to the deaths of her entire family cast
something of a pall over the serving of the soup, but Miss Bickle
picked up the dropped thread of conversation and began working
it into something at least polite, if not wholly connected to reality.
"I am not sure Mae can have been in any real danger, can she? She
told me she was with the naiads, and they would not let her come
to any harm."

"Perhaps." The Duke of Annadale looked thoughtful. "Certainly I think they have an undeservedly poor reputation. Nymphs
are, after all, far more often abducted than abductors. But I fear
Miss Mitchelmore had angered them, and those who anger divinities seldom end well."

"It was not my intent to anger anybody," Miss Mitchelmore
protested almost reflexively. "I plead special exemption by reason
of wasps."

"If anything, it was my fault." Mr. Bickle, who fancied himself
to possess an artistic soul, stood quite unnecessarily. I should say
that I like Mr. Bickle *almost* as much as I like his daughter. "Had I
known there were still spirits in the river I should never have
dreamed of intruding. I should have kept the picnic to twenty—
perhaps thirty—guests at most. Instead I damned near, pardon my

language, damned near got your daughter killed, Ned. I feel terrible, truly terrible."

"He does," Mrs. Bickle confirmed. "He hasn't slept since. It's been fearsomely inconvenient."

"Don't be an ass, Billy." Mr. Mitchelmore had sat just as his friend had stood and was now standing again just as the other man was sitting, making it look rather as though they were at either end of a seesaw. "No harm came of it, thanks to Lady Georgiana."

An almost coy expression crossed the Duke of Annadale's face, which quite surprised Miss Mitchelmore, who had assumed her quite incapable of reticence. "Please, I am unused to gratitude. Somebody change the subject before I am tempted to do something unforgivable out of habit."

With the grace of a seasoned hostess, Lady Jane turned to the Caesars. "What news from the abolition?"

The elder Mr. Caesar laid down his soup spoon. "Much done, much yet to do."

"I'm sorry, you must think me very ignorant." Again, the expression on the Duke of Annadale's face was less composed than Miss Mitchelmore ever remembered seeing it. "I should have thought the work is mostly finished? The slave trade was abolished years ago."

"Seven years ago. But for four of those years it was punishable only by a fine." His expression grew grave. "And what, Lady Georgiana, do you think a man does when he is fined for every slave on his ship?"

The Duke of Annadale pondered the question for a moment. For all that she had lost the knack of social niceties, her mind ran easily to dark places. It was one of the few qualities I admired in her. "I expect he throws them overboard the moment he sees a Royal Navy vessel approaching."

Mr. Caesar nodded. "And so we fought to have the trade made a *felony.* And we won. Now we fight to end not only the *trading* but the *holding* of slaves. And not only in the British Empire but across the globe. And we will win there, too, though I may not live to see it."

"Oh, don't be so morbid, Papa," said Miss Mary Caesar, the older of the two girls and the one that most favoured her father. "You're barely fifty."

Her father laughed, a deep, sincere laugh that started in his stomach. "When you are fifty, my dear, you will realise that the world cannot be changed in one lifetime. But enough of this"—he clapped his hands—"we are at dinner, and weighty matters make for heavy dining. Let us talk instead of trivial things. Tell me, Lady Georgiana, how is the *weather* in your part of the country?"

The Duke of Annadale looked, frankly, as if she would rather be discussing politics. "Dire, or so I presume. I have not been back since my father died."

"Too many painful memories?" asked Mrs. Bickle.

"Or too much evidence?" added Mr. John Caesar.

"John!" Miss Mary shot her brother a reproving look. "What a vile thing to say."

"John is always vile," said Miss Anne Caesar. She was the younger of the two, and had more of the kind of prettiness the ton favoured. "I think he got it from Mr. Ellersley."

Mr. Caesar glowered at his sister. "I did *not* get it from Mr. Ellersley."

"But you admit you *are* vile?" observed Miss Mary.

Setting down her spoon, Lady Mary Caesar turned to her children. "Girls, stop needling your brother. John, it is *extremely* poor table etiquette to accuse one's fellow diners of murder."

"My apologies, Lady Georgiana." From my perspective, Mr.

John Caesar did not seem terribly apologetic. "This must be a difficult matter for you to discuss. I simply find it hard to believe that you were so well placed to leap to my cousin's aid *twice*."

The Duke of Annadale set what remained of her soup aside and helped herself to a fillet of fowl. "None necessary. I am quite used to the world thinking me wicked." She shot a glance across the table at Miss Mitchelmore. "And as it happens, the second time was no coincidence. No disrespect meant, Mr. Bickle, but I doubt I would have attended your picnic had I not wished to see if there would be a recurrence of the earlier event."

For once, the normally affable Mr. Bickle was taken aback. "I say, that's a bit off. What was wrong with my picnic?"

"It took place next to a river I knew to be home to a school of naiads who would not appreciate the intrusion, it was full of people who hate me, and I have no time for Wordsworth."

This was a step too far. Mr. Bickle paled visibly. "No time for *Wordsworth*? I—that is I—I mean to say—of all the—I suppose you will tell me next that you have no time for—for joy or for sunlight, or for little puppies playing by a fireplace, or for the very essence of happiness itself."

"I do find most of those things rather dreary, yes." Again, the Duke of Annadale caught some of my own feeling in this matter. Although puppies and fireplaces *can* cause amusement in the right combination.

Mr. Bickle's mouth was still moving but no words were coming out.

"Perhaps," Lady Jane suggested, "we could refrain either from accusing one another of murder or from insulting Wordsworth."

"I find some of Coleridge acceptable," the Duke of Annadale offered by way of conciliation.

Mr. Bickle choked on thin air. "*Acceptable?*"

"And I think Lord Byron has real promise, although his heroic works are pompous and, while 'Maid of Athens' has a compelling passion to it, the verse is somewhat marred by the knowledge that he wrote it to a twelve-year-old girl."

The conversation proceeded in this fashion, Mr. Bickle continuing to defend Wordsworth whenever he could make his lungs function and the Duke of Annadale dancing with limited delicacy around her distaste for him. The guests picked their way through the first course, and the servants cleared the settings to make way for the second.

"So, am I to take it aright," Mr. John Caesar hazarded when he felt the conversation had come to a place where he could return to the question of the curse, "that you have been *following* Maelys all this time?"

"'Following' is such a strong word." The Duke of Annadale leaned forward and speared a quail. "I contrived to be present at an event to which I had been invited—"

"You should not have been," Mr. Bickle spluttered through his lemon soufflé, "had I known your *vile* opinions regarding the lyric poets."

"Oh, I have no problem with the lyric poets." The Duke of Annadale gave him an easy smile. "I am a *great* admirer of Sappho. But as for Miss Mitchelmore, I thought she might be in danger, and that I might be able to ameliorate said danger. I was right on both counts."

"But you understand it still looks suspicious." Mr. John Caesar was, it seemed, determined not to be swayed on this issue.

"Yes. As the deaths of my father and brothers looked suspicious. I truly was not offended when you suggested I might be doing her harm."

Lady Jane, having eaten her fill, was now sitting back in her chair with her hands folded in her lap. "*I* was offended. You're in my house John."

The Duke of Annadale raised a hand. "That's sweet of you, Lady Jane, but this is a serious matter and he's right to be concerned. I am . . . not trustworthy."

"I'd say not——" Mr. Bickle began, but Mr. Mitchelmore cut him off.

"Billy, if you mention Wordsworth one more time, I swear I shall rub your face in the gelée de framboises."

Throughout the meal, Miss Mitchelmore had been notably quiet. It was generally considered proper to allow the gentlemen to carry the conversation, but the Mitchelmores had never been a conventional household. On this particular evening, however, Miss Mitchelmore had every reason to withdraw into herself. Dining with the Duke of Annadale, hearing her talk of poetry and quarrel and shy away from difficult subjects like any other woman might made her seem more human than she had before. And by *more human* I mean it in the flattering way that mortals use the phrase, not the more accurate, disparaging way in which it is used amongst my own kind.

So it was easier, all of a sudden, for Miss Mitchelmore to notice the little details. The way the lady's eyes shone when she thought she had said something particularly cutting but shrank back if she thought she had caused real hurt. The sorrow she could not quite keep from her voice when she spoke of the deaths of her brothers, no matter how brazen she tried to be about it. The way she would, throughout the meal, cast little glances in Miss Mitchelmore's direction and look gratified and almost surprised if she glanced back. And Miss Mitchelmore noticed that the Duke of Annadale, for all her scandalous reputation, was *young.* Not by the standards of society, of course—she might have been so old as four-and-twenty—but she spoke as one who had lived decades and seen worlds.

She was a contradiction. And in spite of the danger, Miss Mitchelmore made a private vow to resolve her. "Lady Georgiana," she found herself saying, "when you rescued me from the river, you implied that you knew what was—what had been done to me. Is that correct?"

"In part. I cannot *know*, but I have several strong inklings."

Lady Jane leaned towards the Duke of Annadale. "I'm sorry, I'm sure this makes me a terrible hostess, but if you knew what was afflicting our daughter all this time, then I think I'd like to know why the bloody hell you haven't told us anything yet?"

"To be fair, dear"—Mr. Mitchelmore laid a hand on his wife's arm—"Billy was talking about poetry for rather a long time."

"And if I'd known our guest had the secret to protecting Maelys's life and reputation and was concealing it from us I'd have told him to *shut up.*"

At the end of the table, the Duke of Annadale looked tense and more than a little withdrawn. "I am not concealing anything. But . . . these are secrets hard won and not normally discussed over dinner."

"You see?" Mr. John Caesar waved a hand in frustration. "How can *any* of you trust this woman?"

Miss Mitchelmore glanced from her cousin to the Duke of Annadale, to the other members of the party, who were all starting to grow restless. "Please, give her a chance."

"I am *giving* her a chance." Lady Jane's tone was icy. "But I increasingly concur with John. You seem to be toying with us, Lady Georgiana, and I for one do not appreciate being toyed with."

"As I have told your daughter, I may play games, but I never *toy.*" Realising, perhaps, that she had struck the wrong tone, the

Duke of Annadale stared fixedly downwards. "My apologies, Lady Jane. I will say what I can but ask that you press me no further. What I speak of is witchcraft, and to tell you too much would be to hand every person in this room a loaded pistol."

Mr. John Caesar arched an eyebrow. "And you would prefer to be the only one armed?" In the lady's defence, it was a sensible strategy.

"I would not endanger you. It is all very well"—here her gaze turned to the Bickles—"to speak of playful nymphs and fairy rings, of old gods and strange magics as though they were things of wonder and beauty, and they *are* things of wonder and beauty. But they are also deadly. I know full well how deadly they can be."

As much as I would love to lull my readers into a false sense of security, she is right on both counts. Sensing the conversation was about to take a turn for the tempestuous, I fled my position in the candle flame and darted towards the ceiling as a wisp of vapour.

"Perhaps," Lady Jane offered, "you could explain a little of this to us."

The Duke of Annadale was breathing slowly now, and carefully. "It is most likely that your daughter is being tormented by a god. A goddess, more precisely."

"Which goddess?" This was Mr. Mitchelmore, who had taken his wife's hand beneath the table.

"Sulis. Called Sulis Minerva by some."

At the other end of the table, Mr. Bickle brayed with laughter. "The *bathwater* goddess? The one who blesses the hot springs and cures old men of gout? Throw the lady out, Ned, she's playing with you."

"I would not speak so flippantly." The Duke of Annadale's eyes were shadowed. "This is her city."

"This is King George's city," Mr. Mitchelmore replied, with

more patriotism than I might have expected from a man of science. "She merely lives in it. Or under it. I'm not familiar with the particulars."

The Duke of Annadale had grown very still indeed, but an observer paying keen attention—and Miss Mitchelmore at least was paying attention *very* keenly—may have noticed a tremor in her shoulders. And it was a tremor that spoke well of her, for it was never wise to disparage deities. "If you believe that," she said, "then with apologies for the discourtesy, you are a fool."

"Lady Georgiana." Lady Jane rose with all the hauteur of an earl's daughter. "Whatever your station may be, you will not speak in such a way to my husband in his own house."

Rising also, the Duke of Annadale nodded once in agreement. "I think, perhaps, I should not have come. It has been many years since I have been visiting, and I have grown unaccustomed to courtesy."

The Mitchelmores, the elder Mitchelmores at least, nodded a silent assent, and the Duke of Annadale took her leave. She had been gone only a moment when Miss Mitchelmore stood and made for the door herself.

"Sit down, Mae," said Mr. Mitchelmore. "There is nothing to be gained by pursuing her."

"She saved my life, Papa." Miss Mitchelmore did not pout anywhere near so well as Miss Bickle, but when pressed she had a fine line in indignation. "And you all treated her like a . . . like a . . ."

"Suspected murderess and accused witch?" Miss Mitchelmore was unaccustomed to her father being so harsh. But then she had never before placed him in quite this kind of situation.

"The word there," said the elder Mr. Caesar, "is *suspected.* Society is not always kind and not always right. Nobody in this room is entirely respectable."

His son gave him a sharp look. "There is a difference, Papa, between being born African, or making one's fortune in the tin mines, and having murdered one's entire family."

The accusation stung Miss Mitchelmore more than it should have. "A crime of which she may be entirely innocent."

"*May*, Mae"—now Mr. John Caesar turned his sharpness to his cousin—"is an extraordinarily small word on which to risk your life."

And to this, Miss Mitchelmore had no answer. She had only the strange and stubborn sensation that if her trust were to prove misplaced, it would be a disappointment she could not bear.

CHAPTER

7

To my discomfort, Miss Mitchelmore seemed once again stricken with indecision and, worse, a preference for restraint over rashness. Of all the flaws mortals may possess, wisdom is by far my least favourite. My expectations were lifted marginally when Mr. Caesar and Miss Bickle called upon her, since I had some reason to hope that they might goad one another into doing something dangerous but entertaining. To my distress, an hour had already passed, and they remained in the drawing room drinking tea and debating strategies. Miss Mitchelmore, still not entirely willing to concede that the Duke of Annadale was the most promising suspect, had made a spirited attempt to make the case for its being literally anybody else, up to and including raising her mother's suggestion that Lord Hale might be responsible. But his absence from Bath had become a sticking point, and so in the end that part of the discussion had become circular and they had progressed from considering who might be responsible for the curse to considering what might be done about it. Realising that they might be about to talk themselves into actual action, I started paying attention.

"You simply can't remain locked inside forever," protested Miss Bickle. "It will be *so* dreary. And there are illnesses one may catch in confinement, I am certain."

Miss Mitchelmore let her shoulders slump in resignation. "If I am being hounded out of society by an angry divinity, I scarcely see how I can avoid it."

On this occasion, I had resisted the temptation to disarrange Mr. Caesar's attire. He was proving a greater source of amusement to me than I had expected, and so I thought it more meet to let him go on unmolested.

"I propose an experiment," he began. He was pacing the room; I would not have pegged him for a pacer but here he was, his half-boots tapping a quick rhythm across the floor. "Thus far you've had . . . incidents only when in the presence of the Duke of Annadale."

"Lady Georgiana," Miss Mitchelmore corrected. "And not *only* Lady Georgiana. Miss Worthing and Mr. Clitherowe were present in each case also. Although I believe Miss Worthing may be safely discounted."

Stretched out on the divan, Miss Bickle struck a melancholy pose. "Such a shame. I was so looking forward to duelling her upon the moors."

"Once again, Lizzie"—Miss Mitchelmore gave her friend a warm smile—"we're a good day's walk from any moors, and I have no desire to run wild across the heath screaming pleas to nameless gods."

"But it would be such *fun.*"

"What I *propose*," Mr. Caesar continued, trying to pretend that there had not been a long digression about hilltop witch-battling, "is that we attend some event at which none of your possible tormentors are present."

"Can you *think* of such an event?" asked Miss Mitchelmore. "Mr. Clitherowe is of sufficient reputation as to be welcome anywhere despite his station and Lady Georgiana is of sufficient station as to be welcome anywhere despite her reputation."

"Which is why we will not be attending an event to which one is *invited*. The dress ball at the Assembly Rooms will suit our purpose."

Miss Bickle clapped her hands. "Oh John, *really*? I've been wanting to go for simply weeks but you keep saying it isn't the done thing anymore."

"It's certainly no longer as fashionable as it was," Mr. Caesar admitted, a somewhat pained expression on his face. "People of quality still attend, but I cannot imagine that either the Duke of Annadale or Mr. Clitherowe would think to seek Maelys out there. Indeed it is likely that neither has even bothered to pay their subscription, the one being of too limited means and the other too much a misanthrope."

Setting her teacup aside, Miss Mitchelmore regarded her cousin with justifiable scepticism. "And what do you think it will prove, if I am able to pass the evening unmolested?"

"That human agency is responsible for your misfortunes, and that the Lady Georgiana is either lying or mistaken."

"Well, I am glad," retorted Miss Mitchelmore, "that you are at least open to the possibility of error. And if I am attacked, will you concede that she may be correct?"

Mr. Caesar nodded. "That she may be, certainly. But it will take more than one evening to make me trust her."

This being all of the concession she could reasonably expect from her cousin, Miss Mitchelmore nodded and gave a quiet sigh. And for a few seconds silence fell over the drawing room before Miss Bickle clapped her hands and exclaimed, "Oh, how wonderful, we're going to a ball!"

———— • ————

I approached the Assembly Rooms early, since once tea had finished Miss Mitchelmore and her little entourage had ceased to be entertaining. As I drew closer to the building, however, I felt a strange sensation creeping over me; something a little like fear and a little like nausea. A few paces shy of its temple-like, columned entrance, I found my knees giving way and I sank, rather indecorously, to the ground.

For some time—I cannot say how long, although I suspect it was mere minutes however eternal it seemed—I remained in this wretched state until at last a corpulent man in a white fur hat emerged from the building. In one hand he held an oaken wand tipped with a pinecone, and in the other he held a glass of wine. About his neck hung a golden medallion bearing an inscription I could not read.

"Spirit!" he bellowed, "reveal yourself. We will have no unseen trespassers in this place."

Well, fuck.

My understanding of the rules of the Assembly Rooms was that ladies were more welcome than gentlemen, so it was a woman's form I adopted. Tall and fair and slender, a cast to my face that one might have called elfin.

"My Lord," I told him, half rising, "I am the Lady Boann of the Tuatha de—"

"You bloody well are not," he said without even doing me the courtesy of listening to the entire lie. "You think I don't know a hobgoblin when I see one?"

I bowed my head. "Forgive me. I meant, of course, that I am the Lady Rowan of the Court of Queen Titan—"

"Piss off."

I stiffened my back and looked affronted. "That is no way to speak to a lady, sir."

The gentleman's visage reddened, a shade I ordinarily enjoy, when I am less visible. "You are no lady. You are a devil."

"I am an honest, plain country sprite, and harmless. Besides, *devils* are from another cosmology altogether and my folk have nothing to do with them."

Striding forward now with a confidence that I hadn't expected from a man clearly already several glasses of wine the better, he lowered his pinecone wand towards my chest. "Out, spirit," he demanded, "out, knave."

Behind him, the doors of the Assembly Rooms opened again, and another figure emerged. This one was a man I knew well. He had the look of a youth, although he was older by far than my present oppressor. His heritage, long ago, was of India, but his eyes were as green as summer grass, a consequence of his long years in the court of my former lord. His given name has been lost (those who stay long amongst my kind learn to wear names lightly, as we do), but we call him the Ambassador, as do those mortals he reveals himself to.

"Let her in, Guynette. She won't cause trouble"—he fixed me with an emerald glare—"*will you?*"

"Me?" I pressed my hand to my bosom in what I counted a reasonable facsimile of feminine courtesy. "Have I *ever?*"

"Not when properly bound." A playful smile crept across his lips. "You'll say the words, of course."

I'd hoped to avoid that. "Very well: I swear by oak, by ash, and by thorn, by both sides of the sky, by the beard of Zeus and the blood of Christ, that I shall abide by all laws and customs of the house I am about to enter. Does that satisfy you?"

"Entirely." The Ambassador descended the steps and took my arm. Then he leaned a little closer and whispered, "This guise looks well on you, Robin."

"Thank you, I rather enjoy it."

Mr. Guynette ushered us both inside, but as the doors were about to close, a carriage pulled up outside, and—

"*See now,*" I said, not entirely able to help myself, "*the lady emerges, and here her companions. I shall conceal myself by yonder pillar and watch what misadvent—*"

"Robin"—the Ambassador yanked me away—"what in the name of all the gods are you doing?"

Well, this was embarrassing. "I am collecting a story."

"Could you possibly"—he waved a hand—"not?"

I couldn't, as it happens. I had chosen to make Miss Mitchelmore's story my subject, and ancient compacts bound me to tell it. The version you are reading has been adapted slightly for the written format. "You've lived at court for—*they approach the door, see how she bites her lip and watches the shadows for—*dammit," I shook my head. "You've lived at court since the days of the Amazons, you *know* how this works."

"Then can you be *quieter*? It's *very* annoying."

I clenched my jaw. If it was annoying to the Ambassador, reader, imagine how much more annoying it was to me. "I will attempt to but—*come, they pass us, let us follow them and mayhap we shall—*sorry."

We followed them inside.

The Assembly Rooms are, as their name suggests, plural, with

card rooms, billiard rooms, concert rooms, and coffee rooms spinning off from the main ballrooms. The halls were decorated, I
could not help noticing, with the signs and sigils of the old gods—
there a statue of Venus Verticordia, watching over those young
maidens who wished to preserve their virtue, there an ivy-wound
effigy of Bacchus, watching over those who did not. This, at least,
went some way to explaining why the Master of Ceremonies had
been so prepared for my coming; this place was clearly some kind
of makeshift temple, and actively used. As I progressed deeper into
the complex, my kind's instinctive and frankly unhelpful sense for
rules and laws and oaths started to push needles of certainty into
my mind. There was to be no hazard played, nor any illegal games.
Subscription to dress balls set at one guinea. Additional tickets
transferrable to ladies only. A minuet to be danced before—fuck.

You mortals see my kind as capricious creatures, but we are not.
We lie, most certainly, but what we tell you three times is true. We
are beings of rules in a way that you merely think yourselves to be.

And I was just remembering why it is foolish indeed for my
people to swear to uphold mortal laws, and for mortals to ask it.
Your codes rely so much on discretion, on understandings, on *gentlemen's agreements*.

I caught the Ambassador by the arm. "There must be a
minuet."

"A *what*?"

"A minuet. It's a court dance."

The Ambassador pinched his temples. "I know what a minuet
is. But nobody's bothered with the damned things in fifty years.
Why must there be one *now*?"

"Because *you*"—out of the corner of my eye I saw Miss Mitchelmore turn away a man hoping to mark her dance card, and my
other duties overtook me again—"*she demurs, thinking perhaps of other*

arms about her—insisted I swear to uphold the laws of this place and—*her cousin watches, were he a hawk he'd surely grace the*—fuck, fuck, fuck. Some *bastard* decided to make a rule they didn't intend to uphold, and believe you me if they don't uphold it I will be forced to unleash *havoc.*"

"You said you wouldn't be any trouble."

Unusually, I was in the right here even by the unenlightened standards of mortals. It didn't happen very often. "No, *you* said I wouldn't be any trouble. Then you made me swear to do something that will, in fact, cause trouble. Now, can we please ask the band"—to consist of twelve performers, my oath-bindings were telling me, including harp, tabor, and pipe—"to play a sodding minuet, or else every man and woman in this room is going to find themselves trapped in the Dance Without Surcease and I think we can all agree that such an eventuality *might* rather annoy the authorities."

Dragging me by the hand, the Ambassador forged his way across the ballroom, pleasingly heedless of the attention he drew.

"*What a figure he cuts,*" I opined without warning, "*all eyes turn to him. Miss Bickle in particular perhaps sees in his fairy-touched—*"

He stopped, wheeled around. Had I not been wearing the form of a woman I suspect he would have struck me. "Oh, no you don't. Tell all the fucking stories you want, hobgoblin, but leave *me* out of them."

"Right. Sorry. Just, music, please?"

Leaving go of me entirely he stormed away, and I tried to avoid describing him aloud as he left. I watched as he exchanged a few short words and then slightly more rather longer words with the band and, to my relief, the music began and Mr. Guynette stood before the assembly and asked that the ladies and gentlemen in attendance please take their partners for the minuet.

"At *last*," exclaimed a man who, if he had seen one summer, had seen ninety. "Come on, Gloria, let's show these young upstarts what's what."

So the couples made their way to the floor. One or two of the younger gentlemen gamely took the hands of equally game young ladies, fumbling their way through the steps of a dance they had never been taught while their elders looked on with either scorn or pity.

For my part, I kept my teeth together and tried to resist the urge to narrate.

It was going to be a very long evening.

———— • ————

To my dismay, and the dismay of the younger dancers, the not-normally-enforced codes of the Assembly Rooms required that the evening *end* with a minuet as well. Thanking the Ambassador only slightly grudgingly for his only slightly grudging assistance, I left on the spot of eleven and, the moment I was beyond the confines of the walls, returned myself to blessed invisibility.

Gods and powers, how I miss being able to become invisible. I was in a *shop* yesterday buying *food* and I had to actually *pay* for it.

Watching from my shape of mists and shadows, I saw Miss Mitchelmore and her companions leaving the Assembly Rooms looking rather merry. As well they might, for that evening I was the only one to have been troubled by supernatural interference.

"There," Miss Bickle was observing triumphantly, "was that not delightful? And look at this lovely myrtle bough a gentleman gave me."

"I don't think you should have taken that," warned Mr. Caesar, "I'm sure it's symbolic of something."

This was precisely the wrong way to dissuade Miss Bickle from anything. "Oh but that makes it so much more charming. Do you think he has put me under a love spell? I believe I should rather like to be under a love spell."

They are certainly one of my own preferred forms of entertainment, although they must be handled delicately if things are not to get out of hand.

"Would that not lead to one being taken advantage of by a person by whom one would prefer *not* to be taken advantage?" asked Miss Mitchelmore.

"Oh." Miss Bickle's face fell. "Yes that is rather difficult. If I were to be taken advantage of, I should like to have final say in the advantage taker."

They made their way to their carriage and I followed them inside, taking the shape of a few motes of dust that settled discreetly in a corner. For a while they sat quietly, but Mr. Caesar was regarding his cousin with such a look of vindication that she was eventually compelled to respond.

"I concede," she said at last, "that this evening's relative lack of incident does suggest that Lady Georgiana may have been mistaken."

"Or . . ." prompted Mr. Caesar.

"Or actively deceitful. But we cannot rule out the possibility that Mr. Clitherowe—"

Mr. Caesar leaned back in his seat and turned his eyes towards the roof of the carriage. "Mr. Clitherowe is a clergyman. Lady Georgiana is the last surviving heir of a man who was almost certainly struck down by witchcraft. Make of that what you will." The carriage rattled on and, after a little while, Mr. Caesar continued. "What I don't understand, Mae, is why you're so determined to think well of the woman."

"She has developed a tendre for her," explained Miss Bickle.

Miss Mitchelmore made a surprisingly sincere show of affront. "I have *not*. I simply find her . . ."

"Just so you know Mae"—a note of understanding crept into Mr. Caesar's voice that had been absent previously—"there is no possible adjective that you can use that will not make it sound as though you are infatuated with the woman."

"Interesting?" tried Miss Mitchelmore.

Extending her myrtle bough, Miss Bickle tapped Miss Mitchelmore on the head. "Infatuated."

"Unusual?"

Another tap. "*Doubly* infatuated. Nobody ever calls a person unusual if they aren't secretly aflame for their caress."

Miss Mitchelmore folded her arms. "I am not *aflame* for anything."

The myrtle bough came down once again. "Infatuated."

And in this vein they continued as the carriage rolled on through the streets of Bath. Expecting little more entertainment from them this evening, I slipped out through the window, took the shape of the bird that is my namesake, and flitted away.

CHAPTER

8

The new day dawned bright and hopeful. And since, Miss Bickle had argued, the curse upon Miss Mitchelmore fell only when she was in the company of the one who had cursed her, there could be no possible harm in taking a stroll along Milsom Street to see whether a new bonnet or suchlike might help Maelys put the troubles of the last few days behind her.

"I still have an enemy out there," Miss Mitchelmore had pointed out, "who may pose a real danger to my life and reputation. I think my troubles may have progressed beyond the point that they can be remedied by headgear."

Mr. Caesar who, despite my having left him alone, was once again inspecting his attire in the long mirror in order to be certain that every line of cloth fell *just so*, gave a gasp of disbelief. "These are grave matters, Mae, but there is *no* problem that is not better faced in the proper hat. Besides, it would be well for you to be seen in public. After last night, most of society is *relatively* certain you are not dead, but it would do no harm to reassure them."

"Yes," Miss Bickle agreed. "It will be so awfully hard to get invitations to parties if people think you deceased. One simply *can't* invite a corpse to a ball because they have such a tricky habit of turning up, and that makes the evening so sour for everybody else."

They did, Miss Mitchelmore reflected, have a reasonable point. And curse or no curse, she could not live her life bouncing back and forth between her home and the Assembly Rooms. Of course, even leaving the risk of supernatural punishment aside, there was one *other* drawback to a day out shopping with Miss Bickle. . . .

"Besides," Miss Bickle went on, "you simply *must* let me treat you to a new gown. The one you lost at Lady Etheridge's will need to be replaced anyway, and your taste is *so* dreary."

Thus it was that Miss Mitchelmore found herself at a somewhat obscure modiste being fitted for a dress made from a fabric that iridesced in colours both unnatural and unfashionable while Miss Bickle looked on approvingly (her own gown was a comparatively modest affair by her tastes, although the goblins who crafted it had spun pure gold into the hem and decorated the bodice with beetle carapaces) and Mr. Caesar tried not to smirk. Or at least, he tried not to smirk until Miss Bickle insisted upon purchasing for him a hat of quite unseemly height in a shade of purple that no mortal dye could reproduce, at which point the desire to smirk fled him entirely.

I, needless to say, thought he looked wonderful. And indeed I consider the prejudice against fairy-wrought garments in mundane society a product of rank snobbery. A fairy-stitched dress can be embroidered with an intricacy and a delicacy that mortals were quite unable to replicate at the time. Later, of course, you would develop fabulous machines for sewing that would allow you to rival our craftsmanship, which I consider frankly spiteful—eventually one of you will find a way to turn straw into gold and then I don't know how we will be able to trick you into giving us your children *at all*. But I digress. The point is that our work, in its day, was exceptionally wonderful but, perversely, for this very reason, was considered vulgar by polite society. It comes too cheaply and too easily, they say. Which is ironic, since my people are famous for charging unexpected prices.

Doing their best to steer Miss Bickle away from any more milliners, modistes, or haberdashers, the three companions continued down Milsom Street and Miss Mitchelmore permitted herself to feel almost comfortable. If she truly was cursed, and she still thought it most likely, she was perhaps vulnerable only at large gatherings and still quite able to enjoy the company of friends and a pleasant day's walk in Bath.

They had gone only a little way along the street when Mr. Caesar stopped short. "I say"—his voice dropped to a stage whisper—"isn't that Mr. Clitherowe over there?"

He did not, of course, point the man out directly, as that would have been an unforgivable rudeness. Instead he inclined his head gently towards him, although, since he was now wearing a garish mauve hat, the gesture was in some ways even more offensive.

"I believe it is." Miss Mitchelmore was not quite sure what she wanted to do about this observation. He *was* leaving a booksellers, but unless he happened to be clutching a copy of *Laying Curses Upon Innocent Ladies, a Guide for the Discerning Gentleman,* it was unclear what they could learn by confronting him.

"Oh, if *only* we had thought to bring cloaks." The tone of vexation in Miss Bickle's voice was, Miss Mitchelmore felt, rather out of proportion with the problem. "Then we should have been able to spy upon him."

Mr. Caesar gave her a cautious look. "How would cloaks help?"

"They should make us look inconspicuous," Miss Bickle explained. "We should draw them up over our faces and by that ruse prevent anybody from observing us."

"And you do not think," asked Miss Mitchelmore, "that a gentleman and two ladies, all cloaked and hooded, a little after midday, in late May, on a public street in Bath, creeping stealthily behind an otherwise unremarkable clergyman, might draw just the *tiniest* bit of attention to ourselves?"

Miss Bickle blinked, twice. "Of course not. We should be cloaked and hooded."

Across the way Mr. Clitherowe looked up and, whether as a result of Miss Bickle's persistent staring, Mr. Caesar's unconventional headgear, or his afore-established affection for Miss Mitchelmore, began approaching the trio.

"Blast it all, he's seen us." Mr. Caesar lowered the brim of his hat. "Do either of you have any idea what we should say to him?"

Miss Mitchelmore thought as quickly as she could but came up short. "I suppose *Sir, have you perchance put me under a curse?* lacks subtlety?"

They were able to strategise no further, as Mr. Clitherowe was now well within earshot. He was a short man, although it had not been this specific detail that had made Miss Mitchelmore turn him down. Nor had it been his relatively lowly station, for neither her mother nor her aunt had cared for such considerations in matchmaking. Indeed, there was much about him that was charming, if you were the sort to be charmed by an intellectual bent and a sober temperament. No, Miss Mitchelmore was increasingly convinced that his gender had been the primary count against him, and that realisation had significant implications for her future marriage prospects.

"Miss Mitchelmore," he greeted her with stiff enthusiasm. "And Mr. Caesar, Miss Bickle. It is a fine day, is it not?"

They all agreed that it was indeed a fine day and was indeed not *not* a fine day.

"And it is so good to see you recovered from that little . . ." Unable to find a polite way to say *time you were attacked by a swarm of magically summoned wasps and driven into a river wherein you nearly drowned*, he changed the subject entirely. "My, what a fascinating hat."

Miss Bickle grinned. "Does he not look well in it? You see John, I told you that you should look well in it."

"As may be apparent, it was Miss Bickle's choice," Mr. Caesar explained, with the careful tone of a man walking the narrow line between offending a lady and accepting responsibility for a sartorial faux pas. "And I am glad you find it . . . noteworthy."

"I do." Reaching up on tiptoes, Mr. Clitherowe peered at the hat more closely. "Fairy work, isn't it? I'm sure you can't get those colours any other way. Absolutely remarkable."

"I didn't know you were a follower of fashion, Mr. Clitherowe." This was the most polite way that Mr. Caesar could have expressed the sentiment. Mr. Clitherowe was clearly *not* a follower of fashion. His collar was limp, his breeches ill-fitting, and his boots, while clean, did not shine as a gentleman's boots should shine.

Stepping back to a respectable distance, Mr. Clitherowe laughed. "I'm not. But I do have an interest in the otherworldly. It's necessary in my calling."

"I'd have thought it the opposite," said Miss Mitchelmore. "Surely a good Christian should not run around playing with fairies and pagan gods?"

"Some of my fellow clerics concur," Mr. Clitherowe admitted, "but I am of the opinion that those parts of the world that people deem *magical* are as much a part of creation as any other. God must have made the fairies, after all. He must even have made the other gods and, provided we do not violate the first or second commandments, he sets no laws against learning of them." He presented the book he had just purchased. "This, for example, is Cornelius Agrippa's *Fourth Book of Occult Philosophy.* It speaks of geomancy, of the conjuring of spirits, and all manner of other sorceries. But are such things any more wondrous than . . . than gunpowder? Or a galleon under full sail? To say nothing of the new discoveries being made every day by the Royal Society?"

Perhaps that, Miss Mitchelmore reflected, was another reason she had refused him. He reminded her on occasion of her father. "But you do not practise, surely?"

"But a little. I do not *quite* concur with Agrippa's assertion that magic is a form of worship, but I have, I confess, been tempted at times to attempt minor conjurations. I made a candle go out once."

"Might it not have been a breeze?" If Mr. Caesar was more than usually arch, blame could be placed entirely on his hat.

"Oh *no*, John." Miss Bickle seemed, if not offended, then at least a little taken aback. "The quivering of a candle flame is a sure sign of an invisible presence. Its extinguishing proof positive that something has manifested. I always make sure to have a candle by my bedside so that I may know if some spirit is watching while I sleep."

As it happens, we very seldom watch mortals sleep. Even awake you are, at best, occasionally diverting. Asleep you are dull. Unless we have some potion to drip in your eyes or beast's head to watch you wake with, we leave you quite alone until you start moving around.

Mr. Clitherowe gave her an approving nod. "A sensible precaution, good lady. But I fear I have taken too much of your time. Miss Mitchelmore, if you were at all interested—and I quite understand that you may not be—I am leading a small party to Stanton Drew later this week to observe the druidical remains there. If you or any of your party would care to join us, it promises to be most edifying."

"I should *love* to see druidical remains," declared Miss Bickle with a sincerity that nobody present came close to doubting. "I shall *certainly* come even if Mae does not."

"Then I shall be delighted to see you there." And with that Mr. Clitherowe took his leave of the party, leaving them to hold their tongues exactly long enough for him to move out of earshot before beginning their dissection of his person and character.

Drawing in a long breath, Mr. Caesar finally said, "I still think Lady Georgiana is the most likely suspect, but he *has* to go to second place on the list. He openly studies magic and clearly still has eyes for Maelys."

"Does that not place him *above* Lady Georgiana?" asked Miss Mitchelmore. "She does *not* study magic and . . ." She hesitated. The question of whether the Duke of Annadale had *eyes* for her was one she was trying not to consider in detail. "Well, at any rate she does not study magic and Mr. Clitherowe does."

Miss Bickle, who had been pondering the matter while everybody was speaking, came at last to a conclusion. "I believe he's still too obvious. I mean, he was carrying a book of spells."

Still a little sore from the hat, John responded more harshly than he might otherwise have. "You can't keep ruling out suspects for being *too obvious.*"

"I can and I shall. You mark my words, the true perpetrator will turn out to be"—Miss Bickle did some brief calculations on her fingers—"I should say it will be the second or third person Mae speaks to who she believes at the time to have nothing whatsoever to do with the mystery."

Narrowing her eyes, Miss Mitchelmore tried to do some calculations of her own. "I think that would mean I'd been cursed by my lady's maid."

"No, I mean somebody significant."

"I think Sarah would consider herself reasonably significant."

Miss Bickle made an exasperated sort of huff. "Somebody new, I mean."

It wasn't until she was halfway through a mental inventory of her recent social encounters that Miss Mitchelmore realised that this exercise was entirely pointless. "I sincerely don't believe that it works that way. Now, what do you say we pay a visit to Mollands?"

The confectioner's was some way to the opposite end of Milsom Street, but the walk was enjoyable enough, and with the midday warmth and the not-exactly-shock of the not-exactly-confrontation with the affably suspicious Mr. Clitherowe, Miss Mitchelmore felt herself very much in need of refreshment. Besides, going indoors awhile would provide Mr. Caesar with an excuse to remove his hat.

Miss Bickle and Miss Mitchelmore took a table by the window, while Mr. Caesar took a moment to enquire of the proprietor whether they sourced their sugar from the West Indies and, having been reassured that they did not, returned to join them.

"My apologies." Mr. Caesar settled somewhat awkwardly into his chair, and used the opportunity to nudge his offensive hat just a little further under the table. "I just like to check. Because of Papa."

Miss Mitchelmore nodded. "I quite understand. We've been the same ever since I was a girl. Your parents convinced our parents, I think, before I was born."

They continued in this vein for some while, doing their best to distract one another with idle conversation, but the ordinarily

pleasurable diversion of watching the people of Bath go to and fro
outside took on an altogether darker edge now that Miss Mitchelmore was in the habit of scanning them for any evidence of who
was mystically influencing her.

At least, it had taken on a darker edge for Miss Mitchelmore
and Mr. Caesar. Miss Bickle was busy tilting her teacup to odd
angles and then manoeuvring her head to meet it.

"Lizzie"—Mr. Caesar turned to her with a look of familiar
bemusement—"perhaps one day there shall come a point when I
have known you long enough to stop asking this, but what on *earth*
are you doing?"

"I am attempting to drink sunlight," explained Miss Bickle as
though it were the most natural thing in the world.

With the doomed will of a man who should have more sense,
he pressed the matter. "Why?"

"Well, it must surely be healthful. Everybody knows sunlight is
good for you."

Miss Mitchelmore was glad of the opportunity to focus on anything but invisible enemies. "I'm not sure *why* is the question, so
much as *how.*"

"Well, *that* is what I am endeavouring to work out. Nobody ever
discovered how to achieve a thing without first attempting it."

Sometimes Miss Mitchelmore worried that she, Mr. Caesar,
and all the worthies of the ton were merely pieces in an elaborate
game that Miss Bickle was playing with all of them. "Then by all
means carry on. Although I fear we are getting some very queer
looks."

"Well, so did Lady Godiva, but history has been remarkably
kind to her reputation."

Mr. Caesar set his own teacup down gently. "I certainly hope
you do not intend to ride naked through the streets of Bath."

"And," Miss Mitchelmore added, "she *didn't* get queer looks. The good people of Coventry averted their eyes, save Peeping Tom, who was struck blind."

"Which just goes to show it's other people's fault for looking." The expression of triumph on Miss Bickle's face was a sight to behold, and I say that as one who has beheld a great many interesting sights.

Before the question of Miss Bickle's sunlight-drinking habits could be explored any further, the marchpane arrived, and the question of tea was quite forgotten.

"Now, isn't this delightful," observed Mr. Caesar, cracking the glaze on the marchpane with his knife and serving an appropriate slice to each of the ladies, and then to himself.

"Yes, although"—Miss Mitchelmore paused—"I confess that I have been nervous of it ever since Papa told me that the scent of almonds was a sign of the presence of prussic acid."

"Now, *that* would be an excellent basis for a mystery." Thoughtfully, Miss Bickle chewed her marchpane awhile before continuing. "A man—or I suppose a lady—collapses dead at a confectioner's and the only clue is a smell of almonds. And a dashing Bow Street runner must investigate the crime with the help of a charming society lady."

Suppressing her childhood fear of almonds, because she did in fact rather *like* marchpane in spite of its toxicological associations, Miss Mitchelmore raised a slice to her lips and took a bite. It tasted bitter, and its texture was hard in places and moist in others—beyond unpalatable, it was almost inedible, although she swallowed the mouthful anyway since the alternative would have been unforgivably indecorous.

Mr. Caesar was staring at her aghast, although all he could manage to say was: "I say."

Fearful that she already knew what had elicited this reaction, Miss Mitchelmore looked down. The fragment of marchpane she was holding bloomed with mould and crawled with maggots. As did the block from which it had been cut. And the tea in their cups had turned to a dark, viscous liquid that she tried to pretend was not blood.

Cautiously, all three of them got to their feet. But the shrieking and retching from other tables told them that the corruption was spreading. Fighting down both her rising nausea and the knowledge that every eye in the establishment was now firmly on her, Miss Mitchelmore did her best to remain composed.

"My apologies," she said to the room in general and then to the proprietress, "if you would be so good as to send my father the bill for any damages this little . . . I'm most . . . that is . . ."

She turned and fled into the street, the taste of rot and maggots still coating her tongue and writhing in her throat. Her companions followed soon after and hurried her back to the carriage, which waited at the other end of the street. The moment she was out of sight she threw herself into Miss Bickle's arms and burst into tears.

9

Events at Mollands had undone much of the certainty about her predicament that Miss Mitchelmore had earned the previous evening at the Assembly Rooms. It was possible, of course, that Mr. Clitherowe had taken the opportunity to direct some hex against her during their brief conversation, but unless "what an unusual hat" was an incantation of ancient and unknowable power, it seemed improbable.

A tiny shred of comfort came from the fact that her being mystically attacked while *not* in the company of the Duke of Annadale made it substantially easier for Miss Mitchelmore to persuade both her parents and Mr. Caesar that calling on the Lady Georgiana was not only safe, wise, and proper, but wholly necessary. Thus, the next day Miss Mitchelmore arrived at the Duke of Annadale's residence on the Royal Crescent with your humble narrator merged seamlessly into her shadow.

Her card accepted and all formal announcements made, Miss Mitchelmore ascended to the first-floor drawing room, where she found the Duke of Annadale awaiting her. Or perhaps not awaiting her, for she stood by one window, facing outwards, hands clasped tightly behind her back.

"I considered refusing you," she remarked, "but I feared that would compound discourtesy with discourtesy."

"I should not have known you were at home. That is the advantage of servants."

"Where else should I be? You have seen how unfit I am for company." The Duke of Annadale turned from the window and for a moment the light framed her in a way that made Miss Mitchelmore quite unsteady. Her dress, although darker than fashion or the season dictated, was of modern cut with full sleeves and intricate lacework at the hem, but Miss Mitchelmore's eyes were drawn to the line of the lady's neck. To the way her hair, worn high but uncovered, caught the sun for a moment like a dark halo. "If you are here to ask me about the goddess, I will answer. As much as I may."

Not certain whether to stand or to sit, and conscious that a visit should not properly be overlong, Miss Mitchelmore tried to articulate the reason for her presence. "I—if half of what you say is true, if you are correct in your surmises, then I hope you will tell me what you know. Since we last spoke I have been attacked again, and I am unsure how much longer I can bear it. You likened this knowledge to a pistol, but if such a weapon is already trained against me I should surely be told how to defend myself?"

"You cannot defend yourself. As one cannot defend oneself from a pistol." There were moments when Miss Mitchelmore found the Duke of Annadale almost readable. This was not one of them. "One may fire *back*, but that does not stop a bullet. It simply creates a second corpse."

"I . . . I was defended somehow when I visited the Assembly Rooms," Miss Mitchelmore ventured. "And that was a pleasant enough evening. If I could simply pass the summer there—"

"The master of ceremonies," was Lady Georgiana's only reply.

"I'm afraid I don't understand."

"Since the days of Beau Nash, the master of ceremonies has held the favour of—well, of various divinities, Venus, Bacchus, even Cybele at times, entities either chthonic or ecstatic—and through this has been granted some power to enforce his rules on the city. Assaulting you at the Assembly Rooms would have violated the master's rules. But you say you have been attacked again since?"

Miss Mitchelmore nodded. "At Mollands. In company with only my cousin and Miss Bickle."

"Deities do not like to be thwarted."

Deciding that sitting was preferable, given the topic of conversation, Miss Mitchelmore lowered herself onto a sofa. "I had not considered it that way."

"Your safest course of action is to retire from society until the party who cursed you is satisfied, or else to discover who they might be and how they may be stopped, although even that may prove impossible."

"I cannot retire from society—I could give up balls and picnics, but it seems this curse wishes me also to forego the society of my friends, and that would be too cruel a sentence. But why might it be impossible to undo the curse even if I can find the one who laid it?"

"Because it is, in all likelihood, Sulis's curse now. And she will have an offering before she is content."

"Then can I not simply make the required offering and have done with it?"

And perhaps I should caution the reader here, because the events of this story are soon to stray into arcane specificities that, if followed incautiously, could lead a foolish person into supernatural peril. And that is something I would *certainly* not take any kind of pleasure in watching or imagining. Do you consider yourself duly warned? Then I shall continue.

More hesitantly than Miss Mitchelmore might have expected, the Duke of Annadale crossed to the sofa, seemed to consider sitting, then stood by the opposite end looking down. "It will depend. What do you know of the baths, or the temple beneath?"

"Little. I know that there is one. I know that the goddess blesses the waters, and that this gives them their restorative properties."

"That is one way to put it, certainly, but gods are complex creatures."

Gazing up at the Duke of Annadale, Miss Mitchelmore was suddenly and bizarrely aware of the shape of her own tongue inside her mouth. "Are we not all complex creatures?"

"Precisely so. And Sulis is not merely a healer any more than you are merely a daughter, your mother merely a wife, or I merely . . . whatever it is that you believe me to be."

Half unconsciously, Miss Mitchelmore slid along the sofa towards her . . . "companion" was not the right word, but she could think of no other. "I am not certain what I believe you to be. I confess I had hoped if I came to call on you that you might reveal a little more of yourself."

"Did you?" The Duke of Annadale half chuckled to herself. "Hope is a strange thing. The last prisoner of Pandora's box. Be careful of hoping for things, Miss Mitchelmore."

"You need not be so obtuse."

The Duke of Annadale turned away again. "You are correct. So I shall be plain. Beneath the baths lies a temple. Those who believe themselves wronged—who believe, more specifically, that another has stolen from them, taken a thing that is rightfully theirs—may descend to the sacred spring and inscribe their grievance upon a tablet, pronouncing a curse upon the one they say has injured them. If it suits the goddess, she will do the rest."

"But I have injured nobody."

"Neither had Arachne. Neither had Medusa. Look how they turned out."

At least part of the allusion was lost on Miss Mitchelmore. "I thought Medusa was a monster."

"She was made a monster. Punished by Apollo for the crime of being ravished in his temple. The gods, my dear Miss Mitchelmore, if you will pardon my coarseness, are shits. If somebody has set one against you, then you cannot appeal to reason or to justice, only to the petty selfishness of a being old as time whose goals and motivations we mortals cannot comprehend."

"Might I not find a protector? The master of ceremonies—"

"Can ward you for the length of a single ball, and only so long as the goddess remains content to wait. The moment she does not, he will be very much motivated to hand you over to her. Nobody can protect you from an angry deity, not truly."

"*You* protected me." With a boldness inspired at least partly by hopelessness, Miss Mitchelmore rose and reached out a hand to catch the Duke of Annadale by the arm.

The Duke's reaction was immediate. She pulled away and spun to face Miss Mitchelmore, her eyes blazing a mix of fear and fury. "Do not touch me. It is impertinent and imprudent."

"You have just told me that I have the enmity of a goddess, and that I can do nothing to overcome it. I do not see what I have to lose by touching whomever I like." Miss Mitchelmore stepped towards the Duke of Annadale. "Unless I am mistaken, and you do not *wish* to be touched."

The Duke of Annadale's jaw tensed, as though she were fighting for self-mastery. "If you knew a tenth of what I wished, you would flee this house and not return."

"Perhaps"—Miss Mitchelmore looked up, doe-eyed—"but how can we be certain if you will not tell me?"

Once more the Duke of Annadale pulled away. "Gods and devils, I do not know if you are the rankest of ingénues or the worst of temptresses."

"I hold myself neither," replied Miss Mitchelmore coolly, "and would thank you to do the same."

"How prettily you speak. But whatever you may have told yourself, I am not what you want."

This was precisely the kind of mortal foolishness that I was hoping Miss Mitchelmore would find herself caught up in. This endless push and pull of wanting and fearing and hoping that makes you do such ill-considered and amusing things. Pressed past the point of tolerance with people telling her what she wished and what was best for her, Miss Mitchelmore came forwards with more certainty than she felt until she was close enough to feel the Duke's breath on her lips. "Dismiss me all you will, but I am soon to be nineteen. I have seen two seasons and danced with half the eligible men in the ton, and not one of them has done to me what you did the night you took my hand."

"Congratulations." The Duke of Annadale was perilously close to sneering. "You have experienced your first girlish infatuation. Take my advice: Marry a rich man and use his money to support your mistresses."

"I can marry nobody unless I can reenter society, which you say I cannot do with this curse over my head."

"Then grow old a spinster," the Duke of Annadale told her, "and fuck your maids."

And that, for a moment, shocked Miss Mitchelmore into silence. Until she laughed.

"What, pray, is so funny?" asked the Duke of Annadale. I would have asked the same myself. Jokes offend me when I am not party to them.

Stepping back a moment, and wiping genuine tears from her eyes, Miss Mitchelmore gathered herself. "You. I see it now, and you are *absurd*. Worse, you are a *coward*."

The Duke of Annadale looked as though she had been stung by a wasp. Or perhaps a cloud of wasps. "A coward?" She snatched at Miss Mitchelmore, catching her by the wrist and dragging her close again. "Reduced my circumstances may be, but I am a duke's daughter and will not take these insults."

Miss Mitchelmore was still laughing. "I am sorry, but you are doing nothing to change my mind." She laid her hand on her own wrist, covering the Duke of Annadale's fingers. "You will touch me to tease me, to command me, even to rescue me. But the moment I stop flinching or running or trembling"—she leaned forward, bringing her lips to the Duke of Annadale's ears—"the moment I look you in the eye and say *yes*, you spurn me."

The Duke of Annadale sighed heavily against her. "Paler than grass, I am dead or seem to be. Do not offer me this. It will destroy you."

"But you will not tell me why."

"Curses take many shapes. It may seem cowardice to you, but I am trying to do what is right. To be less cruel and less wicked than my nature bids me to be." By some path neither woman could remember, her hands had found their way to the nape of Miss Mitchelmore's neck, where they rested, her thumbs tracing gentle circles along the line of her hair and sending tiny shudders through her body.

"Kiss me," demanded Miss Mitchelmore, "or leave me be. We cannot stand like this forever."

The Duke of Annadale's lips curled into a soft, perplexed smile. "I confess I am no longer certain who is holding whom."

Closing her eyes, Miss Mitchelmore leaned forward one last time, hoping for a closeness that never came.

The Duke of Annadale slipped out of her arms, crossed to the pianoforte, and sat on the stool with her head in her hands. "Go. You are right about me. In every particular you are right. And you must go."

"You said you would help me."

"And you said I already had. But look around you, Miss Mitchelmore—"

"Will you at least call me Maelys? You saved my life. It seems wrong to stand on formalities."

For a moment, the Duke of Annadale was still, but when she looked up her face was a mask of impassivity. "Look around you, Maelys. I am not a witch. I am not a murderess. I am not even— despite what the ton calls me—a duke. I am a wreck of a woman presiding over the slow decline of my family's legacy. And I am worthless to you."

Miss Mitchelmore took half a step towards the Duke of Annadale before thinking better of it. "May I not decide for myself what is of worth to me?"

"Not in this world. Society determines the value of your name. The exchanges determine the value of your property. The gods determine the value of your life. All three have judged me unfavourably, and you should not shackle yourself to me. If you seek answers, you will find them at the temple beneath the bathhouse, but if you would go, bring an offering."

"What manner of offering?"

The Duke of Annadale took another breath, slow and trembling. "A heifer, if you can manage it, although the stairs will prove tricky. A side of beef may be an acceptable substitute, but for large requests it is best to use a live beast. When Wellington consulted the goddess in '09 he drowned nine doves and a peacock."

"I am not sure I could bring myself to drown a living creature."

Now it was the Duke of Annadale's turn to laugh, although her laughter was hollow where Miss Mitchelmore's had held at least a spectre of joy. "And yet you think yourself ready to meddle with gods, and with those they have touched?"

"I do not know." Miss Mitchelmore turned to leave but, stopping a moment in the door, turned back. "For whatever it matters, I . . . I am not sorry I met you."

"All the more reason to go. I wish nothing more than for you to continue feeling that way."

And so Miss Mitchelmore left, taking what comfort she could from the knowledge she had gained. And I, your humble narrator, remained curled peacefully inside her shadow. It had been, for me, a wonderful day. For I enjoy nothing more than watching you mortals torment yourselves.

That night I walked again in her dreams, and saw that they were vivid, and dark, and sensual.

10

"And she did not even *try* to kiss you?" asked Miss Bickle, sitting on Miss Mitchelmore's bed with a half forequarter of beef sat awkwardly between them. I myself was nestled within the meat disguised as a piece of gristle. I will occasionally take this shape in order to stick in old men's throats and make them sputter.

"No. Although I believe she was tempted."

"Well, isn't that selfish of her? How are you to know for certain if you truly favour ladies if none of them will so much as kiss you?"

Miss Mitchelmore shut her eyes and cast her mind back to the previous day, to the heat of the Duke of Annadale's breath on her cheek, and the touch of her fingers on her neck. "I am increasingly satisfied on that score. Evidence is mounting somewhat."

"Then *you* should have kissed *her*." A thought occurred to Miss Bickle. "Unless you wish to wait for a more apposite moment, such as when she whisks you away to the ancient seat of her family, which I am *sure* must be some crumbling castle on a mountain somewhere haunted by the ghosts of twelve generations."

"If I recall correctly, her father was only the third Duke of Annadale. And the Landrake family home dates only from the late 1600s."

"I'm beginning to think you must find yourself another woman, Mae. This one is sounding shabbier and shabbier. Although I suppose one may acquire one or two ghosts in a century. They probably have a grey lady at least. Everywhere has a grey lady."

Miss Mitchelmore touched her hand to her forehead as though chastising herself for her foolishness. "Oh la. Somehow I allowed all of our conversation to revolve around how I could prevent a goddess from destroying me, and how deeply I yearned for her touch, and completely forgot to raise the questions of how many ghosts she had."

"Mae!" Miss Bickle clapped her hands excitedly. "Do you truly *yearn* for her? I'm so glad. Yearning is such fun. It's far the best part of courting in my experience. I fear I shall miss it terribly when I am married."

"I am given to understand that marital relations have their own pleasures," observed Miss Mitchelmore. I am given to understand the same, although from my personal perspective their chief pleasure is that they cause mortals to make some exceedingly silly faces.

"Yes, but one only gets to experience those with a single person, whereas one may yearn for simply heaps of people and I swear it never becomes tiresome."

"I hope so. I fear it may be all I have for some time. Perhaps my whole life."

Miss Bickle's face fell. "Yes, I can see that would be dreary."

Hoisting up one end of the slab of beef, Miss Mitchelmore stood, listing slightly. I allowed myself to enjoy the rocking motion and to imagine myself in a ship on the sea. "Come on. John will be waiting for us."

Downstairs, Mr. Caesar was indeed waiting for the two ladies in the drawing room. He greeted them as warmly as one might expect to greet two women who have appeared in a fashionable town-house carrying over a hundred pounds of raw meat between them. "You will forgive me," he said, "if this question has an obvious answer, but what in the world is that supposed to be?"

"I'm not sure it's *supposed* to be anything," Miss Bickle explained. "It's beef. Quite a lot of beef, actually."

"It's a whole cow." Mr. Caesar stared in confusion. "What on earth do you intend to do with a whole cow?"

"It is *not* a whole cow," insisted Miss Mitchelmore. "It is an eighth of a cow at best. And we shall need it to placate the Goddess Sulis."

"You told me we were taking the waters."

Miss Mitchelmore nodded. "And so we are. But it is very rude to take something and give nothing in return." She was right about this, and it is a lesson too many mortals have forgotten.

Fond as he was of his cousin, Mr. Caesar was not without his suspicions. "You're not telling me everything. If this is the Duke of Annadale's idea . . ."

"Lady Georgiana's idea." Miss Mitchelmore leapt to her . . . acquaintance's defence with an alacrity I personally only associate with the passionate and the officious. "And yes, after a manner of speaking. She explained the nature of the curse to me, and I believe we may learn more about who did this to me if we go to the baths."

"And . . . the meat?"

"She intimated that the goddess may be hostile if I come before her empty-handed."

"And the goddess eats beef?"

Miss Bickle shrugged. "Well, who doesn't?"

Several beings don't, in point of fact. Otherworldly entities often have rarefied and esoteric tastes that mere meat seldom satisfies. In this regard the gods of old were rather pedestrian.

"She said a young heifer, or a live bird. And since I have no wish to drown a bird with my bare hands, I choose to offer cattle."

Mr. Caesar folded his arms. "Very well. I am going to ask you this one last time, Mae. Are you *certain* that you trust this woman? She could easily be leading you into a trap."

"If she wished to harm me, she could have done so several times over. And besides she—that is I—towards her. I mean, I am beginning to feel . . ."

"They're in *love* John. Isn't it marvellous?" Miss Bickle remembered, just in time, that she could not clap her hands in glee without dropping an eighth of a cow onto the drawing-room carpet. Still being ensconced within the ungulate in question, I considered that a blessing.

"We are *not* in love. We—I do not know what we are to one another, but I do not believe she would harm me."

The words hung in the air until Mr. Caesar nodded. "Then I shall trust you and, in trusting you, trust her. But if she is playing you false, I will—well, I do not know what I can do; I can scarcely call her out."

"Why not?" asked Miss Bickle.

"Because ladies do not ordinarily fight duels."

As often happened, Miss Bickle had a look in her eyes that said she knew somebody was being very silly and was not wholly certain it was her. "Ladies also do not ordinarily court other ladies."

"In my experience"—Mr. Caesar moved to assist the two young

women with the beef—"a person who defies the expectations of their sex in one area does not necessarily defy it in others. By the way, is there a reason we aren't getting a servant to carry this?"

Miss Bickle gave the kind of long-suffering sigh one could only give if one had never suffered save for short, intermittent periods. "Don't be silly, John. It would be terribly gauche to bring a servant into the pump room."

"But not to bring a dead cow?"

"An eighth of a dead cow," Miss Mitchelmore reminded him. "And I'm sure we can work something out when we get there."

One uncomfortably meaty carriage ride later, they got there. They had, however, yet to work anything out. Arriving at the pump room with an offering was not, in and of itself, wholly unheard-of— it was known that a goddess dwelt beneath it and that she was responsible for the rejuvenating properties of the waters, and the practical folk of the ton knew a lot about pandering to capricious patrons. The oblations fashionably offered, however, tended more towards the floral and less towards the bloody. It was only those who desired personal communion with the divinity who needed to bring something more substantial.

As was typical for the time of year, the baths were crowded. One of the surest ways to locate *anybody* in Bath at the right time of year was to wait in the pump room; they could be relied upon to appear eventually. As a consequence, the party attracted more than a few raised eyebrows as they carted their gift up the steps and into the long hall where the waters were served. As a further consequence, Miss Mitchelmore was not surprised to glimpse the Duke of Annadale in one of the adjoining rooms, although neither woman moved to approach the other.

"I suggest," said Miss Bickle, "that we promenade once or twice for appearances' sake, then descend to the baths proper, and from there see if we may find our way to the temple. Did Lady Georgiana tell you where you were actually supposed to *put* the cow once you got here?"

"She did not," confessed Miss Mitchelmore. "And I am not sure promenading is entirely practical, given our encumbrance."

"We can go in shifts. I will guard the meat while you walk the room with John, then he shall guard the meat while you walk it with me, then you shall guard the meat while I walk it with him."

"Can you stop saying *guard the meat?*" Mr. Caesar pleaded. "It sounds peculiar."

Looking about the room, Miss Mitchelmore was not sure she felt up to promenading at all. "Why don't you and John take the first turn. I am a little tired from recent events and, given how my last two society outings finished, I am not certain I should be dallying."

They agreed amongst the three of them that this was indeed the wisest course of action, and Miss Bickle and Mr. Caesar set off to make the customary showing while Miss Mitchelmore stood by the half-forequarter, wondering if she should at least have secured herself a glass of mineral water first.

"If I might"—the voice belonged to a tall, shrewd-eyed man, just old enough that you could not call him young—"you are far too beautiful a woman to be standing alone beside a chunk of slaughtered animal."

"You are too kind, sir." Hastily, Miss Mitchelmore searched her mental almanac for the man's name and, to her relief, found it. "My apologies, I have had a trying few days—you are the Viscount Fortrose, are you not?"

He smiled, and there was something about his smile that

reminded her of the Duke of Annadale, although it stirred less in her. "Guilty as charged. I feared you would not remember me."

"Not at all. You very sweetly asked me to dance at Lady Montgomery's ball. I am sorry that I had to refuse you, but my card had filled early that evening and although I was flattered by your invitation, it would not do to slight other gentlemen."

He waved a dismissive hand. "Think nothing of it. I quite understand, and the wonder of being a viscount is that one is never left in want of a dance partner."

"You are most gracious."

There was a moment's quiet. "Forgive my impertinence, Miss Mitchelmore, but I am forced to ask. Why *have* you brought a hundred and forty pounds of prime steak to the baths? Are you intending to slow-cook it?"

"I am not sure that would prove edible. But no, its purpose is oblative, rather than culinary."

"Most people bring flowers."

"Most people are trying to alleviate their gout. I am trying to break a curse."

He cocked his head to one side. "I had heard . . . speculations about your recent public spectacles. Society seems divided as to whether you have been the victim of supernatural mischief or are simply delighting in the scandal."

This was very much what Miss Mitchelmore had feared. "Do people really imagine that *any* lady would delight in scandal?"

"Many do, when they are not the subject of them." He was right on that score. I, for example, delighted in every scandal of the Other Court, save for my last. "And candidly I have heard Lord Hale say some very uncharitable things."

Gentlemen of a certain rank all knew each other, and so it shouldn't have surprised Miss Mitchelmore that the man was on gossiping terms with her uncle. Still, it set her a little on the back foot. "Are you a friend of his, then?"

"More an acquaintance. We belong to several of the same clubs. And I should clarify that speaking *personally* I have no doubt that your present predicament is the result of malfeasance."

"Thank you." The release of tension in Miss Mitchelmore's voice was quite audible. "Would that I were confident everyone else would come to the same conclusion."

The viscount still seemed to be considering something. "I remain uncertain what the beef has to do with the affair."

"A friend thinks I may—that is, she thinks that the Goddess Sulis may assist me, if I am able to access the inner temple. But she suggested also that I might need to bring an offering, and that a heifer was traditional."

"Your friend knows her classics."

"Yes, I believe her quite knowledgeable."

"Although that is almost certainly a bullock."

Miss Mitchelmore shrugged. "It was the best I could do at short notice. After all, where does one even *find* a sacrificial heifer in the nineteenth century?"

"I suspect one would need to make special arrangement with a farmer. Although I understand there are still one or two professional victimarii in the city. One can, after all, find anything in London."

At more or less this juncture, Miss Bickle and Mr. Caesar returned from their tour of the room. Uncertain if her friends had been formally introduced to the viscount or not, Miss Mitchelmore provided the necessary niceties and various *pleasures* and *delighteds* were passed around the little group. Mortal pleasantries always amuse me; they are so full of nothing, and sufficient quantities of nothing, properly harvested, can achieve so much.

"An honour though it has been to make all of your acquaintance," the viscount concluded, "I see that you have pressing business to attend to. I hope fervently that your endeavour ends well, Miss Mitchelmore."

After he had gone, Miss Bickle glared at Miss Mitchelmore accusingly. "Mae, you're not being unfaithful to Lady Georgiana *already,* are you?"

"As yet there is nothing to be unfaithful *to.* And no, I was merely making polite conversation with a gentleman. Now, shall we descend?"

"Oh yes." Miss Bickle looked troublingly excited. "This dress is woven of mermaids' hair and I cannot wait to see how it responds to the water."

"*I,*" Mr. Caesar protested, "did *not* come out expecting to bathe. There is a gantry around the bath and I fully intend to walk along it."

Miss Bickle hoisted up her end of the beef. "Oh, but it's so *good* for you. It's wonderful for rheumatism."

"I do not *have* rheumatism."

"Well, you shall surely develop it if you persist in avoiding the waters."

Miss Mitchelmore had also intended to skirt the bath rather than immerse herself. "Are you *certain* your dress is woven of mermaids' hair? It seems rather unlikely." Although, looking at it, not entirely impossible. Miss Bickle's gown was made of a very strange fabric, which shimmered unnaturally when the light caught it.

"That's what the man who sold it me said."

"The man who sold it you?" Mr. Caesar had the hesitant tone of somebody asking a question to which he was quite certain he would not like the answer.

"Yes. I met him by the beach one day, and he swore to me that the dress he was carrying was woven of mermaids' hair and I saw no reason to disbelieve him, so I bought it at once." This, reader, was very sensible, and is an example you should all follow.

"Lizzie," Miss Mitchelmore exclaimed, "you cannot go around buying dresses from strange men you meet on the beach. What if he had been some kind of ruffian?"

"Then the selkies would have protected me."

Miss Bickle's stubborn belief, in the face of mounting evidence, that all supernatural entities are benevolent and wondrous never ceased to frustrate her friends, although speaking *as* a supernatural entity I found it quite charming. We do, in fact, have a soft place in what you may call our hearts for the innocent. Or perhaps we simply like those who like us.

It had taken a little asking around to find directions to the spring itself, since while it was not exactly forbidden to visitors—it was not, after all, the business of the corporation that ran the baths to keep petitioners away from the goddess—it was not a normal attraction. They were eventually directed past the King's Bath, where men in linen suits and women in linen dresses mingled neck-deep in hot, sulphurous water, and down a staircase that cut through the modern building and into an older and altogether eerier structure.

The staircase itself had not been well maintained, with overspill from the various baths being permitted to trickle down the steps back to the source. The deeper one progressed, the more the air smelt of sulphur and iron and just a little of blood. The party came at last to a wide chamber wherein was a deep, circular pool, rivulets running off in many directions. A bronze statue stood in its centre. The woman it depicted had a cold, imperious expression, and Miss Mitchelmore noted with some confusion that although the statue must have been ancient, the woman's hairstyle had, by some quirk of fate, returned very much to fashion.

"Now what?" asked Mr. Caesar with growing impatience. "Do we throw the cow in and pray?"

"I think—I think there is something I must find first." Hoping that its depth was not deceptive, Miss Mitchelmore lowered herself into the pool, glad that she had chosen a simple walking dress for the occasion. The water was warm, almost uncomfortably so, but it was shallow enough that she could stand and keep her head and shoulders dry for the moment. As soon as her feet touched the bottom, she felt hard, rectangular objects sliding beneath her and concluded that these must be what she had come for.

"Mae, are you quite sure you know what you're doing?" Mr. Caesar's enquiry was a fair one, and the truth was she did not.

She dived anyway, coming up a few moments later with water streaming from her cap and a number of small tablets clutched in her hands. "Here." She handed them to her friends. "One of these carries the curse that is on me. If we can find which, we may find how to break it."

"This is Latin," Mr. Caesar observed. "Worse, it is *bad* Latin. But I believe it says *to the Goddess Sulis Minerva, I give to your divinity my bathing tunic and cloak.* Are you absolutely certain this is what we are looking for?"

"Whoever laid a curse on me believes I have stolen something. What they believe I have stolen, I do not know, but they have asked the goddess to punish me for stealing it."

"I can't read this one at all," said Miss Bickle. "And I think it's old. Very old. Can you find a newer one? One would expect, I think, that the newer ones would be closer to the top?"

Miss Mitchelmore returned to the pool, trying to be more selective this time. Now she was more used to the water, she could tell that some tablets seemed more modern than others—less worn, less faded with time and caked with the silt of years. She re-emerged. "Try these."

"In English, at least." Mr. Caesar read aloud. "*I give to your divinity six shillings and fourpence, which I swear I had when I came into the baths last Tuesday. Do not allow him sleep who has taken it, be he man or woman, unless he brings them to your temple right quickly.*"

Miss Bickle tried another. "*I give to your divinity my best beaver hat, which some blackguard did nab off with while I was bathing. Be he man or woman, let his teeth fall out and his*—oh, I say this *is* vulgar—*until he brings it to your temple.*"

On the right path at least, Miss Mitchelmore dived one more time. Then one more, and then . . .

"I have it, Mae. Or I think I . . ." Mr. Caesar's voice trailed off, and then returned with force. "But this is *vile.*"

"Read it to me, John."

"I am not sure I can."

"If I can be influenced by it, I can surely hear it."

Looking now very drawn, Mr. Caesar read. "*To the Goddess Sulis Minerva, I give to your divinity and majesty the body and heart of Miss Maelys Mitchelmore, who has slighted my dignity and offended my honour. By night or day, in town or country, on land or on sea, let ignominy hound her and shame pile upon her, let ruin follow her until she comes before you in your temple or submits to my desires.*"

I had, by this juncture, left my seclusion within the beef and taken on my most natural form of mists and shadows, the better to observe the comings and goings in the spring. Thus it was I who first noted the change that had come over the statue. Where once she had been bronze, she was now flesh. Where once immobile, she now stepped forward from her pedestal and descended to the pool, her robes flowing about her like the stinging fronds of a jellyfish.

"Don't mind me," I told her, "I am merely the narrator."

She shot one glance in my direction and then returned the whole of her attention to Miss Mitchelmore, who, at last, noticed her.

"Are you—am I in the presence of the Goddess Sulis?"

The goddess nodded.

"I have been cursed," Miss Mitchelmore explained, "and wrongly." Behind her, Miss Bickle and Mr. Caesar hurried to fetch the half forequarter, which was beginning to look like a wholly inadequate sacrifice. "I bring an offering to your name and hope that—"

"You bring me scraps from your table."

The voice of the goddess came from everywhere and nowhere, like a river underground or a storm in the far distance. I am more accustomed to such things than most, and it troubled even me. I avoid the gods when I can.

"I meant no disrespect." Miss Mitchelmore was backing away slowly, but the sides of the sacred pool were slippery, and the waters moved like a vortex to hold her in place. "I have been cruelly mistreated and came to ask for your grace."

Steam began to fill the air, and Miss Mitchelmore felt the pool grow hotter. Much hotter. Even in the baths above, the goddess's anger made itself known. The King's Bath grew suddenly so warm that three people fainted and in the pump room a gout of steam from one of the fountains caused an elderly dowager a nasty injury.

"I am not," said the goddess, "your dying god."

Water began to flood down the stairs. I sincerely considered retreating.

"I do not trade in grace or words."

Miss Mitchelmore's feet were swept from beneath her, and she vanished below the surface of the pool. Mr. Caesar and Miss Bickle rushed forwards to intervene, but grasp though they might, they could not reach her.

"I have been offered your body and your heart. I shall take it."

"Don't." This last interjection came from the stairwell, from which the Duke of Annadale had just emerged. Her dress was soaked, and she had clearly slipped badly on the descent. In her hand she held a cage bearing three white doves.

Stone cracked beneath the weight of divine displeasure. "You do not command me."

The room was filling with water now. Hoping that the goddess would not take it as an insult, I adopted an airy form and rose to the ceiling.

Mr. Caesar, who had submerged himself in a futile attempt to rescue Miss Mitchelmore, surfaced for a moment. "If you have a means to end this, then for the love of God do it."

"I offer you three doves for three days. This woman is yours only if she was cursed justly. I say she was not, and I ask three days to prove it. Then I will deliver her to you myself."

"*That* is your plan?" The whole enterprise had been a terrible trial of Mr. Caesar's patience, and it had now been tried past enduring. "A three-day reprieve and then *fine, let the goddess have her*?"

Miss Mitchelmore's head burst through the surface of the waters. She fought for breath, but it was not a fight she was certain to win.

Sulis Minerva inclined her head in bare acceptance. "Three days."

The Duke of Annadale waded forwards and plunged the cage of doves into the sacred pool. As the waters swallowed them, the birds beat their wings wildly against the bars of the cage, though they must surely have known that escape was impossible. It took several long minutes for the offerings to be done, and then the waters subsided, the room cooled, and the statue was once more on its pedestal, once more lifeless.

"If it pleases you," said the Duke of Annadale to the room in general, "I would have Miss Mitchelmore brought to my carriage. There are things we need to discuss."

CHAPTER

11

I was, all in all, very glad to be able to leave the temple complex. Little in the mortal world is a danger to me (I have mentioned before that the rumours about iron are just a comforting myth) but no being with any sense tangles with a god if they do not have to. Perhaps as a consequence of my discomfort, I elected—on my entering the Duke of Annadale's carriage—to adopt the shape of the smallest insect I could think of and burrow myself securely into a corner.

Miss Mitchelmore, her companions, and the Duke of Annadale, all rather wet and lightly steaming, for the water had been hot to near-scalding, climbed into the carriage and, with a word from the Duke, set off on an apparently aimless tour through the streets of Bath.

"Where are you taking us?" asked Mr. Caesar, still somewhat too flustered to be haughty but nowhere near trusting.

"In a wide circle, for now. We need time to talk."

"I should . . ." Miss Mitchelmore looked down, abashed. "I should thank you for saving me, again."

The Duke of Annadale gave a cold facsimile of a laugh. "This time you were following my advice. If anything, you should be berating me."

"Don't think I haven't considered it," observed Mr. Caesar. "Your presence was, once again, convenient."

"I knew she would be attending. I suspected she would need help. I also thought it probable that she would lack the spirit to make a live offering." With this last comment, the Duke of Annadale shot Miss Mitchelmore a look that carried an edge of challenge.

"*She,*" Miss Mitchelmore replied, "is present, and so should be addressed directly. She also did not think that this was a test of spirit."

"It is a test of everything."

The carriage rattled on, turning in a wide loop that would eventually bring it back to the baths.

"Well?" Mr. Caesar had recovered some of his composure, despite the dampness of his coat, and was staring at the Duke of Annadale pointedly.

"Well what?"

"You said there were things you needed to discuss."

Miss Bickle, whose dress really did seem strangely dry despite the day's events, beamed. "You should probably discuss the fact that you're *desperately* in love with each other."

"We are not," Miss Mitchelmore and the Duke of Annadale said together.

"Then *why* do you keep *rescuing* her?" asked Miss Bickle, as though she were playing a trump at whist.

A little more self-consciously than she perhaps intended, the Duke of Annadale developed a sudden interest in the passing scenery. "Ennui?"

"Whatever your reasons," said Miss Mitchelmore, growing more than a little testy, "I would know what you have to tell me."

For a moment the Duke of Annadale looked out of the window, pretending she had not heard. Then at last she said, "Nothing."

"Stop the carriage," Mr. Caesar demanded. "She's playing with us."

"I have nothing to tell you," the Duke of Annadale went on, "but I am hoping you have something to tell me. Unless you are even greater fools than I fear, you must have some theories about who is behind this and"—she raised a hand to check Mr. Caesar's interruption—"yes, I am quite aware one of those theories is me. You may investigate my personal habits in your own time. But if you will let me, I have resources that I would put at your disposal."

"What manner of resources?" Miss Mitchelmore's tone was guarded.

"Money. Servants. Connections, not all of them in good places. Tell me who you suspect"—once again she raised a hand—"*other than me,* and I will do what I can to help you uncover their secrets."

"And what of your secrets?" asked Miss Mitchelmore, a little more boldly than I might have expected.

"You are welcome to them. Well, to those of them you can find in Bath." She called out to the coachman, "Carter, home."

The coach changed direction and began to make for the Royal Crescent. Miss Mitchelmore watched the Palladian architecture and druidical groves of the Circus drift past the windows. "I hope you are not abducting us, Lady Georgiana."

Perhaps I reveal my own predilections, but I do not believe she did, in fact, hope that at all.

"If you would rather be released to the mercy of Bath and its patroness without my assistance"—the Duke of Annadale and Miss Mitchelmore were now conversing out of opposite windows—"then I shall happily set you down at the place of your choosing."

"That will not be necessary," Miss Mitchelmore told the view outside the carriage. "And yes, I believe our misgivings would be assuaged somewhat if you let us search your premises for signs of malfeasance."

"And don't try to tell us not to open the locked door in the west wing," added Miss Bickle. "Because we shall open it in spite of you."

This, at last, drew the Duke of Annadale's gaze back from the window. "It's a townhouse in Bath; it has no wings, west or otherwise."

Disappointment spread across Miss Bickle's face. "Then where do you keep the bodies of your former wives?"

"The tower."

This answer seemed wholly satisfying to Miss Bickle, at least until they arrived on the Royal Crescent and she was reminded that not a single tower was present on any of the buildings. The carriage pulled to a halt in front of a disappointingly un-betowered house a little way along the crescent, and the four mortals alighted. I became a sparrow and flew out after them.

The group, alongside your humble narrator, were let into the Bath residence of Lady Georgiana Landrake by an efficient and unobtrusive servant. Miss Mitchelmore, no doubt acutely aware that the last time she had been in the house she had called its mistress a coward and challenged her to kiss her, proceeded a little hesitantly. By contrast, Miss Bickle ran forward with all the enthusiasm of an ill-trained puppy, and Mr. Caesar went after her, still radiating determined scepticism. This left me with something of a quandary. It seemed that the party would be dividing itself, and that I would need to decide between observing Miss Mitchelmore, alone with the Duke of Annadale, or Miss Bickle and Mr. Caesar, who would be getting up to all sorts of mischief in a strange house.

I elected, in the end, to follow Miss Mitchelmore. Hers was, after all, the story I had chosen to tell, and I had an inkling that either Mr. Caesar or, more likely, Miss Bickle would shout if they discovered anything interesting.

While her companions set about exploring the house for evidence of murder, Miss Mitchelmore followed the Duke of Annadale into the drawing room, where she perched herself on a settee and waited for her hostess to speak. I observed silently from aslant a curtain.

"I'm sorry," said the Duke of Annadale at last, "you're soaking wet. I should have let you go home and change rather than bringing you here. If I should have brought you here at all."

Miss Mitchelmore was indeed still rather dripping, having dived into the sacred spring and been near broiled. "No, no, I am quite well."

"I would suggest that I provide you with fresh garments, but I fear you would take it as an advance."

"I would if it were intended as one."

Either unwilling or unable to look at Miss Mitchelmore directly, the Duke of Annadale returned to the window where she had stood during the lady's earlier visit. "I hope you would credit me with a little more creativity, were I to attempt to undress you."

"And is a lack of creativity your only objection to the suggestion?" asked Miss Mitchelmore, one hand coming reflexively to the damp neck of her walking dress.

The Duke of Annadale heaved a deep sigh. "And what would you have me say, Miss Mitchelmore? That yes, if I could work my will I would have you stripped and brought to my chamber, there to be tied to the foot of my bed, whereupon I would come to you once or twice daily, as was my wont, and pleasure you until you wept before departing without a word? That since I first saw you that night in the garden, I have wanted to kiss you and, when I kiss you, to taste myself upon your lips? That, put simply and artlessly"—she turned and stalked towards Miss Mitchelmore, standing close enough to touch her—"I want to *fuck* you." Reaching across the short distance between them, she caught a lock of Miss Mitchelmore's hair that had come loose in the water and wound it tight about her fingers, twisting Miss Mitchelmore's head up to face her. "That, years from now, when you lie abed with your rich, tedious husband grunting and sweating atop you, I want your thoughts to be only of me."

For a moment, Miss Mitchelmore seemed lost as to how to reply. And well she might be, for such talk was unconscionable even in the relatively permissive household of the Mitchelmores. But for all the deficiency—or propriety, depending on one's perspective— of her upbringing, she had not been raised to be easily silenced. "These are words," she said. "Just more words."

"Be thankful they remain so."

"I am thankful for my health and the good fortune of my family." Miss Mitchelmore moistened her rapidly drying lips. "I see no reason to thank you for . . . for mocking me in this way."

"You think I am mocking you?"

"I think you mock me very wickedly."

The Duke of Annadale tightened her grip on Miss Mitchelmore's hair and half sneered. "*I think you mock me very wickedly,*" she echoed. "Must you speak so girlishly?"

"I am, in fact, a girl, Lady Georgiana. Or had it escaped your notice?"

"You are a young woman," replied the Duke of Annadale. "Although perhaps that is just my vanity speaking. Still, you are old enough to tell mockery from plain truth."

"And the truth is you want to"—Miss Mitchelmore bit her lip— "to do to me as you have said?"

At that the Duke of Annadale gave a sharp, almost vicious laugh. "My God, she cannot even bring herself to say the words. And you wonder why I pull away from you."

Miss Mitchelmore blushed. "Just because a person cannot say a thing it does not mean that they do not . . . that is, that they would not want to . . . at least the possibility . . ."

"Seek me out when you are older, child. Or at least when you have the stomach to ask for what you want." And with that, the Duke of Annadale released her grip on Miss Mitchelmore's hair and turned away again. "Or at the very least when you have more than three days to live."

"If I have only three days to live," observed Miss Mitchelmore, "then surely I should pursue what earthly delights are available to me while I can."

"Then we shall strike a bargain. If we reach midnight on the third day, and we are no closer to freeing you from the goddess's embrace, I shall take you to my chamber—or, for that matter, any other place you wish—and despoil you thoroughly. Until that time, perhaps we should focus on saving your life."

Resigning herself to dampness and—in this matter at least— dissatisfaction, Miss Mitchelmore conceded that the question of her impending doom was rather more pressing than whatever tangle of longing lay between herself and the Duke of Annadale. "Quite so. But I confess I have been hoping you will lend me your expertise, if you have any."

"I am no expert. Merely an interested party."

"Then I had hoped you would share your interest."

At last relaxing enough to sit, the Duke of Annadale lowered herself into a chair. "There are books in the library that may prove helpful to you, although I suspect your personal knowledge of your enemies will prove more useful in the long run."

"I am not certain I have any enemies."

"Oh darling, everybody has enemies. *Not* having enemies just attracts the enmity of a different sort of person."

"What sort of person would be one's enemy merely for the crime of having no other enemies?" asked Miss Mitchelmore, eyeing her companion cautiously. It was a fair question, although I could think of several answers. There was me, for a start.

The Duke of Annadale gave a laconic shrug. "Vindictive rakes. Jealous mamas. Capricious sprites. Really, the possibilities are—"

A loud bang echoed through the house.

"Ah." The Duke of Annadale rose. "We should go. It appears one of your friends has found my pistol."

12

Travelling as air and shadow I was able to move substantially faster than Miss Mitchelmore and the Duke of Annadale in their clumsy bodies of flesh and sputum (how I am learning to *loathe* physicality; I swear you must be born to it to bear it). I found Miss Bickle in the Duke of Annadale's bedchamber—a rather spartanly appointed room, given the lady's wealth, its only decoration of note being a large portrait of a handsome young man in military raiment. The frame of this portrait was now somewhat marred by a bullet hole.

Miss Bickle put the offending weapon down gently and continued rummaging beneath the Duke of Annadale's bed. Resisting the urge to kick her in the backside (some jokes are timeless, and kicking a person who is bending over is nearly as hilarious as a prudish person breaking wind), I took up an inconspicuous position in the corner and waited for other arrivals.

The first to respond was Mr. Caesar, who was still clutching both Miss Mitchelmore's curse tablet and a slim volume he must have picked up elsewhere in the building. "My God, Lizzie, are you all right?"

"Quite well," replied Miss Bickle from beneath the bed, "although I find myself a little disappointed that I have thus far found nothing incriminating."

"There was a shot."

"Oh, yes." Casually, Miss Bickle indicated the baize-inlaid box that lay open just behind her. It still contained one unfired pistol. "I found those under the bed and wondered whether they were loaded. It seems they were."

Mr. Caesar picked up the box and examined it, not that he seemed to know what he was really examining it for, as he wasn't the kind of gentleman who goes about armed. "She keeps loaded and primed pistols under her bed?"

"Only during the day," observed the Duke of Annadale from the doorway. "By night I keep one beside my bed, in case it is necessary."

"Necessary for what?" Mr. Caesar closed the box and set it down alongside its missing occupant.

"I have yet to find out."

A disappointed Miss Bickle backed out into the open air and sat on the floor, looking up accusingly. "It is very shabby of you to have so little in your bedchamber. I had felt certain you would at least have some letters from former lovers, even if you do not have any corpses."

"My former lovers are not the kind to write letters," explained the Duke of Annadale.

"Lack of interest, or lack of ability?" asked Mr. Caesar, raising an arch eyebrow.

"Depends on the lover." She looked down at the book Mr. Caesar was holding. "Ah, I see you have been raiding my library."

The surprise of the initial gunshot over, Mr. Caesar recovered himself. "I have. And I've found something *rather interesting.*"

Miss Mitchelmore edged into the room, making her way around the Duke of Annadale to where her cousin was standing. "What is it, John?"

"A book." He held it out in order that Miss Mitchelmore might examine it, and I hovered over her shoulder and read the title. It was called *The Curse-Tablets of Bath: A Study of the Ancient Method of Score-Settling.* "One whose presence I think you *might* want to explain. Especially since I found it open upon the desk."

Clasping a hand to her bosom, the Duke of Annadale gasped. "Alas, my most secret hiding place, however did you find it?"

"Still I should like to know why you were reading it," said Miss Mitchelmore, giving the Duke of Annadale an earnest, searching look.

"I have made my interest in you quite plain," the Duke of Annadale began, and then, when Miss Bickle gave a tiny yelp of delight, continued, "my interest in *your predicament,* rather. And I had the book in my library already. Indeed I had several."

Mr. Caesar looked justifiably mistrustful. "And why might that be?"

"Because"—the Duke of Annadale heaved an exaggerated sigh—"I used the power of the goddess to kill my father and all three of my brothers, along with my lady's maid, my old governess, a greengrocer with whom I quibbled over the price of carrots, and a prying magistrate. There, you have my confession, does it satisfy you?"

"Not remotely." If the Duke of Annadale had been attempting

to bait a reaction from Mr. Caesar, she failed entirely. He remained the image of sceptical propriety. "And even if it is a coincidence, it seems so fortuitous a one that you will forgive me for questioning it."

For the merest moment, the Duke of Annadale eyed Miss Mitchelmore, as if gauging her reaction. "I should think you a fool if you didn't. But I should also think you a fool if you accepted any answer I gave at face value."

"Even so"—Miss Mitchelmore looked almost pleading—"you might try for just a little sincerity? I do not like to think that you are mocking me or my predicament."

"Oh, my dear sweet thing, all I have ever *done* is mock you." I do not, as I have said, like the Duke of Annadale, but she is at times a woman after my own heart. "But since you ask so nicely"—she turned to Mr. Caesar and bobbed a brief curtsey—"in the years since my brothers' deaths I have had precious little to occupy me, and so I have read. I have dabbled a little in the mystical because the world is cruel and arbitrary and learning what I can of its underlying principles comforts me. Besides, it would be remiss indeed to spend much time in Bath without understanding the nature of Sulis Minerva."

"Then you must think me very remiss"—Miss Mitchelmore bowed her head in mock contrition—"for I knew nothing before my recent encounters. I wonder, would you let us borrow whatever texts you might have on the subject?" She gave a small smile. "Or if you prefer, we could stay here and peruse them."

Miss Bickle, having convinced herself that the bed hid no trapdoors or summoning circles, got to her feet. "Oh that sounds like a splendid idea. John and I shall leave, while you and Lady Georgiana"—she made an entirely artificial *ahem-ahem* noise—"do some reading."

"Lizzie." Miss Mitchelmore gave her friend a stern look. "You're being unhelpful."

Weary, perhaps, of strangers poking through her things and bickering at her, the Duke of Annadale took a step towards the door. "Perhaps it would be best if you all went home. Two of you are still damp—a good thought, by the way, Miss Bickle, mermaid hair may be unfashionable, but it is eminently practical for bathing—and I am beginning to grow tired. I shall, perhaps, call upon you on the morrow, when we are all rested."

Mr. Caesar bowed stiffly. "You may be right. Will you object if I take those volumes I feel will be useful to us when I go?"

The Duke of Annadale said that she would not, and while her guests saw themselves out, she returned her pistols to their case and then, once alone, moved to inspect the damage that Miss Bickle's incautious handling had caused to the portrait frame.

For a moment she stood there, fingertips running along the wood and flaking splinters out of the crack. I briefly considered mending it for her—such things are within my capability and I often bestow such kindnesses on mortals who earn my favour (or so I will insist if questioned, if you have *not* earned my favour yet I urge you to keep trying)—but thought better of it. There was no sense in drawing attention to myself; it would compromise my position as a neutral and trustworthy storyteller.

"Who is he?" asked Miss Mitchelmore, who had returned quite without the Duke of Annadale noticing. I, of course, had been more perceptive, but chose not to mention anything until now in order to preserve the sense of surprise.

"Some ancestor," the Duke of Annadale replied.

Miss Mitchelmore regarded the painting. "For a wicked woman you are a poor liar. The uniform is modern. I have seen soldiers wearing it."

"Some *recent* ancestor."

"He would need to be very recent indeed."

Once again, they were neither of them looking at one another. Both were looking up at the fresh-faced young man in the portrait. Even if he were not a lineal ancestor, there was a resemblance between him and the Duke of Annadale, something about the eyes—although his were bright where hers were shadowed.

"He is my brother," the Duke of Annadale explained. "Was my brother. Does that satisfy you?"

Gently, Miss Mitchelmore reached out and put a hand on Lady Georgiana's arm. "Yes. Thank you. What did—that is—how did . . ."

"I murdered him. Haven't you been paying attention?"

Miss Mitchelmore pulled gently, turning Lady Georgiana to face her. "I refuse to believe that."

"What you will or will not believe is no concern of mine."

"Tell me about him." Miss Mitchelmore pressed the issue with a tenacity that I could not help but admire. Stubbornness is a virtue amongst my kind, possibly because we are as a rule so easily distracted.

"There is nothing to tell. He died in Spain."

"In the war?"

"In a fire." Lady Georgiana turned her attention back to the portrait. "It was . . . improbable."

With an almost surreptitious slowness, Miss Mitchelmore sidled closer to Lady Georgiana. "Is that why you were suspected of witchcraft?"

"I was suspected of witchcraft because my entire family died within a year, leaving me vastly wealthy and, were it not for the attached risk of death, one of the most marriageable women in the kingdom. That gave me ample motive, and since the proposed method of assassination was *unspecified magical interference*, means and opportunity were rather immaterial."

"I am sorry." Miss Mitchelmore drew closer once more. They were nearly hip-to-hip now, the breadth of a lie between them.

"Be careful, Maelys," said Lady Georgiana, turning to face her once more. "I could still be a murderess."

Miss Mitchelmore shook her head. "I do not believe so."

"You don't believe I could be so wicked?"

"I don't believe you could be so clumsy." She smiled again. It was the most pixieish smile I had seen on her, and pixies are *immense* fun. "If you wanted to kill so suspiciously large a group of people, I cannot imagine you would choose to do it in so suspiciously short a space of time."

"You flatter me."

"I am trying to."

A wary look crept into Lady Georgiana's eyes, as though she was no longer certain whether she was hunter or prey. "But perhaps I was simply in a hurry."

"Perhaps." Miss Mitchelmore took Lady—my apologies, reader, I appear to have lapsed into using the Duke of Annadale's right name and, worse, nearly permitted myself to do so fully seven times, and that would *never* do—she took the other lady's free hand in hers and laced their fingers together. "But I think you have shown a commendable capacity for restraint."

"You may be the first person ever to say such a thing of me."

"Certainly," Miss Mitchelmore went on, "you have greater patience than I."

And before the Duke of Annadale could protest, Miss Mitchelmore kissed her.

———— • ————

A handful of moments later, she was downstairs and letting the coachman help her into the Duke of Annadale's carriage. I had followed her at a polite distance.

"Well?" demanded Miss Bickle, the moment the doors were closed. "Did you?"

I was, in honesty, impressed with how well Miss Mitchelmore feigned innocence. "Did I what?"

"You *know*." Miss Bickle made a wide-eyed, slightly over-eager face. "Did you *ask* her what you intended to *ask* her."

"Perhaps we should not pry," suggested Mr. Caesar, who was sitting next to rather a large pile of books appropriated from the Duke of Annadale's library. "Indeed it may be for the best if we know as little as possible."

Miss Mitchelmore gave a demure little nod. "Thank you John. But yes, Lizzie, I did . . . umm . . . ask what I felt I needed to ask."

Either unable or, as was more likely, unwilling to contain her excitement, Miss Bickle clapped her hands. "Oh Mae, I'm so pleased. I've been tinging you for simply ages."

"Tinging?" Miss Mitchelmore did not sound like she thought the question was wise, but she asked it regardless.

Miss Bickle nodded. "That's what I call it when I strongly believe two people should be courting but they aren't."

Joining the group of people asking questions they knew they should not ask, Mr. Caesar closed his book. "And what does this process involve exactly?"

"It's not really a process," Miss Bickle explained. "It's more sort of a . . . a mental state. It's just rather useful to have a name for it."

"Is it?" From her tone, Miss Mitchelmore didn't seem to think it was.

"Oh yes. Do you never—that is—are you never reading a novel

and think to yourself *Oh, but those characters would be simply perfect for one another, if only they ever actually had a conversation on page.*"

"And this happens to you a lot?" asked Mr. Caesar.

"All the time."

"So often," added Miss Mitchelmore, by way of clarification, "that you need a special term for it?"

Miss Bickle nodded again, rather exaggeratedly. "For example, last year I was reading the new novel by the anonymous lady who wrote *Sense and Sensibility* and, well, once I'd got over my disappointment that it didn't have *any* of the same characters as the first book—"

"Is that an expectation one would ordinarily have of a second novel?" asked Mr. Caesar.

"Oh, I should think so. I always like to think that each of a writer's novels takes place in a kind of . . . a kind of connected universe, even if it is not made explicit. But as I was saying, once I got over my disappointment at neither Elinor *nor* Marianne being so much as *mentioned* in it, I started to develop the strongest conviction that Mr. Wickham would be simply *perfect* for Mr. Willoughby."

"They're in different books, Lizzie," Mr. Caesar reminded her.

"But in the same *universe*. Anyway, the point is that I ting them. I ting them heartily."

Miss Mitchelmore adjusted her position slightly as the carriage turned a corner. "And you do this . . . tinging to people in the real world as well?"

"Only people I know wouldn't mind."

"I think I *might* mind, actually." Miss Mitchelmore seemed almost surprised at her own assertiveness. "Whatever has— whatever might—what is between me and Lady Georgiana is not really *for* you. If that's all right."

Miss Bickle's eyes widened and her face paled into a look of dismay. "Oh Mae, have I been hurtful? Say I haven't been hurtful."

"Not at all. I'm just"—Miss Mitchelmore moistened her lips—"this is all rather new to me."

"It's new to everybody at first," observed Mr. Caesar. "Especially to those of us who . . ."

"Make up the numbers?" suggested Miss Bickle.

Not having been present for Miss Bickle's making-up-the-numbers theory of human sexuality, Mr. Caesar simply nodded politely. "These things are harder without the ordinary mores of society to guide one. And I suspect in some ways it must be even more difficult for ladies than it is for gentlemen."

"Why would that be?" asked Miss Bickle.

"Because gentlemen are expected to go out and fuck," Mr. Caesar replied, rather more bluntly than I had previously heard him be in mixed company. "And ladies are not."

Miss Mitchelmore coloured at that. "I confess it has been . . . confusing. But I think I would rather not dwell on that now."

Opening his book, Mr. Caesar returned to his marked page. "If I were to ask, Lizzie, who you *ting* me with, would I regret it?"

"Oh yes," Miss Bickle gave him a cheerful grin. "Deeply."

13

Once Miss Mitchelmore had returned home and her companions departed for their various establishments, I found myself struck by a curiosity as to what the Duke of Annadale was doing. This, however, places me in something of a quandary. I am, above all, a narrator. My function is to collect and relate stories to those who may be amused by them. But a vital part of amusement in a narrative comes from surprise, and if I reveal too much of what I observed it may ruin the anticipation of those of you who remain uncertain about the Duke of Annadale's trustworthiness.

I could, of course, simply not relate my observations at all, but that would violate old bans and deep oaths that have bound me since before time was time. Besides, used judiciously, these glimpses into the hidden sides of the story can serve to whet the appetite.

It was late evening when I returned to the Duke of Annadale's residence, but I was unsurprised to find her awake and active. If there was ever a mortal who would sleep but little and lightly, it was the Duke of Annadale. Only slightly less expected was that I found her dressed for travel. Her coach had returned and she was cloaked and shod, ready to depart into the night. Merging into her shadow, I followed.

The carriage left Bath and headed south through Somerset for a little over an hour. On the ride I detached myself from the darkness and looked out at the countryside rolling past in the moonlight. It is a commonly held belief amongst your kind that creatures like me are primarily rural beings, and there is some truth in that. Certainly we keep to our groves and our barrows much of the time. But I have, myself, always loved the city. Well, I always loved the city until I was so recently and so rudely cast out into it. It turns out being surrounded by the ruck and run of humanity is much less entertaining when you have no power to prevent it from rucking and running all over you.

As we passed a crossroads, I felt a slight lurching in what, had I been mortal at the time, I should have called my stomach. The ways between worlds are weak in such places, and being carried past one involuntarily is always a little awkward. Our journey ended at last outside an isolated farmhouse. And it was a farmhouse I recognised. It belonged to a woman named Margaret Mason, and she was a witch.

Not wishing to reveal myself to the Duke of Annadale but knowing full well that Sweet Maggie, as I had once known her, would be able to see me, I ran ahead and slipped in through a half-open window. Although I was nothing but mists and figments, a set of chimes rang at my passing and the house's occupant—so much older than I remembered her, so much more worn—looked around at me and smiled.

She had been a fascinating creature in her day, quick and

audacious and full of life. Now she sat in a rocking chair, tying knots in a long, fine thread, and when she rose to greet me it was slow and stiff and almost painful to look upon.

"Robin." The sound of my name—or the name I give to mortals at least—was strange in that moment. "It has been a long time."

"Where you live, perhaps," I told her. "But I—"

She waved a hand dismissively. "Yes, yes, you dance on the cusp of the dawn, where fire is cold and *never* gives way to *always*. What do you want, O merry wanderer of the night?"

"Well, in approximately thirty seconds Lady Georgiana Landrake is going to knock on your door and—"

Sweet Maggie gave me a knowing nod. "And you're collecting her for one of your stories, and you would rather I let you observe."

"Will you stop interrupting me?" I asked. I did not sound at all petulant.

"I learned long ago that if I never interrupted you, I would never speak." A knock sounded at the door. "Come in, Georgiana. It isn't locked."

The door opened and the Duke of Annadale slipped into the one room of Sweet Maggie's little cottage. "I suppose some spirit told you I was coming?"

"In a manner of speaking."

"And did it tell you anything else?"

I cupped one hand against my mouth and stage-whispered the salient details.

"That there is a young lady involved." Maggie smiled—she had always had a rather wonderful smile, and age had not marred it. "That it involves also a curse laid through the power of the Goddess Sulis, called Sulis Minerva by some. I assume it *is* a curse from the goddess?"

"She has confirmed it with her own lips."

"She the girl or she the goddess?"

Without waiting to be asked, the Duke of Annadale sat down on a stool. "Both, as it happens."

"Well, that makes it simpler. No need to go untying witch-knots from her hair or finding out which goat ran under her bed."

"You may not believe this," said the Duke of Annadale, "but I've had no contact with her bed whatsoever."

That made Sweet Maggie laugh. "Then you are becoming cautious in your old age."

"Belatedly. Or perhaps I am only becoming fearful. Perhaps they are the same thing."

"They may be." Sweet Maggie looked up at me—I was perched on the window-ledge in a manner that I liked to think displayed me to advantage. "But were I a wiser woman, I suspect I would be able to tell you the difference. Why have you come to see me?"

"For advice, Mother Mason." The tone in the Duke of Annadale's voice was oddly respectful, as a child speaking to an old tutor.

"What kind of advice?"

And here, I fear, the conversation takes a turn for the specific, and it pleases me to elide the details of what was discussed. Suffice it to say that whatever the Duke of Annadale's plans for Miss Mitchelmore, be they virtuous or villainous, salubrious or salacious (we are, I am sure we can all admit, hoping for at least a *little* salaciousness), she received good advice from Sweet Maggie, and I was left with a far better understanding of who Lady Georgiana Landrake was, and why she was doing what she was doing. I am sorry if you consider my withholding of this information from you artless, but I am a being of caprice, and will have my satisfaction where I find it.

The morning following Miss Mitchelmore's encounter with the goddess and her less perilous but in some ways equally significant encounter with the Duke of Annadale began early for the lady and her companions. Three days had been the bargain, but being novices in the world of unseen things, they did not quite know when the days began to count and, therefore, whether they had wasted one already. Miss Mitchelmore's parents had been understanding about the situation but, their interests running to the scientific rather than the esoteric, they had been able to provide little practical assistance.

Thus Miss Mitchelmore and her friends sat now in the drawing room of the family's Bath residence, various of the Duke of Annadale's books spread out around them, while Miss Mitchelmore dug through old diary entries and piles of correspondence in the hope of finding some clue to her enemy, or at the very least some clue that might exonerate Lady Georgiana.

Exoneration, however, was not Mr. Caesar's primary concern. "You realise that she has made annotations?" he held up *The Curse-Tablets of Bath: A Study of the Ancient Method of Score-Settling.* "This is a matter she has studied." He held up another text, entitled *The Petitioner's Preceptor: A Collection of Examples and Precepts for They Who Would Petition the Aid of the Old Gods from the Most Celebrated Writers Ancient and Modern.* "Or perhaps you could explain *this?*" He held up a copy of Walton's *The Compleat Sorcerer.*

"Oh, but *everybody* has a copy of that," said Miss Bickle with the dismissive air of the easily distracted. "It's fearsomely old and has hardly any actual enchantments in it. It's just a lot of silly stories about how being a sorcerer is more interesting than being a hunter or a falconer."

Miss Mitchelmore looked up from her old letters, which were providing her with no other suspects whatsoever. "Besides, is it so very unlikely that she'd be researching these things. We know that she's been trying to help me."

"You know she—" Mr. Caesar began, but Miss Mitchelmore cut him off.

"Yes, yes, we know she *says* she's been trying to help me. But coming up with more and more reasons to be suspicious of her will not help our cause, John. It will only slow us down. Besides, we have the original curse now and we know that whoever laid it wished me to"—she coloured, still struggling to say it out loud—"to submit to their desires and . . . well . . ."

"And you have offered to submit to hers already?" asked Mr. Caesar, his tone one of studied neutrality.

Miss Mitchelmore nodded.

"Be careful, Mae. Even if she isn't a witch, Lady Georgiana is not a respectable woman, and a sad fact of society is that a lady's reputation is easily damaged and not so easily repaired."

"Perhaps let us focus on my survival first, and we can return to the question of my honour if I'm still alive three days from now."

Before any of them could argue further, a servant arrived with a card. It belonged, of all people, to the Viscount Fortrose.

"Well, what can he want?" Miss Mitchelmore wondered aloud, packing away her letters and doing her best to look like she was having a perfectly normal morning at home.

Miss Bickle clapped her hands. "Perhaps he's in *love* with you. Except"—her face fell—"oh, that should be terribly awkward because of the business with Lady Georgiana. Perhaps it would be best to tell him that you would be simply *thrilled* to marry him, except that you've already decided you'd rather be ravished by another woman."

There appeared, from Miss Mitchelmore's perspective, to be several flaws in this line of reasoning. Flaws that, once she had arranged for the viscount to be sent up, she set about enumerating. "Firstly," she told Miss Bickle, "I would *not* be thrilled to marry the viscount. I am sure he is a perfectly pleasant gentleman, but my feelings towards matrimony in general are . . . they are presently rather uncertain."

"Because you think you might—" Miss Bickle began.

"*And secondly,* I would thank you to not speak of my being ravished by anybody, especially not in the presence of guests."

The door opened, and the Viscount Fortrose was announced and then admitted.

"Miss Mitchelmore." He bowed. "And Miss Bickle, Mr. Caesar. I hope you are all well. Some very peculiar events occurred after we met at the baths, and I thought it proper to call and ensure that you were well."

The realisation that this may have been an utterly routine social call and, worse, one related to the mundane business of matrimony, quite killed my interest in the proceedings. I diverted myself by seeking for ways in which I might vex or otherwise inconvenience this new, irritating visitor. Miss Mitchelmore, by contrast, seemed more inclined to tolerate the man. "That is most kind of you. But as you see, we are quite safe."

"And," the viscount continued, wincing only slightly when I transformed into a gnat and bit him, "if I may make so bold, are you any the wiser as to your . . . predicament?"

"Some. My encounter with the goddess was eventful, at least. And I am hopeful that I shall be free of my—my liabilities sooner rather than later."

"I am delighted to hear it." Despite my repeated attempts to discompose him, the Viscount Fortrose remained frustratingly composed. "Perhaps—if it is not too forward of me, would you consider accompanying me on an excursion tomorrow?"

Miss Mitchelmore looked a little taken aback, as well she might. "Tomorrow?"

"I am aware the notice is rather short, but there is a group travelling out to Stanton Drew to look at the antiquities, and it struck me that something outside of the city might prove safer for you, were you inclined to risk venturing once more into society."

Glances passed between Miss Mitchelmore and her companions as they tried to communicate to one another, entirely using their eyebrows, how much information each of them thought the viscount could be trusted with and how wise it was to slight him.

"You flatter me," Miss Mitchelmore protested, "although I am sure there are other ladies far more worthy to accompany you."

"Do you really think so?" asked the Viscount Fortrose with a thin smile. "Or are you merely turning me down politely?"

"I am a young woman of no title and little fortune. What qualities could I possibly have that fit me to grace the arm of a viscount?"

Mr. Caesar set aside his copy of *The Compleat Sorcerer*. "The sad thing is she isn't even being falsely modest. It's all quite genuine."

"I believe it," replied the viscount, then turned his attention once more to Miss Mitchelmore. "And even if you did not display such becoming humility, you are the granddaughter of an earl, I am rich enough to care little for your fortune, and the grace with which you have borne your recent travails speaks well of your temperament. Now, do you still maintain that it is because of your own deficiencies that you refuse me?"

Blushing slightly, Miss Mitchelmore looked down. "There is also the matter of the curse. And of the fact that I have already been invited to that particular excursion by Mr. Clitherowe and it would be, I think, unseemly to reject his invitation and then appear in the company of a different gentleman."

For a moment, a sharpness crept into the viscount's eyes, and a coldness into his voice. "In my experience, few gentlemen resent being slighted in favour of a viscount."

"Do not *all* gentlemen resent being slighted?" asked Miss Mitchelmore.

"Some gentlemen resent it more than others." Mr. Caesar stretched out on the chaise longue, putting me rather in mind of a cat. I have mixed feelings about cats; I respect their innate indifference to the cares of others but have spent too much time in the shape of a mouse to think entirely well of them.

"But," Miss Mitchelmore went on, in a tone that I suspected was rather optimistic in its notes of reassurance, "I may attend the excursion anyway, with my friends, on my own account. So, I shall likely see you there regardless, and should you wish to—perhaps— take a turn about the standing stones together, I am sure I should be delighted."

The Viscount Fortrose bowed stiffly. "Then I shall take my leave, and content myself with the thought of renewing our acquaintance at a later date."

When he was gone, Miss Bickle huffed out an aggrieved sigh. "Really, Mae, it is most unfair. That is *exactly* the sort of gentleman who should be proposing to me."

"He *is* rather well formed," agreed Mr. Caesar, "in an austere way."

"He *hasn't* proposed," Miss Mitchelmore clarified, "and if he did I should refuse him, and really, Lizzie, I don't know why you should be so keen for him to propose to you anyway."

Pulling herself up to her minimal full height, Miss Bickle took a deep breath. "Well, the way I see it, I shall need a titled man to propose to me as part of a dastardly scheme to deprive me of my fortune. Then a rough but noble swain can come and thrash him fiercely but appropriately in a duel, and I can marry him instead."

"I wouldn't hold out too much hope on that front." Mr. Caesar swung himself back up into a sitting position. "Rough but noble swains have a nasty habit of being rough when you want them to be noble and noble when you want them to be rough."

Miss Bickle frowned. "How contrary of them."

"Leaving Lizzie's matrimonial ambitions aside, are you certain you want to go to Stanton Drew tomorrow, Mae?" asked Mr. Caesar, in a possibly vain effort to bring the conversation back to the more pressing issue. "It might not be the best use of our time."

"Mr. Clitherowe will be there," Miss Mitchelmore pointed out. "And honestly"—she looked forlornly at the books and papers that still largely surrounded them—"I'm not sure what other way we have of discerning whether he's behind the curse or not."

"Go to his house and ask him?" suggested Miss Bickle.

For a moment Miss Mitchelmore and Mr. Caesar looked as though they were about to raise an objection. But in the end they found none to raise.

"Are we," Mr. Caesar asked nobody in particular, "are we extremely bad at this?"

"I'm not sure being cursed is something one can be good at," Miss Mitchelmore reassured him.

This was, I think, not entirely true. Although I confess I have seldom seen a mortal respond to a curse well. My advice in general, should you find yourself with a supernatural affliction, is to relax, go where fate takes you, and if possible, try to avoid having sex with an ass.

CHAPTER

—·(·C·=========·)·)·—

14

I had been hoping that Miss Mitchelmore and her friends would do something reckless, and going to call personally on a man that they believed to be a malicious sorcerer who had conceived a powerful sexual obsession for one of their party certainly counted.

Well, it counted if he was guilty. If he was innocent, then they were just going to take tea with a clergyman, which promised substantially fewer thrills.

Mr. Clitherowe kept comfortable if modest lodgings not far from the river. Mr. Caesar gave his card at the door and, after a short wait, was admitted even though they were a little after the fashionable visiting hour.

They went up at once, and I fear I missed the earlier part of their conversation because I simply *cannot* enter the house of a clergyman without taking time to explore and make mischief. I went swiftly down to the banks of the Avon, where I collected several frogs (the naiads do not come to the city, so I was able to do this without offending them). Then I returned to Mr. Clitherowe's house, ascended at once to his bedchamber, and placed one of the creatures in his bed, another in his chamber pot, and one more in each of his boots.

Satisfied that I had made enough sport with the gentleman, I descended to his drawing room to spy on his guests and fulfil my primary function as an observer and narrator of fascinating tales. Sadly the tale was not proving fascinating, with Miss Mitchelmore and her friends sitting quite politely while Mr. Clitherowe sent for tea.

I should have reserved one of the frogs for the teapot.

"The reason we are here," Mr. Caesar was in the middle of explaining, "is that your continued . . . interest in my cousin has not escaped our notice, and I thought it best that we come to you directly and ask your intentions."

Mr. Clitherowe said nothing for a moment. Tea was brought into the room and, operating on some clockwork mechanism of etiquette, Miss Mitchelmore poured it.

"Well I . . ." Mr. Clitherowe began, watching Miss Mitchelmore with a frankly conflicted expression. "That is I . . . your cousin is a very beautiful woman."

Setting down her tea, Miss Mitchelmore bowed her head demurely. "You are too kind, Mr. Clitherowe."

"It is no kindness to speak the truth," was Mr. Clitherowe's rather predictable response. For a man who dabbled in sorcery he was unspeakably dull. "I have made my regard for Miss Mitchelmore quite plain, and while I am aware that my station does not make me the most desirable of suitors, I feel I would make a"—he glanced at her with a coyness that made me wish I had not restricted myself to frogs—"a suitable husband. I am temperate in my habits, constant in my affections, and despite my profession I am not, I think, wholly tedious."

"I do not think you tedious, Mr. Clitherowe," Miss Mitchelmore reassured him. I can only assume that she was lying, for I have otherwise found her judgement remarkably sound for a mortal. "Indeed, we are here because there is—that is—because I worry that you may have done something decidedly un-tedious."

"Un-tedious?" He was eyeing her warily now. And somebody with a higher opinion of the man than I possessed might have taken that wariness as evidence of guilt. I, however, refused to believe that Mr. Clitherowe was capable of anything so interesting as cursing a person for lascivious purposes.

Of course, mortals have surprised me before.

Mr. Caesar retrieved the curse tablet, which he had brought with him wrapped in a soft cloth, from beneath his chair. "This matter is . . . delicate. You are aware, I am sure, of the recent difficulties my cousin has faced?"

"A little." Mr. Clitherowe's response came hesitantly, as though he feared a trap. "I have tried not to pry. Whatever misfortune has befallen her, I am sure it can be no consequence of her actions and imply no slight against her virtue."

"Prettily said." Mr. Caesar's tone and his gaze were equally laced with suspicion. "But nonetheless I would ask you what you make of this." Rising, he crossed the drawing room and handed Mr. Clitherowe the tablet.

With a caution that felt to me like nervousness, Mr. Clitherowe unwrapped it. "It's a curse tablet," he said at once. "From the baths. I've read of them, but I didn't think people used them anymore."

"Look closer," instructed Mr. Caesar.

So Mr. Clitherowe read. And as he did his expression shifted from confused to shocked to aghast to—and I fear I have run out of adjectives, so I shall simply say *aghaster.* "But this is awful." He set the tablet down. "Miss Mitchelmore, you cannot possibly believe that I would stoop to such things."

"I cannot possibly believe that anybody would stoop to such things," Miss Mitchelmore replied. Although a moment's reflection and a twist of unpleasant honesty compelled her to add: "Save a very few rakes, dissolutes, and debauchers. But since I know few of those I am forced to conclude that some seemingly respectable gentleman of my acquaintance has, in fact, stooped to exactly such things. Indeed I live even now in the shadow of his stooping."

"Assuming," Mr. Caesar added reflexively, "that it *is* a gentleman."

"Well, it *certainly* cannot be a lady," said Mr. Clitherowe with a closed-mindedness typical of his era and species. "It speaks of—of *desires.*"

"Actually I had a theory about that," chimed in Miss Bickle. "It relates to mathematics. You see if we are to assume that everybody—"

"Not the time, Lizzie." Miss Mitchelmore's voice was soft but strained. "But I believe my cousin is simply trying to make certain that we continue to consider all avenues of enquiry. Besides, even discounting the possibility of ladies, plenty of men exist who are not gentlemen."

"Some of them, paradoxically, gentlemen," Mr. Caesar added.

Mr. Clitherowe was still staring at the curse tablet with a look of disbelief on his face and, if he was feigning, then I doff to him the hat I am not wearing, because he was feigning very well indeed. "But this is *abominable*."

"Abominable things happen," observed Miss Mitchelmore. And I could not help but imagine the words in the Duke of Annadale's voice.

Sitting up primly, Mr. Clitherowe re-wrapped the tablet. "Perhaps, but in a perfect world, ladies should not need to know of them."

"We do not live in a perfect world." Miss Mitchelmore seemed less rueful about this than I might have imagined. Perhaps there were other things a perfect world would preclude that she felt she would miss.

"And I rather enjoy knowing of abominable things," added Miss Bickle. "Lovely things are lovely, too, of course. But abominable things are"—she gave a sort of exaggerated shiver—"well they're so exciting."

Although her friend was, nominally, on her side in this matter, Miss Mitchelmore did not take the interjection kindly. "They are rather less exciting in real life, Lizzie."

Mr. Clitherowe had returned the tablet to Mr. Caesar and was now pacing the room in some agitation, his hands clasped behind his back. "I understand," he said eventually, "why it is that you would suspect me. I believe I should suspect myself, were I in your position. And I can also think of no reassurance I can give you that would convince you of my sincerity."

I could think of several, but they mostly involved binding blood oaths sworn before powers nameless and ancient that it is, on balance, best you mortals know not of.

"Regardless," Mr. Clitherowe continued. "It is clearly necessary that I withdraw my suit immediately."

Despite having evinced no desire whatsoever to wed Mr. Clitherowe, Miss Mitchelmore put a hand to her breast and looked almost taken aback. "Sir, I hope you do not believe I have somehow encouraged—"

"Not at all." Mr. Clitherowe's response was swift. As if he was aware that he had caused the lady distress and, somehow, failed to find the fact amusing. "But the purpose of this curse is plainly to coerce you into matrimony. Or"—he coloured deeply, and stumbled over the next few words—"or its equivalent. And I could not marry a woman who believed her hand was being forced in so callous a way."

From the window seat, where she had gone and stretched herself out luxuriantly, Miss Bickle smiled. "Oh, Mr. Clitherowe, you're a *romantic*. How marvellous. I think you should marry him after all, Mae. Romantics are very fine people."

"I fear I must still decline," Miss Mitchelmore told her friend. Then she turned her attention back to the still-pacing Mr. Clitherowe. "But your understanding does you great credit. Although since we have, I think, concluded that there is no rational way you can allay my fears and it is also plain that my presence is causing you distress, I should leave."

Mr. Clitherowe nodded. "I believe that would be for the best. And—Miss Mitchelmore, I hope that we shall remain friends."

Already making her way to the door, Miss Mitchelmore stopped and bobbed a curtsey. "As do I. And if I should not be unwelcome, I still intend to accompany your party to Stanton Drew tomorrow."

From the look on Mr. Clitherowe's face, I suspected that she would not, in fact, have been entirely welcome, but propriety binds your kind as sure as the rowan and birch bind mine. "I should be delighted if you would come, Miss Mitchelmore. The druidical remains at Stanton Drew are the third largest such site in the country and, while they are not so well known as Stonehenge or Avebury, they have charms quite their own."

Having personally watched all three edifices being raised, I assure my readers that none of them are truly worth the visit. An ancient people, long vanished, put time and effort into hauling big chunks of rock into unlikely positions, but they were no wiser in the ways of the world than you screen-picking fools of the present day, or the Enlightenment-era fools who are the focus of our present story. Mortals like to put big rocks in funny positions. It makes you feel special. There is no great secret, no deeper mystery, and it certainly has nothing to do with *us*.

"Do you really still suspect him?" asked Miss Bickle in the carriage afterwards. "He seemed so ardent."

"Aren't ardent people quite likely to go to extreme ends in the name of their ardour?" asked Miss Mitchelmore.

"Yes, but mostly to romantic ends. Not to *horrible* ends." The collision of the romantic and the horrible seemed to quite upset Miss Bickle, who winced visibly.

Mr. Caesar settled back in his seat, and I resisted the opportunity to try to steal one of his gloves from off his hand. "What's romantic to one person may be horrible to another. But I do agree in this case, Mr. Clitherowe seems like an honourable gentleman. Why would he withdraw his proposal if his aim in cursing you was to make you accept it?"

This question pulled Miss Bickle quite out of the doldrums. "Ooh, I know this one. It's because *that's what he wants you to think.*"

Having had a trying day, Miss Mitchelmore gave her friend a weary look. "I'm not sure I follow, Lizzie."

"Well, if *I* were attempting to coerce a lady into matrimony by magical interference, I should certainly at least consider the stratagem of placing her under a horrible curse that looks as though it was laid upon her by an absolute villain, and then assure her of my not-an-absolute-villain-ness by nobly *withdrawing* my proposal, thus making myself look terribly upright and sincere." She smiled, wistfully. "I think such a stratagem might work rather well."

"It has *not* worked," Miss Mitchelmore observed.

"Yes, but that is because I reckoned without your being the kind of lady who prefers ladies." Miss Bickle looked down at herself, and then continued. "I mean, I in this situation am Mr. Clitherowe, who is not a lady. Rather than myself. Who am. Is. Am."

"Confusing as that explanation may have been, I agree," said Mr. Caesar. "He loses nothing by withdrawing his suit at this stage, and he gains our good opinion. Or will gain it, if he is sincere."

They rode on awhile, and then Miss Mitchelmore called for the driver to take them, not home, but to the Royal Crescent.

Mr. Caesar glared at her. "Maelys, what are you doing?"

"I need to see her."

"You—if you will pardon my language—bloody well do not. We still can't trust her, and we have less than two days to find whoever cursed you and stop them."

Miss Mitchelmore looked out of the window in silence awhile. I normally enjoy seeing mortals in distress, but for some reason this one moved me. Perhaps this was the point I started going soft. "I . . . I do not think they can *be* stopped, John. We do not even know who they might be if Lady Georgiana and Mr. Clitherowe are innocent."

"And if they are not?" asked Mr. Caesar.

"Then what do we do?" A note of despair was creeping into Miss Mitchelmore's voice. "Shall I go back to Mr. Clitherowe and murder him? He denies having cursed me. It is unclear whether he would have the power to withdraw the curse even if he wished to. Or, if that will not persuade you, then let it be this. Lady Georgiana claims that she is working on our behalf. Let us go and see if she has done so, and perhaps that will allay your suspicions. Or confirm them."

Regardless of Mr. Caesar's objections, it was the Mitchelmores' carriage and it was, therefore, to Miss Mitchelmore that the driver answered. And so a short while later the party, still vehemently disagreeing about the wisdom of the proposition, arrived at the Duke of Annadale's residence on the Royal Crescent.

15

"Should you not," asked the Duke of Annadale, staring down at Miss Mitchelmore and her associates with a generous helping of ice split evenly between her gaze and her tone, "be out investigating people, rather than here bothering me?"

"Shouldn't *you* be out investigating people?" replied Mr. Caesar. "You said that you would support us in this."

"I did, didn't I?" she gave him a withering look. "Perhaps I lied. Perhaps I am simply dangling hope over dear Maelys's head so I may have the pleasure of watching her squirm."

Miss Mitchelmore glared up at the Duke of Annadale with an expression that said she had put up with quite enough nonsense to last her a lifetime and that she was not appreciating the turn this conversation was taking. "Georgiana, please. If you have *anything* to tell us, do so. And if you do not, then—"

"*Lady* Georgiana," the Duke of Annadale insisted. "And if I do not, then what? Then you shall succumb to despair? You shall demand that I leave you be? I did not ask you to come here."

"Then I shall not know *what* to do." Miss Mitchelmore's eyes grew wide and plaintive in that way humans sometimes fall back on when they have exhausted all other methods of persuasion. "You, if I am to believe a word you say, have studied these matters for years, we only for days. You *must* know something that can help me."

The Duke of Annadale lowered herself into the one remaining chair and leaned her cheek lazily on one hand. "I have consulted with a witch."

At this, Mr. Caesar and Miss Bickle both exclaimed "Oh, how marvellous," although with wildly different levels of sincerity.

"Is that not illegal?" asked Miss Mitchelmore.

"No. It is illegal to charge money for your services as a witch; it isn't illegal to consult one. Also, you might remember I'm a suspected murderess, so I take legality rather lightly. Regardless, I am looking into protections that might help us if we fail to mollify the goddess within the time limit. Beyond that, I fear you are on your own. I cannot find your enemies for you. Although you may have forgotten it lately, I hardly know you."

Miss Mitchelmore looked down. "John, Lizzie, may I have a moment with Lady Georgiana alone?"

In reply, Miss Bickle gave a little squeak of delight while Mr. Caesar offered a cautious "Mae, are you certain?" but both obligingly withdrew to one of the smaller drawing rooms, leaving Miss Mitchelmore, the Duke of Annadale and—unbeknownst to either of them—myself alone in the main receiving room.

For a long moment, they sat in silence.

"I hope," the Duke of Annadale said at last, "that you aren't planning to kiss me again."

"Would that be so terrible?"

Not being able to resist the urge to discomfort, I sidled across to the Duke of Annadale and blew, very gently, on the back of her neck. "It would be . . . a distraction."

"I may be dead in two days. A distraction would be welcome."

"You will not. I will not permit it."

Miss Mitchelmore allowed herself to smile. "You would defy a goddess for me?"

"No, I would defy a goddess out of a general sense of spite, caprice, and contrarianism. I believe I inherited my father's libertine heart, and so I mislike seeing anybody controlled, especially by the old powers."

"I'm sorry, I know little of your father."

A look that danced between regret and resentment passed across the Duke of Annadale's face. "There is little to know. He was a rich man, and a powerful one, but did not always take his duties seriously. He was not cruel, but he was careless. Had he not died when he did, our family would not have half the wealth it does now. It's one of the many reasons people think I murdered him."

"And the other reasons?" Miss Mitchelmore could not help but ask. Neither, to be fair, would I have been able to in her position.

"My survival, chiefly. And my stubborn refusal to marry, which marks me as something of a deviant."

Miss Mitchelmore cocked her head to one side. "Have you had so many suitors?"

"My estate is still substantial. Most men will risk death for money. And I'm certainly a safer prospect than a commission."

"Yet you accepted none of them?"

With a dismissive shrug, the Duke of Annadale sat back in her chair. "I have no need for the protection of a husband, and no desire for the company of one."

I was, impish sprite that I am, delighted to observe the ease with which Miss Mitchelmore slid along the sofa, bringing herself just that little bit closer to the Duke of Annadale. "Then whose company do you desire?"

The Duke of Annadale arched an eyebrow. "Playing the temptress again, are we?"

"Yesterday, I was given three days to live. Tonight may be my last night on Earth. I feel I have little to lose."

Throwing back her head, the Duke of Annadale let out a laugh that was almost cruel. "'I might die,'" she said in a mocking tone, "'so you should fuck me.'"

Once again, Miss Mitchelmore blushed.

"So, you want me to fuck you," the Duke of Annadale continued, "but continue to play the maiden when I say it?"

"I know you think me foolish."

"Do not assume that you know anything. Least of all what I *think*. Do you really believe me so callous that I could take you to my bed tonight and watch you die tomorrow and think nothing of it?"

"I thought you said you would not permit me to die."

"Then I have no need to grant you a final night of ecstasy."

Miss Mitchelmore turned her face away. "You are impossible."

"You are not so very easy yourself."

There was another moment of silence, shorter this time, and then Miss Mitchelmore began to weep. And though it pains me to admit, I had grown so fond of the lady that I barely even laughed.

"Please don't do that."

Miss Mitchelmore did not accede to her hostess's request.

Cautiously, as though she were approaching, if not a live tiger, then at least an irate housecat, the Duke of Annadale rose and sat on the sofa beside Miss Mitchelmore. "I am not good at being comforting."

Somehow, that expression of inadequacy did not induce Miss Mitchelmore to cease weeping.

"If this is a stratagem to seduce me, then I at once admire and resent it."

Sobbing more fiercely now, Miss Mitchelmore let herself collapse into the Duke of Annadale's shoulder.

"There, there," offered the Duke of Annadale, with an obvious discomfort I permitted myself to relish.

Despite her tears, Miss Mitchelmore let out a half laugh. "Did you really just say *there, there*?"

"It was a moment of weakness. And besides, I told you I was bad at comforting people."

Miss Mitchelmore smiled in a way I couldn't help but think was a little wicked. "Do I at least cry prettily?"

"Actually, you look awful. Fortunately, I am a cruel woman, and I am enjoying your distress."

Miss Mitchelmore looked up earnestly. I cannot personally abide earnestness. "Why do you always say such things?"

"What things?"

"Why are you so determined that I think you monstrous?"

Placing two fingers beneath Miss Mitchelmore's chin, the Duke of Annadale turned her face upwards. "Because, child, I am a very great fool and have forgotten how strongly the young are drawn to things that threaten to destroy them."

"I am threatened with destruction already, and I would thank you not to call me a child. You cannot be more than five years my senior."

The Duke of Annadale's lips curled into a rueful smile. "Five years in which much has happened. The question is not how much *longer* I have lived, dear heart, but how much *more* I have lived."

"And should I not be permitted to live also, to live as much as you have?"

"You will live a long life, Maelys. If I have any say in the matter."

"And if you do not?"

"Then I shall mourn you. For a while, at least."

Pulling away, and still weeping, Miss Mitchelmore rose from the sofa and turned her back. "You were right; you have no facility for comfort, and I am wasting my time expecting better."

"So I have tried to tell you. Whatever you are seeking, I am not it, and it is not me. Gather your friends, go back to your books, or to asking your questions of whichever else of your admirers may wish to harm or coerce you. I shall continue to do what I can, but I suggest you not come here again. What I may achieve on your behalf I may achieve in your absence."

Still, Miss Mitchelmore refused to look at her hostess. "Thank you for your candour."

"Before you leave"—the Duke of Annadale rose and retrieved something from a cabinet near the window. A long thread, to which were bound many smaller threads with a set of complex knots—"I acquired this for you."

"You reject me but ask that I accept your gifts? You would treat a mistress better."

"I treat my mistresses *differently.* This is not an ornament, it's a witch cord. Now, come here and I'll bind it into your hair."

Sensibly, Miss Mitchelmore hesitated but, perhaps equally sensibly, she relented. The Duke of Annadale manoeuvred herself behind Miss Mitchelmore and, taking the cord momentarily in her teeth, unbound the lady's hair. As she began the intricate process of weaving the witch knots into it, I found a kind of veil slipping over my sight, at least as regarded Miss Mitchelmore. I could still see her, but I found it hard to focus on her, and if I looked away I found it hard to remember that she existed. When the last string was tied and Miss Mitchelmore's hair restored to something resembling its original condition, she became more solid again, and I was once more able to make out details. To catch the flush just fading from Miss Mitchelmore's cheeks as the Duke of Annadale's fingers left her neck. To see the look in her eyes as she stepped away and said thank you. To hear the sorrow in her voice.

Curious to test the limits of Miss Mitchelmore's new protections, I reached out to catch at her sleeve, and found a sharp, stinging sensation jabbing from my fingertips to my shoulders. I drew my arm back hurriedly. Whatever the Duke of Annadale had done, it had worked, against my kind at least.

Now that these two mortals had finished their . . . personal conversation, the other two mortals could be shown back in. Miss Bickle went at once to Miss Mitchelmore, looked her square in the face, said, "Oh Mae, you've been crying," then rounded on the Duke of Annadale. "If you have hurt Maelys, then I shall—"

"You shall *what*?"

"I shall be very vexed. And I shall—well, as I have told Maelys myself I have a great many plans for vengeance, some of them involving scorpions."

"Please leave the scorpions out of this, Lizzie." Mr. Caesar had taken Miss Mitchelmore to one side and was making his own inspection of her demeanour. "Lady Georgiana, we thank you for your hospitality but, given the distress you have caused my cousin, I hope you understand why we must take our leave of you."

Miss Mitchelmore raised a hand. "Please, she has caused me no distress. I have—I have simply upset myself."

"There"—the Duke of Annadale waved a dismissive hand—
"she protests my innocence. Now, go."

They returned to the carriage and, once they were safely inside,
Miss Mitchelmore broke down again, laying her head in Miss Bickle's lap and sobbing.

"I take it you did not kiss her again, then?" asked Miss Bickle.

"No Lizzie, I did not. And I believe I made quite a fool of
myself. I may die a day from now, and one of my last acts on Earth
was to make a fool of myself over a woman with no—with no—"

"Taste?" suggested Miss Bickle. "I am sure if I were inclined
towards ladies I should find you quite delightful and very much
want to do complicated and romantic things to you."

"It's for the best, Mae," Mr. Caesar said in the most reassuring
tone he could muster. "She may, I begrudgingly admit, not actually
have cursed you, but that doesn't mean I think she would be *good*
for you."

This did not calm Miss Mitchelmore at all. "What does it matter if she would be good for me? There will soon no longer be a me
for her to be good *for*. All I wanted was to—to—I don't know, to *feel*
something I suppose. Before it's all over."

"There are . . ." Mr. Caesar stiffened awkwardly. "If it was
merely a matter of . . . we could always hire—"

"No." Miss Bickle was firm on the matter. "Well, not unless
Mae very especially wants to, but you cannot simply replace a love
affair for the ages with . . . with paid companionship."

Sitting up, Miss Mitchelmore tried to compose herself. "It was
not a love affair for the ages, Lysistrata. It was . . . I was being silly.
And silliness combines badly with fear." One hand strayed to her
hair, to the witch cord the Duke of Annadale had tied there. "Now,
please, I wish to speak no more about it. I wish only to go home."

So home they went.

For a while they remained in the parlour, reading and rereading the Duke of Annadale's books on witchcraft and curse tablets in the hopes of finding some trick or strategy they had missed, but nothing came of it.

At last they retired, Mr. Caesar returning home and Miss Bickle staying with the Mitchelmores in case Maelys should need company. How well the lady slept that night, I cannot say. For when I tried to walk in her dreams, the witch knots tangled and misled me, and I found myself in quite another part of the slumbering lands.

16

The excursion to Stanton Drew was scheduled to leave a little before noon, the journey being long and the round trip, even by carriage, expected to take several hours. That still left the morning for the investigation of possible occult countermeasures, but Miss Mitchelmore and her friends made, though the observation brings me little joy, poor use of it. Mr. Caesar returned to Miss Tabitha for advice, but neither she nor her goddess were willing to defy Sulis Minerva in her own city. Miss Bickle's attempts to court the assistance of my own kind, meanwhile, proved as unsuccessful as ever they had. We are, by nature, a capricious people and our involvement in your affairs is most likely to come when least desired.

As for Miss Mitchelmore, she was reduced to an indignity that no young woman would suffer unless in great extremity: She confided in her parents. They knew of the curse, of course, but that it had recently taken a turn for the immediate, the personal, and the potentially fatal was news to them. News, I might add, that they bore with commendable equanimity.

"O quam cito transit gloria mundi," observed Lady Jane. "I suppose, darling, that you have tried absolutely *everything* to get out of the predicament?"

Not, perhaps, finding Latin the most comforting language to be addressed in, Miss Mitchelmore nodded. "Everything I can think of. But I know little of curses, and while Lady Georgiana has made some efforts on my behalf, she is not a goddess."

Mr. Mitchelmore set down his copy of Hutton's *Theory of the Earth with Proofs and Illustrations.* "I don't suppose we could achieve something by means of the application of electricity?"

"I am as fascinated by Signor Galvani's experiments as anybody," replied Lady Jane, casting her husband a reproachful look. "But if you are going to suggest that we allow Maelys to die and then reanimate her using a voltaic pile and a suspension of essential salts, I believe I shall be quite peeved."

"Thank you, Mama." Miss Mitchelmore nodded her gratitude.

"After all," her mother continued, "without some means to arrest the decomposition of her brain tissue, she would likely come back a simpleton."

This evoked rather less gratitude. "Mama!"

"Would you rather I did *not* think of such things?" asked Lady Jane, who at times could conjure the imperious air of an earl's daughter despite her idiosyncratic interests and matrimonial choices. "I would be a poor mother indeed if I let your father attempt to reanimate you without considering the physiological implications."

"I wasn't suggesting we reanimate her." Mr. Mitchelmore

looked rather aghast at the thought. "I was simply speculating that some kind of electrified chamber—"

"I am not spending the rest of my life in an electrified chamber." Miss Mitchelmore folded her arms with an air that even she would have to admit was rather huffy. "Can you please behave like ordinary parents for just a short while?"

Lady Jane raised an eyebrow. "If you insist." She cleared her throat. "Oh la! But Maelys, if you are devoured by an angry goddess, how-*ever* will you find a husband?"

"That is *not* what I meant."

"All I was trying to do," Mr. Mitchelmore explained with the doomed fixedness of a man who has yet to realise that no explanation will be helpful, "was to advance the hypothesis that whatever physical mechanism is responsible for transferring the curse-causing elements—"

"I don't believe it has a physical mechanism, Papa." Miss Mitchelmore seemed to be relaxing slightly, allowing the familiar irritation at her parents' manner to displace the less familiar and less welcome sense of distress at her predicament. "I believe it is simply magic."

"Nonsense." The expression of disdain on Mr. Mitchelmore's face was in no way alloyed by familial affection, for while he was an affable man, he brooked no disagreement in scientific matters. "Every physical phenomenon must have a physical cause. Even if that cause is apparently supernatural."

Lady Jane nodded in agreement. "You know the old saying, dear. *Sufficiently advanced natural philosophy is indistinguishable from thaumaturgy.*"

"I do not believe that is a saying at all," Miss Mitchelmore complained.

"Well, it should be," replied Lady Jane. "For it is true."

Sighing, Miss Mitchelmore picked at her gloves. "I still do not wish to live out my life in an electrified prison. Besides, I doubt you would be able to find enough zinc to power such a structure."

"True." Mr. Mitchelmore looked glum. "Still, I feel we should do something."

"It's so hard when one's children come of age," mused Lady Jane. "All of a sudden they're off finding themselves in mortal peril and there's simply nothing one can do about it. I do hope we haven't been shabby parents."

Mr. Mitchelmore peered at his daughter appraisingly. "I think we've done all right, haven't we? I mean, Corantin hasn't got himself into any trouble I know of."

"Given what boys get up to at Eton," observed Lady Jane, "I wouldn't be too sure. Besides, where children are concerned, a fifty percent attrition rate seems at least a little suboptimal."

Having no real choice but to embrace the absurdity, Miss Mitchelmore fought to smile. "It's very suboptimal from my perspective. But I don't think this is your fault, any more than it is mine."

"Perhaps we should have pushed you to marry sooner." Lady Jane was not, as a rule, given to self-recrimination, but she *was*, like her husband, given to listing hypotheses. "This seems to be exactly the sort of thing a husband is supposed to guard one against."

"*Supposed to*," Miss Mitchelmore agreed, "but I don't think *capable of*. I've met a number of eligible gentlemen, Mama, and few of them struck me as having the capacity to defy the gods themselves."

"True." There was a note of not-quite-nostalgia in Lady Jane's voice. "And the ones that do tend to be more trouble than they're worth."

At this, Mr. Mitchelmore flustered, just a little. "Excuse me, I would happily have defied the gods themselves for you if it had become necessary. It just never came up."

"There are many things you would have defied the gods for, Edward," observed Lady Jane. "Curiosity, the recognition of the Royal Society, and perhaps even William Bickle if he had goaded you into it. But I don't flatter myself that you would have defied them for me, nor would I have wanted you to."

"I'm sure Captain Haversham would have defied the gods for you." There was a rueful edge in Mr. Mitchelmore's voice.

"I'm sure he would have," Lady Jane agreed. "And yet I did not marry him. That's the deuced thing of it"—she turned her attention back to Miss Mitchelmore—"The people one wants in one's life when one is *not* being harried unto destruction by an implacable immortal are so different from the people one wants in one's life when one is."

It had not been Lady Jane's intent for this observation to affect her daughter strongly, but affect her strongly it did. Miss Mitchelmore stiffened, bowed her head, and wiped a decorous tear from the corner of her eye. "I fear you may be right, Mama."

Although both of the Mitchelmores were easily distracted by abstractions and given to pettifoggery, they were neither of them the sort to ignore their daughter's tears. "Is there something wrong, Maelys?" asked Mr. Mitchelmore. "I mean, wronger than the imminent risk of death?"

Still a little moist around the eyes, Miss Mitchelmore tried to smile again. "When you put it like that, it does seem a little ridiculous. I think that part of things may just be too enormous to think about. Which means I find myself rather dwelling on more . . . more personal matters?"

Lady Jane raised an eyebrow that, as a connoisseur of suggestive eyebrows, I considered suggestive. "Is this about Lady Georgiana?"

"No." The denial came so quickly to Miss Mitchelmore's lips that it was as good as confirmation, and she knew it. "That is, it is not *wholly* about her. It is about—that is to say—I have been reflecting lately on my feelings about a number of things, especially as they relate to—that is—to issues of marriage."

I have seen many expressions of shock in my time, which is why I am quite certain I was not seeing one now. Lady Jane gave a shrug. "Oh. Well, you're not the first lady to be attracted to another lady." It should not have surprised me that Lady Jane was unsurprised by her daughter's apparent sapphism, nor should I have been surprised at Miss Mitchelmore's lack of surprise at her mother's unsurprisedness. But I was, a little. In my defence, my low expectations of mortals are usually wholly justified.

"Of course," the lady continued, "it raises the vexed question of income but, well, immediate dangers make that rather moot. We can work out how you shall make a living after we work out how you shall live."

"On that matter," Miss Mitchelmore said, "I fear we have exhausted all our options. I am making one last journey today in an effort to flush out my persecutor, but if that fails then, well, then I suppose we shall see how well I fare defying the gods. And if Lady Georgiana will . . ." She stopped, apparently not wanting to find out how the sentence ended.

"If she will defy the gods for you?" finished Mr. Mitchelmore. "I dare say she would; she seems the type."

"But that's a type you think I should stay away from?" This question Miss Mitchelmore directed primarily at her mother.

"I wouldn't say that. Just that you should think twice about marrying her. Not that you really have the option in this case. But young ladies should have love affairs, and I daresay a duke's daughter of scandalous reputation is as fine a subject for a dalliance as any. Better than the usual soldiers, at any rate."

Miss Mitchelmore sighed. "It is, unfortunately, immaterial. She steadfastly refuses to dally with me."

That did not sit well with Mr. Mitchelmore. "Why? What's wrong with you?"

"I believe she worries that she will be a corrupting influence."

"I'm not sure that's her decision to make." Lady Jane seemed genuinely offended. "I've half a mind to seek her out right now and tell her to corrupt my daughter *immediately.*"

"Please don't, Mama." Miss Mitchelmore had, at least, stopped crying. "I think it would be awkward."

To Miss Mitchelmore's relief, it was at this moment that the footman announced the arrival of Mr. Caesar and Miss Bickle. And so she bid a fond farewell to her parents who, for their part, wished her luck in averting her possible demise and then went back directly to their reading.

———•———

The journey to Stanton Drew being, in theory at least, a pleasure trip was to be made in the Caesars' barouche. It was also, somewhat awkwardly, to be chaperoned by Mrs. Wilberforce, who had been quite upset at being left out of their visit to the Assembly Rooms a few days earlier.

This made the journey out from Bath a little difficult, for while the countryside was picturesque, the more pressing matters of the curse, the goddess, and the tiny additional detail of Miss Mitchelmore's ever-intensifying desire to feel the Duke of Annadale's lips tracing lines of stinging passion the length of her thighs needed, for reasons of propriety, to be circumlocuted.

"So," asked Miss Bickle with the subtlety of—to take a wholly arbitrary example—a man awaking with the head of a donkey, "who do you think we should be *especially certain* to look out for once we arrive at the antiquities? I feel we should perhaps be *especially certain* to look out for Mr. Clitherowe in case he turns out to be . . . the person we should be looking out for?"

Mrs. Wilberforce gave Miss Bickle a concerned look. "Lysistrata, are you quite well?"

"Oh yes, definitely." She nodded enthusiastically. "I'm just trying to formulate a strategy for"—she hesitated, apparently not certain how to say *defeating a curse in order to prevent Maelys from being consumed by an irate deity* in a tactful way—"improving our marriage prospects?"

"I wonder," offered Mr. Caesar, "if rather than looking out for any one person we shouldn't be watching the crowd in general. There may be a—a potential *suitor*"—from the look on his face, Mr. Caesar found the hastily adopted marriage code a little demeaning—"who we have not hitherto considered."

"You *see*?" The often-worn but seldom-justified look of vindication came once more to Miss Bickle's face. "I said that we should be considering the last person we would suspect."

"Suspect for marriage," Miss Mitchelmore reminded her.

Miss Bickle nodded again. "Why yes. I have always felt quite certain that the individual who is trying to *marry* Mae is far more likely to be somebody we do not think would wish to marry her at all than somebody who we know to have strong cause to wish to marry her."

If she found this line of discussion at all confusing, Mrs. Wilberforce gave no sign. "That's how it was with me and Mr. Wilberforce, rest his soul. Why, until the day he proposed I scarcely knew he liked me, though I had always rather liked him."

"How romantic." Miss Bickle clasped her hands together joyfully. "Did you elope?"

"No. He approached my father like a respectable gentleman." Miss Bickle's face fell. "Oh."

"We may," said Mr. Caesar, making a concerted effort to bring the conversation back to the matter at hand, "at least be reasonably certain that the individual we are looking for will not have approached Maelys's parents."

"Only because nobody has approached them, to my knowledge," replied Miss Mitchelmore. "Otherwise a slighted suitor remains a very probable candidate."

Mrs. Wilberforce looked perplexed. "Oh, I shouldn't think so. Once one has slighted a gentleman he seldom wishes to marry one afterwards. Assuming, of course"—her expression grew dark—"that you are actually *discussing* marriage, and not planning some kind of untoward assignation."

"I can say with confidence," Miss Mitchelmore reassured her chaperone, "that I am planning no untoward assignations. Indeed, I am trying my best to avoid assignations altogether."

Nodding sagely, Mrs. Wilberforce commended Miss Mitchelmore for her judicious avoidance of assignations, and then went back to watching the scenery roll past. It was, by mortal standards at least, a pretty part of the country, all gentle hills and quiet fields dotted with farmhouses. Of course, being an entity of rather advanced years, it all felt rather modern to me. I remember the days when the land was nothing but primordial forest haunted by creatures ancient and hungry and lost. But those days are gone, save a few happy bands of barghests that from time to time savage foolish travellers on the moors. On this day, however, packs of hellhounds were in short supply and so the journey was sadly devoid of screaming, howling, or the rending of flesh.

At least, it was until the party arrived at their destination. Those who tamper with circles of ancient stones, after all, do so at their peril. But that is a part of the story to which we shall return later.

CHAPTER

17

The party of antiquities appreciators was small and select, consisting as it did of Mr. Clitherowe, Miss Mitchelmore and her company, the Viscount Fortrose, and a smattering of bookish gentlemen and bluestockingish ladies to whom I paid no attention. To my surprise and consternation, the Ambassador was also present in the company.

I bowed courteously. "If you could just ignore me," I said. "I'm here in a strictly observational capacity."

Smiling, he tapped the side of his nose in a gesture that I can only assume he had picked up from his time amongst the mortals but gave no other acknowledgement of my presence.

Once everybody had gathered outside the village church, Mr. Clitherowe took up a spot at the head of the party, cleared his throat, and began what I suspected was a long-rehearsed introduction.

"Thank you all so much for attending my little excursion. And may I say I am especially grateful to the Ambassador of the Other Court, the illustrious Viscount Fortrose, Mr. Blessop of the archaeological society and"—his gaze alighted briefly on Miss Mitchelmore, but he faltered—"and all the rest of you."

"So you're especially grateful to everyone?" observed the Viscount Fortrose, dryly.

To his credit, Mr. Clitherowe rallied well. "Gratitude is a virtue," he pointed out. "At any rate, we are beginning our afternoon's observations here because if you will look behind you"—he paused just long enough for everybody to look, a little awkwardly, behind them—"you will see three stones standing not so far from this very building. This is the first of our *druidical remains*. This *cove*, scholars believe, was once the site of ancient rituals—"

"What *sort* of rituals?" asked the Ambassador impishly.

"Ancient ones?" replied Mr. Clitherowe, squirming. "Of course, I wouldn't claim to have the same knowledge of otherworldly affairs as our distinguished visitor from Elsewhere."

As a rule, our people do not go in for *ritual* in the way humans do. We seem to, because our laws and customs are opaque to you, but there is no more ritual to a ring dance or a wild hunt as there is to a butcher carving meat or a greengrocer opening their shopfront.

"At any rate," Mr. Clitherowe continued, "the stones are very ancient and were certainly very important to the druids, or to people who might have been at least a little druidlike. And they are also terribly picturesque, and I notice several of the ladies have brought their sketchbooks and, well, I feel the stones with the church in the background make for a rather fine study and so I suggest we take some time to admire them before proceeding to the site proper."

Neither Miss Mitchelmore, nor Miss Bickle, nor for that matter Mrs. Wilberforce had brought their sketchbooks, but Mrs. Blessop had, and at least one of the ladies from the archaeological society had brought a full folding easel, so the excursion was rather committed to remaining in place for some time while the artistically inclined pursued their artistic inclinations.

Miss Mitchelmore occupied herself by circulating amongst those attendees who were not presently distracted with painting and trying to ascertain whether any of them were doing anything occult. But as ever her profound ignorance of what occult doings would actually look like proved an impediment.

"I am pleased you came," offered the Viscount Fortrose when Miss Mitchelmore's circumambulations brought her at last to his side. "I had thought you might not. I know that I am not the only gentleman in the party who has paid attention to you, and I feared you might find the experience overwhelming, even leaving aside the possibility of . . ." He let the words *direct supernatural intervention* go unspoken, but they hung in the air anyway.

"I will admit the thought was a little intimidating," Miss Mitchelmore offered. Intimidating wasn't really the correct word, but letting a titled gentleman know that she was not only uninterested in him but was, most likely, uninterested in gentlemen altogether, did not seem like a sensible stratagem. "I have, however, decided that whatever may befall, I shall not hide away. I will go out, and visit druidical remains if I wish, and no curse and no mystery shall stop me."

The Viscount Fortrose gave an approving and, to Miss Mitchelmore's eye, slightly condescending nod. "Spirited woman," he said. "Would that all your sex had such boldness."

"In my experience," Miss Mitchelmore replied, before quite

being able to stop herself, "most of us do. Of course, it is possible that I simply have little opportunity to make the acquaintance of wallflowers owing to my spending little time in the vicinity of walls."

At that, the viscount laughed. "Miss Mitchelmore, be careful. Continue to speak in such a way and people will begin to think you wilful, and from there it is but a short step to being thought wicked."

The mention of wickedness must have stirred unexpected associations for Miss Mitchelmore, for she grew quiet. "Still," she continued eventually, "it is a comfort to me to know that nothing unnatural has yet occurred."

"Perhaps there is safety in seclusion?" suggested the viscount. "We are some way from the city, after all. Or perhaps there is protective power in these"—he arched a sardonic eyebrow—"*druidical remains.*"

"You think they may not, in fact, be druidical?" asked Miss Mitchelmore, at least a little relieved to be able to speak of something other than her inevitable doom.

"I think druidry is ill-remembered and worse understood. Besides, the locals tell quite different stories about the stones."

"What kind of stories?" The curiosity in Miss Mitchelmore's voice was a little forced, although not entirely feigned.

"That long ago a wedding party came to this place on a Saturday evening and, as midnight approached, the devil came to them in the shape of a fiddler and persuaded them to carry on dancing into Sunday morning. For which transgression they were all turned to stone."

Miss Mitchelmore examined the rocks. They did not look very much like people, one being very flat and low to the ground and another being very tall and shaped more like a gigantic hatchet than anything else. "That seems rather harsh."

"Some transgressions are deserving of harsh punishment."

"Perhaps, but I think dancing should not be one of them. Besides, it feels out of keeping for God to do such a thing. And we are taught that the devil does not truly walk the world as other spirits do." In that much she is correct. Angels—even fallen angels—are notoriously arrogant beings, and seldom lower themselves to take on physical form. Still, I would counsel my readers to beware the devil in all his guises. He is a bore, and it is very unlikely you have committed any sin so serious as to deserve listening to him drone on and on about how awful it is not to be able to get back into heaven.

But I digress. This is Miss Mitchelmore's story, not mine, and not Samael's.

I watched as the viscount led Miss Mitchelmore away from the church to take a closer look at the stones. He stood nearer to her than was, perhaps, proper by mortal standards, but not so close that any could have reasonable objection, especially not in light of his station.

"Are you so certain," he asked, "about the devil?"

"Of late I am certain about little," Miss Mitchelmore confessed. "But I take some comfort in the notion that if malevolent forces *are* at work in the world, they must surely be so numerous and fractious as to regularly come to cross-purposes."

The viscount laughed again at that. "Miss Mitchelmore, you never cease to surprise me." He laid his hand on the largest of the stones. "What do you think. Bride, groom, or parson?"

The correct answer, of course, was none of these things. The rocks are ancient, certainly pre-dating church weddings or any silly mortal taboos about Sundays, but Miss Mitchelmore played along regardless. "I should like to think the bride."

"You think this part," he gestured at an outcropping on the stone, "might represent a train?"

Miss Mitchelmore shrugged. "Not especially. I just like the thought of her standing so much taller than her husband."

"You see? Wicked. You must be careful, Miss Mitchelmore, or you may find yourself turned to stone."

"I shall endeavour to avoid it if possible."

The party stayed in the grounds of the church long enough for those who wished to sketch, to sketch, although not long enough for those who wished to watercolour to colour water, which led to a small amount of disagreement amongst the party until Mr. Clitherowe repeated his assurances that the stone circle itself was even more picturesque, more fascinating, and a better subject for painting.

It wasn't, really. Rocks are, at the end of the day, rocks. But the circle was wide, and to some mortals width is impressive on its own account.

"There are twenty-six stones in all," Mr. Clitherowe explained from the centre of the ring, "although local superstition holds that they are quite impossible to count."

"Yet people accept that there are twenty-six of them?" asked Mr. Caesar, who had already spent far too long in the countryside for comfort and was looking on the prospect of further hours in a muddy field with only hunks of dolomite for entertainment with increasing dismay.

"I did say superstition, rather than knowledge," Mr. Clitherowe pointed out. "I suspect it comes from the simple fact that it *is* rather easy to lose count when one is attempting to enumerate a large number of similar objects standing in a wide circle."

With that peculiar human perversity that I have so enjoyed exploiting, most of the gentlemen in the party (and some few of the ladies) responded to this assertion by immediately attempting to count the stones for themselves. This led to several minutes of fussy men twirling in circles tallying slabs on their fingers and periodically muttering things like "Dash it all, I'm sure I've done that one already."

In the end the stones did indeed prove surprisingly uncountable. A property that should, as Mr. Clitherowe suggested, be attributed *entirely* to their similarity and positioning and not at all to the intervention of any sprites, spriggans, airy spirits, or hobgoblins that might have happened to be in the vicinity for unrelated purposes.

"I'm sure I saw that one move," Miss Bickle told the Ambassador, whose time she had, I thought, somewhat monopolised. "There, tell me I am wrong."

The Ambassador looked down at her, somewhat indulgently. "Something I have learned in my long-yet-short years in the Other Court is that if a seemingly inanimate object is trying to move without your noticing, it will think you very rude for pointing it out."

Miss Bickle looked crestfallen. "Oh, but that will not do at all. It was never my wish to be impolite to the poor thing. I'm sure it was only trying to go to the river for a drink."

She may have been right. They have been known to at times.

Hurriedly, Miss Bickle scampered towards the stone whose peregrinations (that I had, I should stress, in no way been assisting) she had interrupted and dropped a somewhat exaggerated curtsey. "My profoundest apologies, Master Monolith. It was not my intent to make you self-conscious."

The monolith seemed unmoved by this apology but, then again, it had seemed unmoved by the original offense.

Wandering amongst the stones in the various companies of her friends, affable strangers, and at least two men who seemed to be interested in courting her, Miss Mitchelmore was able to feel, for a moment at least, like an ordinary person again.

"Miss Mitchelmore"—the Viscount Fortrose had circulated once more to her side—"if I might make so bold, you have something in your hair."

Miss Mitchelmore reached reflexively for her head, and there felt the woven witch knots that the Duke of Annadale had set there. "They were a gift."

"A strange gift. But I think they are in need of adjustment. May I?"

"With all due deference, sir, I think that would be improper."

The viscount turned his head to one side and gave Miss Mitchelmore an amused, cynical look. "You are a paradox, lady. At once so spirited and so coy."

"Again, sir, you flatter me when truly I am neither."

He had moved closer as he had been speaking. He did not touch her, that would have been unseemly, but he could have, had he chosen to. He leaned nonchalantly against the stone that Miss Mitchelmore was presently inspecting. "I assure you, Miss Mitchelmore, what you call flattery stems from genuine esteem." Then he said something else, but I fear that I did not catch it, because I was distracted by something that was happening within the circle.

In ages past, the stones which our little party of amateur antiquarians had chosen to visit were part of a far larger, far more complex site with concentric rings of wooden columns leading inexorably inwards towards—well, that I shall elide, for fear of disquieting my more sensitive readers. Suffice it to say that what distracted me was that I was now seeing that ancient structure, shimmering and spectral, coalescing into existence in the centre of that otherwise unremarkable field.

Being more attuned to such happenings than mortals, I was the first to notice the change, with the Ambassador perceiving it almost as swiftly and hastily advising Miss Bickle to move aside in case the spirits grew angry. By the time the manifestation had become complete enough that even Mr. Clitherowe and the members of the archaeological society could see it, I had adopted the shape of a sparrow and withdrawn to a safe height. There were ghostly figures moving amongst the ghostly pillars, and in my experience compounded ghostliness was invariably the worst form of ghostliness.

On the periphery of the field, by the twenty-third stone (or perhaps the ninth; they do, after all, move) the Viscount Fortrose stepped boldly in front of Miss Mitchelmore. There was, I noticed, already blood on his hand that seemed to be flowing from a straight, shallow cut. That Miss Mitchelmore did not notice it also cannot be held against her. She is mortal, and thus more prone to distraction by inconsequential things like hordes of angry spectres.

"Stay back, Miss Mitchelmore." He put an arm out in order to prevent her from wandering past the boundary of the stones and into the gathering crowd of spirits. "Whatever these things may be, it is likely they wish you ill."

She did not look like she was in any danger of rushing forwards. "Thank you, I had worked that much out for myself."

The spirits—cowled and indistinct and not at all as picturesque and druidical as, I suspect, the excursioners had hoped—were indeed turning their attention towards the stone where Miss Mitchelmore was standing. They had knives in their hands. Or rather they had things that looked like knives in things that looked like hands. The people who raised the stones, I seem to recall, were no better or worse than modern mortals, but beings long dead mislike disturbance, and the will of the old gods makes these things turn bloody. They did not, however, seem to notice Miss Mitchelmore, although they made immediate motions to menace several of the other visitors.

"If I might"—the viscount went swiftly to Miss Mitchelmore's side, reached into her hair and yanked out the witch knots—"I believe whoever gave you these has betrayed you most cruelly." He tossed them into the ephemeral circle and the things within swarmed forwards. "You see, they are drawn to such magics."

They were certainly drawn to something, since the moment the knots were removed from Miss Mitchelmore's hair, the shades turned their baleful gazes towards her. And Miss Mitchelmore watched, an expression of shock turning to one of alarm as the beings progressed past the knotted thread and towards her. And to her credit, the look of shock did not last for long, either, since the moment it became apparent that the creatures were not, in fact, stopping to play with string, she took to her heels.

From my vantage point in the sky, I was able to maintain a watch over events as they unfolded and, since I cared not one whit if any of the humans present lived or died, I was able to observe them with a clarity and detachment that those on the ground certainly could not. Various inconsequential mortals scattered to the corners of the field, although Mr. Clitherowe made at least some attempt to locate Miss Mitchelmore. The Ambassador made a valiant attempt to protect Miss Bickle—well, relatively valiant since it was unlikely the spirits would risk the ire of the Other Court by harming him directly—while Mr. Caesar made a still more valiant, if also rather briefer, effort to find his cousin amongst the ever-growing crowd of angry revenants. When, however, he discovered that, as insubstantial as the creatures were, their knives still drew blood and their fingers could still clutch and catch and choke, he recalled Falstaff's admonition regarding valour and discretion, and retreated.

The antiquers and archaeologists had been woefully unpre-pared for supernatural intervention, and even Mr. Clitherowe, for all of his dabbling in the mystical, was at a loss as to what might be done about the incursion (there were, in point of fact, at least six countermeasures he could have taken, although since two of them involved blood sacrifice and a third relied on a weapon that has not been seen in the waking world for more than a thousand years, it was not entirely his fault). As a consequence, Miss Mitchelmore found herself quite alone as the things-out-of-time bore down upon her.

The dramatic convention, in such a moment, would of course be for her to turn—eyes wide with shock and a cry of panic on her lips—only to stumble and to lie, just a moment, helpless as the creatures drew closer. But really, what are the chances of so thrill-ing a sequence of events occurring naturally?

Even so, it is precisely what happened. Isolated from her friends, without even the Viscount Fortrose to defend her, the angry shades of a forgotten past swarmed towards Miss Mitchelmore and she turned—eyes wide with shock and a cry of panic on her lips—only to stumble and to lie, just a moment, helpless as the creatures drew closer.

Is that not a thrilling end to a chapter? And I assure you it all occurred just as I say, and quite without my intervention. And reader, if there is one thing you have learned by now it must surely be that I would never deceive you.

18

A hand reached down to Miss Mitchelmore as she recovered herself. "This way."

Seeing little alternative, she took the hand and went the way. A thick fog was gathering now, and from the direction of the standing stones Miss Mitchelmore could hear a low chanting and a high screaming.

I followed her as she let her benefactor lead her through the chaos, back to the church and, at last, into a carriage. I adopted the shape of a curl of mist and went after her, watching to see exactly what would happen when she regained her composure.

She regained it with adequate speed. Although not quite adequate enough that she could get out of the carriage again before it began to move.

"There now," said the Viscount Fortrose, "that wasn't so bad, was it?"

"By comparison with what?" asked Miss Mitchelmore. Now that the immediate need for self-preservation had passed, she was able to take more careful stock of her surroundings, and to recognise that she was alone in a moving carriage with a man to whom she was neither married nor related.

"With the alternative," replied the viscount.

They had gone some distance from the stone circle now, making their way swiftly through the village of Stanton Drew. "My lord," Miss Mitchelmore began cautiously, "it seems that I am out of danger, and if you would stop and leave me somewhere in the village, I am certain I will be able to reconvene with my friends and—"

The viscount raised a hand. "You must surely already have realised I have no such intention. You seem, after all, to be an intelligent woman."

"You continue to flatter me, but I would sooner be released than flattered."

Settling his hands neatly on his lap, the Viscount Fortrose gave Miss Mitchelmore a cold smile. "You may also have realised that your wishes do not mean a great deal to me."

"That much I had indeed surmised. Am I to take it, then, that I am addressing the architect of my present misfortunes?"

"That's a very formal way to put it."

Miss Mitchelmore's eyes narrowed. "Did you curse me?"

"Yes."

"Why?"

The Viscount Fortrose gave a shrug that I might almost have called insouciant. "Because I could. I am no great occultist, but the curse tablets are well known in certain circles. As, for that matter, are the dangers of shedding blood on standing stones."

"That is an answer unbecoming of a gentleman."

And again, the viscount smiled. "You have clearly met few gentlemen."

"Perhaps." Miss Mitchelmore remained carefully impassive. "Certainly I am coming to the conclusion that they are of less use to me than I had once assumed they would be. But regardless, *because I can* is, I think, a half answer at best. That explains why you have decided to prey on a vulnerable woman. It does not explain why you singled me out for your spite."

The glare he turned upon her was rage tempered by disbelief. "Can it be," he mused, "that not only do you slight me, but you then *compound* the slight by forgetting it?"

"My lord," Miss Mitchelmore said, touching one hand to her breast in the socially mandated gesture of submissive femininity, "I am quite certain I have never—"

"And now you compound it again. There is spirit, Miss Mitchelmore, and there is impudence. Do you not recall Lady Montgomery's ball last season?"

I did. But then I have a good memory for casual details mentioned in my presence. Miss Mitchelmore took a moment longer. "I recall that you asked me to dance, but my card was already full and it would have been the height of ill manners to pass over another gentleman in your favour."

"I am a *viscount*, Miss Mitchelmore, I am entitled to considerations that other men are not."

"With respect, my lord, my grandfather is an earl, and I have never heard him express such sentiments."

The viscount sneered at that. "Given the indignities he let his daughters bring on your family, I do not think Elmsley is a fit point of comparison."

"My mother brought no indignity on anybody."

"Did she not? She married a man without fortune or conse-

quence, all because he indulged her vainglorious interest in schol-
arship. And as for your *aunt*. Well, the least said there the better.
And yet despite all of this—despite the paucity of your connections and the modesty of your expectations, you think yourself
above me."

Despite her real and mounting danger, Miss Mitchelmore was
able to muster some measure of defiance. "I assure you, I thought
no such thing. Until today."

"Now, that was sanctimonious. I would prefer that you were not
sanctimonious."

"And I would prefer that I were not being abducted. But in life,
as in piquet, we play the hands we are dealt."

That made him laugh. I have heard a great many unpleasant
laughs in my time and, honestly, his rated poorly. Yes it was cruel,
and furthermore was that mix of cruelty and real pleasure that
always seems so particularly petty. But I have heard the Queen of
Shadows laughing at the death of worlds, and so the scale by which
I judge such things is rather different from yours.

After that they fell into a silence until at last Miss Mitchelmore
asked: "Where are you taking me?"

The viscount raised an eyebrow. "Don't ask questions to which
you already know the answer."

"To the baths, then?"

"To the baths. There I shall present you to the goddess, and you
shall choose between us."

"And what will this choice entail?"

Another laconic shrug. "You have read the tablet, I presume. I
believe it makes that quite clear."

"On the contrary, your language was rather euphemistic. It
asserted your claim over my body and my heart, both of which I
personally consider my own and neither of which I am inclined to

bestow upon you." The coach rattled along in silence a moment, and then she added: "Also, I find it hard to believe that my *heart* is truly your object."

"Oh, but Miss Mitchelmore, you do me a disservice." The viscount's expression was one of wounded amusement. "I will confess that when I began this venture my interest was primarily in"—his gaze swept across her body, lingering on her lips a moment before sweeping downwards and lingering once more—"the more *yielding* parts of your anatomy. But in the interim, Miss Mitchelmore, I have honestly come to admire you."

"If this is your admiration, I am loath to imagine your contempt."

A sly smile spread across the viscount's face. "Perhaps you *should* try to imagine it. I am not one to brook defiance, and a little reflection might help you to choose wisely."

Miss Mitchelmore did not, in fact, need to commit any great amount of energy to imagining how much worse her fate might be should the Viscount Fortrose cease to find her amusing. She was, after all, alone in his carriage while he was accompanied by servants who were, no doubt, well paid for both silence and, if necessary, assistance. "So this is, from your perspective, a proposal of marriage?"

"An unconventional one, I will admit. But you are not a conventional woman."

"I am sure you intend that as a compliment, but if being unconventional to you means abducting, molesting, and tormenting people who have done you no wrong, then I shall continue to pride myself on my conventionality."

"Yet how many other women would speak so defiantly to a man of my station? And in such straits?"

Miss Mitchelmore looked up, making, for a moment at least,

direct eye contact with her captor. Something she had thus far avoided. "More than you think, my Lord. My mother would, I am certain, as would both of my cousins despite their youth, and all of my friends. Indeed I can think of few ladies of my acquaintance who *would* hesitate to express their displeasure at this kind of treatment. And if any did remain silent, I assure you it would be from fear and not from respect."

With an air of exaggerated theatricality, the Viscount Fortrose clutched a hand to his breast. "And still she persists in denying her own exceptionality. Beautiful, spirited, and humble. Truly, no man could ask for more. And allied to my name and fortune, Miss Mitchelmore, think what wonders we could accomplish."

"Pretty words for one who as good as admitted that he started all of this out of a desire to punish and"—she looked down again, bit her lip hard enough that I almost thought she would draw blood, and then looked the viscount in the face once more—"and to fuck me."

Her use of such language prompted a raucous peal of laughter from the viscount. "My lady, if you intend to put me off with such vulgarity, you have chosen an ill strategy. A whore's mouth in a gentlewoman's face is every man's private fantasy."

Miss Mitchelmore gave him a look of naked revulsion. "You are disgusting."

"Men are disgusting. Women are weak. I thank the gods every day that my sex got the better half of the bargain."

"If you think your behaviour bespeaks strength, then I fear this is another matter on which we will have to disagree."

And again, the viscount sneered. "You say that, but who laid a curse upon whom? Who is in whose carriage being taken, even now, to face the judgement of an indifferent goddess? You retain an element of choice in the matter, certainly, but let us be very clear: You will—to use your own language—be *fucked* either way."

I could see the tension in Miss Mitchelmore's neck and shoulders. For all her defiance, she was certainly feeling the pressure of her predicament acutely. Had I cared one whit for mortals, my heart would have been breaking for her. "Then I assure you," she said, "I should rather be fucked by a goddess."

"So you say now. But I suspect you will choose more wisely when the time comes. Especially since giving your heart to a deity is often more *literal* than giving it to a husband."

The afternoon's excursion, for all it was cut short, had been a leisurely one and the journey from Bath to Stanton Drew was long, which meant the sun set well before the viscount and his hostage arrived in the city. Since the pair had lapsed into a relative silence I permitted my own attention to wander, expecting that little more of note would occur or be said before they arrived at the baths.

One of the things I resent the most about my exile to your tawdry world of steel and dirt is that I have lost much of my mobility. Time was I could put a girdle round about the Earth in forty minutes (for those who wish to indulge in a little light mathematics, the circumference of the physical part of your planet is some twenty-five thousand miles: how fast did that make me?) whereas now if I want to travel any distance I will instead wait forty minutes for a ride-share. But back in the happier days when this story takes place, I was able—on those occasions when my attention wandered and whimsy overtook me—to disappear and find some other diversion without serious risk of missing anything important.

Thus it was that I was able to leave the Viscount Fortrose's carriage, make several stops in Bath, travel briefly to London, interfere in a wholly unrelated (but I assure you equally fascinating) set of events unfolding at the time in Paris, pay a short but satisfying visit to a mermaid of my acquaintance, and return via dreams to Bath just in time to reach the carriage as it rolled to a halt, its doors opened, and the Viscount Fortrose led the unresisting Miss Mitchelmore into the street and through the wide-open doors of the pump room.

As they approached, I became aware of a certain energy in the air. The sense of an old god stirring, of old hungers waking in anticipation of satiety. I was, gentle reader, taking a real risk by entering that place, for the anger of a goddess can be indiscriminate and, while little in your world can possibly harm me, the old powers are a different matter entirely.

Still, I went forward. Because above all things I am a storyteller, and I would never leave my audience with half a tale. Boldly and, if I may take the liberty of saying so, selflessly, I walked into that ancient temple without fear or regard for my personal safety.

Truly, I am a wonder.

19

That the doors were open at so late an hour was not itself remarkable. The houses of the gods are never closed unless the gods will it, and while technically the bathhouses remained the exclusive property of the corporation who administered them, their divine resident felt otherwise, and it had been some while since any of the mortal proprietors had made the mistake of defying her.

Within, a haze of steam filled all the rooms and chambers of the house. This was not unheard-of in the baths themselves—it was, after all, a hot spring—but now it hung in the air like a miasma, and for those who watched carefully (and I do, for all my protestations as to my own caprice, always watch carefully), shapes formed in the mist that both warned and beckoned.

The Viscount Fortrose half-led, half-dragged Miss Mitchelmore through the pump room, down the steps to the King's Bath, and then on and down the narrower, older stairs to the ancient and sacred structure that lies beneath. Adopting a misty form I swiftly overtook them, made my own brief obeisance to the lady of that place, and then retreated to the darkest crannies of the spring cave in order to better observe without dying.

The sacred well was already overflowing, and so Miss Mitchelmore and the viscount were both ankle-deep in water when he spun her around, pulled her close, and demanded to know her ultimate choice.

"Well, lady, what will it be? Me, or the well?"

"The well."

No sooner had she spoken the words than the air roared with the sound of rushing water and the statue of Sulis Minerva that stood watch over the shrine turned from bronze to flesh in a shift so subtle that few could truly say it had changed at all.

"You have returned."

The voice of the goddess came, once more, from everywhere.

"I have," replied the viscount and Miss Mitchelmore both, each assuming, as mortals are so wont to do, that they were the one addressed.

In the end, whether out of some vestigial social grace on the part of the viscount or as a result of her will genuinely being the stronger, it was Miss Mitchelmore who continued. "I have brought my tormentor to face you," she said. This wasn't entirely true; she had more been brought *by* her tormentor, but in her place I, too, would have elided that particular detail. "He has no claim over me, and has offered me to you without cause. I hold that my heart and my body are my own to give as I will, and not his to offer up."

While Miss Mitchelmore had been speaking, the viscount had stepped neatly to the side, and now he dropped to one knee in the slowly flooding chamber and bowed his head in a surprisingly sincere display of submission. "Great Goddess Sulis Minerva, this girl defies us both. I offered her to you in humble supplication, in recognition of your majesty—"

"You offered me to her out of spite." Miss Mitchelmore could put up with an attempt to murder her, but not with a *disingenuous* attempt to murder her. "It is craven to pretend otherwise."

"Great Goddess," the viscount continued, "this ungrateful creature is clearly blind to your magnificence and considers you unworthy of her respect and submission."

That the viscount's argument was little more than mewling, self-serving flattery was obvious but, as Miss Mitchelmore was beginning to learn, mewling, self-serving flattery was coin the old gods prized highly.

"An offering has been made," said the voice of the goddess as the water deepened and the air grew hotter and more humid. "An offering will be taken."

"I am not an offering," insisted Miss Mitchelmore. "And I have had enough of this." She turned to leave, but as she did, water began to flow down the stairs to the shrine and the Viscount Fortrose rose from his knees to catch her by the hair, dragging her backwards and casting her to the floor.

"It is over, Miss Mitchelmore. You could have made this easy on yourself"—he stepped closer, standing over her and looking down contemptuously—"but you chose not to. What becomes of you now is entirely your—"

"Step away from the lady." The voice belonged to the Duke of Annadale. And so did the pistol; loaded, primed, and cocked.

The Viscount Fortrose turned slowly. "What in the name of God and the Olympians are you doing here?"

"Making a sacrifice." She glanced past the viscount to the goddess, who was still watching from her pool. The deity's countenance was not serene, exactly; it was more the detached curiosity that I was used to seeing on the faces of immortal beings when mortals fought for their amusement. It was an expression I had worn myself more than once. "Great Goddess Sulis Minerva"— she brought the pistol to aim directly at the viscount's heart—"I offer to your glory this man's blood, in payment for all debts owed."

And then she pulled the trigger.

And then nothing happened.

A triumphant grin spread across the viscount's lips. "You should really have kept your powder dry, my lady. Now, do you wish to watch while I finish what I started, or will you leave us our privacy?"

"As you must surely be aware, I will do neither."

"And how do you intend to stop me? You had, quite literally, one shot. And it failed."

The Duke of Annadale glanced down at Miss Mitchelmore and then back up at the Viscount Fortrose. "Maelys," she said calmly. "Run."

Before Miss Mitchelmore could either obey or disobey, the Duke of Annadale rushed at the viscount. She was not, all in all, a large woman, nor an especially swift or graceful one, and her skirts were already sodden half through so the attack was more ungainly than anything else. Still, it caught him off guard, and she managed to drive him backwards far enough that they both came to the lip of the sacred well where Sulis Minerva waited, more expectant than patient.

As he struck the slick stone of the well, the Viscount Fortrose stumbled, but recovered himself. For all the Duke of Annadale's fearlessness and for all her dark reputation as a murderess, he was still the taller of the two, and the stronger, and so when they fell at last to struggling together at the feet of the goddess, the advantage was certainly his.

I am not, it may shock you to learn, a great afficionado of physical combat (although I do enjoy the balletic quality of the modern entertainment that you like to call *professional wrestling*), and so I fear my summary of the exchange that followed will be woefully inadequate. The Viscount Fortrose contrived by some mix of main force, brute strength, and leverage, to pitch the Duke of Annadale past him and over the side of the well into the steaming, ever-flowing waters. She, for her part, was able to cling to him tightly enough to drag him in after her, and then they both vanished for a moment beneath the surface.

The Viscount Fortrose arose first, gasping for air, flushed from the heat, but holding his enemy beneath the water. Not, until recently, having had any need to breathe myself, I was at the time uncertain as to precisely how long the Duke of Annadale would be able to survive the arrangement, but I did not give her long.

And neither, it appeared, did Miss Mitchelmore, who had ignored the Duke of Annadale's admonition to run as much as she had ignored the Viscount Fortrose's admonition to submit. She returned to the fray now, scrambling into the well and clawing at the viscount's collar, dragging him back just enough to let the Duke of Annadale break the surface before the viscount caught Miss Mitchelmore a backhanded blow across the cheek, knocking her back into the water.

While all of this was going on, the goddess looked down beatifically. As, I suppose, did I. The viscount, having stunned Miss Mitchelmore at least temporarily, had returned his attentions to the Duke of Annadale, seizing her by the throat and attempting to dash her head against the stone wall of the well, with only the drag of the water and his uncertain footing stopping the attack from being a fatal one. Even so, the impact was enough to cut the Duke of Annadale deeply across the scalp, and as her blood began to mingle with the spring-water, the eyes of the goddess turned hungrily down. Gods are, in many ways, like sharks and, in many more ways, like cats. They are drawn to blood, and love to toy with the wounded.

Glancing frantically around, still not —if I was any judge and, being the narrator I am, in a sense, the only judge who matters— quite confident that he was in command of the situation, the Viscount Fortrose saw Sulis Minerva step forward from her pedestal, her feet hovering on a thin layer of steam above the surface of the pool.

"Great Goddess Sulis Minerva," he called out as she approached, forcing the Duke of Annadale's head beneath the waters while she thrashed and struggled, "I give to your divinity—"

He got no further. Rising behind him, Miss Mitchelmore lifted an ancient stone curse tablet that she had retrieved from the bottom of the well and brought it down with all the force she could muster on his head.

It was a messy thing. Mortal skulls are strange, durable and fragile all at once. The first blow staggered him but left him standing, and angered him enough that when he turned, the blood from his own torn scalp masking his face like a huntsman blooded from the fox, she almost lacked the wherewithal to strike him again.

But only almost.

Where the first blow had staggered, the second amazed. "You little—" he managed before the third blow fell, dropping him back into the pool.

For a moment he floated, quite still, and Miss Mitchelmore stood breathing heavily in the too-hot air. The Duke of Annadale drifted over to stand beside her, the blood from her wounds dripping into the waters and mingling with the ever-expanding cloud from the viscount's own injuries. "You need to say the words," she said.

Miss Mitchelmore looked at her with an expression of innocence that she seemed to be feigning, but fervently wishing could still be sincere. "The words?"

"Yes."

Staring up at the deity who seemed now to tower impossibly large above them all, despite the cramped conditions of the spring cave, Miss Mitchelmore drew in an unsteady breath and began. "Great Goddess Sulis Mi—"

She got no further. Sensing, perhaps, that his time was running out, the Viscount Fortrose summoned the last of his strength to rise from the waters and strike.

Miss Mitchelmore brought the tablet down for a fourth time and then, not daring to look, dug her fingers in the tangled mass of the viscount's torn, bloody hair and held him under. "Sulis Minerva," she continued. "I give to your glory and majesty the . . . the . . ."

The Duke of Annadale laid a hand on her shoulder and, in the waters beneath, the viscount struggled ever more feebly.

". . . the blood of this man, in payment of the debts I owe. I— I beseech and implore you to remove your curse from me, to withdraw your gaze from me, and leave me in peace. This I offer in your sacred name."

The viscount grew still, and around the two ladies the water began to churn, dark with mineral salts and blood and old magic. Beneath her fingers, Miss Mitchelmore could feel something cruel and strong and confident pulling the unconscious viscount from her grip, dragging him somewhere not quite of your world and not—I should make very clear—quite of mine either.

"The offer is made," said the voice of the goddess, echoing as off of long-dead stone, burbling as though through gore and ichor. "The sacrifice is accepted."

Around them, the ladies felt the water heat past wilting to scalding and, as they retreated as quickly as they could manage in their sodden skirts and ruined petticoats, to boiling.

"Go."

And so they ran, holding to one another for support and for whatever, in that place of drowned offerings and callous bargains, counted for comfort. Behind them they heard the sounds of rushing water, and a woman's laughter, and the wingbeats of a great bird and, just on the edge of it all, a man screaming.

20

The Duke of Annadale commanded the carriage to go with such urgency that the driver set off without asking where, precisely, it was that they were going. The coach ran through the nighttime streets of Bath to the Royal Crescent, with Miss Mitchelmore huddled in the back fighting her tears. Her companion said nothing, staring fixedly out the window with the air of a woman in deep and complex contemplation.

When they arrived at last outside the Duke of Annadale's Bath residence, she turned to Miss Mitchelmore, said simply "wait" in a tone of absolute command, and, before Miss Mitchelmore could reply, left the carriage and hurried inside.

Being still wet, bloody, and shaken, Miss Mitchelmore had little choice but to obey. So for several minutes she huddled into herself, trying to shrink as far as possible into the shadows (an instinct I understand and respect greatly; the shadows are where all of the most *interesting* things are). Eventually, when curiosity began to out-weigh despair, she inched over to the window and peered out. There were lights in the house, and a flurry of activity appeared to be taking place within. Then, after what had felt an age to Miss Mitchelmore but could not in fact have been even a quarter hour, the Duke of Annadale emerged once more, hurried to the carriage, gave a set of rapid instructions to the coachman, and then climbed aboard.

"What are we—" Miss Mitchelmore began as they rolled off into the night.

"Fleeing," the Duke of Annadale told her.

Miss Mitchelmore gazed down at her dress still soaked in blood and mineral water. "Is that truly necessary?"

"You murdered a man. Worse, you *sacrificed* a man to an ancient goddess and that has been very, very illegal for over a millennium."

"He was trying to kill me." Miss Mitchelmore's tone was flat, as though she didn't quite accept the excuse herself.

"Actually, he was trying to kill *me,* and as such I am grateful to you. But unless you wish to stand before a magistrate and declare *I offered the Viscount Fortrose's blood to the glory of Sulis Minerva in self-defence,* I strongly suggest we run."

"You told me to." It wasn't wholly an accusation.

"He would not have stopped otherwise. I said you broke the law, not that you did wrong. Still, we may evade censure yet."

Miss Mitchelmore looked up at her companion with little hope. "How?"

"The usual way the people of my set avoid censure. Corruption, coercion, and lies. The viscount's coachman will be a problem, but I have asked my man to pay him for his silence, and if he will not accept money, he will accept that his word counts for little against a duke's daughter and an earl's granddaughter. The viscount himself will be missed, of course, but the goddess did us the courtesy of removing the body, and so evading justice seems likely. But for this evening, at least, I believe we would do well to be out of town."

"Out of town?"

"To a friend this evening. From there I need to think."

"You are taking me away from Bath?" Miss Mitchelmore laughed with far more irony than mirth.

"You find the thought amusing?"

"A little. It appears you have abducted me far more effectively than the viscount did."

That drew a cold smile from the Duke of Annadale. "Well, what can I say? I am clearly the more accomplished villain."

"You know I do not think you villainous."

"You did not think the viscount villainous, either, until it was too late. And you observed yourself that it was I who encouraged you to perform the sacrifice. You would be prudent to assume that I mean you ill and that I am simply trying to lure you away from your friends and family."

The allusion to friends and family brought Miss Mitchelmore up short. "You jest, but it will be a cruel thing indeed to vanish in the night and let everybody believe me lost."

"Cruel, but safe. And I have dispatched servants to reassure your parents that you are well. Of course, they may be disinclined to believe me, but there is little we can do about that. There is still a chance that somebody has alerted the law, and so we would be wise to remain in motion if we wish to remain at liberty."

"That sounds like something an abductor would say."

"Yes, it does. And I reiterate, you would be wise to treat me as one."

Miss Mitchelmore slid across the seat and laid her head on the

Duke of Annadale's shoulder. "It is late, and I am too tired to think ill of you. If that is my undoing then, well, it is a better undoing than many others I can imagine."

"You are too trusting. But I shan't chide you for it."

For a while they travelled in quiet company, then Miss Mitchelmore raised her head. "How—how did you know I was at the baths, that I needed you?"

A shiver ran through the Duke of Annadale's body. "I am not entirely certain. I had fallen asleep somewhat earlier than I normally do, and I dimly recall a dream of some kind, and waking with a peculiar certainty as to where I should go and what I should do. I would have dismissed the notion but for its remarkable vividness."

"I am glad that you did not. For all the difficulty of my present situation, it is infinitely preferable to . . . to whatever the Viscount Fortrose must have had in mind."

Neither of them wished to dwell excessively on the details of the viscount's intentions, and so they lapsed once more into silence. As they sat, the one resting against the other in a scene that could almost be taken for companionable by an observer with no knowledge of the context, the carriage wound its way through the Somerset night, past dark fields and through quiet villages, over a crossroads that still made me feel momentarily nauseous, and to rest, at last, outside a lonely farmhouse.

"We're here," announced the Duke of Annadale.

"Where is here?"

"Somewhere we will not be looked for." She opened the door and let the coachman help her down.

Miss Mitchelmore followed and, when she looked up at the coachman to thank him, was distressed to notice a look of worry on his face. It would not normally have been proper to speak to him, but propriety was becoming less and less of a concern. "Is there something I should know?"

The man shot a conflicted look at his mistress, who nodded. "You can tell her, Carter, it isn't a secret."

"Well, it isn't really my place to say, miss," Carter offered, "but word is that this is a witch's house. And as I see it, no good can come of staying here."

Rounding on her companion, Miss Mitchelmore looked at the Duke of Annadale with accusatory alarm. "Is this true, Lady Georgiana? Have you brought me to a place of witchcraft?"

"Given tonight's events," the Duke of Annadale replied, "I don't quite see why you scruple so. You'll have full use of the stables, Carter, and whatever you might imagine the other horses won't bite. After that you'll be welcome amongst the company; Mother Mason is no great respecter of station."

"If it's all the same to you, milady, I'll sleep in the coach."

The Duke of Annadale sighed. "At least permit me to send you a blanket."

"I've me coat, and I'd not trust a witch's blankets neither."

For all his superstition, the man had a point. One is seldom so vulnerable to enchantment as when one has accepted a gift. Sweet Maggie would not, I am certain, have transformed him into anything unnatural but, in the absence of credible assurances to the contrary, I found his reticence both explicable and wise.

Leaving Carter to his own devices, the two ladies made their way up the path to the front door.

"The hour is late," called Sweet Maggie from inside. "And I'm expecting no visitors."

"It's Georgiana," explained the Duke of Annadale. "I have urgent need of assistance."

"Alone this time, are you?" asked Sweet Maggie.

The allusion to my presence at their last meeting was, thankfully, lost on the Duke of Annadale, who simply replied: "What? No, I'm not. I have brought Miss Mitchelmore with me."

The door swung open eerily. Or, at least in a manner I am sure was eerie to the mortals present, who would have been unable to see the bored-looking goblin who opened it. All three of us went inside, the Duke of Annadale taking the lead and me bringing up the rear.

"Oh, it's *you*," said the goblin as I passed. I recognised him as Colm Peppercorn, one of the almost definitionally numberless Peppercorns who inhabited the Queen's Court.

"Yes, it's me. How on earth did you wind up on door duty?"

Colm shrugged. "Lost a wager." He peered at Miss Mitchelmore and the Duke of Annadale. "So which are you following this time?"

"The younger one."

"Seems like she'd be good sport."

I nodded. "She is. And almost entirely without my interference."

In the parlour, the Duke of Annadale had just finished explaining the sequence of profoundly improbable events that had brought them to their present situation. In response, Sweet Maggie cackled, which, frankly, I thought was overplaying it.

"Well, well"—she turned to Miss Mitchelmore—"you're a *witch* now, m'dear."

"I most certainly am not." From my observations to that point, I would have considered Miss Mitchelmore far from prudish, but her indignation here was positively conventional.

"You *did* just sacrifice a man to a pagan goddess," the Duke of Annadale pointed out. "And in order to achieve a specific magical effect."

Apparently Miss Mitchelmore did not consider this a fair comment. "In order to stop him from doing the same to us. And the only magical effect was to lift a curse that he had laid in the first place."

Sweet Maggie shrugged. "A woman who sews her own clothes is a seamstress. A woman who lifts her own curses is a witch. Accept it, you'll be happier. Tea?" She cast a meaningful glance at Colm, who obligingly lit the fire and filled the kettle.

This apparently sourceless activity quite startled Miss Mitchelmore, who tensed in her chair.

"Oh, stop showing off," chided the Duke of Annadale. "Maelys, these are parlour tricks designed to toy with you. Mother Mason may be a crotchety old woman, but she won't harm us either in body or in spirit."

"*Crotchety?*" protested Sweet Maggie. "You knock on my door after midnight and I invite you in, gentle as you please, and you call me *crotchety.*"

"It was an observation about your general character, not your present demeanour. I shall revise my assessment to *mercurial* if you prefer."

Rocking back in her chair, Sweet Maggie cackled again. "Mercurial I will take. I think I might enjoy being mercurial."

Miss Mitchelmore watched in amazement as Colm, quite invisible to mortal eyes, poured the tea. "You have been most kind," she conceded with the instinctive grace of the well-brought-up. "And I am sorry if I have been ungrateful. You understand that I know little of witchcraft, and certain habits of mind are difficult to overcome."

"Ooh, she speaks prettily, doesn't she?" said Sweet Maggie, shooting the Duke of Annadale what I can only call a suggestive look.

"She is also in the room," Miss Mitchelmore reminded her. "And she has had a very long day in which she has nearly died several times and while she is grateful to you for your hospitality, she is not happy to be ignored."

Sweet Maggie rocked forward again. "Quite right, quite right. We'll make a witch of you yet, m'dear. But it's true, you've had a terrible time of it. What do you say I draw you up a bath and see about sorting you out some fresh clothes? You can't go about with a man's blood on your gloves. People will talk."

"By 'What do you say I draw you a bath,' " Colm said to her, "you mean 'What do you say I have my fairy servant draw you a bath,' don't you?"

She gave a curt nod but didn't speak.

"Mortals," I offered by way of consolation. "They have no manners."

Miss Mitchelmore observed that a bath would indeed be welcome, but I was momentarily distracted by Colm glaring at me. "I don't suppose you want to *help*, do you?"

"Master Peppercorn, I am a *storyteller* not a . . . a toter of bathtubs and a warmer of waters."

He continued to glare.

"I have duties. Ancient duties. Ancient and *sacred* duties of profound importance to—"

The glare continued. You have never been glared at until you have been glared at by a goblin.

"Fine. You fetch the tub. I'll do the rest."

And oh, reader, how I miss the days when being asked to draw a bath for a young woman was the greatest indignity to which I had been subjected. Since my exile in your world, I have experienced a thousand things more terrible. Only yesterday I was forced to stand in a queue. In a shop. It was dreadful.

CHAPTER

21

In a fit of misplaced and inconvenient pride I fetched water from the Dead Sea, warmed it with fires I stole from the heart of Mount Vesuvius, scented it with lavender from Rome, and garnished it with rose petals swiped from Titania's own gardens (it was a small transgression, but vexing the lady was part of my charge in those days). It was, in my own humble estimation, the best fucking bath any mortal could ever have experienced in their entire sad biological life, but, true to humanity's ingrateful heritage, Miss Mitchelmore barely noticed.

The tub had been set up in the same cluttered spare room in which she and the Duke of Annadale were to spend the night. This meant that Miss Mitchelmore found herself disrobing amongst bundles of dried herbs, stacks of mouldering leather-bound books, and at least a dozen taxidermied animals whose eyes, I could not help but observe, were most definitely not their own but were also not glass.

She did, at least, offer a sigh of relaxation as she lowered herself into the water, and being invisible I suppose I had to take that in lieu of gratitude. The Duke of Annadale entered only after her companion was fully immersed, then stood somewhat awkwardly at the side of the room, taking great care to look anywhere but at Miss Mitchelmore.

"How are you feeling?" she asked, staring fixedly into the face of a stuffed raven.

"A little better for this, I think. But the conversation will prove difficult if you keep your back to me."

"I was thinking only of your modesty."

"I have been undressed in front of other ladies before. Indeed it is quite normal to bathe with one's maid."

The Duke of Annadale continued to focus on the raven. "I am not your maid. The circumstances are quite different, and I believe you know that full well."

"I know full well that you will take any excuse available to you to slight and overlook me."

For a moment, the Duke of Annadale did not reply. Instead she bit her lip and held her breath. Finally, she exhaled. "Believe me, if I thought myself capable of overlooking you, things would be far simpler."

"They could *be* simple," Miss Mitchelmore maintained. "You surely cannot still think me an innocent after all I have experienced."

The Duke of Annadale actually scoffed. "If there was one quality about society I could alter, it would be the peculiar quirk of language and propriety that makes us equate *suffering* with *guilt*. You have been mistreated, Maelys. That does not make you a debaucher. It does not even make you a witch, for all Mother Mason might claim otherwise."

"Could it not, at least, make me a woman who knows enough to make her own decisions?"

Perhaps unable to bear the restraint, perhaps simply unable to cope with the cold gaze of the dead raven, the Duke of Annadale turned at last. "And do I not know enough to make mine?"

Having no good reply to that, Miss Mitchelmore resorted instead to non sequitur. "I have said the words, you know."

"What words?"

"You told me once that I could not see myself as ready to perform acts I could not even name. Well, I have, now, named them. When the viscount had me in his coach, I told him that he was acting not from gallantry but from a desire to punish and to"—for all her bravado, she stumbled over the phrase again—"to fuck me."

The casualness of the Duke of Annadale's response belied the tension I saw in her eyes. "And I should be impressed by this?"

"You should be chastened by it. I am, as you see, not so missish as you have imagined."

The Duke of Annadale barked something that may have been a laugh. At the very least, it would transcribe as "hah" if I chose to transcribe it. "You are asking me to take your behaviour in extremis as evidence of your desires in general. Believe me when I say I would very much like to. But it would be wrong. Profoundly wrong."

"You are still treating me like a child."

Hesitantly at first, and then with greater confidence as she seemed to make up her mind about what to do next, the Duke of Annadale approached the bathtub and crouched, a little uncomfortably, beside it. "Were I feeling sharp-tongued I might point out that objecting to being treated like a child is itself a rather childish characteristic."

"You are——" Miss Mitchelmore began, but the Duke of Annadale raised a hand to stay her.

"I am not," she said. "I assure you I am not. You"—she shut her eyes, moistened her lips, and then looked at Miss Mitchelmore once again—"you are quite the most beautiful creature I have ever beheld, and it is taking all of my strength not to reach into this water and show you quite which elements of my reputation are deserved."

"Then why *won't*——"

"Because"—the Duke of Annadale stood up again—"less than three hours ago you were abducted by a man who, to speak plainly, made no secret of his desire to rape you. A man you were, ultimately, forced to murder in order to spare my life and your own. I am not denying you or belittling you when I say that whatever you are feeling right now, even if it is real, is hopelessly entangled with fear and guilt and perhaps a little of the excitement that always comes with danger. And that is not how I want you when—*if* we are ever together."

Miss Mitchelmore looked down. "Oh."

"I promise that I am doing my best to protect you as far as my power allows, and to comfort you as much as my temperament permits. But for tonight, at least, whatever happens will have that man's shadow cast across it. And that is not a context in which I would wish to make anybody my lover, least of all you."

"I understand," replied Miss Mitchelmore. And to my mild surprise, it seemed that she did.

"Thank you. I think, perhaps, I should leave you be. I am . . . I am feeling rather like Tantalus at the moment." The Duke of

Annadale pressed a kiss against Miss Mitchelmore's forehead, then bowed her head and retired.

And I myself, although I am by nature an observer and a recorder, felt that in this moment it was meet to give the lady some privacy and so, after applying one last touch of fire to keep the waters warm, I withdrew also.

———— • ————

Colm brought Miss Mitchelmore a nightdress of fairy manufacture, a slip of sheer grey spider silk that caught the light in ways mortals cannot perceive. There was, I should stress, no actual enchantment upon it, but it was perhaps a trifle less modest than mortal fashions of the day dictated.

When the Duke of Annadale reentered, she was dressed similarly, although the silks she had been given were of a somewhat darker hue—we fairies like to keep to certain conventions, after all. Miss Mitchelmore, by this time, was already beneath the blankets.

"I . . ." she began. "That is . . . I am not certain how you would be most comfortable."

"My comfort should not be your concern. I am content to be directed by you in this matter. If you pass me a blanket, I will sleep on the floor. But if you would find my presence soothing, on the understanding that nothing . . . intimate will happen, at least not in the physical sense, then I will—"

"I would like you to come to me, Lady Georgiana."

"I think we can, at last, dispense with the *lady*? After everything that has happened, it seems foolishly formal."

"I would like you to come to me, Georgiana."

And so she did. More hesitantly than I might have expected from a lady of her reputation. Although for the sake of my own pride I shall try to avoid clichéd analogies about maidens on their wedding nights. Besides, it would be an inapt comparison. This was not the timidity of a virgin; it was the caution of one who fears that they are poison.

The Duke of Annadale eased herself into the bed, and Miss Mitchelmore curled reflexively into her arms. And there, before long, Miss Mitchelmore began weeping. Decorously at first, then in uncontrollable and frankly unladylike bursts.

"I feel I should say something," said the Duke of Annadale, stroking Miss Mitchelmore's hair in the least sexual way she could manage, "but also know that I am as like to make things worse as better."

"I just—" Miss Mitchelmore tried, and then by way of clarification added, "It's only . . ."

"A lot has happened. It's natural to feel overwhelmed."

Miss Mitchelmore was shaking now, as though alone and naked on the ice. Only, not as funny. "I don't feel overwhelmed. I feel *weak.*"

"Maelys, my darling, you killed a man with your bare hands. I don't see how that can be weak."

I know little of mortal emotions, but even I could see it was the wrong approach. Miss Mitchelmore curled even smaller and for some time lost the capacity for speech. "I was just so scared."

"Anybody would have been."

"And I didn't know what to do."

"Nobody would have."

"And I can still"—she shuddered again, as though nauseous—"I can feel him fighting. I can feel it burned into the palms of my hands."

More a physical creature than a verbal one, the Duke of Annadale ran a hand down Miss Mitchelmore's arm and to her wrist.

She raised her hand, gently unfurled the clenched fingers and stroked one thumb over the palm. "Does that help?"

Miss Mitchelmore shivered again, but in a less ice-like way. "Some. But I thought you said—"

"This is different."

"It is still . . . intimate, I think."

"But an acceptable intimacy?"

Rolling onto her side, Miss Mitchelmore looked up at the Duke of Annadale through eyes stained with tears. "The prohibition against intimacy is yours, not mine."

"Even now you play the temptress." The tone in the Duke of Annadale's voice was more teasing than rueful, but rue was not wholly absent from it.

Nonetheless, the remark drew a laugh from Miss Mitchelmore. "I cannot look so very tempting like this. I am sure my face is quite swollen."

"You really do think I am lying about my penchant for tears, don't you?"

"I confess it is not a preference that makes much sense to me."

Gently, the Duke of Annadale raised Miss Mitchelmore's hand to her lips and kissed her palm. "Although I am trying my best, given the situation, I am not a kind woman. There are things I find pleasing that I would rather I did not find pleasing. For now, however, I am trying only to be a comfort to you."

"Like a sister?"

"I have never had a sister, but if I did I do not think I would look on her as I look on you, and I hope she would not behave towards me as you behave towards me. But for tonight, yes. Let us be sisters."

Miss Mitchelmore pressed herself close against the Duke of Annadale, and let herself settle into the comforting circle of her arms. "I do not think my sister would have kissed my hand like that."

"You're right. I was—that was excessive of me. But I find your hands beautiful, and I misliked the thought of your misliking them."

"They are just hands."

"I mislike the thought of your misliking any part of yourself, body or spirit."

Breathing deeply, Miss Mitchelmore allowed herself to relax. "I did not think you a spiritual woman."

"I am not. But when first we met you asked me about the state of my soul. And so it felt appropriate to think also about the state of yours."

"And what do you think of it?"

A brush of movement in the dark, and the Duke of Annadale laid a kiss against the back of Miss Mitchelmore's head. "I think that you remain an innocent in all ways that matter. That to have experienced cruelty has not made you cruel. That to have killed does not make you a killer."

"I believe the law and the dictionary would disagree with you on the latter count."

Laying her head against Miss Mitchelmore's shoulder, the Duke of Annadale smiled to herself. "My father was a duke. I learned at a young age to scoff at the law, and my old governess would tell you terrible things about my distaste for the dictionary."

"I find it hard to imagine you as a child. Were you a terror?"

"No, no I was actually rather dutiful. Not that it helped matters."

In the dark, Miss Mitchelmore shut her eyes, only half focusing on the continued conversation. "What matters?"

"My father cared little for me. My brothers he . . . valued after a fashion. At least, he valued their ability to continue his name and his line. But me, he largely ignored."

"What of your mother?"

The Duke of Annadale fell silent a moment. "I have few memories of her."

"Were you very young when she died?" asked Miss Mitchelmore.

There was another, slightly longer pause. "I shall let you know if I ever see her body."

Miss Mitchelmore rolled over, tears forgotten, at least for the moment. "I don't understand."

"My mother was . . . from what I have been told, she was a passionate woman, but a capricious one."

Somehow, Miss Mitchelmore avoided making the obvious comparison.

"When I was eight years old," the Duke of Annadale continued, "she disappeared. The rumour was she went to the Continent, or perhaps to the Other Court." She sounded uncertain. I, on the other hand, am entirely certain, although I shall not share my knowledge with you for it is quite immaterial to this story. "Darker whispers suggested that my father had done away with her, but I never countenanced them."

"Why not?"

"It did not please me to do so. And—you will forgive me if this sounds asinine—it does not *feel* like she is dead."

Softly, Miss Mitchelmore nestled her head against the Duke of Annadale's neck. "It doesn't sound asinine at all. Although, if she lives, it seems ill of her to have left you in such a place."

Unaccustomed to sympathy, the Duke of Annadale drew a slow, calming breath. "It was long ago, now. And my parents' marriage was a miserable one. I don't begrudge her for taking freedom when she could. Besides, mine was not so awful a childhood. I read a great deal. I walked a lot."

"That sounds lonely."

"It was, sometimes. But I met people on my wanderings."

Pulling the blankets tighter, Miss Mitchelmore permitted herself to smile. "Did you seduce the fair maids of the villagery?"

"One or two. And some of the less fair ones—fairness is rather in the eye of the beholder, after all. And I think I was seduced as often as seducing."

"Yet you have resisted seduction so vehemently."

The Duke of Annadale returned to her strategy of caressing Miss Mitchelmore's hair and hoping that the chaste trace of connection would soothe her and prevent her mind from wandering too far back to the baths and the temple and the blood. "My resistance is finite, I assure you. But rest now."

And rest, at last, Miss Mitchelmore did.

Purely from curiosity, I permitted myself the luxury of a stroll in her dreams. And it was, I should emphasise, entirely for reasons of my *own* comfort that I shooed away the shadows that threatened to creep into them and the echoes of the cold, distant voice of the goddess that would otherwise have set such a repetitive tone.

I am a creature of the Other Court, after all, and the needs of mortals do not concern me.

CHAPTER

22

They rose early that morning, although not so early as Sweet Maggie. Witches seldom sleep a great deal, for they know what things lurk in dreams (my kind are by far the least of the terrors which dwell in that place) and spend time amongst them only out of dire necessity.

Taking their leave of the farmhouse, our delightful heroines found that Carter had passed a comfortable enough night in the carriage; for all his fear of the old woman's enchantments, she would not have allowed harm to come to him, as most witches—like most humans—are selfish but not wantonly malicious.

"Home, Carter," the Duke of Annadale instructed as they embarked.

"Home?" Miss Mitchelmore echoed. "We are returning to Bath?"

"I think it best."

Miss Mitchelmore shuddered. "Are you certain? I have—that is we—what if I am accused?"

"Then you will be accused. Since the Viscount Fortrose abducted you under the cover of a supernatural event, I think it will be very hard for anybody to prove you were together. The safest thing I think—the best thing—is for me to return you to your friends and family, for you to concoct between you a satisfying explanation as to where you have been and what occurred, and for you to simply stick to that story as though your life depended on it." She turned and looked out of the window, not distracted exactly, but melancholy. "Because, let us be clear, it does."

This sobering thought sat with Miss Mitchelmore all the way back to Bath. All the way back to her parents' house, where the Duke of Annadale stopped the carriage and the two women alighted once more.

"I should deliver you," the Duke of Annadale told her. There was a coldness in her tone that Miss Mitchelmore had clearly noticed but could not muster the courage to address. "And should be present at least so long as is necessary to explain my role in the narrative. You will have been seen exiting my carriage, so you must have an explanation."

Miss Mitchelmore looked at the Duke of Annadale with eyes uncomprehending. "I would hope you would stay longer than that. There are—that is—we still have things to discuss that are not mere matters of misdirection."

Already sweeping towards the door of the Mitchelmore residence, the Duke of Annadale turned her head a fraction towards her companion. "Perhaps. But now, I think, is not the best time to discuss them."

"Then when shall be?"

A footman opened the door and, seeing Miss Mitchelmore, admitted both ladies at once.

"Quite possibly never."

Before Miss Mitchelmore could challenge this, the two of them passed through into the drawing room, where Mr. Mitchelmore and Lady Jane were waiting. Unusually, neither of them was reading.

"Maelys." Her mother rose, rushed forward, and embraced her. "We didn't know *what* had happened, we were *frantic.*"

"It's true," agreed her father. "I've been so distracted I damn near blew myself up."

"Well"—Lady Jane let her daughter go and turned back to her husband—"if you *will* persist in trying to manufacture explosives when you are in an ill mood . . ."

"I find chemistry calming," he protested. "You know I find chemistry calming."

"I am well," Miss Mitchelmore assured them both, not wishing to give her father any more excuse for self-detonation. "Lady Georgiana rescued me."

"Rescued you from *what,* exactly?" asked Lady Jane. "Your letter was unspecific in the extreme."

The Duke of Annadale bowed her head in apology. "It was necessary. Or at least I believed it so at the time. The circumstances in which your daughter came into my custody were . . . complex."

An expression crossed Mr. Mitchelmore's face that normally only crossed it when he was engaged in an especially troubling piece of calculation. "Complex in what way *precisely?*"

"May we sit down?" asked Miss Mitchelmore. "I believe this conversation would certainly go better were we all sitting down."

They sat down and, for extra preparedness, had tea brought in.

Then Miss Mitchelmore, with the occasional support of the Duke of Annadale, explained the events of the previous evening, starting with the visit to Stanton Drew and ending with the death of the Viscount Fortrose.

Afterwards, there was a long silence.

"And," her mother asked at last, "are you all right? After—after everything?"

Miss Mitchelmore nodded. "I have been well looked after."

"Although were I you," added the Duke of Annadale, "I should ask her that again after I have left, so you may be certain."

"And were you *seen*?" Lady Jane continued. "It was late, but from what you have said, not so very late as all that, and the viscount's coachman—"

"Has been advised to remain silent," the Duke of Annadale said.

Mr. Mitchelmore hadn't drunk so much as a sip of his tea, but he picked up the cup and then set it down again to give himself something to do with his hands. "It seems scant protection, simply to hope nobody connects her to the death."

"That was my thought, initially," confessed the Duke of Annadale. "And I had intended to remove her to my estate, but she would have had little protection there, either, in truth. Her best options now are to flee to the Continent, or to brazen it out." It should surprise nobody that my personal preference would have been for the option that required the lady to be *brazen.*

"The climate *is* more agreeable on the Continent," Mr. Mitchelmore observed. "And I understand one can get fine views of the stars in the alps."

"I do not wish to run to the Continent, Papa," protested Miss Mitchelmore. "However conducive to astronomy the weather may be."

Lady Jane nodded her agreement. "Probably for the best. Besides, running away would make you look guilty, and while that might seem romantic at the moment—"

"—living with a pall of suspicion over you is not, in fact, especially pleasant," finished the Duke of Annadale. "Take it from me."

"Which leaves me with brazening," said Miss Mitchelmore. "Although that will also require an explanation for my absence and, for consistency, an explanation of my being delivered home by Lady Georgiana."

At that, all eyes turned to the Duke of Annadale.

"Well," she began, "your faith in my ability to improvise alibis for murders is heartwarming. I might suggest that we remain as close to the truth as possible; that's normally the best way to lie about things. We shall say that Miss Mitchelmore was taken by— well here I suppose Maelys shall have to supply the details. I would recommend vague but tantalising. Ideally, other people should embellish your story for you."

"So, I should say *I was taken by the spirits in the mist, I don't know what happened only that I found myself . . .* "

"At the crossroads a little south of Bath," said the Duke of Annadale. "It is a known place of fairy intriguing"—she was right on that account; we do love a little intriguing, and a crossroads is as fine a place to do it as any—"and if you had been taken by something otherworldly, it is where you would be found. And it will not seem so very unlikely to the ton to imagine that I was at a crossroads by moonlight for my own purposes."

"And then you brought her back home?" asked Lady Jane.

"And then I arranged suitable accommodation for her overnight and brought her home as soon as would be proper to avoid disturbing the household."

Mr. Mitchelmore frowned. "We found our daughter disappearing quite disturbing as it was."

To that, the Duke of Annadale gave a dismissive half-shrug. "Then you are free to say that I was insensitive to your needs. Or, if you prefer, you could say that I wanted to wait to be certain we were not being hunted as murderesses, but then that might involve further explaining *why* I would think that."

A few minutes further discussion ironed out the details, such as were necessary, of Miss Mitchelmore's cover story and, when the fine points were agreed, the Duke of Annadale rose, gave a curt nod, and made her excuses.

"I should be taking my leave of you," she said. "This visit has already exceeded the proper duration, and I should not like to give the neighbours yet more cause to talk."

Lady Jane and Mr. Mitchelmore did not, it seemed, have any great desire to check her, but Miss Mitchelmore reached out a hand. "Stay, Georgiana, please."

Her omission of the lady's title did not, I think, go unnoticed.

"I shall not. Take time to rest, Miss Mitchelmore. And tell your friends that you are alive; their concerns are far more pressing than mine."

"But—" Miss Mitchelmore began.

It did no good. The Duke of Annadale curtseyed, turned, and walked away.

———— • ————

"And were you truly drawn into another world by cruel spirits?" Miss Bickle was asking later that day. Both she and Mr. Caesar had been sent for shortly after the Duke of Annadale departed and they had both rushed to the Mitchelmore residence to confirm that the lady was indeed alive, whole, and not transformed into any-thing squiggly. Although this latter detail had—to Miss Bickle at least—been a source of mild disappointment.

"No, Lizzie," Miss Mitchelmore explained for what she was certain must have been the twelfth time. "I was in a carriage. But it is imperative that everybody *believe* I was carried into another world by cruel spirits, or I shall hang for murder."

Speaking as one accustomed to deception, I personally ques-tioned the wisdom of letting Miss Bickle in on the truth of the matter. She was guileless to a fault (and guilelessness is *always* a fault) and inclined to trust those who should not be trusted.

"Well," she said, once again demonstrating how suited for pout-ing her lips were, "it seems very ill-mannered of the cruel spirits not to take you anywhere interesting. I am sure there was a time when cruel spirits were more considerate tormentors."

Mr. Caesar seemed less concerned with the quality or otherwise of the cruel spirits, and more with the safety and security of his cousin. "And you are quite sure," he asked—also convinced that it was for the twelfth time—"that you do not wish to fly to Paris? I believe I could arrange it if it were necessary."

"No, no, I do not think it will be. Flying to the Continent feels like it should be a last resort rather than a first recourse."

"True." Mr. Caesar nodded a thinking kind of nod. "But flee-ing the law is rather easier if you do it before the law knows it is being fled from."

Miss Mitchelmore looked down, sighing. "I think, if there is a hope that I might keep my life in England, I should take it. I am sure France is a fine place, but I have little of the language and know nothing of Parisian society. If indeed we were even to go to Paris. Papa has rather a yen to go to the alps."

"That," Mr. Caesar replied, "would perhaps be a step too far.

Quitting England is one thing, quitting society altogether would be intolerable."

"It has been hard enough these past weeks," Miss Mitchelmore agreed. "Indeed, if there is one bright point in all of this, it is that the curse upon me has at least been lifted."

Mr. Caesar nodded. "Yes, we should get you seen in public as soon as possible. The Vicomte de Loux is arriving in Bath shortly and will doubtless be hosting a ball of his usual extravagance. It would be a good way to reenter society and, in extremis, it could be your best opportunity to arrange passage out of the country."

"If it is all the same to you, John," said Miss Mitchelmore, "I shall refrain from throwing myself on the mercy of a visiting Frenchman unless I am extremely certain that it is my only choice."

Miss Bickle, whose attention had wandered a little over the course of the conversation, looked up from where she was now kneeling behind a chaise, searching for something invisible. "There's also the Ambassador, of course. I'm sure the Other Court would protect you if you needed it."

She was right about this. For certain definitions of "protect."

This suggestion did not delight Miss Mitchelmore. "I have had quite my fill of magic. I am sure the Ambassador is a perfectly trustworthy gentleman, but I think I would rather take my chances with the mortal authorities than with immortal ones."

"Oh, but immortal authorities are so much more interesting," declared Miss Bickle. She was right about this also.

"My life has been interesting enough recently. I am ready for it to be merely safe."

Miss Bickle was about to protest, but despite her enthusiasm for all things wondrous, she did have the sensitivity to understand when her friend wished to speak of some other subject. And for a while they did exactly that, contriving to converse as though Miss

Mitchelmore had *not* murdered a man less than twenty-four hours previously, that the man she had murdered had *not* laid her under a curse designed explicitly to coerce her into either matrimony or ruin, and that she had not then fled into the night in the company of a woman she desired but who seemed, once again, to have decided to have nothing to do with her.

But it was only for a while, and as the afternoon became evening, the darkening of the skies led to a darkening of thoughts and so, when at last her friends departed, Miss Mitchelmore found herself near brooding. Unable to sleep, but not—despite her recent adventures—so insensible of propriety as to leave the house alone at night, she sat at a table, took ink and paper, and wrote a letter to the Duke of Annadale.

It was not long. It was, however, intense and quite personal in its contents, filled with words of longing and some honestly rather explicit passages that I had not at all believed that the lady had in her.

I am, of course, a being of far too much sensibility to go into details. I trust that you will understand.

23

The next day, Miss Mitchelmore almost destroyed the letter but, with a resolve that did her credit (and had served her well on that unfortunate occasion when she had needed to drown a man) she screwed her courage, as that plagiarising prick Bill once put it, to the sticking place, sealed the letter, and gave it to a servant to carry to the Royal Crescent.

She received no reply.

She received no reply the following day either. Nor the next. And when on the third day Miss Mitchelmore decided to take matters into her own hands and call on the Duke of Annadale directly, she discovered that the object of her attentions had quit Bath entirely, returning for the first time in four years to her family seat at Annadale in Yorkshire.

Thus it was a despondent Miss Mitchelmore who prepared,

alongside Miss Bickle, for the Vicomte de Loux's ball the following Tuesday.

"Cheer up, Mae," Miss Bickle offered while admiring her new gown in the mirror. Like all her gowns it was of fairy creation, an explosion (in the strictly metaphorical sense) of pink silks that defied gravity, reason, and the paltry sensibilities of mortal taste. "I am sure there shall be plenty of fine young ladies at the ball."

"And I should, what, approach one of them and say, *My dear, may I have this dance, and then would you perchance accompany me home and do things to me with your tongue that I am still not entirely able to articulate?*"

The intended hyperbole was lost on Miss Bickle. "Grandpapa says 'don't ask doesn't get.'"

"Your grandpapa was raised very differently from the people who will be at the ball."

"Perhaps, but he says he was always very *popular* with ladies."

Miss Mitchelmore checked her own reflection and adjusted the ribbons in her hair and the flowers at her temples to better advantage. "But I am not sure what it meant for your grandfather to be popular with ladies is the same as what it would mean for me to be popular with them."

"I think it depends on how good you are at climbing walls and running from dogs," offered Miss Bickle.

"Not terribly." Miss Mitchelmore looked rueful. "My slippers are unsuited for it, and I have had little opportunity to practise."

"Well, perhaps now is a good time to start. I have heard Miss Penworthy is given to dallying with ladies."

"Erica Penworthy has little conversation and no accomplishments. I suspect dallying with ladies is the most interesting thing about her."

Miss Bickle brightened. "Then perhaps she is very, very good at dallying."

That thought did, at least, give Miss Mitchelmore pause. After all, if she was to commit herself to abandoning the marriage market in favour of some more independent and less certain destiny, learning to dally well might be a sensible course of action. "Perhaps people simply find her so dull that they are speculating in order to make her more interesting."

"Oh, but that would be very unfair." Miss Bickle frowned exaggerated disapproval. "Think of the harm such rumours would cause to any poor girl who *wanted* to dally with Miss Penworthy and found she couldn't."

"I am concerned more about the harm such allegations could cause Miss Penworthy. If they are unfounded, then she will be the subject of unwanted advances *and* face increased difficulty in finding a husband."

For a moment, Miss Bickle considered this. "Perhaps. Then again, I'm sure there are some gentlemen who would consider a wife who likes to dally with other ladies a rather jolly thing to have."

"Yes, but I suspect many of those gentlemen are ones a lady would be very ill-advised to marry."

They continued their debate of the merits or otherwise of dallying or not dallying with Miss Penworthy, and of marrying or not marrying a gentleman who would or would not enjoy having a wife who dallied with Miss Penworthy, when they were called downstairs by Lady Jane and Mr. Mitchelmore. Mrs. Wilberforce had been informed that her services would not be required that evening, Miss Mitchelmore's parents deciding, belatedly, that perhaps if they had paid more personal attention to their daughter's movements in society she would not have found herself drowning a man in a sacred spring.

"Are you looking forward to the ball, dear?" asked Mr. Mitchelmore once they were loaded into the carriage. "Or is that a silly question? And if it is I'm not sure what direction it's silly in. Sorry, you see there really *is* a reason we normally sit these things out. I *do* wish you'd let me bring a book, Jane."

"You are *not* going to sit around at a ball reading the *Dialogue Concerning the Two Chief World Systems*. It would be rude."

"No, it wouldn't," Mr. Mitchelmore countered with the misplaced confidence of a physical scientist, "it's a very old book, so nobody would feel awkward about distracting me from it."

"It would *still* be rude. And we are here to show the world that Maelys is no longer cursed with supernatural misfortune. It would be very unhelpful to demonstrate that she remains cursed with a disagreeable father."

Mr. Mitchelmore was seldom truly offended, partly because he was seldom truly paying attention, but he huffed at that. "I am *not* disagreeable. I just find people uninteresting."

"I think, Papa," Miss Mitchelmore offered, "that many would say that's rather the *same* as being disagreeable."

"Well, as Galileo observed, many would say that the solar system is geocentric. They are assuredly wrong."

Lady Jane rested her head on her hand. "Edward, please tell me you won't be talking like this all evening."

"This is how I talk."

"And yet I married you anyway." From her tone, Lady Jane seemed as bemused about the fact as anybody.

The Vicomte de Loux was not staying in Bath itself but had instead let a manor house within a few miles of the city. It was an ancient, sprawling sort of place, with unusual topiary. I dimly recalled having once enchanted a former owner to fall in love with a duckpond. But that had been centuries past, and neither he nor the pond were there any longer.

The Mitchelmores' carriage pulled up in the grounds, and its inhabitants noted two familiar carriages. One belonged to the Caesars, and the other . . .

"Look alive, Jane," Mr. Mitchelmore observed, "your brother's here."

Lady Jane scowled. "So I see."

Still, having braved supernatural reprisal, it seemed foolish to have gathered only to be frighted off by a mildly unpleasant relation, so they disembarked from the carriage and proceeded into the house.

Although the let itself had been peculiarly furnished—its owner had a strange fondness for Florentine embroidery, and employed it on every surface on which it could reasonably be employed and several on which it could not—the vicomte had spared no time in making such alterations as he saw fit. But a lifetime's idiosyncratic taste could not be overturned in a few days.

The ball was conspicuously well attended; ever since the Peace of Paris, the ton had been able to indulge its infatuation with all things French without feeling unpatriotic, and so the arrival of a continental aristocrat was cause for much excitement. Miss Penworthy was indeed in attendance, and despite herself Miss Mitchelmore couldn't quite escape the temptation to look at her with new eyes, as a potential ally if not a potential partner. In one corner, Mr. Caesar was already conversing with the vicomte. The vicomte's house was one of the few in fashionable society in which the Caesars were readily accepted even *without* the influence of the Earl of Elmsley; not only did they do things differently on the Continent, but the vicomte was himself the son of a French nobleman and a woman of the gens de couleur libres whom he had met in the colonies, and so had less inclination to look down on the family than many aristocrats.

While the Earl of Elmsley was absent, his only son was most

decidedly present. He noted the arrival of the Mitchelmore party and moved towards them with the slow inevitability of a spider approaching a group of socially embarrassed flies.

Lord Hale was younger than his sisters, and from the perspective of a person who gave two figs for such things, had borne much indignity on their behalf. That the one had married a gentleman-scholar with no name and little fortune had been bad enough; that the next had married a freedman had proven too much to bear. Thus he had little interaction with his sisters' families if he could avoid it, although on the rare occasions where their social circles could not help but overlap, he defended his territory fiercely. His wife, Lady Hale, followed behind him. Being even more her husband's junior than he was his siblings', she was closer to Miss Mitchelmore's age than her parents', a fact that had always caused both women a certain amount of discomfort.

"Jane." The baron offered an ingratiating smile. "And Edward. How wonderful that you could make it. And after everything that has *happened* recently."

"Yes, well"—Lady Jane looked at her brother with a precisely calculated level of civility—"we have always been a resilient family, and it takes more than a little magic to fright Maelys away."

Her brother nodded sagely. "Quite so. Although, the most recent events *do* seem to have frighted away the Viscount Fortrose."

A quiet fell across the party a moment, but Miss Mitchelmore was first to recover. "Have they? I am afraid I lost track of him."

"Really?" asked Lord Hale. "It seemed for a while that you were rather close."

Despite her parents' idiosyncrasies, Miss Mitchelmore had still learned well the techniques of polite impassivity that were necessary for survival in society. She blinked and looked uncomprehending. "Not at all. He called on me once, I think he may even have liked me a little, but we were never more than acquaintances."

"That's not how he saw things." Lord Hale's tone and eyebrows were both moving in suggestive directions.

"I am sure I do not know how he could have seen things in any way but the one I have described," Miss Mitchelmore maintained. In matters such as these, it was generally best to avoid even the hint that one might be at fault. "We cannot have spoken more than a few hundred words to one another."

"Marriages have been built on less," observed Lady Hale.

"And polite indifferences built on more," replied Miss Mitchelmore. "I am truly sorry, Uncle, I had not expected to be called on by the Viscount Fortrose and so I have not noticed his absence."

They stood watching each other in a kind of tense but polite standoff, and then Lord Hale bowed somewhat stiffly, said a few formal words of parting, and parted.

Miss Bickle was staring up at Miss Mitchelmore with her eyes wide but, to her credit, managed to avoid saying anything incriminating. The extent to which young ladies could circulate at balls when not dancing was limited, but Miss Mitchelmore managed to secure Mr. Caesar for the first of the country dances and thus had a moment to converse with him under the cover of music and movement.

It was, unfortunately, a longwise dance, and so they each of them spent much of their time moving in circles with people with whom they had no wish to converse, but snatching fragments of dialogue in motion was a technique both had long practised.

"My uncle is here," Miss Mitchelmore explained as they crossed paths briefly on their way to cast around the second couple.

"What does he *want*?" Mr. Caesar replied when they reconvened on their way to cast around the third.

They came to a position parallel to one another, not quite close enough to whisper but sheltered enough to speak relatively freely as they danced up between their companions. "He asked about the viscount."

They led through to the top and crossed again in the middle, their paths intersecting just long enough for John to offer a quick "fuck, damn the man" and Miss Mitchelmore to throw back an equally brief "which?" before returning to their positions.

One more round gave the opportunity for them to exchange a quick "What does he know?" and a "Little, but he suspects more" with a final "But what can he prove?" before they were parted and remained so for the rest of the dance.

They were able to discuss the matter in more depth as Mr. Caesar walked Miss Mitchelmore back to her parents, although with a lull in the music they needed to keep their voices lower.

"I think it likely," Miss Mitchelmore whispered, "that he is simply attempting to scandalmonger, but it concerns me."

"As it should. He could make life difficult for you, Maelys. He is not without influence."

Miss Mitchelmore returned to her parents' side, where another gentleman—a Mr. . . . you know, I shall be honest, the man is not important, and you must remember that I met these mortals some two hundred years ago, let us call him Smith and have done—asked for her hand for the next dance. She obliged him because to *not* oblige him for any reason other than a prior engagement would have been an unforgivable violation of social convention. Indeed, as she had recently learned to her cost, failing to oblige a gentleman even *for* the reason of a prior engagement could cause offence with potentially disastrous consequence.

And it was this last consideration that grew in her mind as the evening progressed, as she danced with one gentleman after another, all perfectly respectable and all perfectly forgettable and none of them the person she wished to be dancing with. When the event paused for supper, she permitted Mr. Caesar to escort her through to the supper room and there made an increasingly futile effort to amuse herself.

In something approaching desperation, she sought out Miss Penworthy, who was also largely ignoring the gentlemen and focusing instead on the excellent array of French patisserie.

Seeing her approach, Miss Penworthy bobbed a curtsey. "Miss Mitchelmore."

"Miss Penworthy."

Not quite certain what was expected of her, Miss Penworthy smiled. Miss Mitchelmore did her best to find her pretty, which she probably was in a straightforward sort of way. But she lacked the darkness of eye or the feigned cruelty in the curve of the lip that Miss Mitchelmore was truly seeking. "Can I offer you something?"

"What sort of something?"

Half a smile in return, something that Miss Mitchelmore wasn't sure whether she was meant to read as flirtation. "Well"—she indicated a selection of continental pastries—"these are all—I think they're various sorts of French cake."

"Oh."

Miss Penworthy picked up something small and brightly coloured, holding it out and offering to pop it into Miss Mitchelmore's mouth.

For a moment it seemed like she might accept, but at the last moment she closed her lips and turned away. "No. Thank you. It— that is you—I mean, it looks delicious, but my life is rather complicated at present."

"I understand." Miss Penworthy ate the dainty herself. "You should—you should probably know that I've been hearing things."

Suddenly wishing she'd taken the pastry, Miss Mitchelmore paused. "What sorts of things?"

"I was warned off you," Miss Penworthy explained. "Apparently people who become close to Miss Mitchelmore come to bad ends."

"What sort of people?"

Miss Penworthy glanced about conspiratorially, then whispered, "*The Viscount Fortrose.*"

Marshalling all her self-control, Miss Mitchelmore guided her expression into one of exactly the most innocent amount of surprise. "Oh? What do they say of him? I confess I hardly know the gentleman."

"Well"—Miss Penworthy leaned a little closer—"they say he was courting you."

"That is news to me," Miss Mitchelmore half lied. It depended, after all, very much on what you considered *courting.*

"And then he disappeared without a trace."

"That is news also."

Miss Penworthy unfurled her fan and fluttered it coquettishly. "I know, is it not scandalous? I confess it made me quite desirous to speak with you."

"Really?" In candour, Miss Mitchelmore could understand why. Had she less personal experience of scandals and mysteries, she might have found it intriguing herself.

"Oh yes. It gives you quite the air of danger."

There was something about this conversation that was striking Miss Mitchelmore as familiar, but she was at a loss as to what to do with that familiarity. "As one who has experienced much of it recently," she tried, "danger is a lot less entertaining when it is happening to one than when it is happening to people one may observe from a safe distance."

Miss Penworthy peeked over the top of her fan. "Then I shall be sure to observe you safely."

And with that, Miss Penworthy took her leave of Miss Mitchelmore and went in search of—of whatever it was that particular lady was actually searching for. And Miss Mitchelmore was left alone to watch the company and, the more she did, the more she fancied she saw them watching her in return. Watching her, and speaking in hushed tones.

It was an unfamiliar sensation. And an unpleasant one.

Or so I imagine. I, after all, have always rather enjoyed being talked about.

24

The ball passed as such things always pass, which is to say joyously for some, interminably for others. I myself oscillated between both categories, since whenever the evening threatened to grow dull, I was able to entertain myself by tripping somebody during a dance or slipping something laxative into a person's blancmange.

Miss Mitchelmore, however, had no such recourse, and as the evening progressed she found little to bring her joy. She took to refusing to dance, citing tiredness and the after-effects of her recent magical trials, but that merely gave her more time to watch the company and to wonder whether they were whispering about her, and *what* they might be whispering. Certainly Lord Hale was wasting no time doing his rounds, and every so often he would glance in her direction and the gentleman or lady he was talking to would glance also, and then laugh, or cover their mouth, or make an expression of shock or scandal.

Or perhaps that was only her imagination.

She slept poorly that night, and I remained outside her dreams for fear that they would bore me.

Over the next several days Miss Mitchelmore, along with her friends and her parents, attempted several times to engage in the kinds of activities that one would ordinarily undertake at Bath if one were there and not under a curse. They dined with other families, they took walks and went to the theatre. They avoided the pump room assiduously and visited the Assembly Rooms only once, and while nothing happened to Miss Mitchelmore that was so immediately distressing as those events that had originally drawn her to my attention, there was a continual discomfort around her. A growing sense that perhaps not all was quite right with the young lady, that she was a person to be *accepted* but not *embraced.*

There remained also the question of the Duke of Annadale, who had still not returned and seemed likely never to, at least for that season. It was becoming increasingly apparent to Miss Mitchelmore that even if she could, perhaps, eventually reconcile herself to the ordinary occupations of a lady of her age and station—to relearn the habits of flirting decorously with suitable gentlemen while making cold, unflinching calculations regarding their net worth and broader reputation—she could not do it *now.* The wounds of her recent travails were too fresh, her mind was too much disordered, and Lady Georgiana Landrake preyed too much upon her thoughts.

"I'm getting the impression," Lady Jane observed one evening, looking up from the frog that she was dissecting on a small folding table, "that you might not be totally happy here."

Miss Mitchelmore, who was at work on her needlepoint and trying to ignore the smell of the strong mixture of alcohol in which her mother's specimen had been lately preserved, did her best to look like she was not in the middle of an existential crisis. "Oh no, Mama. I have just—things have been so difficult recently and so I have been rather tired."

Setting down her scalpel, Lady Jane gave her daughter a stern look. "I went to the same finishing schools as you did, my girl. I know what *I have been rather tired* means. It means you're miserable and too polite to say it."

"Really, I am not. I am merely . . ."

Her inability to finish the sentence rather spoke for itself. "Please stop trying to be courteous, Maelys. Your father and I are only here for you, so if you aren't enjoying yourself and are happy to wait a little while—or indeed a *long* while—before thinking too hard about marriage, then I see no reason why we should remain."

"But would it not be terribly inconvenient?"

"We shall need to arrange to end our lease on this house a little early, but that's manageable. And frankly your father will be overjoyed at being free to return to London. There are very few interesting lectures in Bath."

Despite the generally high opinion in which society held maidenly reticence, Miss Mitchelmore permitted herself to accept that, in this case at least, her desires and her duties truly did align.

Thus arrangements were made. And it did not, in the end, take so very long at all. She apologized to her friends, but both were quite understanding and reassured her that from Bath to London was not so far and that, at any rate, the season would soon be over and they would be reunited.

And indeed, she did not have long to wait, for summer began in earnest and the fashionable set who had been passing the winter and spring months in Somerset soon began to filter back either to their country estates or to town, depending on where they were most needed or most comfortable.

While this time was passing, I began to wonder if I had, in the end, backed the wrong metaphorical horse in pinning my hopes on Miss Mitchelmore. True, she had already murdered a gentleman, and that had been diverting, but as days passed in which she sat pining and sighing like a sapphic Lady of Shalott, I began to despair of her doing anything foolish or reckless again.

———— • ————

Events became mildly more diverting towards the middle of June when Miss Bickle—who had found little difficulty in persuading her father to let her summer in London rather than Cornwall—returned to the city and dragged her friend by one arm and one ear to a card party on Warwick Avenue. My joy at seeing the lady leave her house was marred when I realised it was to be an entirely respectable evening and that its hosts—the Fitzhamptons—were two of the dullest people I had encountered all year. Wealthy enough to have no need to learn a trade, inconsequential enough to have no involvement in politics, they were the kind who spent their evenings drinking tepid lemonade and making tepid conversation.

Worse, Mr. Clitherowe was in attendance. Worse still, Mr. Clitherowe was in attendance and was one of the more interesting members of the company. Reader, I nearly fled. Cold iron holds no power over my kind, but we are quite repulsed by dull people.

Hoping, perhaps, that he would be an agreeable companion, Miss Bickle and Miss Mitchelmore took the opportunity to form a four with him at whist. But when he won the contract on a frankly ambitious bid of four spades, making his partner the dummy, they found themselves a more awkward trio than either of the ladies had anticipated.

"Well, this is jolly," declared Miss Bickle, with the air of a woman who believed she could will jolliness into existence by sheer force of personality.

"Quite," Mr. Clitherowe replied, laying the nine of hearts.

Miss Mitchelmore followed with the two and Miss Bickle with the four.

"I am glad," Mr. Clitherowe continued, keeping his eyes very firmly on his cards, "that you were not harmed after"—he fell silent for long enough that Miss Bickle had to nudge him into starting the next trick—"after the events of . . . after the events."

"Thank you." Miss Mitchelmore did not sound especially thankful, but then Mr. Clitherowe had not sounded especially glad.

"Although, of course"—Mr. Clitherowe led with a hesitant six of clubs—"the viscount does not seem to have—that is—you must understand that I—it was . . ." He stood. "I fear I will have to concede this hand. My apologies, Miss—my apologies."

When he was gone, Miss Mitchelmore tried not to cry and Miss Bickle tried not to draw attention to the fact that Miss Mitchelmore was trying not to cry while also comforting her as best she could. Reaching across the card table, she took her friend's hand and said simply, "I'm sorry, Mae."

"He could not even look at me." Despite her efforts, a few tears glistened at the corners of Miss Mitchelmore's eyes.

Miss Bickle squeezed Miss Mitchelmore's fingers just a touch too tightly. "He was . . . the events at the excursion must have been hard for him too."

Cursed as she was with that mortal tendency towards empathy, Miss Mitchelmore nodded. "I know, Lizzie. I just . . . not two months ago he was proposing marriage, and now he plainly thinks me—" She did not finish the sentence; the room was small and, even whispering, it would have been impolitic to describe oneself as a murderess.

"We should go," Miss Bickle insisted.

For a moment, Miss Mitchelmore was about to protest, but it would have been so plainly self-destructive that she did not. "Thank you."

Making only the most perfunctory of goodbyes to their hosts, the young ladies departed forthwith in Miss Bickle's father's carriage. Once within, Miss Mitchelmore laid her head on her friend's shoulder. "I'm sorry," she said again, "I fear I have not been myself lately, and I have been sleeping very poorly."

A great believer in dreams and portents, Miss Bickle looked around attentively. "I am sure that means something. Whenever I sleep ill, it always means something. Why, just last week I spent all Tuesday night tossing and turning, and then I woke in the morning to discover that one of my best peach gloves had gone missing."

"That doesn't seem *very, very* meaningful," Miss Mitchelmore observed.

"Oh, but it is. For I am sure it was misplaced only through supernatural agency." She was right on this account. In my defence, I was bored.

"Gloves do sometimes go missing, Lizzie, especially where you're concerned. I recall you once left a pair in a tree outside Falmouth."

"That was a gift to the dryads, as I told you at the time."

"They seemed to have little use for it."

Miss Bickle frowned. "So it appeared to *you*. But from that day forth I have never once had a splinter from a beech tree."

"Have you had much opportunity to?"

"Well"—for a moment Miss Bickle's ironclad faith in supernatural providence collided with empirical reality—"no, not as such. But I feel certain I shall not in the near future either." Recalling herself, and concerned she had let her whimsy override her friend's distress, she put a supportive arm about Miss Mitchelmore. "But you were speaking of your lack of sleep. Was it strange dreams? Did you feel something beneath your mattress? Has there been an otherworldly presence in your room?" There was. Again, I'd been hoping she'd do something interesting. "Or is it still—that is, I should not have pressed you to return to society. But you should not give a thought to Mr. Clitherowe; hardly anybody listens to him because he's so very . . . unassuming." "Unassuming," reader, was a euphemism. For "terrible."

A look of contemplation settled over Miss Mitchelmore. "It is not that, I think. Not exactly. And I do not blame Mr. Clitherowe for his . . . his reticence with me. Nor would I truly wish him to be otherwise. I rather—I feel Lady Georgiana has been very present in my mind of late."

"Well, of course she would be," Miss Bickle agreed. "You are in—"

"Please, Lizzie, do not say I am in love with her." There was genuine entreaty in Miss Mitchelmore's tone, and not a little sorrow.

"But you *are.*"

"I may be? But I cannot be certain. I feel—in candour, Lizzie, I feel a great many things that I am sure a young lady should not but, were it not for the discomfort of being parted from her, I do not think I should be so very sorry to go on feeling them."

Miss Bickle seemed to think about this a long time, although what Miss Bickle was thinking of when she seemed to be thinking was often not quite what another person would be thinking of in her place. "Well," she said at last, "then I shall *not* say it sounds very much as though you *are* in love with her, since you are plainly not of a mind to hear it. But may I say that if you are open to the possibility, then it seems only good sense that you should go to her and test the supposition."

By way of reply, Miss Mitchelmore said only: "She is in Yorkshire."

"And?" From her expression, Miss Bickle apparently considered this no answer at all. "Has Yorkshire sunk into the sea?"

"Well, no but—"

"Has Napoleon escaped Elba and landed all his armies in Yorkshire?"

Miss Mitchelmore gave her friend a reproving look. "Don't be silly, I'm sure Napoleon shan't escape Elba and even if he did, he would have far better places to go than the North of England."

"Really? It is quite lovely this time of year."

"I'm sure. I don't think that makes it a vital strategic point in the European theatre."

"But"—Miss Bickle grinned triumph—"you *do* concede its loveliness."

Fearing she had been tricked and wondering, for neither the first time nor the fiftieth, if her friend was in fact a secret genius, Miss Mitchelmore was forced so to concede. "I am sure that part of the world has many attractions. And from what I know of Annadale it is very pleasant. But I cannot simply pick myself up and run the length of the country."

"Why not?" And now Miss Bickle had adopted her attitude of defiance, one that I had, during some of my earliest reconnaissance, seen her practising in the mirror. "You plainly are no happier in London than you were in Bath."

"I *am* finding society a little wearing."

Miss Bickle nodded sagely. "Which is only natural. Although in truth, Mae, I think very few people of consequence consider you a murderer."

"I believe in the very best of company," Miss Mitchelmore returned, "nobody should consider one a murderer at all."

"Well, yes, but that is slightly harder to achieve when one actually *is* a murderer. At least a little bit."

Miss Mitchelmore sighed at that. It was a wretched thing, she was discovering, to have all the guilt of a crime and none of the imperviousness that she had always imagined would come with being a criminal. In abstract it seemed like it should be a source of strength, to be able to say *Yes, I killed him because he wronged me, because he would have harmed me and a woman I cared for.* But it was not. It was instead a wound that she hoped would one day heal but felt certain would scar instead.

"Thus, my discomfort," she said at last.

For a moment, Miss Bickle let that sit there, and then segued gracelessly to: "Miss Penworthy has been asking after you. I think she wants to ravish you."

"Really?" Miss Mitchelmore raised a sceptical eyebrow.

"Or for you to ravish her. I'm afraid I'm still not certain how it is between ladies. I have been reading Sappho to understand it better, except I have little Greek and it can be rather hard to find translations. So far I am coming to the conclusion that it involves something to do with singing songs to Aphrodite and paying very close attention to gentlemen at weddings."

Miss Mitchelmore could not help but laugh at that. "I lack your father's love of the lyric poets. I'm afraid I have been navigating these matters without the help of the ancients."

"I don't think you've missed much." Miss Bickle wrinkled her nose. "I daresay I found it all very confusing."

"Either way," Miss Mitchelmore tried to wrench the conversation back towards her present predicament, "I am certain that while she is not perhaps so dull as I once thought, I have no desire to either ravish *or* be ravished by Miss Penworthy."

"And by Lady Georgiana?" asked Miss Bickle.

That was the heart of the question, was it not? And for a long while Miss Mitchelmore did not answer it. And after that while had passed, still the only answer she could manage was "She is in Yorkshire," which was not truly any answer at all.

"Then go to Yorkshire," Miss Bickle told her, as if it was simple. Which it was, from my perspective, but then distance means little to me.

This suggestion did not, however, meet with Miss Mitchelmore's approval. "I cannot travel the length of the country alone; it would only compound scandal with scandal."

"Then I shall come with you."

There were innumerable practical reasons why Miss Bickle's company was not the sure ward against danger or rumour that Miss Bickle seemed to think it would be. Most practical of those reasons by far being Miss Bickle's utter personal disdain for practicality.

But it was, Miss Mitchelmore had to admit, tempting.

"It shall be a holiday for us," Miss Bickle went on. "More than a holiday, it shall be an adventure."

"I have had my fill of adventure," replied Miss Mitchelmore, with less conviction than she had, perhaps, expected from herself. "But . . ." She drifted a moment, her thoughts meandering back to dreams and fancies that had entered her sleeping mind quite of their own accord and barely assisted at all by the guile or glamours of fairykind. "But it would be good to *see* her."

"Then it is settled," Miss Bickle declared, despite its being nothing of the sort. "And Mae, you need do nothing at all, for I am sure I can make all of the arrangements myself and we shall want for nothing on the journey and—oh, *Maelys*, it will be *such* fun, I am *sure* of it."

Miss Mitchelmore, for her own part, was rather less sure. But it was, she was finding, a sweet unsureness. An uncertainty grounded in the hope of better, rather than the fear of worse. And that, she allowed herself to believe, made it worth pursuing.

25

Miss Mitchelmore had shared her plans with her parents the following morning and they had been broadly supportive of the notion. While they lacked the Bickles' reflexive romanticism, they could both see the sense in their daughter's removing herself from London for a time, even without considering the matter of the Duke of Annadale. And true to her word, Miss Bickle had arranged everything. Or, more precisely, people who worked for Miss Bickle's grandfather had arranged everything, which meant that it was actually extremely well arranged. The elder Mr. Bickle, unlike his son, was an eminently practical man, and so had provided his granddaughter not only with a suitable carriage but suitable servants suitably armed, in case there should be highwaymen on the road. He had arranged also for suitable lodgings at suitable coaching-inns making it, in the end, the most expedient trip across country that Miss Mitchelmore could have imagined.

"You are quite sure that this is what you want?" Mr. Caesar asked as he helped Miss Mitchelmore into the carriage. He was not joining the party himself, having studies to attend to and a life in town that could not be put down at a moment's notice.

Miss Mitchelmore looked at him with nothing but doubt in her eyes. "In truth, I am not. But I am sure that I want to be sure, if you see what I mean."

"I do see," Mr. Caesar reassured her. "I see very well. In which case, I wish you luck."

And with that they set off.

Despite Miss Bickle's determination that the journey be, in her words, "a jolly one," Miss Mitchelmore found it at most "comfortable." Her longing to be, once more, with the Duke of Annadale made all the pretty scenery and interesting landmarks that her companion took pains to point out seem little more than an ill-painted backdrop in an ill-acted play.

The elder Mr. Bickle's itinerary had set them a measured pace, breaking the journey into three legs and always ensuring that they would reach an inn before sunset, a stratagem which Miss Bickle grew increasingly to resent.

"Had we travelled by night," she explained to Miss Mitchelmore as they settled into their room at the end of the second day's journey, "we might have been waylaid by highwaymen." Expressed like that, I, too, came to regret their prudence.

"Is that not exactly why we are *avoiding* travelling by night?" Miss Mitchelmore asked, although she could already anticipate her friend's answer.

And, sure enough, here it came. "Oh *no*, Mae. A lady should *certainly* experience being waylaid by a highwayman at least once in her life. To have a dashing ruffian ride out of the dark and demand either your jewellery or a kiss . . ." She drifted off into rapture.

"I think that would be less romantic in reality than it may feel," Miss Mitchelmore suggested. "To have a gentleman make advances on one under the threat of violence is . . . not pleasant."

With the shocked look of a true innocent who feels she has caused unintentional hurt, Miss Bickle bounded across the room to kneel by Miss Mitchelmore and beg her forgiveness. "Oh Mae, I'm sorry, I wasn't thinking. That must have been terrible for you, truly. It's just . . . well . . . I am soon to be twenty and have never had either an adventure nor any real kind of love affair and, well, I think I should at least like to experience it."

"I am not sure you would," Miss Mitchelmore replied, trying not to think too hard of the feeling of the Viscount Fortrose struggling in the water, the sick knowledge that at most one of them could leave that pool alive. "Experienced personally, adventure can be rather nauseating."

"Oh." Miss Bickle looked genuinely sad for about an eighth of a second, then brightened at once. "Then I shall strive to make the best of this journey and find wonders where I may." She squeezed Miss Mitchelmore tightly and fell back with her onto the bed in an embrace far more companionable than carnal. "And we *are* having a fine time, are we not?"

Miss Mitchelmore, desiring to be permitted to breathe, conceded that they were, but she did so with such an undercurrent of melancholy that Miss Bickle, although she loosened her grip enough to avoid asphyxiating her companion, maintained a level of bodily contact that communicated *I am here for you, whether you wish it or no* in a very direct, very literal way.

"Dear Mae," she whispered, gently stroking Miss Mitchelmore's face in a manner I would not personally have found comforting (too many things in my part of reality can do very strange things to a face, and if you don't wish to wake up with the wrong head in the morning, be very careful what you allow to touch yours) but which Miss Mitchelmore apparently did. "I am quite sure all will end well for you. If it does not, nothing in this world makes any sense."

Having lived in this world since before time was time, I could—had I the heart and the desire to expose myself—have told Miss Bickle there and then that nothing in it *does* make sense (take, for example, my own exile from the Other Court for transgressions so minor that they are still not at all worth discussing). But the reasoning seemed to suffice for her and, while it was unlikely to suffice for Miss Mitchelmore, the sentiment behind it was a balm to her, and they passed their second night on the road in quiet and comfort.

To Miss Bickle's disappointment, their third day's journey ended with as little violence or romance as the first two and they arrived in the North Riding just as the sun was beginning to dip towards the horizon. The country seat of the Landrakes, Leighfield Hall, was situated—as its name suggests—in fields beside a little river called the Leigh, and its magnificent grounds, wide and green and far less gothic than Miss Mitchelmore had been fearing and Miss Bickle hoping, spread before the travellers now like the emerald gardens that lie on the far side of the moon.

My apologies, that analogy may not be terribly meaningful to mortal readers.

They were large, and green, and pretty.

Although less haunted by monsters.

The elder Mr. Bickle had shown enough foresight to write ahead to the Duke of Annadale to inform her of the ladies' coming, but had also shown enough shrewdness to make it clear that they would be leaving too soon to have waited for any return letter. It was something of a shabby strategy by the standards of polite society, but then he was also, by the standards of that society, something of a shabby man, having made his fortune in tin instead of inheriting it from the misdeeds of his forebears like a respectable gentleman. Thus it was with a reasonable certainty that they were expected but somewhat lesser certainty that they would be admitted that Miss Mitchelmore and Miss Bickle pulled up at last at the gates of Leighfield.

They were met by a footman at the carriage, and by another at the door, and shown through at once to the northwest drawing room, where the Duke of Annadale was waiting.

She stood by the fireplace beneath a portrait of a smiling man in a deep-blue riding coat. He held a crop in one hand and looked like he did not give one single solitary shit what anybody thought of him. I'd have admired the fellow immensely were it not for my instinctive disdain of all mortals.

"I was informed you would be coming," she told Miss Mitchelmore. "You should not have."

Miss Bickle clapped her hands. "Oh this is wonderful, it's going *exactly* as I expected."

"Edward"—the Duke of Annadale looked at one of the footmen coolly—"please escort Miss Bickle to the French Guest Room. I think this conversation would be improved by her absence."

"*Exactly* as expected," Miss Bickle repeated as she was led away, leaving Miss Mitchelmore and the Duke of Annadale alone in a spacious but, to Miss Mitchelmore's eye, seldom-used drawing room.

When she was gone Miss Mitchelmore spent rather longer than was comfortable or useful staring at the carpet. "I am sorry," she said. "I should not have come, but Lysistrata can be as persuasive as her namesake."

"But by different methods, I hope," replied the Duke of Annadale.

And this, of all things, triggered something in Miss Mitchelmore. She looked up sharply, her eyes all defiance and her lips all—well, let us be honest, they were mostly just lips. "I do not see what concern it would be of yours if she *had* chosen to use . . . conjugal coercion to sway me. You have made no claim on me or, if you have made one, you have failed to act upon it. Or even to admit to the *possibility* of acting on it."

"And you still can barely speak of the possibilities you are discussing." The Duke of Annadale hovered on the edge of a sneer. "*Conjugal coercion* indeed."

"I see you maintain your perverse insistence that vulgarity is the same thing as confidence."

That earned a smile, at least. "And you maintain your girlish assumption that avoiding bad words is a magic that wards against bad outcomes."

"Very well, if you insist." Miss Mitchelmore took a deep breath and a single step towards the Duke of Annadale. They were still some distance apart, but there was an energy in the air between them. "If I were *fucking* Lysistrata Bickle, then I should at least have the gratification of knowing that she enjoyed and welcomed it."

"That girl seems like she enjoys and welcomes anything."

"She has a sanguine temperament, but she is a better judge of character than I think I sometimes give her credit for. She knew my feelings for you before I did."

"A clock left unwound," replied the Duke of Annadale, herself taking a step closer, putting the women mere feet from one another now, "will still show the correct time twice a day."

"She also said I should come to you."

"Which demonstrates that twice a day is not all day."

Still emboldened, Miss Mitchelmore took a step closer. Then another. She reached out and took the Duke of Annadale by the hand, twining their fingers together. "You want me, Georgiana. You have said as much. I know as much. And I want you and"— she put a hand up to stifle the Duke of Annadale's inevitable reply—"before you say I do not know what I want, I do. I have travelled three days through—admittedly—clement weather and no danger whatsoever, with several servants to protect me and a lady companion for company, but I have still travelled all this way to be here. With you."

The Duke of Annadale took hold of Miss Mitchelmore's wrist, moved her hand away from her mouth, and held it a moment, thumb pressed along the pulse-line. "And you think me so cloistered that I would have nothing better to do than indulge you?"

"Well"—Miss Mitchelmore risked a smile—"I cannot say that you seem overbusy from where I am standing."

"I inherited an excellent steward from my father. The estate needs little attention. But even so, I have diversions enough here without you."

There was no room to step closer, but there was room for half a step and Miss Mitchelmore took it. "What manner of diversions?"

"I read," replied the Duke of Annadale coolly, "and sew."

Which surprised a laugh from Miss Mitchelmore. "You sew?"

"On occasion."

"You shall have to make me a shawl."

Unable to help herself, the Duke of Annadale let her lips curl into half a smile. "Come now, you have had two of my cloaks already, I cannot be constantly robing you."

Had I taken the form of a shadow, I could not have slipped between the two women, so near one another were they standing now. "You realise," Miss Mitchelmore observed, "that I could kiss you from here very easily."

"Yet you have failed to."

"I was testing your resolve."

One of the Duke of Annadale's eyebrows arched. "And what did your tests determine?"

"You could have stepped away, but you did not. You could have kissed *me*, but you did not. I think you are irresolute, Georgiana."

"Perhaps you are failing to measure my resolve relative to my temptation."

Unweaving her fingers from her companion's, Miss Mitchelmore laid a hand gently over the Duke of Annadale's heart. "And to what do I tempt you?"

"Ill-considered action."

And Miss Mitchelmore, considering her actions, perhaps, less well than she might have done, leaned across the last of the distance separating her from the Duke of Annadale, and kissed her.

26

They had kissed once before, but it had been a brief and perfunctory thing, an experiment in crossing lines and living as one ought not. This was different. It was a challenge, a standing forth and saying in the strange mortal language of lips and hands and sighs, *I am here and I will not be ignored.*

It was, I thought, mostly the Duke of Annadale's will that moved them in the direction of the chaise longue, but it was Miss Mitchelmore who drew them down, the Duke of Annadale kneeling beside her.

"And is this," the Duke of Annadale whispered in her ear, "what you were hoping for?"

Miss Mitchelmore gave a hesitant nod. "I think so."

That stopped the Duke of Annadale. She laughed and sat back. "You think so? I can't tell if I'm offended."

"I did not mean—" Miss Mitchelmore blushed. "I am glad that you are—we are rather running to the edge of my experience."

"And what of your imagination?" asked the Duke of Annadale.

"It has not been entirely specific."

A look of mingled lust and doubt crept across the Duke of Annadale's face. "You are not, I think, making the best case for my ravishing you."

"I thought innocents were prime subjects for ravishment."

"They are." The Duke of Annadale gave a regretful sigh. "But I have been trying to avoid—"

"Spoiling me?" suggested Miss Mitchelmore, a little indignant. "Depriving my future husband of his rights?"

"Leading you into anything you might not have chosen."

Miss Mitchelmore propped herself up on one elbow and, with her other hand, reached out to run her gloved fingers down the Duke of Annadale's cheek. "I choose this, Georgiana. I choose everything. You have stopped touching me only for a few moments and already I mislike it intensely."

"Everything is rather a lot to request."

"Even so, I request it. If it is too much, then we can stop, surely?"

And at that the Duke of Annadale laughed again. "Oh, my dear, if only it were that simple. The problem with *too much* is that one so often only sees it *too late*."

Miss Mitchelmore raised an eyebrow. "For a woman who claims to harbour dangerous passions, you are being curiously timid."

"It pays to be timid around dangerous things."

Miss Mitchelmore cocked her head to one side. "Does it? I should have thought that the moments of danger were the moments when timidity could prove most perilous. Decisive action has much to recommend it."

A glint of joyful cruelty caught in the Duke of Annadale's eye, and she reached beside the chaise longue to a small basket. From it, she withdrew a roll of ribbon and a pair of long scissors.

"What are you . . ." Miss Mitchelmore began.

"I did tell you I sewed." And without further explanation she gathered up Miss Mitchelmore's hands, guided them together, and bound them with ribbon, securing them first to one another, and then, via a length of the same material, to a decorative curl of wood that protruded from the chaise. This left Miss Mitchelmore with her arms raised, her elbows bent, and her hands held behind her head in an attitude that left her stretched and—to the eye of a capricious fairy at least—eminently vulnerable.

She did not struggle, but she did look up at the Duke of Annadale with some apprehension. "This is . . . unexpected."

"But not unwelcome?"

"I don't . . . I don't think so. Just unfamiliar. And I am not certain *why.*"

A smile crept across the Duke of Annadale's lips. "You said you wanted everything. And if you will recall, I once said that I wanted you naked and bound."

"If I draw attention to the fact I am still clothed," Miss Mitchelmore observed, "I suspect I would only be making myself look foolish."

Taking up the scissors, the Duke of Annadale snipped neatly through Miss Mitchelmore's sleeves. "You would. But I might have enjoyed that."

"I am beginning to think your reputation for wickedness is more deserved than I had imagined."

"Disappointed?" asked the Duke of Annadale. Without waiting for an answer, she used the scissor blades to slip Miss Mitchelmore's dress down past her shoulders, cold steel gliding against warm skin, and then laid soft, tantalising kisses the length of her collarbone.

Miss Mitchelmore did not reply, but made sounds that suggested disappointment was not, at least, an immediate risk.

Slowly, the Duke of Annadale peeled Miss Mitchelmore's dress the rest of the way down, Miss Mitchelmore arching her body to aid the process in a manner that spoke of hunger. When the dress was gone, and Miss Mitchelmore was reduced to her stockings and stays, the Duke of Annadale rose, turned, and walked away.

"Georgiana?" Miss Mitchelmore's voice had more than a little shock in it. "What are you doing?"

The Duke of Annadale turned back. "Exercising control. You asked for passion and, for me at least, a certain element of passion is power."

"You intend to leave me tied to a chaise longue?" Miss Mitchelmore did not sound distressed, but neither did she sound entirely credulous.

"Think of it as a charming reference back to our first meeting."

"When you left me weeping in a garden?"

The Duke of Annadale moistened her lips. "You did weep so very, very prettily."

"And would you stay now if I wept again?" From the look in her eyes, Miss Mitchelmore did not seem close to weeping.

"I might."

Within the restrictions imposed upon her, Miss Mitchelmore arranged herself as decorously as she could. She said nothing, but the Duke of Annadale, she noted, did not turn away. "You do not appear to be leaving."

"No."

"Afraid I'll escape?"

For a moment the Duke of Annadale hesitated. "No. But I confess I am finding it harder to stop *looking* at you than I thought I would."

"You have looked at me before."

"Not in such flattering light. And I have long believed that you were made to be looked at."

Turning as best she was able with her hands bound, Miss Mitchelmore faced the Duke of Annadale. "That is not the compliment you think it is."

"No? You are very beautiful, Maelys."

"So are sunsets. I am not sure I would wish to be one. I do not want to be *looked at*, Georgiana, I want to be *touched*."

With a last glance at the door, the Duke of Annadale walked back to Miss Mitchelmore's side. "It seems I have misjudged who, precisely, has the power here."

"I am a woman of hidden depths."

Kneeling, the Duke of Annadale removed a glove and brushed one fingertip along the exposed edge of Miss Mitchelmore's upper arm, making her shiver rather prettily. "And what do you intend to do with these new-revealed depths and new-found powers?"

"Command you to please me." Miss Mitchelmore was doing her best, I felt, to convey confidence, but there was uncertainty beneath the bravado.

"Commands is it now?" The Duke of Annadale gently kissed Miss Mitchelmore on the arm, the shoulder, and then *almost* on the lips, before drawing back just further than Miss Mitchelmore's bindings would let her rise to reach. "But such a *broad* command." She let her hand wander the length of Miss Mitchelmore's body, coming to rest just above the tops of her stockings, and traced idle patterns on her thigh. "After all, there are many things you might find pleasurable."

In illustration, the Duke of Annadale moved her hand upwards, and Miss Mitchelmore responded first with anticipation, then with surprise, and then with surrender, arching herself into the Duke of Annadale's touch with an enthusiasm that bordered on abandon.

"You like that, then?"

Miss Mitchelmore gave a short, somewhat distracted nod.

"Good. This will work a lot better if you can tell me when you like something."

And that, it seemed, Miss Mitchelmore could do very well indeed.

All the while, the Duke of Annadale never took her eyes from Miss Mitchelmore's face, and I never took my eyes from the Duke of Annadale. In part, this was something resembling courtesy. Mostly, though, it was because, while I have no compunctions about sneaking into mortals' bedchambers and watching them do whatever nocturnal, organic things humans do, it does not *interest* me a great deal, at least in its mechanics. Its *dynamics,* however, the push and pull of wanting and withholding and all the pretty alchemies of desire? *Those* fascinate me.

And the Duke of Annadale's face was very, very fascinating. I am familiar with wanting, although my wants are often fleeting. What I saw in her eyes as she whispered Miss Mitchelmore's name, as she asked her softly where her pleasure lay, was the strangest kind of wanting I had ever beheld. A desire to possess and to serve and, perhaps more than anything else, a desire—a deep and impossible and unfulfillable desire—to flee.

At last they were done, and Miss Mitchelmore subsided, her cheeks wet with the kind of tears mortals enjoy shedding.

"I always thought you wept prettily," whispered the Duke of Annadale.

"Had I known this was what you meant," replied a still-flushed Miss Mitchelmore, "I would have let you move me to it more readily."

"And you have no regrets?" asked the Duke of Annadale.

"Only that I waited so long."

Half smiling, the Duke of Annadale withdrew her hand from between Miss Mitchelmore's thighs, skimmed it the length of her body, and brought it, at last, to her lips. Miss Mitchelmore, still straining a little against her bonds, leaned forwards and took the Duke of Annadale's fingers in her mouth. When she had cleaned herself from her lover's hands, the Duke of Annadale leaned over her once more and kissed her, deeply this time. Claiming, or trying to claim.

But Miss Mitchelmore was not, it seemed, in a mood to be taken so easily. And she made clear with her lips and her tongue and, in at least one moment, her teeth that she considered herself owning as much as owned.

"Gods and horrors," the Duke of Annadale sighed, gazing down at Miss Mitchelmore's satisfyingly ravished body. "You are a wondrous creature."

"With you," she replied, "I confess I sometimes feel like one. But I'm still just me."

"In my experience, *just me* is a lot more than most people give it credit for." Saying no more, the Duke of Annadale rose and, for the second time that evening, walked to the door.

Miss Mitchelmore looked at her with confident circumspection. "I'm sorry, Georgiana, but I will not fall for that a second time."

"I shall see you in the morning," she said. "If you manage to free yourself, then ring for a servant, and they will show you to your rooms."

"You expect me to show myself to a servant naked?"

"I expect you to work something out. You have proven yourself a resourceful woman. Good night, Maelys."

Before Miss Mitchelmore could reply, the Duke of Annadale had gone, leaving her tied to a chaise longue with her postcoital glow rapidly fading.

Electing, as Miss Bickle would have done, to view her present predicament as an adventure and trusting, perhaps against her better judgement, that the Duke of Annadale would not leave her in a position of real danger, Miss Mitchelmore focused her efforts on liberty.

Now that she was making an earnest attempt to free herself, rather than making—to some extent at least—a play of struggle for her own and her partner's gratification, she found escape easy enough. The loop to which she had been attached was wide and smooth, and it took only a little leaning to slip her hands free and back over her head.

Untying the knot was trickier, since the Duke of Annadale had tied it with—and I say this with grudging admiration—practised expertise. In the end, the knot itself proved intractable, but by an awkward process of sliding a pair of scissors between her wrists and operating them with thumbs and teeth, she was able to remove the ribbons. Watching them flutter to the floor felt strangely celebratory, like unwrapping a gift. Albeit one, in this case, that Miss Mitchelmore had already received.

Her nakedness was the next obstacle to be overcome, but this was fixed easily. The cuts to the sleeves of her dress had been straight and neat, which meant with a few pins they were restored—if not to beauty or fashion, then at least to their minimal functionality of remaining over her shoulders.

That left only navigation. She rang for a servant and then waited, apprehensive, for one to arrive. She was becoming uncomfortably aware that the chaise was rather damp and she herself smelled unmistakably of carnality. She settled into a different chair and tried to pin her sleeves more firmly in order that she not expose her shoulders to a stranger.

The stranger arrived in the shape of a wide-eyed girl of perhaps fifteen who seemed as perplexed by the situation as Miss Mitchelmore. "You rang, milady?"

"I'm not a lady," Miss Mitchelmore corrected.

"You rang, miss?"

"Yes." Not entirely sure what tone was appropriate for a guest in the house of a dead duke whose daughter had just fucked her near senseless, Miss Mitchelmore opted for one of calm detachment. "Will you escort me to my room?"

"Of course, miss. Though truth be told I'm a bit unsure as to the way myself."

That was discouraging. "Are you new then?"

"Yes'm. Her ladyship brought me in special when she heard you'd be coming. Said I was to do for the guests."

Rising, Miss Mitchelmore went to the young girl's side. "And your name?"

"Polly, miss. From the village. And I hope you'll be pleased with me, miss, as I've not worked in a big house before and it's far better than farm work."

"And you were brought here for me?"

Polly nodded. "Her ladyship said as she was expecting a young lady visitor and as she'd need taking care of. And she's known of my family for years on accounts of how we live on her land—well, her father's land as was, am I talking too much?"

"For most mistresses, yes. But I am in a new house with only one friend with me and in honesty am glad of the company."

Miss Mitchelmore needed to say no more. With little deference to rank or station, Polly launched into an extended quasi-monologue about her history (brief, since she was young and ill-travelled); her family (two brothers, three sisters, parents, and a grandmother living in the same house); her education (minimal); and her hopes of marriage (a charming young man in the next village). She attempted to draw Miss Mitchelmore forth on similar subjects, but since her own answers would have been *I have recently murdered a man, one brother presently at Eton, my parents are eccentrically devoted to the sciences but my governess ensured I acquired accomplishments* and *I am fucking your mistress,* she demurred on most of them.

It was, by most standards—especially those of a young lady who would otherwise have been wandering a stately home alone and unescorted—a genial conversation. So genial, indeed, that it was not for some time that Polly realised that they were lost.

"I'm terribly sorry'm"—she shrank a little, not quite trusting Miss Mitchelmore's otherwise informal manner to shield her from censure—"I think we've taken the wrong turn. This is the mistress's rooms."

It was a natural enough error for a girl new to the house, but Miss Mitchelmore was nothing if not alert to serendipity. "It's quite all right, Polly. I can find my own way from here."

Fortunately—or at least fortunately for the direct progression of Miss Mitchelmore's proposed plan of action; how fortunate it was in the overall scheme of things may be another matter—Polly had not been instructed to *prevent* her charge from wandering unescorted and therefore obediently left Miss Mitchelmore alone.

It was not really the done thing to surprise a lady in her chamber. But the Duke of Annadale had left her tied to a chaise longue, and that surely required at least a little payback. Although in hindsight, Miss Mitchelmore should probably have remembered that the Duke of Annadale slept with a pistol beside her bed.

CHAPTER

27

Of the new experiences Miss Mitchelmore had discovered in her brief time at Leighfield, being held at gunpoint was definitely the least pleasant. She raised her hands and hoped that the light from the doorway, while making her an easier target, would also make it clearer that she was not a threat.

"It is impolite," the Duke of Annadale told her, "to enter a lady's bedchamber unannounced."

"It is impolite to tie ladies to items of furniture as well."

"Really? I don't recall it being mentioned in any of the normal handbooks."

"I think it can be taken as a specific case of a general principle."

The Duke of Annadale returned the pistol to its place on the bedside table. Her room was in full darkness and so Miss Mitchelmore could make out little beyond her shape and the shadow of the pistol. "So you have come to complain in person."

"I have come to show you that I have my own will."

A laugh echoed from the shadows. "Your decision to travel the length of the country to track me down and demand that I fuck you already demonstrated that quite admirably."

"Perhaps. But since you did"—the hesitation was momentary but noticeable—"fuck me, I thought it important to show that I am still . . . still myself."

There was a rustle of bedclothes as the Duke of Annadale turned and sat up. "Who else would you be?"

"That's what concerns me," Miss Mitchelmore admitted. "Your mistress, perhaps?"

"Oh, you're *definitely* my mistress. But you are also certainly yourself. Nell Gwynn remained Nell Gwynn even when she was riding Charles's sceptre."

Miss Mitchelmore shifted uncomfortably. "I am not sure *mistress* sits well with me."

"You came to my house and offered yourself to me with no expectation of marriage. What else would you call yourself?"

"An innocent girl of whom you have taken advantage?" suggested Miss Mitchelmore with more irony than rancour.

"I think that appellation does us both a disservice."

Deciding that she had loitered in the doorway long enough, Miss Mitchelmore took a decisive step forwards. I slipped in behind her just in time to avoid being shut out. Not that mortal doors are any great hinderance to me. "What if we were to say that *you* were *my* mistress?"

"Sadly, the rigid orders of precedence are against you. I am the daughter of a duke, you merely the granddaughter of an earl."

"Alas, station thwarts us once more."

For a moment, there was silence. Then the Duke of Annadale said, "I note that you are still in my bedchamber."

"Yes."

"Do you, perhaps, intend to return to your own?"

"It is a possibility I have considered. But it would not be my preference."

There was another sound in the darkness, a shifting in the Duke of Annadale's position, her posture almost defensive. "Thank you, but I do not sleep with my lovers. It sets a bad precedent."

Miss Mitchelmore smiled to herself in the darkness. "I like *lover* better than *mistress*. But we have shared a bed before."

"That was different. You were distressed and I was not—we had not . . ."

"Now who is shying away from wicked words?"

The comment was, in my estimation, fair, but it provoked a disgruntled growl from the Duke of Annadale. "Forgive my delicacy. When we last shared a bed, it was before I spread you upon a chaise longue and fucked you until you wept, is that better?"

"It is more like you."

Another sound of disagreement echoed from the darkness. "You know little of what I am like. That is why I propose we limit our relationship to carnality henceforth."

"That seems cruel."

"I am a cruel woman."

Miss Mitchelmore crossed the room almost hurriedly. "You are not cruel, Georgiana. You have protected me, and comforted me, and kept my secrets and asked nothing of me in return."

"Oh, grow up." The contempt in the Duke of Annadale's voice was palpable, so palpable it felt, to my ear, almost forced. "I am given to lasciviousness, and I desired you. Any good I have done you flowed only from that motivation, and while I flatter myself that you have profited by the arrangement, you should not make it more than it is."

To that, Miss Mitchelmore had no reply.

"Go back to your room, Maelys. I will speak with you tomorrow."

"But this—"

"Tomorrow."

"I do not know where my room *is*. Polly got lost, that's partly why I am here."

At last that stirred a laugh from the Duke of Annadale. And a proper laugh, rather than the haughty *hah* she would sometimes fall back on. "Very well." She rose and lit a candle. In the dim circle of light, she was revealed to be wearing a long, white nightdress that, combined with her distant manner, made her look like her own ghost.

Silently, she led Miss Mitchelmore out into the halls. Leighfield was, at its heart, a modern building with little of the labyrinthine layout that one might find in older or more haunted manors. Miss Bickle, I'm sure, had found this fact profoundly disappointing. As such, the walk was short and the path easy to remember. They stopped outside the door to Miss Mitchelmore's room and stood, in the candlelight, looking at one another.

"Goodnight, Georgiana," whispered Miss Mitchelmore.

The Duke of Annadale raised a hand and brushed her fingers gently across Miss Mitchelmore's cheek. "Goodnight, Maelys."

And in the fatal few seconds in which Miss Mitchelmore was debating whether to lean in for a kiss, the lady was gone.

With a sigh—more frustrated than despairing, I was glad to observe—Miss Mitchelmore went into her room, lay down, and failed to sleep.

She was awoken, or at least stirred from that fitful half-rest that is the domain of the harried, the hunted, and the deeply peeved, by the arrival of Polly, who informed her that breakfast was served, that she was here to help miss get ready if miss required it, and that the other miss, the one with the big eyes and the habit of talking about queer things if miss doesn't mind her saying, was outside hoping to see her.

"Show her in, Polly."

So Polly showed her in and Miss Bickle barrelled over to embrace Miss Mitchelmore. "Well?" she demanded. "How was it? Was it marvellous? Was it everything you dreamed?"

Miss Mitchelmore cast a significant look at Polly.

"Pretend I'm not here, miss."

"You're not furniture," Miss Mitchelmore replied. "And I mean no slight, but speaking unguardedly in front of servants can end badly."

Polly nodded. "I understand miss. And I can go. But"—she looked down and shuffled her feet—"if it's a matter of you and her ladyship then, well, I shan't say anything. She's—that is—I've an older sister, miss, who she was fond of at one time so I do understand how it can be."

"You see." Miss Bickle gave a broad, happy smile. "She's quite to be trusted. Now, tell me every single detail of all the lewd, sweaty things you did to each other."

Miss Mitchelmore removed her nightdress and allowed Polly to help her into her stays and stockings. "I most certainly shall not. And I shall neither confirm nor deny the lewdness nor sweatiness of any activities we may have partaken in."

"My sister was the same," Polly confirmed. "But she always said as her ladyship was a very satisfying person to be around, and I took that to be a good thing for her."

A cynical, perhaps even unworthy suspicion was creeping over Miss Mitchelmore. "Polly," she asked, "what *happened* to your sister?"

"Married a fellow from Bayesridge. Nice man. Good teeth."

"Oh that's fortunate." Miss Bickle had seated herself on the end of Miss Mitchelmore's bed and was busying herself picking loose threads from the counterpane. "Grandpapa always said I should be certain to find a man with good teeth." She stopped, blinked, and thought for a moment. "Or was it a horse?"

"A horse with good teeth?" asked Polly. "Or a man with a good horse?"

Miss Bickle gave an apologetic smile and shook her head like a dog drying itself. "I'm sorry, I simply can't recall."

"But she is well?" Miss Mitchelmore continued, not quite willing to let her friend derail the discussion wholly into matters of equine dentistry. "She is not—that is to say nothing has—Lady Georgiana was not unkind to her."

"Not as she's let on," offered Polly, whose attention was now turning to Miss Mitchelmore's outer garments. The dress from the night before had been discreetly set aside, to be replaced with another in powder blue. "And she isn't a timid woman, my sister. If her ladyship had done her wrong, she'd've said. Wouldn't have done anything, of course, on account of there being nothing the likes of us *could* do, but she'd have not let me take a place at the house if she'd thought her ladyship would use me ill."

A notion uncomfortably like jealousy crept into Miss Mitchelmore's mind. "How *has* she used you?"

"Just brung me in to take care of you miss. I'm not like my sister, and her ladyship hasn't tried to make me like her, if that's what you're asking."

It had been, although Miss Mitchelmore rather wished it hadn't. It was a line of questioning that reflected poorly on everybody concerned. "I'm sorry Polly, that was indelicate of me."

"Not at all, miss. You've got to ask these things, else how'll you know 'em. I should also say in case I've not made it clear that I'll be accepting no improper instructions from yourself neither."

"I wasn't intending to give any."

"Not that I'm saying you're not very pretty miss, I'm sure you and the other miss are both very pretty indeed for them as has eyes for that kind of thing, but I don't and shan't."

Dressed, Miss Mitchelmore settled in and let Polly start work on her hair. "I really wasn't intending to."

"Nor I," added Miss Bickle, who seemed a little put out that her lack of interest in coercing the staff into sapphic entanglements had been merely assumed. "Although if you had a change of heart, then I for one would be delighted to keep an open mind about such matters. For I have never kissed a lady before and am certain it must be a diverting experience."

Over Miss Mitchelmore's shoulder, Polly gave Miss Bickle a helpful look. "I know a couple of girls in the village might be up for it."

"Shepherdesses?" asked Miss Bickle hopefully. "Or milkmaids?"

Polly's expression turned apologetic. "Neither."

"Oh. Then I'm not sure there's much point."

Trying to turn towards Polly without moving her hair into an unhelpful position, Miss Mitchelmore flexed her neck slightly. "Don't mind Lizzie, she's given to these fancies."

"All the best people are, miss."

"There." Miss Bickle grinned. "Have I not always said as much? Tell me, Polly, are you familiar with any fairy rings in the vicinity?"

There are some questions, in some company, which act very much as sparks to tinder, and so it was with Miss Bickle, Polly, and the question of fairies. Within a few short minutes, minutes during which Miss Mitchelmore found herself having to put the finishing touches to her own hair, the visitors had learned of a half dozen local sites of supernatural interest, all of them—I can vouch—authentic, and several of them supremely deadly.

Miss Bickle's overweening desire to visit at least one of these locations was the entirety of her conversation on the way down to breakfast and, when the Duke of Annadale failed to materialise and the housekeeper—a tall, severe woman who looked like a smartly dressed razorblade and went by the name of Mrs. Scott— informed them that Her Ladyship had not, since her return, been in the habit of arising before the early afternoon, and even then was inclined to haunt her chambers in silence, Miss Mitchelmore had acquiesced. Indeed, in many ways she had been glad of the distraction.

There were, after all, few ways to make oneself feel more like a person's mistress than to sit demurely in the drawing room and wait to be summoned to her pleasure.

28

That morning, the two ladies went walking. And there was, in those days, much to see in Yorkshire if one had a mind to wander. Of course, my people would, in general, rather you *didn't*. The dales—as far as we are concerned—belong to the boggarts and to my own hobgoblin kin, and while there are times and hours and seasons when we care for visitors, when we can even be hospitable, mostly we prefer that you keep to your places, and let us keep to ours.

But mortals do not take instruction well and seldom heed warnings that are not backed in blood. And so Miss Bickle and Miss Mitchelmore roved across the hills, heedless of the things that dwelt beneath their feet, and into the woods somewhat *less* heedless of the things that could hunt them there. Miss Bickle was, it seemed, very keen to see a barghest, although I could have told her it would be quite unworthy of her time. All dogs look alike.

They came at last to a swift and narrow river that flowed through the woods a little way out from Leighfield. It was here, they had been told, that they might see kelpies that make their way down from the Scottish borders in order to drown a slightly different kind of traveller.

"And why," asked Miss Mitchelmore as they walked along the banks of the river—although they were not banks, in truth, but rocky overhangs slick with moss that concealed the deep gate to the lost kingdom of Queen Janet—"are you so very keen that we be exposed to risk of drowning?"

"I am sure we shall not *actually* be drowned," Miss Bickle asserted with her customary confidence in her own indestructibility. "A kelpie will only drown you if you climb onto its back, and I see no reason why either of us should unless it took the form of an exceptionally fine horse indeed."

"I sometimes wonder if you don't think altogether too much of horses."

Miss Bickle looked plaintive. "Oh, but Mae, they're such beautiful creatures, and if I had a magical one I should be the happiest girl in the world—assuming of course that I avoid drowning during its acquisition. Although I think I mostly invited you on this walk so that you might feel inclined to share more about your personal experiences of"—she made a polite clearing-the-throat sound—"being swept away on currents that threaten to dash you apart."

Coming to an abrupt stop, Miss Mitchelmore folded her arms and glared at her companion. "Lizzie, did you bring me out to a potentially haunted stretch of river because you thought it would inspire me to confide in you about my intimate life?"

Miss Bickle blinked. "Is it not working?"

"Why would you expect it to work?"

Crestfallen, Miss Bickle turned her attention to the river,

perhaps seeing in her mind's eye some echo of the strange, drowned palaces that would await her if only she had the courage to leap. "Well, it's so . . . torrential."

"Torrential?"

"Yes. You know"—she waved her hands as if to imitate the elemental majesty of the river—"that sort of intense, sort of . . . rushing, sort of . . . pounding."

"Lizzie, I declare you think far too much of horses *and pounding.*"

Huffing in a manner that secured her position as one of the nation's great huffers, Miss Bickle tossed her head. "I have no siblings and spend half the year in Cornwall, where my only society is Papa's artistic friends. Thoughts of pounding are one of my few diversions."

"I thought you went for a lot of walks."

"I do!" Miss Bickle nodded fervent agreement. "And then I spend hours sitting by rivers and thinking to myself how quiet and simple my life is and how marvellous it would be if some broad-shouldered, iron-thewed water spirit with green hair would rise from the briny deeps and—"

"Rivers aren't briny," Miss Mitchelmore pointed out.

"It's my fantasy"—still huffing for England, Miss Bickle sat down on the mossy ground, blissfully unaware of the ecstatic deaths that lurked in sunken caves beneath her—"and I shall make my river as briny as I please. And in that fantasy I shall be carried away by a lusty river spirit and shown pleasures the like of which mortal women only dream of."

Miss Mitchelmore came and sat beside her friend. "In a . . . poundy way?"

"I don't see what's so very wrong with that." Miss Bickle had, I suspect, never seen what was wrong with anything.

"Well, my experience is limited," Miss Mitchelmore began, acutely aware that she was about to allow herself to be drawn on the very topic she had determined not to be drawn on, "but from what I have seen and . . . well . . . felt so far . . ." she trailed off, looking down and blushing.

Reaching out, Miss Bickle shook her friend encouragingly but impatiently by the shoulder. "Come on, Mae, you can tell me. And there's nobody around to hear except the fairies."

"I am sure that there are no fairies around *either.*" Miss Mitchelmore was, of course, spectacularly wrong in this regard. "But if it will help with your . . . hydraulic fixations then, well, in my very limited experience, those particular kinds of pleasures are less a matter of pounding than they are of—I'm sorry, Lizzie, I really don't think I can talk about this."

"Please?" Miss Bickle gave Miss Mitchelmore her biggest, most imploring eyes.

"Than they are of attention to detail," Miss Mitchelmore finished. "And communication seems to be important."

"Oh." The answer did not seem to have satisfied. "That all sounds very complicated."

"A little, I suppose. But I'm learning that Georgiana is a complicated woman."

Miss Bickle made a wordless sound of curiosity, prompting her friend to continue.

"After we'd—after she and I had—she wouldn't share a bed with me."

"Oh." And then Miss Bickle brightened. "But then you should have come to my room. That would have been so jolly."

"I love you, Lysistrata. But you weren't quite the company I was looking for in the moment."

With a sense of empathy that far outstripped her senses of

decorum, tact, or for that matter her sense in general, Miss Bickle wrapped a comforting arm around her friend. "I'm sorry. Is she being beastly to you?"

"Not beastly, no," Miss Mitchelmore admitted. "Just . . . I don't know, cold? In a strange way I felt she cared for me more when we were in Bath."

"You were in danger in Bath," Miss Bickle pointed out. "Perhaps that brought out her protective side."

"Perhaps." The thought was a gloomy one, and Miss Mitchelmore allowed it to gloom her.

Miss Bickle, on the other hand, lived in a world made entirely of lemonade and silver linings. She cast a significant glance at the river, which roiled only a few feet away, promising sweet asphyxia in its cold embrace. "Why don't—"

"No."

"But I haven't—"

"You were going to suggest that I throw myself into the river which we have been *explicitly told* kelpies drown people in and see if she comes to save me. She won't. She's back at the house. And if I get dashed to pieces on the rocks, then, while my romantic difficulties will, I suppose, definitely be over, they won't have ended in a way I find pleasing."

Deep in the rushing waters, the queen of that drowning kingdom laughed a laugh made of rocks and algae.

"I suppose it would be rather a risk," admitted Miss Bickle. "But then isn't love *worth* taking risks?"

"Some risks," Miss Mitchelmore half agreed. "But not those *specific* risks."

A broad grin was already spreading across Miss Bickle's face. "Oh, *Mae*, that's wonderful."

Suspecting she had walked into a trap, but not certain how

deep or dangerous a one, Miss Mitchelmore gave her friend a questioning look.

"I said that love made it worth taking risks, and you *didn't* respond by denying that you loved Lady Georgiana."

For a while Miss Mitchelmore said nothing. Then, when she had said as much nothing as she was able, she added, "No."

"So you *do* love her?"

"I—in Bath I was discontent being only somebody she cared for. Here I find myself discontent being only somebody she . . ."

"Pounds?"

"I told you there was very little pounding involved. Here I find myself discontent being only somebody she fucks."

Miss Bickle gave a little squeal and clapped her hands over her mouth. "Maelys *Mitchelmore,* where did you learn such language?"

"From a briny river spirit." Turning to Miss Bickle, Miss Mitchelmore put her hand on her friend's. "But I think you may be right. I am still not certain what the proper word is for—for anything between me and Georgiana, but any lesser name seems inadequate to it."

Tears began to well up in Miss Bickle's eyes. "Oh, Mae, I'm so *happy* for you."

And then she threw her arms around Miss Mitchelmore and refused to let go for far longer than was necessary or seemly.

I have always liked Miss Bickle.

———— • ————

They returned to Leighfield in midafternoon, where they were greeted by Mrs. Scott, who informed them that the mistress was awake and requesting the pleasure of Miss Mitchelmore's company at her earliest convenience.

After a brief discussion with Miss Bickle about the relative merits of coyness versus boldness, Miss Mitchelmore ascended to the Duke of Annadale's bedchamber, knocked, and entered.

Inside she found the Duke of Annadale reclining on the bed dressed in a gown of fashionable cut but unfashionable colour. The lady had always favoured darker shades, but this was an evening dress in sheer black, details picked out in gold to match the embroidery on her gloves and the necklace at her throat.

"Undress," the Duke of Annadale said.

Miss Mitchelmore had slipped her gown from her shoulders before it occurred to her that she did not, in fact, have to obey the Duke of Annadale's instructions. "And if I do not?"

"Then you may leave."

"That seems a rather stark choice."

"Yes."

Despite her hostess's ultimatum, Miss Mitchelmore elected to do neither.

"Well?"

"Is this truly what you would have of me?"

Still reclining in an attitude of almost studied loucheness, the Duke of Annadale flicked a dismissive wrist. "I did not ask you to leave London. You came out of an express desire to become my lover. This is how I *treat* my lovers."

"Polly says you fucked her sister."

"I hope the girl has better sense than to have used those exact words. But yes. I did. Does that bother you?"

"Why would it?"

The Duke of Annadale shrugged with one shoulder. "Jealousy?"

"It would have happened long before you met me. And you

think too highly of yourself if you believe I value your attentions so much that I would keep them from others. Especially when they come with such clear lack of regard."

One of the Duke of Annadale's eyebrows curled into a thin arch. "You read lack of regard into my attentions then?"

"You call and dismiss me like a servant. And there are words for the kind of servant you would make of me."

Finally un-reclining, the Duke of Annadale swung her legs off of the bed and sat forward. "Words like 'harlot'? Like 'whore'? In my years outside polite society I have known many such ladies, and the bulk of them were good people."

"That does not mean I wish you to treat me as one."

The Duke of Annadale rose from the bed and walked towards Miss Mitchelmore. "And I do not mean to make you feel like one." She smiled. "Well, not in a bad way. Although if it helps, I was always far more . . . utilitarian in my handling of my paid companions."

Not quite convinced this wasn't a trick, Miss Mitchelmore stood her ground. "More utilitarian than '*Undress*'?"

"Much. But I am sorry if I made you—" She broke off, apparently not quite willing to articulate any specific emotion. "Regardless, I see you are in a mood to be seduced." She took Miss Mitchelmore's ungloved hand and kissed it, sending a shiver up her arm and through her spine. "Come."

With a care that could not quite be called *loving*, the Duke of Annadale led Miss Mitchelmore to the bed and bid her sit. When sit she had, the Duke of Annadale knelt at her feet and began to unlace her boots.

"You have been walking, I see."

"You gave me no pressing reason to remain indoors."

Removing the boots entirely, the Duke of Annadale traced her thumbs along the line of Miss Mitchelmore's arches. "I am sorry, I have been a poor hostess."

"You haven't even spoken to Lizzie."

"Miss Bickle is lucky that I don't cast her out of the house entirely. She is not the individual who concerns me." As she spoke, the Duke of Annadale was continuing to rub Miss Mitchelmore's left foot. "Was it a very long walk?"

"Not very, but over rough ground some of the way." A thought struck Miss Mitchelmore, and she looked down. "Is this your attempt to make me feel less like a servant?"

"I am kneeling at your feet"—the Duke of Annadale looked up, a playful kind of malice in her eyes—"I am asking about the day you spent with somebody I know little of and care nothing for. I could practically be your wife."

"You have a cynical view of marriage."

"My father made my mother's life by turns tedious and miserable, raised my brothers to be brutes, wastrels, or absent, and he ignored me entirely. So no, I do not think well of marriage."

With her free foot, Miss Mitchelmore tried to stroke the Duke of Annadale's arm in what she hoped was a comforting way, although the gesture came out rather awkward. "I'm sorry. I believe my parents have always got on rather well."

"Then they are fortunate."

"I also do not think I have ever seen my mother kneel to anybody."

"Then think of this as mere apology."

Drawing her legs up, Miss Mitchelmore pulled her foot away. "Why must you be this way?"

"What way?"

"Why must one of us always be kneeling?"

That earned a laugh from the Duke of Annadale, and almost an affectionate one. "If I remember rightly, I have been the only one on my knees so far. You have been standing or lying."

Miss Mitchelmore only glared. "I meant that there did not— I admit I know little of these things, but from what I have learned from books, my mother, and my governess, they do not always need to involve such . . . explicit exploration of power."

"My darling Maelys, sex *is* power. Sometimes that power is vested in law, sometimes it comes from money changing hands, sometimes from the simple fact that when two people fuck, one of them almost *always* has more to lose than the other."

"I do not think I like this philosophy."

Still very much on her knees, the Duke of Annadale took hold of Miss Mitchelmore's foot again and drew it into her lap. "Then don't think of it as philosophy. Think of it as a game." She walked her fingers up Miss Mitchelmore's calf, then beneath her skirts and up her thigh to her garter and stocking tops. "Is there not, after all, some part of you that likes this view of me?"

Miss Mitchelmore looked down and seemed to take the question seriously. "I could, perhaps, grow accustomed to it. Although I would not like it to be the only view I ever saw."

Gently, the Duke of Annadale eased down Miss Mitchelmore's stocking, lowered her head, and pressed her lips to the top of Miss Mitchelmore's foot.

"Please don't, I've been on a long walk and I'm sure to be trail worn."

The Duke of Annadale looked up. "Maelys, Maelys, Maelys. I don't want you to be some spirit made of light and alabaster." She leaned down and kissed Maelys's foot again, along the arch and across the ankle then slowly up the calf. "I want you to be flesh and blood and sweat." She brushed up Miss Mitchelmore's leg towards the knee, sweeping petticoats back as she went. "I want you to walk where you wish and go where you wish."

Miss Mitchelmore had, I think, stopped listening at this point, focusing instead on the sensation of her lover's lips working across her skin.

"I want you to speak freely"—the Duke of Annadale's mouth inched upwards—"and live freely." She inched further. "I want you to feel freely, to touch freely, and to be touched." Further. "I want you to beg and to cry, and to call my name."

And, over the course of the next short while, Miss Mitchelmore obligingly did all of those things, while the Duke of Annadale gave up on speaking entirely and put her mouth to other uses. When they were done, and Miss Mitchelmore—her dress at least more intact than it had been after their last encounter—lay spent on the bed, the Duke of Annadale kissed her once, told her she was beautiful, and then sent her away.

CHAPTER

29

This pattern repeated itself most days for the next week. And for all Miss Mitchelmore would begin with fine thoughts of defiance, the Duke of Annadale's commitment to keeping their relationship a purely carnal one had been absolute.

It was a most vexing situation, and Miss Mitchelmore found herself most vexed by it. Or at least, she found herself intermittently vexed by it when she wasn't lost in a haze of distracting fucking. And even then she was vexed by certain elements of the arrangement. Like that she was always touched and seldom touching—at least, not in the ways that the Duke of Annadale touched her—and that she would, after every encounter, be dismissed.

Aside from that, she was left to the company of Miss Bickle, Polly, and occasional other members of the household staff. It was not an uncomfortable life, but nor was it one, Miss Mitchelmore was increasingly deciding, that she would wish to be permanent.

"She doesn't even . . ." she began confiding to Miss Bickle as they walked back from church on Sunday; the Duke of Annadale, caring little for gods of any kind, had not joined them. "That is to say, I have never even seen her undressed."

Miss Bickle clasped her hands to her bosom. "Oh Mae, how romantic."

"It doesn't *feel* very romantic."

"But she's so dark and brooding and Byronic."

"Which"—Miss Mitchelmore flushed—"I admit it has its attractions. But I fear it is rather more wearying in practice than I might have hoped."

"That," Miss Bickle said, "is because you're not approaching it correctly. You need to be seeking for the source of her inner darkness so that you can overcome it with the power of your ardour."

Miss Mitchelmore looked the opposite of convinced. "I'm not sure it works that way."

"But it has to. Else why have we come?"

Despite the pastoral beauty of the dales, the sunlight stippling the road back to Leighfield with a hundred shades of gold, Miss Mitchelmore did have to admit that her friend had a point. Alternating cycles of ecstasy and despondency, punctuated by short, strengthening walks in the countryside, were not the basis for long-term happiness. "And how do you propose I uncover this all-important darkness source?"

"Speak to the ghost?"

"There isn't a ghost."

"That you *know of.*" The certainty in Miss Bickle's voice was unassailable, but Miss Mitchelmore nonetheless did her best to assail it.

"You think hunting hypothetical ghosts is the most productive way to address my misgivings?"

Miss Bickle nodded.

"You don't think I should, perhaps, talk to her?"

"I was assuming you'd tried that already."

She had. And it had not worked. "Even so, it feels like conjuring the dead is rather an extreme next step."

"Well, if you'd had the sense to fall for a *proper* brooding aristocrat we'd be in a much older castle and there would be ghosts all over the place."

"But there aren't."

"Which is why we shall have to conjure them."

Miss Mitchelmore looped her arm through her friend's and drew her closer. It was a companionable walk in many ways. "Do you *know* how to conjure ghosts?"

"No, but it cannot be so very difficult."

"I think I may try speaking to the servants first."

A sound of intense disappointment emanated from Miss Bickle's general direction. "Oh, yes. I suppose that *would* be more sensible."

"I promise that we will resort to ghosts if the servants prove unhelpful."

Miss Bickle brightened. "Do you promise *faithfully?*"

"I promise faithfully."

It was a promise that she would soon be obliged to keep, since their investigations made little progress that day. Polly knew nothing and the other servants were always sufficiently busy that Miss Mitchelmore felt uncomfortable approaching them. Thus she was entirely unsurprised that night when Miss Bickle arrived in her room with two candles and insisted they go ghost hunting.

Leighfield was strange by night, as most houses are. Miss Bickle had a very clear sense of what constituted a sign of otherworldly manifestation—doors rattling, beams creaking, disembodied laughter echoing down the halls, that kind of thing.

The disembodied laughter, I confess, I provided myself.

"I think," Miss Mitchelmore declared after an hour of searching, "that we may have to concede the ghostlessness of the house."

"Just a little longer," pleaded Miss Bickle. "It is not so far past midnight, and I am certain that this is the hour when the walls between the living and the dead are at their thinnest."

"Certain on what basis?" asked Miss Mitchelmore, with more than a note of scepticism.

"Intuition." Miss Bickle snatched at her friend's hand. "Come on, I've an idea."

She dragged Miss Mitchelmore through the empty halls of Leighfield and into the room that the Duke of Annadale referred to as the small gallery. There was, as far as Miss Mitchelmore could tell, no *large* gallery, but then the Landrakes were a relatively young family with barely more than a century's worth of ancestors to commemorate.

"There." Miss Bickle thrust a candle towards a portrait of a man with a thin moustache and his hair falling in curls to his shoulders in a style that would have been fashionable sometime after the Civil War. "See how the eyes follow one about the room. If there are spirits here, they are certain to be watching us now."

Miss Mitchelmore did not feel especially watched by spirits, but since I *am* a spirit and I had been watching her for some while without her feeling anything untoward, that feeling by itself proved little. "And if we find them, what should I say to them? *O spirits, please tell me why my lover refuses to let me undress her.*"

"Perhaps you could try *What is the terrible pain that lies over this house?*"

There is something about candlelight which casts all things favourably, from people of questionable beauty to ideas of questionable merit. For this reason, if no other, Miss Bickle's suggestion sounded perilously close to sense. "In any case, the question is moot, as no spirits are forthcoming."

"Not *immediately*," Miss Bickle conceded. "But give them time."

So Miss Mitchelmore gave them time, walking the length of the small gallery and staring up at the faces of the Duke of Annadale's immediate ancestors, in the male line at least. There was a quality, she felt, that linked them—most of them—a look she could, especially by candlelight, call devilish. It varied from face to face, generation to generation, but it was always there in the curl of a lip or the cast of an eye. At the far end of the hall she found herself lingering in front of a face she recognised. A young man she had last seen depicted in military dress but shown here a civilian. His hair styled in loose curls, lace at his chin, a grey coat over a grey jacket. He looked happy, she thought, and free, and unaware that he would soon burn to death in a Spanish field.

"*Mae*." Miss Bickle's voice, although a whisper, still felt loud in the still of the night. "I hear a spirit."

It was not the first time that evening that Miss Bickle had heard a spirit, but thus far all of them had turned out to be breezes, branches, or, well, me. Even so, Miss Mitchelmore was well used to humouring her friend and fell quiet a moment to listen.

There was, indeed, a sound, but to Miss Mitchelmore's ear it was not a spirit. It was footsteps. "I think," she whispered back, "that it might be a living person."

With a sudden look of panic, Miss Bickle dashed across the gallery and took Miss Mitchelmore's hand. "Quick, hide."

"Where?"

"Behind the tapestry."

"What tapestry?"

Miss Bickle brandished her candle. "How can there be no tapestry? What kind of gallery doesn't have any tapestries?"

"One built in the seventeenth century?"

"They should have installed some anyway for just this purpose."

The gallery door opened and a light entered, followed by the slim figure of Mrs. Scott.

Miss Bickle ducked behind Miss Mitchelmore and whispered very firm instructions that she should pretend to be a statue.

"Is there something you need?" Mrs. Scott asked. "It's very late to be about, and if you require assistance, you need only ask."

Since Miss Bickle was optimistically clinging to her presumed invisibility, Miss Mitchelmore replied for the both of them. "No, we were just . . ." There seemed no point in lying. "We were looking for ghosts?"

"There are no ghosts at Leighfield, miss."

Craning her neck around, Miss Mitchelmore looked at Miss Bickle. "You see."

"I'm sure that's what she would say if there *were* a ghost."

"Why?" Miss Mitchelmore asked. "Many houses have ghosts. It's usually not a secret."

Miss Bickle considered this, crouched behind Maelys as though she considered herself still in hiding. "Perhaps *she* is the ghost."

"She," offered Mrs. Scott softly, "can hear you."

Miss Bickle shot up. "You see? Ghostly hearing."

"Are ghosts renowned for their hearing?" asked Mrs. Scott, her voice still determinedly impassive.

Miss Bickle thrust out her chin defiantly. "I'd have thought you should know better than anybody."

"I'm sure she's not a ghost, Lizzie," Miss Mitchelmore said, and then, remembering her friend's tendency to seek immediate physical proof of non-ghostliness, added, "but you should not poke her to check. It would be invasive and unseemly."

"What if she were to poke me?" Miss Bickle asked earnestly. "That would achieve the same effect without subjecting Mrs. Scott to intrusions unbefitting her position."

Miss Mitchelmore cast the housekeeper an apologetic look. "Would you mind? It will save us all a tremendous amount of time in the long run."

Unfazed, Mrs. Scott walked over to Miss Bickle, extended one finger, and poked her firmly in the shoulder.

Miss Bickle nodded approvingly. "See, that wasn't difficult."

"Thank you," added Miss Mitchelmore.

"I've been in this house thirty years," Mrs. Scott replied. "I've had far stranger requests."

At that, Miss Bickle emitted a sound that I can only describe as a squeal. "You see, I *knew* ghost-hunting would work. Can *you* tell us what Lady Georgiana's terrible secret is?"

Miss Mitchelmore buried her head in her hands.

"I'm not sure," Mrs. Scott tried, her tone now wavering just a little, "that she really *has* a terrible secret."

Miss Bickle did not look disappointed, but only because she plainly didn't believe it. "Then why is she so tempestuous and Byronic?"

"You do recall that her mother left and then the rest of her family died mysteriously?" Mrs. Scott reminded her.

"But that's not a *secret*," insisted Miss Bickle. "A secret is something we don't already know about."

In a gesture she hoped would signal the need for quiet—or at least quiet from one of them—Miss Mitchelmore laid a hand on Miss Bickle's shoulder. "I think what Lizzie means is that I'm aware of Lady Georgiana's personal history but was worried that there might—that is—if there is some context to it which I am not understanding."

Mrs. Scott looked down at Miss Mitchelmore with a look of enigmatic loyalty. "How long have you known her ladyship?"

"A few months?" It was, Miss Mitchelmore was certain, a trap, but she had no other answer to give.

"Then yes, there is almost certainly context you are not understanding. It's the twenty-four years she was alive before she met you. Miss."

Chastened, Miss Mitchelmore looked down. "Of course. That was foolish of me. But I don't suppose—that is, you have clearly known her a long time. Would you be at all willing to . . ."

"Discuss the intimate details of my mistress's personal life with a stranger at midnight in the small gallery?"

Miss Mitchelmore made no reply, but Miss Bickle nodded and said yes, as if no request could be more reasonable.

Turning to Miss Bickle, Mrs. Scott inclined her head a fraction of an inch. "In my position, miss, you keep your job by keeping your confidences."

Miss Bickle seemed about to protest, but Miss Mitchelmore cut her off, thanking Mrs. Scott for her attentiveness, assuring her that their ghost-related curiosities were quite satisfied, and that they would, of course, put her under no pressure to violate the terms of her employment.

There followed a brief struggle of wills as to which party would leave the small gallery first, a struggle which Mrs. Scott won, rather pointedly seeing the two guests back up to their rooms before returning to her own.

Once she had gone, Miss Mitchelmore lay on her bed for some minutes staring at the canopy above her. It had been, on reflection, entirely fair (if, in the joint opinions of Miss Bickle and your humble narrator, wickedly unsporting) for Mrs. Scott to refuse to be drawn on the subject of her employer's personal history. But it also meant that she had no alternative but to pursue more direct redress.

With, I was delighted to realise, no need for my personal intervention, she rose, took a moment to straighten her hair, and then made for the Duke of Annadale's bedchamber.

This time, at least, she remembered to knock.

CHAPTER

30

There was, initially, no answer, and so Miss Mitchelmore called through the door and, when she was certain that, were she to be shot, it would at least be design rather than accident, she went inside.

Lady Georgiana had, on this occasion, left the pistol alone. She was sitting up in bed with the covers drawn to her waist and looking—if either Miss Mitchelmore or I were any judge—as though she had not been sleeping either.

"Maelys?" The tone in her voice was a mixture of apprehension and reproach. "If you intend to offer yourself to me, then that is a seductively bold choice, but I find myself not in the mood."

"I am not here to offer," replied Miss Mitchelmore, hoping that the Duke of Annadale would continue to consider her both bold and seductive, although in this moment the former was of greater import. "I am here to demand."

"Are you?" It was dark enough that Miss Mitchelmore could not see the Duke of Annadale's expression, but I, since I perceive the light that comes from the other side of midnight, noted well the arch of the eyebrow and the curl of the lip. "Well, that, too, can be a pleasant game, but for tomorrow perhaps."

"I am not here for games. I am here to talk."

A frown and, in the light-beyond-light, just a trace of worry. "I told you that was not part of the bargain."

"And I am telling you I no longer find that acceptable."

"She finds things acceptable now?"

Miss Mitchelmore had begun walking towards the bed. "She does."

"Then she is free to leave."

"And I will," replied Miss Mitchelmore, deciding that it had become tiresome to refer to herself in the third person. "Tomorrow morning I shall make the arrangements and Lysistrata and I shall be gone before sunset."

"I meant you were free to return to your own room."

Miss Mitchelmore stopped. She did not *hesitate*, but she stopped, just within reach of the Duke of Annadale's bed. "And I will do that also if you ask me to. But I would rather you give me what remains of the night."

"You want me to fuck you one last time?"

"I want you to speak to me."

"I *am* speaking to you."

Steadying herself, Miss Mitchelmore drew in a short breath and held it a moment before continuing. "Confide in me then."

"There is nothing to confide. I am a woman of few virtues, Maelys, but simplicity is one of them."

Striking a balance between her own comfort and the Duke of Annadale's, Miss Mitchelmore sat down on the end of the bed at what she hoped was a respectful distance. "When I—that is—after what happened with the Viscount Fortrose, I found myself in great need of comfort, and you comforted me. As did my friends. But you . . . after your father and brothers died—"

"After I killed them, you mean."

"I refuse to believe that."

"Believe what you will."

Although she could not see the Duke of Annadale in the darkness, Miss Mitchelmore turned to face her anyway. "Very well. Let us say that you are indeed a murderess. That means that we are *both* murderesses and, though I may speak only for myself, I found *being* a murderess easier having somebody to talk to."

"You are no murderess, Maelys."

"The law would say otherwise."

"The law is for the foolish and powerless, and I am neither." The blankets shifted in the night and the Duke of Annadale moved down the bed to take Miss Mitchelmore by the hand. "Although I will say that it is guileful of you to subvert my misgivings by abusing yourself."

"That was not my intent," Miss Mitchelmore replied, half-honestly.

"It was, and you needn't be so coy about it. It was effective." She made a somewhat grudging sound. "Well, moderately effective."

Pressing her luck a little, Miss Mitchelmore slid slightly further along the bed towards the Duke of Annadale. The bedclothes rucked up between them and so she could feel only the gentle pressure and attenuated heat of the lady's body as they grew closer, but it was something. It was enough for the moment. "Then will you not at least accept that if you do not wish me to think *myself* a murderess, it is perverse to wish me to think *you* one?"

"I thought you rather enjoyed my perversity."

"I enjoy your company," Miss Mitchelmore corrected. "I enjoy your passion and your touch. I consider none of what we do together perverse. Only that you will not speak with me afterwards."

The Duke of Annadale made a dismissive sound and tightened her grip on Miss Mitchelmore's hands a little. "I would not have thought you so starved for conversation."

"I am not starved for conversation, Georgiana, I am starved for *you.* And if I cannot have you outside of these moments behind closed doors—"

"You'd rather I fucked you in public?"

"I'd rather you were *with me.* And yes, in public. I would rather you joined us for breakfast. Came for walks with us. Sat with me in the drawing room while I read or sewed or made polite conversation about the charming people we had met in the village."

"You wish me to be dreary. To be ordinary."

"I wish you to be *mine.* To be mine always, not only in one room."

The Duke of Annadale's grip grew harder now, almost painful. "And what of my wishes, Maelys?"

For a moment, Miss Mitchelmore said nothing. On the one hand it was selfish of her to focus only on her own wants, on the other . . . "As you are so fond of reminding me, you are a rich woman, a powerful woman, and one with the will to make your wishes quite manifest should you choose to."

"You came here—"

"Of my own free will, I know. And now I am leaving of my own free will. And all I am asking from you is one night in which you trust me."

"I trust you Maelys, I don't—" She was, I am sure, about to say that she didn't trust herself. But she never got that far because Miss Mitchelmore kissed her.

By the light that is not light, I watched as the debate moved from words to bodies. As hands and lips and limbs formed arguments and counterarguments and objections and rebuttals.

Clothing proved a sticking point. Their arrangement to date had been marked by both its clarity and its inequality, but through the featherlight negotiation of whispers and kisses, Miss Mitchelmore conveyed that this night they would have equity or nothing. And so the Duke of Annadale relented and for the first and, for all she knew, last time, Miss Mitchelmore let herself bask in the new joy of lying skin to skin to skin with the woman she was forced, at last, to admit she loved.

"I—I would like to touch you," Miss Mitchelmore whispered. "As you have touched me."

The Duke of Annadale rolled towards her, and Miss Mitchelmore tried not to dwell on the fact that here, face-to-face in the dark, was as close as they had ever been. "That isn't necessary."

"It is not a matter of necessity, it is a matter of—of desire, I suppose. Unless you would not . . . if you do not want—"

The Duke of Annadale laid her face against Miss Mitchelmore's neck. "What I want is complex, my darling. It is too bound up in what I fear and what I regret. But no, I would like to indulge you in this." She took Miss Mitchelmore by the wrist, raised her hand to her lips and kissed her fingertips before guiding her gently downwards. "Besides, it may be of use to your future lovers."

"I do not want to be of use to future lovers, I want to be of use to you."

The echo of a laugh escaped from the Duke of Annadale. "Maelys, Maelys, my most beautiful Maelys. Are you really this callow, or are you trying to torment me?"

"I am trying to be true. To find *your* truth."

"The truth, my dear one, is that I burn for you, that I have always burned for you, that I want you in all the ways that a woman can want or can be wanted. But the words taste like blood in my mouth and saying them chokes me."

"I do not think that is—I do not wish to—" Miss Mitchelmore could not finish the thought as the Duke of Annadale kissed her again, and guided her hand between her thighs. And for a while Miss Mitchelmore was at a loss as to what to do, but she let her lover lead her and direct her and for a time she let herself forget that the lady she lay with was still in so many ways an enigma.

Even in pleasure, the Duke of Annadale was guarded, biting her lip to stifle herself and, when Miss Mitchelmore had given all that she could, kissing her again with a passion that bordered on ferocity. "Witch," she whispered in the moments her lips were moving from Miss Mitchelmore's mouth to her throat to her collarbone. "You foolish, beautiful witch."

"Have I enchanted you then?" asked Miss Mitchelmore, still not certain what anything meant in this new world she was entering.

"You have ensnared me. Ensnared us both. For all I would have prevented it."

Reaching up, Miss Mitchelmore cupped the side of the Duke of Annadale's face. "Why prevented? There is no harm in this, Georgiana. You have done me no injury, and I have done you none."

Not looking overly reassured, the Duke of Annadale lay against Miss Mitchelmore's breast. "I am not a safe woman to love, Maelys. Still less to be loved by."

"I was not aware that I had ever said that I loved you."

"Nor I you. But let us say that I kept you at a distance for a reason."

Miss Mitchelmore ran her fingers through the Duke of Annadale's unbound hair. "Do you truly fear being cared for so much?"

"Deeply. I was not made to be relied upon. And my affection is . . ." To my ears, and I am sure to Miss Mitchelmore's, the silence that followed was ominous in the extreme.

"Your affection is what?"

"Tainted." The word proved, at last, more ominous than the silence.

The Duke of Annadale had become very still, so Miss Mitchelmore held her tighter and whispered. "There is nothing tainted about you."

"That is sweet of you, but you cannot possibly know that."

"I know you, Georgiana. And you are no murderess, you are no witch, and you are no danger to me."

"I may be."

"Because your scandalous reputation will ruin me for marriage?"

And now the Duke of Annadale was breathing slowly and deeply, as though forcing herself to think of something she had long elected not to think of. "Because my father laid a curse on this house, and I do not know if it holds."

"Your father was a witch?"

The Duke of Annadale laughed a bitter laugh into Miss Mitchelmore's shoulder. "Nothing nearly so disciplined. He was a scoundrel, a vagabond, a gambler, and, when he could be bothered, a rake."

"Did he anger a witch then? Did he"—Miss Mitchelmore, who did not have Miss Bickle's encyclopaedic knowledge of supernatural misfortunes, reached for the only other mythical transgression she could think of—"did he dishonour a priestess of the old religion?"

At that the Duke of Annadale laughed again, dryer and more hollow. "No, my darling, nothing so romantic. He pissed."

Not sure she had heard correctly, Miss Mitchelmore double-checked. "He pissed?"

"He went to Bath, descended through the pump rooms, into the temple, and pissed in the sacred waters. I believe it was a bet—it may even still be on record at White's for all I know."

Miss Mitchelmore looked down at the Duke of Annadale, incredulous. "And he was cursed for this?"

"You think the gods are above such pettiness? Ask Acteon, or Prometheus, or anybody who has made one of them feel slighted. 'As flies to wanton boys,' and all that." Why she chose to end a perfectly good explanation by quoting that shit from Stratford, I shall never know. But then you mortals are creatures of habit, and so often use each other's words when your own fall short.

Slowly, Miss Mitchelmore had begun to piece the story together. "But that can't be how he died?"

"It was how *all* of them died. George was first—George, son of George, heir to the dukedom, my father was never creative with names—a blusterer and a bully all his life, as well as a sanctimonious prig. One evening he wanders lost into a part of London he should never have been anywhere near, quarrels with a man he should never have met, and dies on the end of a knife." There was a bleak note of humour in her voice. That gallows mirth that is the closest your kind ever come to the truly enlightened perspective of my people, the simple knowledge that life and death and comedy and tragedy are all one and that all weddings are, on some level, funerals.

"Then Edward," she continued, "who *should* have died in a brawl if there was any justice, on his way back from trawling the fleshpots of the Continent, sank in the Channel on a clear day, taking a hundred other souls with him. And then there was Arthur. The only one of them worth a damn. Burned in the fields of

Talavera." The mirth was gone now, whatever flirtations with per-spective the Duke of Annadale might have made swallowed by that mortal weakness for sorrow.

Gently, Miss Mitchelmore reached out a hand to offer her lover comfort, and then realised that she had no idea where comfort could be found. "And you think they were all . . . her?"

"I've no proof, of course. We have no courts for gods. But they all died, and all in unlikely ways." A note of something like malice was in her voice now, a bitterness that was easier to bear than pain. "My father went last and went slowly. In his final delirium I think she came to him, to make clear what she had done, and why. I sometimes wonder where his soul is now. If God took it, or the devil, or if she snatched it from the ether between the two and keeps it even now as a plaything."

Miss Mitchelmore tried her best to take all this in and tried, but entirely failed, not to ask the obvious question. "But you were spared?"

"I wondered why, for a time."

"And then?"

"And then my father wondered the same thing. Aloud. To my face. And I took that for my answer."

Drawing her arms still tighter around the Duke of Annadale, for fear the answer would pain her, Miss Mitchelmore asked: "What do you mean, took that for your answer?"

"I mean the Bard was wrong, in a way." This much I could have told her myself. "They do not kill us wantonly; they kill us with clear and singular purpose. My brothers died to torment my father. I was left living for the same reason."

"Then it is done, surely? Your father is dead. The goddess has no more quarrel with your family."

"As Athena was content to confine her wrath to Paris and spare the rest of Troy? My father lost everything he cared for. I have lived the years since determined that neither I nor those around me will suffer similar fates."

"By caring for nothing?"

The Duke of Annadale nodded. "And it was easy enough. When the world reviles you, it is a simple thing to revile the world."

"Until me?" The words felt strange in Miss Mitchelmore's mouth. Presumptuous, almost.

"Until you."

"Why?"

The Duke of Annadale stifled a yawn and then looked up into Miss Mitchelmore's face, her eyes grown more accustomed now to the dark and the light beyond light. "Because I have a weakness for beautiful women," she said. "Because I could feel the hand of the goddess upon you and rankled at it. And because"—she gave half a smile—"I thought you would cry prettily. Now, let's have no more questions."

She lay her head back against Miss Mitchelmore's breast and permitted herself to be held. And although I should have liked it very much had something strange or unexpected befallen them in that little moment of calm, it did not. They lay, all quietness, all stillness, all love-twined and passion-glamoured, until the morning.

CHAPTER

31

They woke the following morning still in each other's arms and did not appear in any great hurry to roll out of them.

"I suppose," the Duke of Annadale said as she blinked the sleep from her eyes, "that you will be leaving today?"

"I suppose I shall." With some reluctance, Miss Mitchelmore slid away from the Duke of Annadale and sat on the edge of the bed. "Unless—that is—if you willed it, if you wished me to stay and would ask me to be with you, then . . ."

Shifting across the bed, the Duke of Annadale laid her hands on Miss Mitchelmore's shoulders and a kiss on her neck. "Was this your plan all along? Tell me you were leaving so you could seduce me into asking you to stay?"

"I barely think it constitutes a plan. A hope, perhaps."

Still trailing her lips along the back of Miss Mitchelmore's neck and shoulders, the Duke of Annadale let her hands wander to the lady's hips. "You are reckoning without my legendary stubbornness."

"And you without mine. I shall stay if you ask me. Otherwise, my mind has not changed."

The Duke of Annadale fell back on the bed, casting one arm across her face in a gesture of what I suspected was deliberate melodrama. "You are impossible."

"This from the woman who has refused to share a bed with me because she fears a curse that most likely died with her father."

"How foolish I must seem," replied the Duke of Annadale in tones that suggested she did not consider herself at all foolish, "to have permitted the sudden deaths of almost my entire family to instill in me an abundance of caution."

Turning, Miss Mitchelmore looked down at the woman she was now at least moderately comfortable considering her lover. "I'm sorry, Georgiana. But I am weary of being afraid of things— *especially* of deities. Your desire to protect me is flattering but I would, perhaps, prefer that you permitted me to take my own risks."

"Then"—the Duke of Annadale uncovered her eyes, the better to cast Miss Mitchelmore a look of rhetorical victory—"you should decide to stay on your own terms and not at my bidding."

Miss Mitchelmore sighed. She had, perhaps naïvely, not expected this exchange to develop into such a battle of wills. "I shall stay," she conceded. "If you will agree to be with me—earnestly with me, not skulking away in your chambers and summoning me when you feel lustful."

"My darling"—the Duke of Annadale propped herself up on her elbows—"where you are concerned I *always* feel lustful. But that aside, I suppose I can agree to your terms. Although should you be struck down by some improbable tragedy I shall reserve the right to be posthumously vexed with you."

Miss Mitchelmore agreed that this was an acceptable compromise and, having been reassured that the servants would not be the least bit scandalised by their arrangement, permitted herself to be dressed for breakfast.

There they met with Miss Bickle, who communicated with her eyebrows a range of insinuations that grew so convoluted that they necessitated a verbal response.

"If what you mean by all that grinning and waggling," the Duke of Annadale said over her coffee, "is that you are pleased that I have joined you for breakfast, then thank you. If you are intending to insinuate something more specific about me or about Maelys, then I might kindly ask you to stop."

Miss Bickle clasped her hands to her bosom and made a strangled but happy noise.

"Lizzie," warned Miss Mitchelmore. "If you are going to make this peculiar, I shall have to write your grandfather and ask that he bring you home."

"I am *not* making this peculiar," Miss Bickle protested. "I'm just happy. That's all. And please don't send me home, there's simply heaps of things I've yet to do in the hills. Why, I've not even seen a single barghest."

The Duke of Annadale took another sip of coffee. "So I deduced. From the fact that you are still alive."

"I'm sure they're terribly friendly once you get to know them."

"They are not."

Despite the Duke of Annadale's manner towards Miss Bickle varying between tepid and arctic throughout breakfast, she was nonetheless persuaded to join her and Miss Mitchelmore on their after-breakfast walk in the dales.

And they made, for a while, rather a picture between them. Miss Bickle frolicked ahead, hopping over stiles and occasionally, when neither of her companions could prevent her, bothering sheep (the lady's penchant for arbitrary mischief was rather commendable, although nothing at all to that of my own people). And behind her—often some way behind her—Miss Mitchelmore and the Duke of Annadale walked arm in arm, speaking idly and of idle things.

They did not, that day, see a barghest, nor a yeth hound, nor any of the—if I am honest—largely interchangeable beasts that roam the high and wild places of the country. But the Duke of Annadale was right that this was, for the most part, a blessing because they are vicious creatures whose primary function is to slake the hunger of a primordial vastness that mortals would do best not to contemplate.

By noon they had come to the crest of a high hill and, although they had not thought to bring a picnic—especially since they were all of them from a world in which a picnic involved folding tables, servants, and multiple courses—they sat awhile anyway and watched the sun playing across the meadows.

It was, in a word, tedious. Had I not been holding out faith that the Duke of Annadale's personal demons, Miss Bickle's reckless curiosity, and Miss Mitchelmore's adamant refusal to be dissuaded from a dangerous course of action would lead them, sooner rather than later, into some calamity or other, I should have quit my observations entirely. I would have pronounced the story closed, stepped forward, and taken my bow, and asked that you, dear reader, give me your hands if we be friends.

But I am a teller of tales, and this tale, my instincts told me, had not ended yet.

Days passed, and for all my hopes and even, I shall freely confess, my occasional provocations, affairs at Leighfield remained stubbornly harmonious. Miss Bickle did, at last, see something that she believed to be a kelpie but which to my more experienced eye was definitely just a drowning horse (the torrent in the upper Leigh is treacherous, its queen as fond of animal lives as human ones). And in the evenings the Duke of Annadale and Miss Mitchelmore engaged in acts of wanton physicality which, while I enjoy observing such things when they form part of a wider tale of mortal folly, I found uninteresting on their own account.

At last, however, my patience—incompatible with my nature though it may have been—was vindicated. One morning a little under a week later, Miss Mitchelmore and the Duke of Annadale awoke, as they had become wont to do, in a glow of romantic complacency, and rolled to face one another. I observed the interaction with little interest until the Duke of Annadale's hand, straying idly across Miss Mitchelmore's breast, came to rest by a patch of discoloured skin, raised nerves radiating from beneath it like spider webs.

"Maelys." Her voice was cautious, almost thin. "How long has this been here?"

Contorting her neck to look at her own chest, Miss Mitchelmore gazed downwards. "It is new, I think."

"Touch it." The Duke of Annadale's tone was commanding but, unusually, not remotely sexual.

Miss Mitchelmore obeyed, pressing her fingers lightly against the patch of skin. "It feels . . . strange."

"Numb?"

Before Miss Mitchelmore could even finish nodding, the Duke of Annadale had risen, slid away, and was now sitting on the edge of the bed with her head in her hands.

"It is Bladud's disease."

Miss Mitchelmore looked up anxiously. "The king, from the Baths?"

"The king who *founded* Bath. Thousands of years ago he contracted leprosy and was exiled from his native Athens. Fleeing to England he lived as a swineherd, where he was cured of the disease by the sacred waters of what is now Aquae Sulis. For whatever reason, it is a disease over which she has specific power."

For a moment, Miss Mitchelmore did not react at all, then gave the kind of laugh that comes only from a place of absolute denial. "That is absurd. Nobody contracts leprosy. Not in England. Not in modern times."

"My father did. The goddess is spiteful, and she wished him to suffer."

Miss Mitchelmore looked down at her chest again with a growing fascination that shaded, around the edges, to horror. It was so small a thing in so many ways, little more than a rash. That it might herald a sickness of quite literally biblical infamy seemed impossible.

"I shall send for a physician," the Duke of Annadale told her. "For all the good it will do. We may need to take more drastic steps."

That shook Miss Mitchelmore out of her daze. "What sort of drastic steps?"

"For all your friend's enthusiasm, she is not wrong that there are many strange and powerful things in this place. I am sure some of them would defy a goddess."

"For what price?" asked Miss Mitchelmore, who to give her due credit had learned the most important rule of magic well and articulated it now plainly and to the point.

"None that I would not pay happily. This was my folly and I shall not let you be brought down by it."

Determinedly stopping herself from prodding the discoloured patch on her skin, Miss Mitchelmore rose and walked around the bed to stand face-to-face with the Duke of Annadale. "It was not your folly. It was your father's error and my choice that brought us to this."

The Duke of Annadale reached up to take Miss Mitchelmore's hand, but the lady pulled away.

"No." Miss Mitchelmore took a step backwards. "I would not have you infected."

"The disease may be contagious," replied the Duke of Annadale—although she was, in point of fact, largely wrong in this regard, as your scholars would eventually learn. "But a curse is not. You suffer this because the goddess wants me to watch you die. If I fall to the same fate it will be because she wills it, not because of some mortal pestilence. Now, come and stand by me."

Miss Mitchelmore, still showing greater caution than either the Duke of Annadale or your esteemed narrator thought necessary, inched forwards again and let her lover take hold of her fingertips. "What are we to do?"

"We are to dress, I am to send for the doctor, and while his ministrations are proving pointless I shall make enquiries elsewhere."

The unqualified *elsewhere* did not escape Miss Mitchelmore's notice. "Where *precisely*?"

"As I say, there are beings of power in this part of the country. I may be able to make some kind of bargain."

"I would not have you striking any bargains on my account."

"I would not be. I would be striking them on my own. If it helps you may think of it as a trade I make to alleviate my own guilt rather than to protect your health."

Hesitantly, Miss Mitchelmore permitted herself to move a half inch closer to the Duke of Annadale. "I should rather you make no trade at all. I have found my way out of one curse; I am sure I can overcome another."

"This is different. It is a goddess acting of her own accord. And unless you are secretly a very, very talented musician, then neither you nor I have anything that might placate her, save our deaths."

"I play the pianoforte," Miss Mitchelmore offered. "But not such that it makes the gods themselves weep. And surely there are other paths open to us that are not needless self-sacrifice?"

"Are you convinced of that," asked the Duke of Annadale, her tone bordering on aristocratic, "or do you merely wish it were true? The world is harsh and indifferent. We are petty creatures of blood and flesh living at the feet of immortals who claim the right to destroy us at their whim. Needless self-sacrifice is the best hope many of us have."

Miss Mitchelmore shut her eyes. She knew, in her heart, that the Duke of Annadale was right. For all that the affliction seemed slight at present, the thought of how it might progress, of where it might lead, did not bear thinking of. "I would sooner not speak of it. Let us at least go to breakfast. Perhaps things will become clearer with time."

Although the Duke of Annadale maintained that Miss Mitchelmore's illness was unlikely to be contagious, both women agreed—with a typically mortal lack of imagination—that it was inappropriate to expose the staff to unnecessary risk of infection. Thus they assisted one another in dressing, an intimacy that would under other circumstances have delighted Miss Mitchelmore but which now had the ugly virtue of necessity.

While breakfast was being served, the Duke of Annadale asked Mrs. Scott to assemble the staff. When they were gathered—and Miss Mitchelmore had not, she realised, understood quite how large a staff Leighfield had, despite its four years' near-abandonment—she addressed them calmly but authoritatively, explaining that like the old Duke, Miss Mitchelmore had been struck down with an illness that, while likely not communicable, had an evil reputation, and that for the sake of the safety and ease-of-mind of the staff, all precautions would be taken to minimise any potential exposure. It was all quite tediously responsible and, had I been less given to indolence, I would have infected the butler with influenza just to spite her.

Once the announcement was completed and the staff returned to their duties, Miss Bickle, who had been listening to everything with the quiet attentiveness of the secretly morbid, turned at once to her friend and rattled off a string of questions, starting with how she was feeling presently, ending with whether she thought she would die soon, and detouring through innumerable digressions on the way.

"I feel well," Miss Mitchelmore replied. "I would sooner not speculate about my demise, and as for the rest, if Georgiana is right and this is a curse from a goddess, it will not progress as a natural sickness"—she stopped midsentence and looked down at the mark on her chest, not able to be certain whether it had already grown since she first saw it—"but regardless, I should not wish to dwell on the question."

"Suffice it to say," added the Duke of Annadale, "that in my father's case the disease set in rapidly, progressed far more quickly than should have been possible, and left him dead within the year from what the doctors referred to as *asphyxia resulting from laryngeal complications.*"

Miss Bickle covered her mouth with her hands.

"That shall not be Maelys's fate if I am at all capable of preventing it." Without waiting for further comment, the Duke of Annadale finished her coffee and rose to leave.

"Will you not stay until the doctor arrives?" asked Miss Mitchelmore. "Or, for that matter, let me accompany you? If you are to seek out otherworldly beings then—"

"No." The Duke of Annadale's tone was sharp and decisive. "You will remain here, where you will be looked after."

"I understand that you are concerned for me, Georgiana," Miss Mitchelmore began, "but you are being very high-ha—"

There was no sense in finishing the sentence, however, since the Duke of Annadale had already departed.

32

Deciding that the doctor would, more likely than not, be a dreary old man who said nothing of value and seeing that Miss Mitchelmore was bearing her new affliction with a disappointing lack of panic, I elected to follow the Duke of Annadale instead, in the hopes that she would do something ill-judged and potentially fatal.

She began inauspiciously, walking—one might almost say rambling—across the estate to a nearby farm where she purchased a young ewe. Had she not bought the animal I might have suspected that she was simply trying to avoid Miss Mitchelmore's company, either from a sense of guilt at having brought a divine curse on the young woman's head, or so as to avoid burdening her with her own sense of helplessness.

With a sheep in tow, however, she had clear purpose. And so it was with some interest that I trailed her over the dales, and with still greater interest that I saw Miss Bickle running up behind her.

"Lady Georgiana." Miss Bickle had inherited good lungs from both parents and so her voice carried well over open ground.

This did not, however, prevent the Duke of Annadale from pretending not to hear her. But the Duke of Annadale's pretending not to hear her was in its turn insufficient to prevent Miss Bickle from calling her name again, and again, and again, and again until at last she was forced to stop, turn, and ask in an exasperated tone: "What?"

"Did you not hear me?" Miss Bickle asked with an ingenuousness that even I, master of dreams and deceptions that I am, could not say for certain was feigned. "I have been following you for some time."

"Perhaps I was distracted," the Duke of Annadale suggested.

This seemed, to Miss Bickle at least, a good enough explanation. "Well, I'm here now, and I wanted to ask what you were doing."

"You dogged my footsteps half a mile across Yorkshire to ask me what I was doing?"

Miss Bickle nodded.

"Why are you not with Maelys? I'd have thought you'd want to comfort her."

Miss Bickle shook her head. "Oh no, Mae is quite comforted enough I'm sure. Polly is looking after her and she's very sweet. But I thought you might be going to do something exciting."

"Well, I am not. Go home."

"I also thought you might be going to do something foolish."

Tilting her head a little, the Duke of Annadale scrutinised Miss Bickle warily. "Perhaps I have formed an overly hasty impression, but I did not think you the kind of woman who much objected to folly."

"I'm not," Miss Bickle agreed. "But if one is to do a foolish thing, one should do it in company."

"That is not a principle I live by."

Refusing even to ask a question for which no could be taken as an answer, Miss Bickle looped her arm through the Duke of Annadale's, taking position on the opposite side from the sheep. "But it is one *I* live by, so I shall accompany you, wherever you might be going."

"You may be pleased," the Duke of Annadale said, "or disappointed. We are going to look for kelpies."

It was technically only half a truth. The kelpies were not, ultimately, the point of their search. The Duke of Annadale, submitting gracefully to Miss Bickle's company, led her and the sheep into the woods that surrounded the upper reaches of the Leigh and, from there, to the narrow and deceptively peaceful waters of the torrent.

Still somewhat excited by the thought of seeing a fairy at last, Miss Bickle looked eagerly up and down the river, but she saw no sign of anything invisible. Then again, how could she?

"If you are that determined to see something mysterious," the Duke of Annadale told her, "perhaps you could assist me with this." She indicated the sheep, which was looking a little perplexed, being accustomed to open fields and bright sunshine rather than woodlands aslant rivers, and finding the mossy rock less to its liking than the green grass they had just left.

Obediently, Miss Bickle hurried back from where she had been kelpie-spotting and knelt down next to the sheep, running her fingers gently through its fleece. "What do you want me to help with?"

"I want you to help me throw it into the river."

Miss Bickle's face fell. "Won't that be rather bad for it?"

"Very bad for it. It will die."

"Oh."

"What did you *think* we were doing with a sheep by a haunted river?"

Miss Bickle looked at the Duke of Annadale as though she had asked a very foolish question indeed. "I thought it was a gift for the fairies."

"It *is* a gift for the fairies," the Duke of Annadale explained with diminishing patience, "but what fairies do with sheep, by and large, is what *we* do with sheep. And that is an arrangement that seldom ends well for the sheep."

For a while, Miss Bickle seemed to consider this and, at last deciding that since she did indeed eat lamb she could not, therefore, deny the fairies the same privilege, agreed to help the Duke of Annadale make her offering.

Between them, they lifted the lamb. Since the Duke of Annadale was hereditary aristocracy and Miss Bickle was the granddaughter of a tin miner, neither of them was especially skilled in the handling of livestock. But the beast was domesticated and had, though it is a fact about which some mortals are oddly squeamish, been bred for the slaughter. It was, therefore, quite placid as the two ladies lifted it into their arms and, with a somewhat hesitant three-count, hurled it into the torrent.

Any temptation Miss Bickle might have been feeling to try the waters herself—for they were narrow and seemed on their surface quite tranquil—vanished the moment the unfortunate animal struck the river. Although *Ovis aries* is not renowned for its strength as a swimmer, the speed with which the beast was caught by the undertow and sucked out of sight, before it was even able to utter a last bleat, demonstrated plainly what fate awaited anyone foolish enough to trespass on the river queen's watery domain. Miss Bickle did not—and she may have counted this a mercy—see what happened to the beast afterwards. The currents of the torrent are vicious and the rocks jagged, and it does not take long for a body to be churned to bloody froth in the darkness.

For a long moment or a short eternity, nothing happened. My people are, as a rule, given to drama, and we will always make an entrance at exactly the right moment. In a summoning, that moment is just when the person summoning you is beginning to think that you will not answer.

The waters of the torrent rippled. Already dark, they faded imperceptibly to red as the queen rose up on her seat of bone and stones. Mortal once, but long ago, Janet still looked *mostly* human. Her hair was long, dark, and lank, her eyes were glass worn river-smooth, and her nails were long and sharp and silver-white. She wore a chemise of cambric, which I knew without looking would have been made without hem or seam, which is often the way with fairy garments.

"My Queen," offered the Duke of Annadale, dropping a polite curtsey. Behind her, I made my own greeting and then pressed a conspiratorial finger to my lips.

The Queen of Falls and Rivers inclined her head just a fraction in acknowledgement. "It has been some years."

"I have been busy," replied the Duke of Annadale. "As, I am sure, have you. But I need advice."

"And what do you offer?"

Standing at the Duke of Annadale's side, Miss Bickle was gazing at the queen agog. I have, I think, in all my many centuries of existence, never seen a genuinely agog expression in the wild, but Miss Bickle was managing it. "Do you want our firstborn children?" she asked. "It's just I don't think either of us are very close to getting married for one reason or another and so I suspect it might take a while."

"Lysistrata." The Duke of Annadale looked over at Miss Bickle with an already-wearied expression. "A general rule in negotiations of all sorts is that one's opening offer should never be an actual human child."

Miss Bickle blinked. "Then what about 'the first thing to greet us when we return home'?"

"That will probably be Maelys."

"Oh. Yes. Then that isn't a good idea."

The Duke of Annadale turned her attention back to the queen. "I don't suppose you want *her*? She's quite annoying but she's decorative."

For a moment, Janet seemed to consider this. "Is she yours to offer?"

"Not remotely."

"I was about to say"—Miss Bickle folded her arms in a gesture of minuscule defiance—"if I am to be sold to an otherworldly monarch, it will be on my own terms."

Not wishing to become distracted by Miss Bickle's protestations of self-determination, the Duke of Annadale did her best to continue. "I can offer blood, gold, or service," she said. "And since my time is short, I would very much prefer blood or gold. I am here only for counsel; I do not believe there is any magic you could work that would aid me in my present need."

It was bait. It was obvious bait. I knew it, and Janet knew it, but there was nothing either of us could do about it, because as well as the iron-and-smoke rules that bind us there are also certain conventions, certain truths, that while not universal are certainly predictable. And we can very seldom resist a challenge.

"And what *is* your present need?" asked the queen, far more eagerly than was wise.

"My lover has been struck down by Sulis Minerva. She has afflicted her with Bladud's disease and if I cannot find a way to relieve her, she will die."

Janet frowned. "Bladud's disease is rarely fatal."

"But the wrath of the gods normally is. Now, do you have some power I do not understand that would permit you to protect her?"

There is bait, dear reader, and there is provocation. The secret of dealing profitably with my kind is knowing how to walk the line between them. The waters of the torrent began to roil, and Janet leaned forwards, her fingers hooking into the eye-sockets of one of the many bird skulls that lined her throne. "Do you wish to see, Landrake, what my protection looks like? Ask me and I shall keep your lover safe from the goddess. This I have power to do. This I swear I shall do if you but ask it."

And this, dear reader, was a trap. An obvious trap. So obvious that even the Duke of Annadale, for all that she was a stubborn and unlikeable creature, did not fall for it. "And on the day I wish to see her turned to stone, or set outside of time, or imprisoned in a crystal jar, I may make such a request. But until then I ask only your advice, and that only if set at a fair price."

"You may have it for a kiss," Janet offered. And if that seems cheap to you, do recall that where I come from a kiss can mean many things.

Miss Bickle looked up at the Duke of Annadale with an expression of rapt betrayal. "But Maelys!"

"Really?" The Duke of Annadale turned her eyes downwards

and somehow managed not to sneer. "It flatters me that you are so invested in my relationship with your friend—"

"I've been tinging you for months," Miss Bickle explained unhelpfully.

"No doubt. But if it helps, see this as proof of devotion. Fairies only ask to be kissed if they know there is somebody else you would far prefer to be kissing."

By accident or by insight, the Duke of Annadale had hit on the precise line of reasoning most guaranteed to earn Miss Bickle's approval. She made the shape of a heart with her hands. A stylised heart, of course, not an actual heart. For some peculiar reason you mortals find real hearts disturbing rather than romantic. A double-standard I consider to be the rankest of hypocrisy.

"I am waiting," the queen said from her seat of bones and stones.

The Duke of Annadale looked at her. Then she looked at her feet, and the rocky overhang that led sharply down to the deceitful waters of the torrent. "Ah," she said at last. "It is to be like that, then?"

Janet nodded.

"And I am to take it on trust that you will not drown me?"

Janet nodded again.

Drawing in a breath, not that it would have helped her in the violent waters of the torrent, the Duke of Annadale stepped forward.

I gave her, on balance, even odds of surviving. Had I breath, I would have held it.

Her foot came to rest on the surface of the water, and the water held. That much did not surprise me; it would be the second step that was telling.

Holding up her skirts, she took another step forwards, and the water held. More confidently now, she went on, making her way to where Janet sat waiting, her cheek resting lazily on the back of one hand. And when she arrived at the seat of bones and stones, the Duke of Annadale leaned forward and kissed the Queen of Falls and Rivers with well-feigned passion.

"What must I do?" she asked.

And Janet, who had always been fond of giving less than she received, smiled and said: "You already know."

CHAPTER

33

Miss Bickle trailed behind the Duke of Annadale as they walked back to Leighfield, asking all the while what, precisely, it was that she—that is, the Duke of Annadale—already knew. Since the Duke of Annadale had resolved to give no answer and Miss Bickle to give no quarter, this made for a somewhat repetitious return journey, but at least neither lady was left with nothing to say.

They arrived in the drawing room to find the doctor still attending to Miss Mitchelmore, who—no longer restrained by the need to dissuade her lover from rash action, had abandoned much of her earlier composure. There were tears in her eyes, and not the pretty kind that the Duke of Annadale favoured. The doctor himself looked scarcely less concerned. He was standing a cautious distance from Miss Mitchelmore, wearing an expression of distress and a patina of perspiration which bordered on the unprofessional.

"Well?" the Duke of Annadale demanded.

The doctor gave her a helpless look. "I have seen nothing like it. Not since—"

"My father?"

He nodded. "Although even then there are . . . there are complications."

"I have *gout,*" Miss Mitchelmore said with the kind of indignation that buries fear. "The goddess gave me *gout.*"

"She also shows early symptoms of scarlatina, typhus, and"—he coloured deeply—"the *French disease.*"

"I believe you may say *syphilis* in my presence," Miss Mitchelmore snapped. "If I am to die of a sickness I would at least prefer to give it its right name."

Looking more and more like a drowning man, both in terms of distress and of general moistness, the doctor turned his gaze from Miss Mitchelmore to the Duke of Annadale and then back to Miss Mitchelmore. "It is worse," he said, "than I remember with His Grace. She is—that is—I can prescribe little except bed rest and, well, I have some patent tonics that may alleviate some of her symptoms but—"

"Leave what remedies you think best with the footman," the Duke of Annadale told him. "For now, you may go. And I am sure it goes without saying that you say nothing of this."

"Madam"—the doctor bowed stiffly—"in candour I am not certain what I *could* say. This is—it is unnatural, plainly unnatural. My only other advice is that you send to London for a specialist in supranormal idiopathies."

"Your advice is noted. Go."

His advice noted, he went. When he had gone, the Duke of Annadale and Miss Bickle both moved to Miss Mitchelmore's side to comfort her, but she waved them off.

"Don't. I am—even if this is magical, we cannot know for certain that I will not infect you."

"It is my curse," the Duke of Annadale told her. "If it strikes me down, that will only be justice."

Miss Bickle, perhaps out of a sense of romantic precedence or perhaps because the danger of lingering had, at last, overmastered her belief in her own imperviousness, kept more of a distance. "We should get you to bed, Mae. There is no sense tiring yourself."

"I am already tired."

"All the more reason to go to bed."

Protestations continued in both directions, but Miss Mitchelmore was eventually persuaded to return to her room, and Miss Bickle sat by her bedside while the Duke of Annadale, almost as uncomfortable with inactivity as I am myself, paced the room like a caged tigress.

"Doctors," she cursed to nobody in particular. "Useless creatures. Arrogant, up-jumped, overpaid—"

"I am not sure what a physician is expected to do against a goddess," said Miss Mitchelmore. Her voice was soft, from physical weakness as much as spiritual kindness. "He did what he was asked to do and could have done no more."

"I do not consider that to his credit."

Miss Mitchelmore looked up with rheumy eyes. "What more could anybody have done?"

"There are steps that can be taken," the Duke of Annadale replied darkly.

For a while, the words were allowed to simply hang there. Then Miss Mitchelmore asked, "What are you intending to do?"

"You see, that's what *I've* been asking," interjected Miss Bickle. "But she's adamant that she shan't tell me."

It had not been a welcome interjection, and Miss Mitchelmore's response was sharp. "Lizzie. Not the time."

"I was only—"

"Lizzie."

Miss Bickle looked contrite. "Sorry."

"Well?" Miss Mitchelmore asked the Duke of Annadale.

"I shall do whatever is necessary to protect you." There was affection in the lady's voice, but there was also distance. A great and echoing distance.

"That is not an answer."

"It is the answer you are getting."

Miss Mitchelmore made an exasperated sound and tried, very briefly, to rise from the bed. It was a bold gesture but a futile one; she managed little more than to sit up before she collapsed back against the pillows, her face ashen and blood beginning to trickle from her nose. "Do not manage me," she was just about able to say. "I thought we had gone past your managing me."

"That was before my actions put you at risk of death."

"It was not your actions that did this."

That, once more, drew the short, harsh laugh that the Duke of Annadale relied upon when no other sound could express her feelings. "But it was. You are deteriorating far more quickly than my father did, because through his death, the goddess meant to punish him, so let him linger. Through your death she means to punish me. And that I will not allow."

Miss Mitchelmore wiped the blood from her face. "I have been at risk of death our whole acquaintance. But if I am dying, I would die knowing that you trusted me, not that you shut me out and treated me like a child."

"I am treating you," the Duke of Annadale replied in her best not-losing-her-temper voice, "like a sick woman."

"A sick woman still deserves to know what medicine she is to be given. If you have a plan to cure me, I demand to know what it is."

The Duke of Annadale sat still and quiet. Then she said: "You already know what it is."

"No."

"It is not your decision."

Miss Bickle glanced from Miss Mitchelmore to the Duke of Annadale and back again. "Why does everybody know what this thing that people already know about is but me?"

"She intends," Miss Mitchelmore explained, "to bargain with Sulis Minerva."

"Her quarrel is with me, not with you," replied the Duke of Annadale coolly.

Permitting Miss Bickle to pass her a handkerchief, Miss Mitchelmore coughed a wet, rattling cough. "She has tried to kill me twice. I believe that constitutes a quarrel."

"And how do you intend to stop me?" asked the Duke of Annadale. "You are in my house, staffed by my servants, even the carriage you came in has returned to London. On top of which, you can barely stand. You could, I suppose, have your friend tie me to my bed, but I believe that we have run out of ribbons."

"And are my words not enough?" Miss Mitchelmore's eyes were watering again, and it was hard to say what was sickness and what sorrow. "Is my asking, my pleading, not enough?"

The Duke of Annadale looked up. "No."

The word, perfectly formed, hung in the air a moment like a smoke ring.

"I shall never forgive you if you do this." Miss Mitchelmore's flair for the dramatic was a pale shadow of Miss Bickle's, but she had her moments and this was one of them.

"I am sure you shan't." The Duke of Annadale turned away,

her eyes closed in something that might almost have been shame. "But I could bear your disdain better than your demise."

Miss Mitchelmore had no reply for that. So she stayed silent, shut her eyes, and waited for her lover to leave. Which, in the end, she did. There was no other way it could be.

———— • ————

That night Miss Mitchelmore and the Duke of Annadale slept in separate beds and, when Miss Mitchelmore woke, much had changed. All of her conditions had worsened overnight, rough lumps and nodules spreading over her chest, across her arms and, when she reached upwards to check, to her nose and the base of her jaw. Her throat was on fire and her head rang, and when she forced herself, with much effort, to rise, she found that her feet were swollen and suppurating, so she returned to bed in frustration until Polly arrived.

"How're you feeling, miss?"

"Unwell," Miss Mitchelmore admitted. "I believe I shall need to remain abed today. And I would not ask you to assist me—the risk of infection goes beyond your duties."

Polly shut the door behind her. "Don't be silly, miss. Her ladyship says it's magic and we can't catch it and I'll not have you lying unattended just because nobody will come be near you."

The mention of the Duke of Annadale made Miss Mitchelmore wince. "Could you—could you send for Georgia—for Lady Georgiana?"

"Gone, miss," replied Polly. "Left this morning."

"She what?" Miss Mitchelmore tried to sound shocked, but in truth she'd known it already in her heart. The Duke of Annadale was not one to be turned aside from a course of action she considered right.

"Had the coach made up moment she rose. Been gone two hours now."

That her lover had left without even saying goodbye was—in the wider scheme of things—the least of Miss Mitchelmore's worries, but it was also the one that it was easiest to focus on. "Then fetch Lizzie. I—just, please fetch her."

Polly bobbed a curtsey and ducked back outside, returning a few minutes later with Miss Bickle in tow. "Will there be anything else, miss?"

"Not now. Thank you."

So, Polly departed and left the Misses Bickle and Mitchelmore alone. Miss Bickle, to her credit, did not react at all to her friend's deteriorated condition, although this may have been as much a matter of obliviousness as kindness.

"Georgiana has gone," Miss Mitchelmore explained and then, before her friend could reply, she raised a hand, trying not to fixate on the lesions at her wrist. "And no, before you say anything, it is not romantic. It is cruel."

Miss Bickle came and sat on the end of the bed. There was a familiarity in the sight that even I found a little comforting, so I'm sure Miss Mitchelmore did also. "Do you miss her very terribly?"

"I have only known she was gone for three minutes, Lizzie. I don't miss her, I am *angry* with her."

Keeping a little more distance than she ordinarily would, Miss Bickle patted the blankets near Miss Mitchelmore's feet. "It's all right. I think I'd be angry too. But what are we going to *do*?"

"There is nothing we can do." A disturbing thought wormed its way into Miss Mitchelmore's mind. "Even were I able to travel, and I am not sure I am, Georgiana was right. This is her house and we are, in a sense, prisoners."

"We will be permitted to leave, surely?"

"But how far can we go without a carriage?" asked Miss Mitchelmore, rather darkly, I thought. Darkness, in my estimation, looked well on her. "Especially in my current state."

Miss Bickle looked uncertain. "In your current state, it might be best if you—"

"If I *what*, Lizzie?" asked Miss Mitchelmore. "Laid abed and waited to die? Or for Georgiana to die in my place? I will not accept it. We *must* find some way to stop her." Once again, Miss Mitchelmore tried to ease herself upright. "If you would help me, Lizzie, I believe I may be able to stand."

Miss Bickle slipped an arm around Miss Mitchelmore's waist and let her lean on her shoulder as she stood, wincing. "Does it hurt very much?"

"Some, but it is a small pain." This was a lie. Her head was swimming and her vision blurring. "Even so, I would very much like to leave."

"And we will," Miss Bickle reassured her. "But perhaps it would be best to take things at least a little slowly. One cannot begin a chase before breakfast."

So Miss Mitchelmore relented. She allowed Miss Bickle to help her into the most appropriate of her dresses, an incongruously formal satin gown chosen for its softness and relative looseness of fit rather than its appropriateness for the occasion. They broke their fast in the usual manner, but then found themselves in the unenviable quandary of being in another person's house with no resources and no authority.

For some while they talked in circles around the question of what they could actually do and, once Miss Bickle had been persuaded that any strategy involving magic of any kind was off the table, they rang for Mrs. Scott.

"Are you well, miss?" was her opening gambit.

Miss Mitchelmore replied, "No, but I am managing. I also require a carriage."

"Where to, miss?" There was a cautious tone in Mrs. Scott's voice, of which Miss Mitchelmore and I were both immediately suspicious.

With a confidence that she was not, perhaps, entirely feeling, Miss Mitchelmore looked the housekeeper in the eye and said: "Bath."

"That is a very long way, miss. And ordinarily her ladyship would have to be consulted."

"Her ladyship is not here," Miss Mitchelmore pointed out.

"No." Mrs. Scott's agreement, in this context, felt rather a lot like defiance.

"London, then."

Mrs. Scott shook her head. "Not in her ladyship's carriage. You can go anywhere in Annadale you wish, but not beyond."

Miss Mitchelmore tried to remain composed. "So we are prisoners?"

"You are guests who may come and go as you will, but the estate's resources are not yours to use. If you want to return home, you must find your own way. Write your parents; I am sure they will make arrangements."

Turning her face up to Mrs. Scott, Miss Bickle made an imploring expression. "But it's a matter of *love*."

"Love does not pay my wages," Mrs. Scott pointed out.

"It may also be a matter of your mistress's safety," added Miss Mitchelmore. "If I am right, then she has gone to Bath to bargain with a goddess, and I doubt she will come back alive."

That, at the very least, gave Mrs. Scott pause. "The mistress may do as she likes," she tried.

"Even if it kills her?" The question would, from me at least, have been cruel, but from Miss Mitchelmore there was sincerity in it. I almost thought I saw tears in her eyes, although that might have been the sickness.

"I have my instructions."

With her various diseases marking her ever more visibly, Miss Mitchelmore did not reach out for fear of frightening the woman, but she leaned forward a little. "You don't agree with them, though, do you?"

Mrs. Scott hesitated.

"You've been here thirty years," Miss Mitchelmore continued, her voice low. "You will have seen Georgiana grow up. Her brothers too."

"Even so—" Mrs. Scott's voice was wavering now, though her posture remained rigid.

"Georgiana is the last of the Landrakes. The rest have already died from the very curse that will soon kill me if she does not act, and will likely kill her if she does. All I am asking is that you permit me to stop her trading her life for mine."

For some while Mrs. Scott was silent. She stood in the drawing room with her fingertips pressed together and her lips pressed closed and her eyes on Miss Mitchelmore watching, calculating. "I have no authority over the coachmen. That is Mr. Stephens's domain."

"Then speak to him," Miss Mitchelmore pleaded. "I cannot remain here knowing Georgiana is in danger and I am doing nothing."

Not quite able to speak her assent, Mrs. Scott nodded. "Will there be anything else, miss?"

Miss Mitchelmore gave a gracious nod of her own. "That will be quite enough, thank you."

When Mrs. Scott had departed, the two young ladies returned to their discussion of what they could actually *do*, even if they were able to return to Bath. In this matter Miss Bickle was inclined to trust to providence, while Miss Mitchelmore attempted, with minimal success, to pin her friend down to a specific plan.

By the time Mrs. Scott returned they had made precious little progress, concluding in the end only that doing something was better than doing nothing.

"I have spoken with Mr. Stephens," Mrs. Scott told them. "And you may have the coach as far as London. From there you will be on your own. I suggest you write ahead and depart in the morning."

And, in the end, that is exactly what they did.

CHAPTER

34

Miss Mitchelmore's condition had worsened again overnight. Her fingers were drawing inwards painfully, her skin was growing increasingly calloused, and her lungs were growing weaker and filling with fluid. She made her way downstairs with the help of a Malacca walking cane that Polly had found for her, and permitted Miss Bickle to escort her to the carriage which waited outside.

They had written—or rather Miss Bickle had written since Miss Mitchelmore had already lost sufficient mobility in her hands that writing was proving difficult—to John in London and to both sets of their parents to inform them of what had happened. For the parents they elided some of the details, like the small matter of the leprosy, scarlatina, and syphilis. For John they had no such qualms, and told him everything.

I am, as I said at the start of this narrative, a connoisseur of mortal folly. I find it amusing in the extreme. I am also, to some extent, a connoisseur of mortal suffering, and I find that amusing also. As the saying has it: tragedy is when I cut my finger, comedy is when you are torn apart by wild dogs under a waxing moon without ever knowing why. But even I found watching Miss Mitchelmore's progress down the Great North Road upsetting. It was not the disfiguring nature of the sickness that bothered me; mortal standards of beauty mean little where I am from. But the jolting and jostling of the carriage caused her such constant distress that even I, after some hours, stopped finding it funny and started finding that it made me sad in a way that first made me angry and then made me bored.

They stopped at a coaching inn at the end of the first day, but Miss Mitchelmore, having all the symptoms multiple illnesses both infectious and ill-reputed, could not be admitted. She offered to spend the night alone in the coach, but Miss Bickle, being very much that sort, would not hear of it. It was, at least, a relatively balmy evening, and the two ladies were able to distract one another with stories of simpler, less divinely accursed times.

The next day saw them facing similar difficulties, for Miss Mitchelmore's appearance was, by this time, ghastly, and even the most generous of innkeepers would have balked at accepting her. When the carriage arrived in London on the evening of the third day, Miss Mitchelmore entered the house cloaked in order not to fright the servants, sent word to her parents that she was home but too tired for visitors, and went at once to her room, where she fell onto the bed and stared upwards, unblinking.

Drawing up a chair, Miss Bickle sat beside her. "How are you feeling, Mae?"

"I am not." Slowly, Miss Mitchelmore moistened her lips. Movement in general was becoming more difficult for her as her nerves gave way to leprosy, her joints to gout, and her lungs to a dozen pulmonary ailments. "Or rather, I am numb in places and ache in others and I fear Georgiana may be dead already but it is a . . . a distant thing like the first half of a dream. I'm sorry I'm not making sense."

"You are ill."

"I'm not ill, I'm cursed."

"You're cursed to be ill, so it's the same thing."

Miss Mitchelmore shut her eyes. The line between weeping and the constant watering of the eyes that attended her condition had ceased to be discernible days ago, but she would have wept were she capable of it. "I just need to rest a little. Tomorrow I shall explain the situation more fully to Mama and Papa, and then I shall proceed to Bath."

"And then?"

"I shall go to the baths and speak to the goddess."

Miss Bickle, for the first time since I had known the lady, looked doubtful. "And you think that will work?"

"I thought you believed in the power of love, Lizzie."

For once, Miss Bickle did not clap her hands at her friend's use of the word. "I do, Mae, of course I do. And I am *sure* all will end happily. It's just—now it's so close it feels rather"—she drew a little into herself—"less certain than it once seemed. After all, the goddess so far has been quite unreasonable."

"I fear goddesses are."

"And I expected the fairies to be far more helpful," added Miss Bickle with genuine rancour. "They have a reputation to uphold that they are not upholding."

"To give the queen her due, she did tell Georgiana what she wanted to know. It was just an answer I disliked."

Another concern struck Miss Bickle. "And you are well enough to travel? You worsened considerably on the way from Yorkshire. I should hate to think what will happen on the way to Bath."

Miss Mitchelmore tried to smile, but found that her face would not respond. "Your concern does you credit, Lizzie. But if you are concerned that I shall be . . . unromantic, you needn't—"

"I am concerned you will *die*, Mae."

"Georgiana will see that I do not. But I *should* rest. There should be a guest room ready for you."

But Miss Bickle shook her head like she was trying to clear water from her ears. "No. I shall stay with you all night."

"There is no need."

"You are my friend, and you are unwell. I shall stay by you until one of those things ceases to be the case."

At that, Miss Mitchelmore laughed. Or as close to laughter as she could get with her muscles weakening and her throat constricting and her lungs filling with phlegm. "After three days together in a carriage, I fear the former would end sooner than the latter. Go, Lizzie. I will be all right."

After two or three further rounds of protestation, Miss Bickle went, leaving Miss Mitchelmore to sleep, for the first time in some while, alone and in her own bed. I did not walk in her dreams that night, for fear that they would go to places I did not want to see.

———— • ————

When she awoke the following morning, Miss Mitchelmore looked down at her hands and wept in earnest. All signs of the disease had passed; her fingers had returned to their normal length, her skin to its normal texture, and she could breathe and feel again, the sheets beneath her and the blanket above a strange, sensory revelation after days of numbness.

She was still weeping when Miss Bickle appeared to call on her. Rushing to her friend's side, Miss Bickle's expression went from elation on seeing Miss Mitchelmore's recovery to sorrow at seeing her tears.

"Oh, Mae"—she reached out a hand and squeezed Miss Mitchelmore's tightly—"you're cured. Why are you sad to be cured?" She cocked her head and blinked. "Or are they happy tears? I am sure I have seen your happy tears, and these do not look like happy tears."

"I am crying," Miss Mitchelmore explained, "because if I am cured then Georgiana has already—already done whatever it is she intends to do in Bath, and we are too late to prevent it."

Miss Bickle covered her mouth. "Oh. Will you think me very cruel if I am happy anyway to see that you are well? I am sad, too, of course, but I have known you far longer and . . ."

Without another word, Miss Mitchelmore leaned forwards and pulled Miss Bickle into an embrace. When they parted she knelt back and said, "Will you still come with me? To Bath, I mean?"

"You're still going? Even though . . . even if . . ."

Miss Mitchelmore gave a decided nod. "Even though and even if. If there is any chance that I might find her, might undo whatever it is she has done, then I must take it."

"I suppose there is a possibility," Miss Bickle began, not quite up to her habitual levels of enthusiasm but getting there, "that she really has solved the problem?"

"You think she has simply persuaded a goddess to stop being spiteful?"

"I think all manner of things are possible with hope and good fortune."

For a fleeting, tempting moment, Miss Mitchelmore permitted herself to entertain the possibility, to imagine simply turning around and riding back to Annadale to find her lover waiting for her, arms wide and eyes wicked, a knowing smile on her lips.

It was not a possibility that she felt bore scrutiny.

"If all is well, I shall find out in Bath. And if all is not well . . . then I suppose I shall find that out also. But whatever has occurred, I must leave today. That is more vital now than ever."

With this new urgency expressed, Miss Mitchelmore rose, and Miss Bickle helped her to dress, and the two of them descended to the drawing room. It was some hours, still, before breakfast would be served, and so Miss Mitchelmore busied herself in writing letters. The first she wrote to the household back at Leighfield, to thank them for their assistance, make certain the carriage had arrived safely, and enquire if the Duke of Annadale had returned. The next she wrote ahead to make preparations for their lodgings in Bath. The last she wrote to her parents and brother, and gave to Miss Bickle for safekeeping.

Although Miss Bickle was not especially quick to apprehend many things, she had an unparalleled sense of the dramatic and knew at once what the missive was for. "In case you die?" she asked by way of clarification.

"Or am otherwise unable to return."

"I shall treasure it. Even if you survive, and I am sure you will survive, I shall keep it by my bosom always."

"There are surely better places for a letter than one's bosom," Miss Mitchelmore observed. "And for that matter, better things for one's bosom than a letter."

Miss Bickle, however, was already sliding the envelope down the front of her gown. "It is the way these things are *done*, Mae. I shall keep it close to my heart until some more significant item of correspondence displaces it."

"And when you sleep?"

"I shall keep it by my bedside and replace it at once in the morning."

The finer details of what was and was not appropriate to store in one's undergarments occupied them until breakfast and, shortly afterwards, they were further occupied by the announcement that Mr. Caesar stood without. Miss Mitchelmore asked that he be admitted at once.

When he arrived, he looked at Miss Mitchelmore with an expression of guarded joy. "You said," he reminded the ladies, "that you had leprosy."

"I did."

"She got better," Miss Bickle added.

"I am no medic," replied Mr. Caesar, "but that seems improbable."

"The goddess giveth"—Miss Mitchelmore held out a hand, representing one half of a balance—"The goddess taketh away." She held out the other. "But I fear to speculate what price Georgiana has paid for my cure."

Mr. Caesar took a short breath and held it in the manner of a man trying to avoid saying something he will regret. "Whatever price she has paid," he said after a moment's reflection, "it is likely she has paid of her own will."

"And whatever price I pay to be reunited with her, I shall pay of my own will also."

"You are nineteen, Maelys"—I chose to interpret the tone of Mr. Caesar's voice as concern rather than command, but I am not sure Miss Mitchelmore did likewise—"you cannot really think that this is the right course for you."

"I can and I do. Georgiana is—that is I—she is dear to me, and I will protect her if I can, as she has me."

Taking a seat, Mr. Caesar regarded his cousin over steepled

fingers. "Does that not become very circular? She sacrifices herself for you, you sacrifice yourself for her. You can't both spend the rest of your lives standing in front of the goddess saying *take me instead.* It will grow tedious."

"I am not intending to ask her to take me instead of Georgiana. I am hoping to—I don't know, make some kind of bargain. The gods do such things, on occasion."

Mr. Caesar gave a *yes but* sort of a nod. "And for how many people *exactly* have such arrangements turned out well?"

"Odysseus was reunited with Penelope eventually," Miss Mitchelmore suggested.

That much Mr. Caesar was forced to concede. "After ten years' journey."

"Still, he was ultimately successful and, from what I recall, happy."

Leaning back in his chair, Mr. Caesar sighed. "Well, I suppose if I cannot dissuade you from this, I shall be forced to assist you. Although I am not certain what I can do exactly."

A look entered Miss Mitchelmore's eyes. A look that said, *Well, I am glad you brought that up, because actually I wanted to ask you a tremendous personal favour.* "I don't suppose that you have maintained correspondence with Miss Tabitha?"

"I have. Do you feel that consulting her again would prove valuable?"

"Valuable or not," Miss Bickle chimed in from her habitual seat by the pianoforte, "I hope I shall be allowed to visit this time. I should dearly like to meet a real priestess of the old gods."

Mr. Caesar frowned. "She isn't a dancing bear, Lizzie. She's an augur."

"I could take you to see a witch, if you'd like that," suggested Miss Mitchelmore.

"Oh Mae, would you?" The notion seemed to delight Miss Bickle as much as it was possible for a person to be delighted.

"Well, I will be consulting a witch, and should like company."

At this, Mr. Caesar buried his head in his hands. "Please, please do not consult a witch."

"She knows Georgiana, and seems to care for her after her fashion."

"Seeming to care," Mr. Caesar observed, "is what witches are known for."

Plinking tunelessly at the piano, Miss Bickle turned her attention back to the conversation. "Isn't turning people into newts what witches are known for?"

"What witches in general are known for is not my concern," Miss Mitchelmore told her friends. "My concern is what this particular witch may do to assist me."

"Which is what?" asked Mr. Caesar.

"I do not know," Miss Mitchelmore replied. "But it would be remiss of me not to find out."

CHAPTER

35

And so find out she did.

The Misses Mitchelmore and Bickle, along with Mr. Caesar, arrived in Bath some two days after Miss Mitchelmore's arrival in London and, the moment they had settled into their temporary lodgings, immediately set back out into the countryside in order that they might consult with the woman they knew as Mother Mason.

I went ahead, slipping through the window on a moonbeam and appearing in the large multifunctional room that served Sweet Maggie as parlour, greeting room, and, on occasion, laboratory. Colm Peppercorn was absent about some errand, and I was thankful for that, since I wished to speak frankly and would rather not have done so in front of a servant of Titania. I mean no disrespect to that lady, of course, but her relationship to my former patron is a complex one and I strive to avoid interfering in it.

"Robin." She acknowledged me with a nod.

"Maggie."

"Three times in one year. It might almost be a sign."

There was no *almost* about it; where my kind are concerned, all things of true worth happen in threes. "Miss Mitchelmore is approaching."

Sweet Maggie threw me a look that gave nothing away. She had been a fine witch in her day and was now, I was sure, a finer one. "Remind me."

"Youngish? Prettyish? Keeping company with Georgiana Landrake?"

That made Sweet Maggie laugh. And her laugh had not aged, for all the rest of her had. "You mean they're fucking?"

"They were. But there was an arc to it. Though I say it myself, it was quite the story."

Sweet Maggie's eyes narrowed. "I'm familiar with your stories, Robin, and I'll not be drawn into another."

"Not even as a supporting character?"

She laughed again, and a hundred tales came flooding back to me. Tales that I shall, perhaps, tell another time. "That, I think, would be a still worse fate than being the heroine. I have some pride, after all. Besides, I know what you do to your supporting characters, and ass's ears would suit me very ill indeed."

"Come now, surely you know I would never make you comic relief."

"I know no such thing. Indeed, I learned long ago that trying to predict your actions was folly. Am I to take it, then, that you have some purpose for Miss Mitchelmore, and that you wish me to aid you in that purpose?"

I nodded. "To the point as always. The lady is on a journey to confront Sulis Minerva in order to win back her lover. It's a pleasing tale, and I have a sense that my master is more in the mood for comedy than tragedy."

"I have no weapons that can fight a god."

"You have wisdom, Maggie, and that is the greatest weapon of all."

Her chair creaked as she rocked backwards. "Flatterer. Although it saddens me to think I have grown so old that you flatter my mind instead of my beauty."

"Mortal beauty is trash," I told her, "and you are fools to value it at all."

"You might say the same of mortal wisdom."

"Oh please, I would never be so crass."

That earned me only a smile. "You would be exactly so crass. But yes, I will give the girl what guidance I can." She sighed. "She is one of the more reasonable deities, you know, if approached correctly."

"*One of the more reasonable deities,*" I pointed out, "is rather like *one of the drier oceans.*"

"With the proper sacrifices she can be quite amica—"

There was a knock at the door, and Sweet Maggie gave me a nod, which, for all its courtesy, translated roughly as *Get that for me, will you?*"

Not wishing to spoil Sweet Maggie's mystique in front of guests, I opened the door, revealing Miss Mitchelmore, in company with her companions, each of whom I identified to Sweet Maggie and about each of whom I provided one or two small biographical details in case she should wish to drop them into conversation.

Thus she was able to greet them each by name, and to tell Miss Mitchelmore that she did indeed already know what her business was and that she would extend what aid she could.

"And how, precisely, do you know so much?" asked Mr. Caesar.

Sweet Maggie's expression was scornful. "I'm a witch, my dear. If we didn't know things we shouldn't, we'd be no use to anybody."

"It's fairies," Miss Bickle added authoritatively. "My grandmama tells me that everything witches know comes from the fairies."

"Your grandmama told you that the funny-shaped stone at the bottom of your garden was a dragon that the king of the elves would ride to his palace on the moon," Miss Mitchelmore pointed out. "I don't think she's a very reliable source."

"You have no proof the stone *wasn't* a dragon," Miss Bickle insisted. "And its shape was very peculiar indeed."

With another creak, Sweet Maggie rocked forwards in her chair. "The dragons did not turn to stone, although where they *did* go it is not my place to tell you."

This, to Miss Bickle, was the greatest injustice in the history of the nation. "Oh, please do. I should so like to see a dragon."

"Try to stay focused, Lizzie," Miss Mitchelmore pleaded. "Unless a dragon can help us with the goddess, we have no need for them."

Showing the flexibility of mind that made her so excellent in her chosen profession, Sweet Maggie gave the matter sincere consideration. "On balance, my understanding is that dragons were far less useful than one might expect. If you wish to confront the goddess, you need proper rites and offerings."

It was not the advice Miss Mitchelmore wanted. "I tried that last time. I brought her a whole half-forequarter of the best beef and she was, if anything, insulted."

"Dead?" asked Sweet Maggie.

"Well, yes. I'm not sure one could quarter a cow and keep it alive."

"Then that was your problem. The gods like their meat fresh. Not all of them require the sacrifice in situ, and some are happier than others with burned offerings, but Sulis . . . no, she needs blood in the water."

"This"—Mr. Caesar was looking apprehensive—"is sounding a lot like a plan we have tried before."

"Not with a live cow," Miss Bickle pointed out. "I'm sure that should make all the difference. Although—shall we really have to kill it ourselves?"

Sweet Maggie nodded. "Ideally the supplicant should do it. If she has the stomach. When the offering is made, bow your head and say that you ask for the chance to earn your lover back."

"It will be that simple?" asked Miss Mitchelmore, somewhat doubtful.

And again, Sweet Maggie nodded. "Simple, yes. But simple is not the same as easy."

"We have to get a cow for a start," said Mr. Caesar, somewhat acerbically from my perspective. "And get it into the baths."

"I can provide a cow," Sweet Maggie told them, although the meaningful glance she cast in my direction suggested that she actually meant *I* was going to provide a cow and she was going to take the credit. This is why I limit my interactions with witches. "And an appropriate blade. But what will really prove a trial are the tasks."

Miss Bickle pulled herself to attention. "Will they be impossible? Would she need to find an acre of land between the strand and the sea, and then plough it with a ram's horn and sow it with a peppercorn and then reap it with a leather sickle and—"

"Something very much like that, yes."

Sweet Maggie was still giving me a pointed look and so I left her to deal with the visitors while I searched for an appropriate sacrifice. How had I been reduced to the state of scouring the English countryside for a cow small enough to put in a carriage and wrangle down a narrow staircase? My pride—pride on which I had no doubt that Sweet Maggie had bargained—forbade me from producing a substandard animal, and so I ranged, in the end, some seventy miles in search of the perfect beast. I found one at last, not quite a calf, not quite grown, its body red-gold and its face white like a mask. Stringing threads from starlight, I bound it and brought it back to Bath. There I left it in front of Sweet Maggie's cottage and watched as Miss Mitchelmore and her friends decided what to make of it.

They were cautious, which in most circumstances would have been wise, although I personally feel that they were already far too deep in the thrall of ancient powers to be concerned about the harm a simple ungulate might cause them. Besides, I had chosen the beast for its docility, and Miss Mitchelmore at least came from a country family, and so should have had some familiarity with livestock. In the end they assuaged one another's misgivings and prevailed upon the coachman to help them move the creature into the carriage. There they all climbed in around it and did their best not to think too much about the smell, nor the proximity, nor the uncertainty of their present situation.

—— • ——

The short return trip to Bath proper had been marked by bickering. Mr. Caesar had initially been discontent at sharing space with a cow, and his discontent had escalated to outright irritation when the creature had relieved itself on his shoes. As if that weren't sufficient cause for consternation, there was some disagreement about whether paying a return visit to Miss Tabitha for a second opinion or pressing on directly to the baths was the more prudent strategy.

At least, the disagreement between Miss Mitchelmore and Mr. Caesar was related to whether it was the more prudent strategy, while Miss Bickle's casting vote was focused more on the question of which choice would better serve her desire for adventure and wonder. Their eventual conclusion was that urgency trumped caution, and that seeking further advice before confronting the goddess was procrastination rather than preparedness.

It was approaching midnight when their carriage pulled up outside the baths. The doors remained open, as temple doors always do, but this was the only convenience that the night afforded them. The cow remained their largest impediment, and the process of manoeuvring it from carriage to entryway to baths was one that necessitated much pulling, goading, and steering, for which none of the gently brought-up socialites had been prepared. The stairs down to the King's Bath proved particularly tricky, since cattle are not climbing beasts by nature and the baths had not been designed with the comfort of bovine bathers in mind.

They managed—with Miss Mitchelmore leading from the front, Miss Bickle prodding from behind, and Mr. Caesar coordinating from the middle—to negotiate the first set of steps, and to lead the animal around the edges of the bath and into the temple courtyard, but the narrower, more spiralling staircase that led down to the sacred spring itself proved both impossible and impassable.

"Well?" Mr. Caesar looked from cow to staircase and back to cow with the air of a man who, when he arose that morning, had hoped his day would include fifty percent fewer staircases and one hundred percent fewer cows. "What now?"

"What if you just popped down to the spring and told the goddess you have a sacrifice for her?" suggested Miss Bickle, practical as ever—for her own idiosyncratic definition of practicality.

Miss Mitchelmore looked doubtful. "I think that might be seen as disrespectful. I think we might"—she glanced nervously back in the direction of the King's Bath—"we might actually have to do it here."

A man of fashion, Mr. Caesar could bear many things, but this was not one of them. "In the *baths*, Mae? The baths where people bathe?"

"All Mother Mason said was that there needed to be blood in the water, and it *is* the same water."

"If you're wrong, you'll have wasted our only cow," Mr. Caesar pointed out. "But it seems we have no choice."

And so they returned to the King's Bath and stood, hesitant, on the edge. The cow lowed ominously and Miss Mitchelmore, witch knife in hand, tried her hardest to work out what she was meant to do next.

"Do you think," she asked, "that I should be standing in the water?"

"That might make it more difficult to actually"—Miss Bickle drew her finger across her throat—"it's quite small and the baths are quite deep."

Gingerly, Miss Mitchelmore touched the blade to the creature's throat, but it shied and she pulled away. "I'm not sure I can do this."

"You don't have to," Mr. Caesar reassured her. "Lady Georgiana has made her choice; you are under no obligation to shield her from it."

Whether it had been his intention or otherwise, it was all Miss Mitchelmore seemed to need to steady her resolve. "Will you both hold it in place for me? I believe I can act more easily if it is still."

With the confidence and enthusiasm of decidedly urban people confronted with a decidedly rural problem, Miss Bickle and Mr. Caesar did their best to restrain the cow.

Holding her breath and biting her lip, Miss Mitchelmore put the blade once more to the animal's throat and, after just a handful of heartbeats' pause, slashed.

The cow screamed a low, bestial scream and struggled forward, pulling itself free of its captors only to stumble into the waters of the King's Bath. There it floundered awhile before its strength gave out at last and it lay in a cloud of bloody water under the waning moon.

Miss Mitchelmore wasn't watching. She had cut deep enough that the arterial spray had caught her, patterning her hands, her face, and her dress with blood that looked black in the night. And since she was not watching, she did not see the water begin to boil, nor the carcass of the unfortunate heifer vanishing beneath the water, nor the goddess, incongruously dry, rising from the centre of the bath.

But she heard, she most certainly heard, when the goddess's voice, echoing from the cloisters all about them, coming from nowhere and everywhere at once, said, "*Speak.*"

With a kind of pious instinct, the three companions fell to their knees on the edge of the bath. It is a gesture more demanded by the new god than the older ones, but these days most entities respect the intention of it.

"Great Goddess Sulis Minerva," Miss Mitchelmore began—it seemed best to retain the formality—"I have reason to believe that Lady Georgiana Landrake has lately come before you and offered some bargain in return for my own life."

The goddess nodded.

"I would know the nature of that bargain and, if it is to her detriment, what I might do to reverse it."

The goddess made no reply. Or rather, she spoke no reply, but the waters of the King's Bath roiled and surged and parted, revealing roughhewn steps leading down and away into chthonic darkness.

Miss Mitchelmore stepped forwards, but Mr. Caesar laid a hand on her shoulder to check her. "Mae, you can't think this is a good idea."

"No," she shook him off. "But I'm doing it anyway."

She kept walking, and when Mr. Caesar and Miss Bickle tried to follow her, the waters rushed back, violent and scalding hot. This was, to your great good fortune as readers, no impediment to your humble narrator. The fires of Vesuvius and the snows of the Arctic are equally meaningless to me. But for the mortals present, it meant clear confirmation that Miss Mitchelmore would be required to continue alone. She turned, just once, to look back at them, and then continued into the darkness.

CHAPTER

— •⟨ • ⟨ •══════════════•⟩ •⟩ •—

36

I hope you are grateful, kind reader, for the very real personal danger in which I placed myself by following Miss Mitchelmore into that strange and unearthly realm. This world our various species share is larger in many directions than your senses or your sciences can detect, and while there is much common ground between the domains of the ancient powers and the domain of my people, we are not the same and our interests do not always align. But I am a storyteller, and I go where the story takes me. And this story was taking me into the underworld.

It is not the Hell of the Bible, or not wholly. And nor is it the Hel of the Norsemen, the Hades of the Hellenes, or even the land at the end of the wide road in the stories of my own people. It is all of these and none of these. A sleeping place and a lying place, in every sense of the word. It is the place where ancient things went and where they wait for their time to come.

It is also a place that few leave.

In Sulis's part of the place-beneath-the-place, the air was filled with the sounds of rushing water and every breath tasted of salt and iron. Miss Mitchelmore followed the goddess through winding caverns and beneath a cascade of green-brown, brackish water to a hollow in the rock, where the Duke of Annadale sat huddled, waiting, outside of time.

"Georgiana?" Miss Mitchelmore's instinct was doubtless to run to the Duke of Annadale, but there are certain circumstances that naturally inhibit spontaneous displays of affection, and being in a primordial prison-cavern in the presence of a bloodthirsty divinity was one such.

"I should have known that you wouldn't have the sense to leave me," the Duke of Annadale replied. "You were safe, Maelys. And now you are far from it."

"You have met my friends. Sense is not a virtue any of us value, and safety has been alien to us for some while."

"Go."

Miss Mitchelmore looked down. "I shall not."

"Stubborn. So what will you do, offer yourself in trade?"

And this, I suppose, was the moment of truth. Gods are, in many ways, even harder to wrangle than cattle, and substantially more dangerous. Miss Mitchelmore turned to the goddess and gazed up at her. "I will make any offering—"

"Maelys, please . . ."

"I will undertake any task."

"This will end badly."

"If only you will return her to me."

There are rules that bind my kind and rules that bind gods. They are not the same, but they are similar, and the Unattainable

Law afflicts us both. If you want it badly enough, are willing to risk enough, then we are all of us bound to grant any wish you can devise, if only you will perform for us an impossible service.

And so the Great Goddess Sulis Minerva turned to Miss Mitchelmore and said, in a voice that whispered from the darkness: "Come before me neither clothed nor naked, neither walking nor riding, neither on sea nor on land, and bring me the moon in a silver cup, the regrets of the man who insulted me, and the most terrible thing in the world."

Miss Mitchelmore bowed her head in agreement.

"Oh, Maelys," sighed the Duke of Annadale. "What have you done?"

"What I had to. I would not let this fall on you alone."

"You have until the moon is full," the voice of the goddess said, "to bring your gifts before me. Fail, and you shall not return to the world above."

It was a classic bargain. One I could under other circumstances have seen myself striking with an irritating human (although I flatter myself that I should have been less imperious about it). And over her lover's protestations, Miss Mitchelmore acquiesced and then, with a final, yearning look back at the Duke of Annadale, let the goddess bring her through the caverns and up to the moonlit waters of the King's Bath.

Above, Miss Bickle and Mr. Caesar were still debating what precisely they should do about their missing companion. They were in broad agreement about the desirability of pursuing Miss Mitchelmore into the underworld, but were in equally broad agreement about the impossibility of progressing beyond a barrier of scalding water.

"—if we blew on it very, very hard," Miss Bickle was suggesting as Miss Mitchelmore emerged, "then perhaps it might—oh Mae, we were so *worried* about you." She swept her into an embrace that nearly unbalanced the both of them and pitched them bodily into the baths.

"I am well, Lizzie. Concerned, but well."

"You are alive," Mr. Caesar observed, "which was never guaranteed."

Miss Mitchelmore reached out and laid a hand on Mr. Caesar's shoulder. "It's sweet that you care, John, but I knew the risks."

From the expression on his face, Mr. Caesar was unconvinced. "Did you though?"

On the way back to the carriage and, from there, to their lodgings, Miss Mitchelmore explained the terms of her pact with the goddess.

Mr. Caesar stretched out in front of the fire, doing his best to forget that a sacrificial cow had recently shat on his shoes. "The full moon is in a little less than a fortnight."

"I know," replied Miss Mitchelmore. "Believe me, I know."

"I'm sure it will all come out right," Miss Bickle reassured them. "Two weeks is practically forever, and besides, impossible things are usually simple when you have the trick of them."

Her companions gave her a look of shared scepticism.

"All of those neither-this-nor-thats," she went on, "there's always some trick. Like, you have to have one foot in a bucket or be standing in a doorway."

"I'm not sure how a bucket will help," Miss Mitchelmore admitted.

Miss Bickle shrugged. "Well, I'm not sure it would. But we might wrap you in a fishing net."

For a fragment of a moment, Miss Mitchelmore and Mr. Caesar stared at Miss Bickle in typically mortal incomprehension.

"Surely," Mr. Caesar said at last, "the solution to *come before me neither clothed nor naked* is not something so . . . so . . . so *asinine* as *come before me wrapped in a fishing net.*"

Spoilers, readers. It absolutely is. The Old Laws are whimsical, and whatever antediluvian powers forged them absolutely *loved* that kind of shit.

"It has worked before, there are simply *heaps* of stories about it." Miss Bickle was entirely correct on this count. The fact that your people dismiss as children's tales such vital advice as *how may I evade destruction should I become ensnared by the Unattainable Law* is but one factor contributing to your limited life expectancy. "And *neither on sea nor on land* is even simpler. Practically a pray-hand-it-me."

"A what?" asked Miss Mitchelmore.

"A pray-hand-it-me. It is what one calls a thing that is so easy to achieve that it is as simple as going up to a person who has it and saying *pray hand it me.* It's slang."

A look of incredulity settled over Mr. Caesar's face. "It is *not* slang. I refuse to believe that you know any slang whatsoever."

Miss Bickle, reclining on a chaise and trailing one hand absently on the floor, was a picture of relaxed defiance. "It *should* be slang. It is an excellent and evocative phrase. But what matters is that Mae need only walk into the baths and she will be neither on land nor on sea, neither walking nor riding. Really, I think the goddess was scarcely trying on that score."

"You think the solution to this whole thing is for me to wrap myself in a fishing net and float in the King's Bath?" asked Miss Mitchelmore, displaying a depressingly human unwillingness to embrace absurdity.

"Yes. Yes I do. Of course, there's still bringing her the moon in a silver cup and working out what the most terrible thing in the world is and finding a way to make a dead man apologise to some-body, but I'm sure those are really very small problems."

Miss Mitchelmore looked doubtful. "They do not feel like small problems."

"Well, of *course* they don't." To Miss Bickle, this was stagger-ingly obvious. "But I am certain that they are. That's how these things work."

"Then perhaps you can enlighten me?" suggested Miss Mitch-elmore, an edge of exasperation creeping into her voice.

"Oh no. You will have to work it out for yourself. That's *also* how these things work."

Rising, Mr. Caesar looked pointedly at the clock. "Well, there is liable to be little worked out this evening. I am going to bed, and I suggest the two of you do the same."

There was a general consensus that this was, indeed, a wise course of action, and the Misses Bickle and Mitchelmore likewise retired. Since notice had been short, neither the Mitchelmores nor the Caesars had unlimited funds, and as Miss Bickle was charm-ingly indifferent to organisation, they had taken only two rooms in a simple lodging house, which left Miss Bickle and Miss Mitchel-more sharing a bed, which was an old, familiar kind of comfort, but not the one that Miss Mitchelmore longed for.

It was reassuring to have her friend with her for companion-ship, but as late night became early morning, Miss Mitchelmore grew increasingly convinced that sleep would not, that evening at least, come for her. Rising in the small hours, taking some pains not to disturb Miss Bickle (although few were necessary, since the lady was a sound sleeper), Miss Mitchelmore dressed herself as best she was able unaided, wrapped a cloak about herself, and set out into the dark.

For a single woman to walk the streets of any city alone after dark was scandalous, but Miss Mitchelmore's tolerance for scandal had grown considerably since her arrival in Bath at the start of the year. It was, after all, rather scandalous also for an unmarried woman to drown a man in a sacred spring, fuck a duke's daughter, and start consorting with witches, priestesses, and ancient deities.

Of course, scandal was not the only danger that awaited a young woman alone on the city streets. And while the risk of violence was not so very great, it would have been an ill end indeed to my tale if its subject had ended up with her throat slit because she had, in a moment of emotional abstraction, taken an unwise walk down the wrong alley.

So I followed and watched over her.

I have seen mortals wandering lost many, many times in my life. It is the state in which your people most often come to the attention of my own. I have seen you fleeing into woodlands, stumbling into valleys, passing all innocent through doors that stop existing when they close. Thus I consider myself something of an expert on the humble wander, and judged this one to be the meanderings of a woman who could not quite bear to be alone with her thoughts, but was rapidly discovering that she could not outrun them.

There were, I think, several reasons that I chose to speak to her. Compassion, I assure you, was not amongst them. I care nothing for the suffering of mortal creatures. But curiosity is a different matter entirely, and there was a certain desire to protect my investment. Miss Mitchelmore's story, after all, was my offering to my lord, and he so hates it when things end inconclusively.

So I huddled into the shadows and took the form of a ragged woman of uncertain but pitiable fortune.

"Show some kindness to a poor creature, sweet lady," I called to her. My voice was clear in the empty streets, and I have a gift for making myself enticing in a hundred different ways if I must.

Miss Mitchelmore stopped, turned towards me, and then, with that sense of self-preservation that had served her so well and me so inconsistently, took a few steps back. "I am sorry, I . . . I have nothing."

"'Tis a strange thing," I went on, "for a fine young lady like yourself to be out so late, however balmy the night."

"I couldn't sleep," she told me.

"When my little girl couldn't sleep, I'd put her on my knee and sing to her till she drifted off." This was, of course, a lie. I have no children, or at least no children of my own. I have *acquired* several, but only fleetingly.

"I am perhaps a little old for such things."

"When my little girl grew older I would ask her to tell me her troubles. And that would work also."

She was looking at me warily, and I wondered if I had, perhaps, overplayed my hand. "Who are you?" she asked.

"Just a poor old woman."

"Forgive me, but I have met many strange things of late, and few were quite what they seemed."

I treated her to my most ambiguous smile, although the light was poor enough and her mind occupied enough that I doubt she appreciated it. "Wise," I told her. "And foolish. There are odd things in the dark, my dear, but some of them turn dangerous only when named."

It was a threat. And I believe she took it in the spirit in which it

was intended. "I have a friend who is a great believer in serendipi-
tous meetings."

"Your friend sounds like a clever young woman."

"I never said my friend was a woman. Or that she was young."

I laughed at that, and it was only half pretence. "But most
young ladies' friends are other young ladies. And you still haven't
told me your troubles."

"I fear if I do it will give you power over me."

When did mortals grow so cynical? Very few things *actually* give
my kind power over yours. And no, I will not tell you what those
things are. "Please yourself."

For a moment I thought she might prove as good as her word
and walk on without me. I need not have been so concerned. "How
do I catch the moon in a silver cup?" she asked.

There are rules to these things. I *could* simply have told her the
answer, but that would have put me at odds with a goddess. "I
would start," I told her, "by buying a silver cup."

"And how do I make a dead man apologise to somebody?"

I gave her a look of profoundest innocence. "I am but a simple
beggar woman. How am I to know how rich men send their
apologies?"

That, I feared, was perilously close to the edge. But if I was
lucky the goddess wouldn't be listening too closely to things a hobgoblin said in the night.

"And what is the most terrible thing in the world?"

I smiled again. Less ambiguous this time, and for just a half an
eyeblink I let illusions slip and allowed her to see me as I am. Or as
close to it as mortals can reckon. "Your world?" I asked. "Or mine?"

Miss Mitchelmore made no reply but nodded, at least half
comprehending. "I . . . I feel I should give you something."

I returned to my play of innocence. "I am but a poor beggar woman. I live on charity but expect none."

Having no coin nor jewellery on her person, Miss Mitchelmore slipped the cloak from her shoulders. "I would not have you freeze come the winter."

I took it and thanked her for the gift. The tiniest part of me was disappointed, because things become so much more *interesting* when mortals behave ungratefully towards us. But sweet Maelys Mitchelmore had paid her debts, or shown an old woman kindness, depending on what you believe that she believed. And that made things square between us.

And I still have the cloak. It was one of the few things I took with me when I left my master's court.

37

"What do you mean you gave her your cloak?" asked Mr. Caesar over coffee and marchpane in Mollands the following day. "That was a good cloak, Mae, you can't just go around giving cloaks to strange women."

Miss Bickle gave him a look of profound dismay. "Oh, but you can. In fact, you *must*. If you do not give a gift to a mysterious beggar woman you will attract all sorts of misfortune." She took a bite of her marchpane. "Well, unless you cause her terrible offense and she transforms you into a garden ornament."

"So I either did exactly the right thing, or exactly the wrong thing?" Miss Mitchelmore gave her friend a sceptical look over the rim of her teacup.

"I believe that's how it works, yes," Miss Bickle confirmed.

Mr. Caesar picked up the silver cup that Miss Mitchelmore had purchased that morning on Milsom Street. "And you think this will work?"

"I think the silver cup is probably the easy part."

On the other side of the table, Miss Bickle was once more angling her teacup in order to drink sunlight. "You say that, but silver cups are only in some places, whereas the moon is everywhere."

Turning the cup upside down, Mr. Caesar inspected it closely. "It isn't *in here*, which is where it needs to be."

"Well *I* think that's a very narrow perspective," replied Miss Bickle. "And I don't think a narrow perspective is very helpful when one is dealing with goddesses."

Mr. Caesar set the cup down. "I do *not* have a narrow perspective."

"Compared to Lizzie," observed Miss Mitchelmore, "I think *most* of us have a narrow perspective."

"Thank you." Miss Bickle grinned. "Now, that just leaves the most terrible thing in the world and an apology from a dead man."

"*And* the moon in a silver cup. Because *that*"—Mr. Caesar indicated the vessel under discussion—"is not the moon in a silver cup. It is a silver cup that remains steadfastly moonless."

Breaking off a piece of marchpane and trying to enjoy the fact that it was no longer rotting to maggots in her mouth, Miss Mitchelmore did her best to divert the conversation from the practicalities of acquiring the moon to the practicalities of virtually anything else. "Perhaps the dead man's apology might be an easier thing to think about?"

"Necromancy?" suggested Miss Bickle with unwavering confidence.

Mr. Caesar gave her an indulgent look. "Do you know any necromancers?"

"Well, no, but I am sure if we walked into the right graveyard at the right time of night—"

"That seems to rely rather a lot on chance," Miss Mitchelmore pointed out. "Might Miss Tabitha . . ."

Pressing two fingers to his lips, Mr. Caesar made a contemplative sound. "She might. I know little of Cybele or her cult, but she was once reckoned to have great power."

"Power over the dead?" asked Miss Mitchelmore, uncertain.

"Who can say?"

I could say, as it happens. Although the answer I would give might not have been helpful. All the gods have power over the dead, either directly or indirectly. Cybele is no different in that regard, but neither does she have any special authority.

Even so, the companions finished their tea and marchpane and set out for Westgate Street.

———— • ————

Miss Tabitha answered the door wearing a yellow robe and an expression of irritation. "I assume this isn't a social call?"

"My fault, Tabitha," Miss Mitchelmore explained. "It's a very long story in which I've nearly died more than once, but you're right, that's no excuse for taking your society for granted."

Ushering them into the sitting room, Tabitha took a moment to allow herself to be introduced to Miss Bickle, who in turn took a moment to bubble enthusiastically about how enchanting it was to be meeting a real servant of the old powers. Once ushered, the guests assembled themselves as best they could on the furniture, although since there was only one chair and one chaise, Mr. Caesar elected to stand in order to leave the seats for the ladies.

Once tea was served and everybody settled, which took longer than it would have done in a household with servants, Miss Mitchelmore told her story. The second half of her story, at least.

"And you didn't think to come to me *before* speaking to the goddess?" Miss Tabitha asked, once Miss Mitchelmore had finished.

Miss Mitchelmore gave her an apologetic look. "Time was pressing."

"And we *had* spoken to a witch," added Miss Bickle. "Actually, what *is* the difference between a witch and a priestess?"

Miss Tabitha gave a one-shouldered shrug. "Perspective, mostly."

"Have we made a terrible mistake?" asked Miss Mitchelmore.

The lack of an immediate answer was not entirely reassuring to the company, but that answer was, at least, "I don't think so."

"Just an average mistake then?" observed Mr. Caesar.

With a casual air, Miss Tabitha rested her chin on her hand. "Involving yourself with the gods is always a mistake without pressing need. But then, love is always a compelling reason for action. If not one that normally leads to good ends."

An irrational uncertainty pricked at Miss Mitchelmore's skin. "I don't believe I ever told you my feelings for the lady one way or the other."

"Of course." Miss Tabitha smiled. "Doubtless you are baiting a deity in her lair out of tolerable regard and detached affection."

"Mae gets very defensive about these things," Miss Bickle explained. "I've been trying to get her to admit that she loves Lady Georgiana for weeks and have managed it precisely once."

"And I," Mr. Caesar added, "have been trying to persuade her not to do anything that will get her killed and have managed it not at all."

Miss Mitchelmore drew herself up slightly. "And I am sorry to have disappointed you. But what's done is done and now I need to find a way to speak with a dead man, catch the moon, and identify the most terrible thing in the world."

"Firstly"—Miss Tabitha began counting on long, elegant fingers—"you don't want to speak to a dead man. Locating specific souls is—if you'll pardon a little unladylike language—a total fucker. It's not only the God of the Bible who takes note of the fall of a sparrow. Divine beings flock to the dead, and unless you have *very* special talents or know some *very* dubious magics, you can never quite be sure what you'll owe to whom if you trifle with them."

"Thank you for the advice," replied Miss Mitchelmore, "but I'm not certain I have any other choice."

Miss Tabitha made a *yes-and-no* gesture. "You have no choice but to give the goddess what she asks. But what she has asked is not for you to conjure a spirit, only for you to bring her a message from a dead man. And the world is full of messages from dead men."

An *it-can't-be-that-easy* look crossed Mr. Caesar's face. "Do you mean letters?" he asked, only slightly incredulous. "That seems—"

"I told you," Miss Bickle cut in, "it will seem impossible but actually be simple."

"*Is* that simple?" From her inflection, it seemed Miss Mitchelmore considered it rather the contrary. "Getting a dead man to write a note also seems like it might pose challenges."

But Mr. Caesar had taken the idea and was already, if not running with it, then at least moving at a brisk walk. "The man was a duke; he would have written letters his whole life. Most of them would have been trivial, but if I am understanding these things correctly, he would need only have put the words *my regrets* in writing."

"It's a little more subtle than that," said Tabitha, "but not very."

Miss Bickle was beaming. "There we are. Now just put the

moon in the cup, give the goddess a letter from the Duke of Anna-dale, and all will be well."

"A letter we still do not have," Miss Mitchelmore pointed out.

That, to Mr. Caesar, was just detail. "But people keep their cor-respondence, especially from the peerage. And the ton is small—grandfather may even have something."

"And the most terrible thing?" Miss Mitchelmore turned back to Miss Tabitha. "Is that—that is, is there an answer I should know?"

Miss Tabitha shook her head. "I'm afraid not. It will be differ-ent for everybody. Which means, in a way, that there are no wrong answers. Of course, there are also no *right* answers."

"Not a comfort, Tabby," Mr. Caesar told her.

"Not intended to be."

There was little more to be said about the immediate problem, but Miss Mitchelmore and her party remained visiting awhile with Miss Tabitha for the sake of propriety and gratitude in Miss Mitch-elmore's case, boundless enthusiasm for the arcane in Miss Bickle's, and renewing an old acquaintance in Mr. Caesar's.

I left them to it. The houses of the gods make me uneasy, and it seemed improbable that anything more of interest would occur that evening.

———— • ————

There are many fables, myths, and legends that speak of the gods, and of the fates that befall those who tangle with them. But what those tales do not speak of is the sheer administrative burden that comes alongside such a mystical curse. There are some, of course, for whom the displeasure of a deity resolves swiftly. Acteon did not,

ultimately, need to fill in very much paperwork between his transgression and his death. Sisyphus, on the other hand, has—since the
Industrial Revolution at least—been buried under an ever-
extending list of forms, dockets, and documents.

In much the same way, Miss Mitchelmore was, on her return to
her lodgings, tormented with the unique curse of correspondence.
She, Miss Bickle, and Mr. Caesar stayed up late into the night writing to everybody they could think of, a long list of individuals
including but not limited to Mrs. Scott at Leighfield, their various
parents and grandparents, and those of their friends who would
still speak with them (this was primarily Mr. Caesar's duty, Miss
Mitchelmore having lately been exiled from polite society and Miss
Bickle never being wholly welcome in it in the first place).

It was not interesting to watch, although when the letters were
sent the following morning, I took some pleasure in following them
to their intended recipients.

Mr. Caesar's friends were not especially helpful, being largely
concerned with their own affairs, and all Mrs. Scott was able to do
was to send messengers to local families in the hope that they had
kept their correspondence from the old Duke. The greatest hope
for Miss Mitchelmore and her lover came from her grandfather,
the Earl of Elmsley.

The earl was a man of somewhat fixed habits. He had stopped
updating his dress in the 1790s, his home in the 1780s, and his
opinions in the 1770s. Every morning he took a short walk in the
same part of the gardens before coming back to eat the same
breakfast in the same room. The letter was brought to him by a
footman as his letters always were and I, perched on the footman's
wig in the shape of a piece of stray fluff, watched him open it. After
taking a moment to marvel that the missive had arrived from Bath

in only two days, when it would certainly have taken three in his youth, and to solicit the opinion of several different servants on recent improvements to the postal service, he read it.

Then he reread it.

Then he consulted his servants once again. This particular ritual was one he had been practising since 1773, and was less a manifestation of uncertainty than of noblesse. They confirmed for him that yes, they remembered Miss Mitchelmore, that yes, she was a very fine young lady, and that yes, he had indeed known the past two Dukes of Annadale and had corresponded with both. That no, it seems it was not *that* Duke of Annadale his granddaughter was talking about but the *other* Duke of Annadale. The younger one. And that yes, he had indeed been a rather rude gentleman but had, even so, on occasion communicated in writing.

Thus the Earl of Elmsley was able to write back to Miss Mitchelmore to tell her that she was more than welcome to visit and look through his old letters if that would please her. The reply was sent, as his replies to correspondence always were, by the first post after breakfast, and when it arrived two days later, I watched Miss Mitchelmore read it at the other end.

I do like it when mortals travel. Standing still frustrates me so.

———— • ————

The Earl of Elmsley lived, as he had always lived, at his ancestral home of Millfield Hall, where Miss Mitchelmore arrived almost exactly a week after she had begun looking for a way to find an apology from a dead man.

When Miss Mitchelmore entered, trailing Miss Bickle and Mr. Caesar behind her, he rose to embrace the ladies and shake hands with the gentleman. "Maemae. Lysistrata, Johnny-lad. Such a wonder to see you. And"—he looked momentarily grave—"after all your troubles."

The fact that word of Miss Mitchelmore's troubles had reached Millfield was unsurprising but still a little upsetting. But she had fond memories of her grandfather and she allowed that to comfort her. "I would have come earlier," she told him, "but—"

"But you are young, and young ladies have far better things to do than come to Elmsley and visit old men?" He smiled as he said it, but he also definitely *meant* it.

"Bath *can* be very distracting," Miss Mitchelmore admitted. "And this year it was even more distracting than usual."

Sitting back down, the Earl of Elmsley frowned. "Quite so. Dicky has been up to see me."

That, too, was both expected and distressing. "I suppose he wants you to disinherit Mama."

"Always has, always will."

Mr. Caesar and Miss Mitchelmore were well used to this; the disagreement between the earl and his eldest son about whether it was appropriate for a man of property to let his daughters starve was an old one. Miss Bickle, however, was unfamiliar with the situation, and responded as she always did to information that contradicted her conception of the world. Her mouth formed a geometrically perfect *o* and she gasped. "But that's awful."

"Richard is an awful person," replied Mr. Caesar.

"He's also your uncle," the earl reminded him. "But yes, he was never the kindest of boys, even as a child."

Miss Bickle was still shivering involuntarily. "I don't think I've ever heard anything so beastly."

"We're here," Miss Mitchelmore reminded her, "because a

goddess has abducted my—my friend, and I need to jump through impossible hoops to save her. There are some quite beastly things in the world."

"Yes, but that's different," declared Miss Bickle with the unswerving certainty of the passionate and naïve, "that's magic. Magic is permitted to be wonderful and terrible. A man who doesn't care for his own sisters is just a—just a—a very bad man."

Miss Bickle's shock at the existence of bad men aside (and I share her contempt here; mortal pettiness is a pale and shallow thing compared to the spite of the Good Folk), they passed a pleasant enough visit before politely bringing up the question of the earl's correspondence. In response, the earl waved over a footman, who sent for another footman, who sent for the secretary, who arrived a few minutes later. Like his master, he was a small, neat man, although he wore fewer stripes and eschewed a wig.

"Ah"—the earl looked up—"Jayes. Take my grandchildren and Miss Bickle through to the office and show them my files, will you? They want a letter from the old Duke of Annadale. I take it we have them?"

"A specific letter, my lord?" Jayes—who had been long in the role—was carefully impassive.

"A specific *type* of letter."

"An apology," Miss Mitchelmore added. "If there was, perhaps, an invitation that was issued and declined? If you would have kept such a thing?"

"It is very probable, my lord. You gave me quite specific instructions never to destroy your correspondence." He looked down at Miss Mitchelmore and gave the slightest of nods. "If you will follow me."

They followed him, as did I. Or rather, I did not follow, I transformed into a mite and bit him on the neck. He did not react.

The earl's office was meticulously kept, with his most recent correspondence filed neatly in drawers designed specifically for the purpose. Older missives, however, were stored elsewhere, and it was, in the end, the work of some hours to have them brought up from the earl's archives, unpacked, sorted, examined, and returned to their proper place.

"I can never tell," Mr. Caesar observed as he leafed through a set of notifications the earl had received from his lawyer about a business matter that had concluded sometime in 1812, "if Grandpapa is a charmingly eccentric man or a deeply tedious one."

"Perhaps he is eccentrically tedious?" suggested Miss Bickle, who was never one to accept one choice when she could make two. "Although I think my own grandfather is similar—he's *always* asking Papa why he doesn't keep better records."

They worked their way backwards through the 1810s until they at last reached the era in which the old Duke of Annadale would still have been alive and thus in a position to send his regrets to a lower-ranking aristocrat. Even having narrowed the scope of the search, there were certain needly and haystackish qualities to the endeavour, but the office was comfortable, and the earl arranged for tea and sandwiches to be served to them as they worked (the latter item being presented with rather more fanfare than they deserved; since the Earl of Elmsley had been a personal friend of John Montagu's, he considered the placing of meat between bread a startling innovation and worthy of perpetual comment).

"I think I have it," Miss Mitchelmore said at last, setting her cold beef aside. *"Elmsley, I have looked into it, and while your daughter's passion in this matter is admirable, I regret to inform you that my present engagements do not permit me to raise the question in parliament at this time."*

"And it's definitely him?" asked Mr. Caesar.

Miss Mitchelmore nodded. "It's his name and seal. I'm not sure I'd know the signature, but it seems likely to be authentic."

"And it will be accepted?"

"Oh, it *must* be." This was Miss Bickle, who had dropped her own pile of letters the moment the task had been deemed over and was already hastening to Miss Mitchelmore's side to peer over her shoulder. "This is *exactly* the sort of thing that solves *exactly* this sort of problem. It should have been easier if Mae had been asked for something that has never been seen before and shall never be seen again, but a letter from a dead person seems almost as good."

Setting down his own letters, Mr. Caesar gave Miss Bickle a wary look. "Should I ask why it would be so easy to offer something that had never been seen before and would never be seen again?"

"Well, then she could just crack open a walnut and eat it," explained Miss Bickle, as if it was the most obvious thing in the world. Which it is, and any of you who have failed at that particular task deserve all of the terrible consequences you suffered as a result.

"Oh, of course," replied Mr. Caesar. "How foolish of me."

Letting her companions discuss the potential loopholes of common otherworldly bargains around her, Miss Mitchelmore stared at the letter. It was a small thing to pin a future on. A fragile thing. But she would need to trust to fate and to fortune that Miss Bickle was right and that small, fragile things truly were the secret to overcoming deities.

CHAPTER

38

Although Miss Mitchelmore and Mr. Caesar were both fond of their grandfather, they stayed only one night with him before returning to Bath. Their round of letter writing and the journey to and from Elmsley had swallowed most of the grace period that the goddess had given them, and by the time they had also resolved the peculiar question of finding a fishing net (it had to be used, Miss Bickle insisted, otherwise it would have been created purely to be a garment and would, therefore, count as being clothed—she was wrong about this, but it was prudent attention to detail) there was scarcely any time left.

In the days leading up to the full moon, Miss Mitchelmore had become very prone to overthinking. She had settled on the net and the water of the King's Bath as means of resolving the essential contradictions of the Unattainable Law, and she had a reasonable sense of how *the moon in a silver cup* might be attained. The apology she was still sceptical of, but she could see no ready alternative. As for the most terrible thing in the world, that she had no notion of at all, and however much Miss Bickle reassured her that she would think of something in the moment, it seemed a very risky strategy.

She broke, at last, a mere day before the full moon, calling for the carriage over the objections of both her friends.

"You have until tomorrow," Mr. Caesar reminded her. He was not quite so ungentlemanly as to forcibly drag her indoors, but from his attitude he looked very much as though he wished to. "Would it not be best to use the time?"

"But I am *not* using it. I am sitting in a parlour we rent by the week, staring at the wall and trying to think of solutions to riddles with no answers. It is driving me quite out of my wits and I would see it ended."

Miss Bickle's objections were less pragmatic but equally strenuous. "But you can't go to rescue your lover from an ancient goddess on the night of a *gibbous* moon. It simply isn't done."

"She never said the moon had to be full."

"She may never have said it, but it should surely be taken as implicit."

"Should it?" Miss Mitchelmore asked, trying and failing to raise an eyebrow.

"Of course it should. Interesting things only happen by the light of a full moon, the dark of a new moon, or when the moon is but a sliver in the sky while clouds roll by like the breath of ghosts."

Mr. Caesar, having concluded that dissuading his cousin from her present course of action was not a viable option, turned his attention to Miss Bickle. "That is demonstrably untrue."

Before Miss Bickle could marshal her arguments for the importance of lunar influence on worldly events, Miss Mitchelmore had descended from the house to the carriage. Mr. Caesar made to follow her, but she refused him on the basis that for all he was her cousin, propriety still forbade him from seeing her robed only in a fishing net.

"Then take Lizzie at least," Mr. Caesar insisted. "You shouldn't be going alone."

Without waiting for her friend to reply, Miss Bickle leapt into the carriage after her. "Shove over."

"I shall not shove over."

Refusing to be deterred, Miss Bickle settled onto Miss Mitchelmore's lap. Finding herself beaten, Miss Mitchelmore shoved.

"You are very vexing, Lysistrata."

"If I am this vexing to my friends, imagine how terrible I must be to my enemies."

Miss Mitchelmore gave Miss Bickle a questioning look. "Do you have enemies?"

"Well, no, but if I had any, I am sure I should vex them thoroughly."

There was little point in arguing. Miss Mitchelmore bade farewell to her cousin, and the carriage rolled out into the streets of Bath. I followed, in this instance, in the shape of a sparrow. It was a fine night, and I was of a mind to enjoy the air. Beneath me, the carriage made its way from the tiny lodging house on the outskirts of the city, along the grand parade, and across the Avon. Bath was quiet by night. Or, at least it was quiet by night once the fashionable set had gone back to their estates and townhouses. From above it was rather beautiful, a place of golden stone nestled amongst verdant countryside, the river winding through it like a ribbon in a maiden's hair.

The carriage pulled to a stop outside the baths, and Miss Bickle disembarked and whispered a few words to the driver, who dutifully put his hand over his eyes. Unencumbered by either loyalty or convention, I perched atop the carriage, and looked down with interest as Miss Mitchelmore, clad only in a fishing net, descended cautiously into the street and hurried up the steps and into the pump room.

I shall not dwell overmuch on the lady's appearance. For all that I love to see mortals humiliated, I confess to holding a certain admiration for how much Miss Mitchelmore refused to let humiliation stop her. And even wrapped in a net with a quite indecorously open weave, even barefoot on cold stone, her hair unbound and her hands ungloved, she held a semblance of dignity. As much as your kind ever do.

Swooping over the rooftops, I came to rest in a less avian shape on the edge of the King's Bath in time to see Miss Mitchelmore lowering herself gingerly into the water, cup in one hand, letter in the other. The paper of the letter was already growing damp in the steam and even I, as little as I cared about any of the people involved in this tale, could not help but wonder if the message it carried would survive. My heart would have been fluttering, save for the tiny detail that I do not strictly *have* a heart.

Floating in the baths, Miss Mitchelmore dipped the chalice into the King's Bath, lifted it out, and angled the surface until the moon reflected in the waters.

"Great Goddess Sulis Minerva," she called out, "I come before you neither clothed nor naked, neither walking nor riding, neither on land nor on sea, and I bring you the moon in a silver cup."

For a moment, nothing happened. And in that moment, I was afraid that I might have chosen a tale with an unsatisfying ending. Not that this would have made a great deal of difference in practice; I am bound to be entertaining, not to be honest. But all else being equal, I would have liked Miss Mitchelmore *not* to have failed at the last.

As it was, however, neither I nor Miss Mitchelmore need have worried. The waters rippled, then surged, then parted, and the Great Goddess Sulis Minerva rose up from the depths all silver and majesty.

Wordlessly, she reached out and took the chalice from Miss Mitchelmore's hands and raised it to her lips. Above, the sky darkened, and I saw the moon bleed red.

"Acceptable," her voice said from everywhere.

"I bring you also words of apology from the late Duke of Annadale." Miss Mitchelmore held out the rapidly disintegrating paper, and the goddess took this also.

A smile played across Sulis Minerva's lips for a moment. And in the shadows I heard a man scream. "There is a final gift," her voice said from the sky.

And Miss Mitchelmore was silent.

There are all manner of awful things in the world, but the wrath of a god is certainly one of the most awful. And Miss Mitchelmore was perilously close to facing it. Sulis Minerva gazed down at her with eyes that had looked out on the cosmos when it was nought but formless chaos.

Awful indeed. But not the most terrible thing in the world.

"You have one chance," said the voice of the goddess.

And still Miss Mitchelmore was silent. There was, in the end, nothing she could say. There had never, loath as she was to admit it, been anything she could say, or anything she could do. Since the first moment the curse had fallen on her, she had been running in circles to keep herself from facing a simple, unencompassable truth. That the world in which she lived was indifferent, that the powers who ruled it were cruel. That there were, everywhere, beings that could harm her at their whim and that she could have against them no recourse and no redress.

It was a blood-quickening, nausea-inducing sense of frailty.

And it was the most terrible thing in the world.

"I offer you helplessness," she said. "I offer you insignificance in the face of a world that thinks nothing of you. I offer you the cold, sick fear of *not knowing.*"

And the goddess took it and was gone.

The King's Bath grew chill, and what remained of the moonlight danced crimson on the waters. From the depths, the Duke of Annadale rose screaming, plumes of steam erupting and condensing around her. Miss Mitchelmore, ignoring the risk of either scalding or freezing—or, divine power being inherently unfair, both—rushed forward to catch her, pulling her close and holding her as tightly as she could in case Sulis Minerva, at the last, reneged on her end of the bargain.

When the screaming stopped, the Duke of Annadale slumped against Miss Mitchelmore's breast, both women breathing heavy and ragged. And for a while they stood there, neither on land nor sea, floating in each other's arms.

"That," the Duke of Annadale was able to say eventually, "was very foolish."

Miss Mitchelmore looked up. "You're welcome."

"I'm sorry, I still don't quite have the habit of gratitude."

"Then you are also forgiven." Leaning forwards, Miss Mitchelmore kissed her, as around them the waters stilled and the moon returned to its natural colour. And I, gentle reader, took the form of a sparrow and rose gracefully into the clear night sky.

———•———

In older, simpler times, ending a story was easy. The prince would enter, stage left, and inform the company that so-and-so was to marry such-and-such and whomsoever was to marry as-it-may-be and that would be understood to be good and just and all would be right with the world.

You mortals used to be much, much easier to please.

There are a thousand and one loose ends to any tale, and no epilogue I could expound would answer every question the astute reader might have about Miss Mitchelmore and the Duke of Annadale, or about the future they would walk into together after they left the baths that evening and returned, by carriage, to Miss Mitchelmore's lodging house.

I can, however, tell you a few things: that the curse was lifted from the house of Landrake, that the Great Goddess Sulis Minerva never again troubled either of the ladies, and that despite Lady Georgiana's best efforts to sabotage her own happiness, they remained together for many years.

And after those years? But that is where you must have mistaken me. I am a weaver of fictions, not a keeper of records. I am not Clotho with her spindle, nor Atropos with her shears. It is not the span of a life that interests me but the moments within it.

I could embellish, of course. I could tell you that they moved to Leighfield and between them coaxed that estate to a prosperity it had not seen in generations. That they travelled the mortal world and even strayed, at times, into the lands beyond, where they faced perils even more awful than Bladud's goddess. I could say that Miss Mitchelmore died tragically young and Lady Georgiana mourned her ever after, or the reverse, that Miss Mitchelmore went on alone after her lover died of a fever in Venice at the age of forty-nine, finding love again in her twilight years with a crofter's daughter from Pembrokeshire.

I could say all of these things, but I would be lying.

Over the coming decades, Miss Mitchelmore's path would cross mine two or three more times, although never so completely or so entertainingly as it did in 1814. She and her lover were destined, ultimately, to leave the centre of my stage and vanish into the wings. To become spear carriers and cup bearers in other people's stories.

I last saw her sometime in the reign of Victoria, in the year they opened the new Westminster Bridge. I was chronicling the adventures of a young street urchin who had just stolen a handkerchief from an unsuspecting gentleman and who would, ultimately, go on to steal far more valuable things from far more dangerous beings, but I caught sight of two women walking arm in arm along the Thames. And as a teller of tales, I never forget a face, not even one that has aged, and I was certain that they were indeed Miss Mitchelmore and the Duke of Annadale. It was a fine, warm morning and, though I am no great judge of mortal sentiments, they looked, to my eyes, happy.

After that, I have no more to tell.

If that bothers you, reader, I am sorry. But there is little I can do. This is, after all, only a dream.

ACKNOWLEDGMENTS

Make no mistake, reader, the fact that this book is in your hands today is for the most part entirely a consequence of my own remarkable powers of perception, recollection, and storytelling. You mortals, with your tedious rules, your officious deadlines, and your stubborn but woefully misguided belief that your lives have meaning are, to me, an endless source of frustration. I do, however, need to work with some of you to pay my bills and so I will grudgingly admit that some few of you, such as my agent, Courtney Miller-Callihan; my editor Sarah Peed; and my assistant Mary are slightly less vexing than the rest of your terrible species.

The greatest of acknowledgments, however, must of course be reserved for my Lord Oberon, who is always wise, kind, noble, bold, handsome, and, above all, forgiving.

ABOUT THE AUTHOR

Alexis Hall is the mortal pen name of a wandering fairy spirit cruelly exiled to the physical world for reasons that were not at all his fault. He is slowly coming to terms with his predicament and feels fortunate that he has found a way to monetize his contempt for humanity.

ABOUT THE TYPE

This book was set in Baskerville, a typeface designed by John Baskerville (1706–75), an amateur printer and type-founder, and cut for him by John Handy in 1750. The type became popular again when the Lanston Monotype Corporation of London revived the classic roman face in 1923. The Mergenthaler Linotype Company in England and the United States cut a version of Baskerville in 1931, making it one of the most widely used typefaces today.